DRAINING THE SEA

ALSO BY
MICHELINE AHARONIAN MARCOM

The Daydreaming Boy

Three Apples Fell from Heaven

DRAINING
THE SEA

Micheline Aharonian Marcom

RIVERHEAD BOOKS

A MEMBER OF PENGUIN GROUP (USA) INC.

NEW YORK

2008

RIVERHEAD BOOKS
Published by the Penguin Group
Penguin Group (USA) Inc., 375 Hudson Street, New York, New York 10014, USA •
Penguin Group (Canada), 90 Eglinton Avenue East, Suite 700, Toronto, Ontario
M4P 2Y3, Canada (a division of Pearson Penguin Canada Inc.) • Penguin Books Ltd,
80 Strand, London WC2R 0RL, England • Penguin Ireland, 25 St Stephen's Green, Dublin 2,
Ireland (a division of Penguin Books Ltd) • Penguin Group (Australia), 250 Camberwell Road,
Camberwell, Victoria 3124, Australia (a division of Pearson Australia Group Pty Ltd) •
Penguin Books India Pvt Ltd, 11 Community Centre, Panchsheel Park, New Delhi–
110 017, India • Penguin Group (NZ), 67 Apollo Drive, Rosedale, North Shore 0632,
New Zealand (a division of Pearson New Zealand Ltd) • Penguin Books (South Africa) (Pty) Ltd,
24 Sturdee Avenue, Rosebank, Johannesburg 2196, South Africa

Penguin Books Ltd, Registered Offices: 80 Strand, London WC2R 0RL, England

Grateful acknowledgment is made to quote from *Let Us Now Praise Famous Men*,
by James Agee and Walker Evans. Copyright 1941 by James Agee and Walker Evans;
copyright renewed © 1969 by Mia Fritsch Agee and Walker Evans. Used by permission
of Houghton Mifflin Company. All rights reserved.

Library of Congress Cataloging-in-Publication Data

Marcom, Micheline Aharonian, date.
Draining the sea/Micheline Aharonian Marcom.
p.   cm.
ISBN 978-1-59448-973-0
1. Armenian Americans—Fiction.   2. Guatemalans—United States—Fiction.
3. Los Angeles (Calif.)—Fiction.   I. Title.
PS3563.A63629D73   2008   2007033674
813'.54—dc22

Printed in the United States of America
1   3   5   7   9   10   8   6   4   2

Book design by Marysarah Quinn

This is a work of fiction. Names, characters, places, and incidents either are the
product of the author's imagination or are used fictitiously, and any resemblance
to actual persons, living or dead, businesses, companies, events, or locales is entirely
coincidental.

While the author has made every effort to provide accurate telephone numbers and Internet
addresses at the time of publication, neither the publisher nor the author assumes any
responsibility for errors, or for changes that occur after publication. Further, the publisher
does not have any control over and does not assume any responsibility for author or third-
party websites or their content.

CONTENTS

BOOK 1   I

BOOK 2   103

BOOK 3   149

BOOK 4   199

BOOK 5   259

Collected Phrases   317

List of Photographs   327

Victims of the Acul Massacre   328

Timeline   329

Acknowledgments   334

FOR LUCO,

born in these Americas

FOR THE IXIL OF ACUL AND NEBAJ,

FOR MARÍA AND HER CHILDREN,

lakoj oon ve't uma't u ak'la tiichajil tetz u tenam Ixil

Oh, take pity on me, the unfortunate still alive, still sentient
but ill-starred, whom the father, Kronos' son, on the threshold of old age
will blast with hard fate, after I have looked upon evils
and seen my sons destroyed and my daughters dragged away captive
and the chambers of marriage wrecked and the innocent children taken
and dashed to the ground in the hatefulness of war, and the wives
of my sons dragged off by the accursed hands of the Achaians.
And myself last of all, my dogs in front of my doorway
will rip me raw, after some man with stroke of the sharp bronze
spear, or with spearcast, has torn the life out of my body;
those dogs I raised in the halls to be at my table, to guard my
gates, who will lap my blood in the savagery of their anger
and then lie down in my courts.

—*Iliad*

In the sound of these foxes, if they were foxes, there was nearly as much joy, and less grief. There was the frightening joy of hearing the world talk to itself, and the grief of incommunicability. In that grief I am now as then, with the small yet absolute comfort of knowing that communication of such a thing is not only beyond possibility but irrelevant to it; whereas in love, where we find ourselves so completely involved, so completely responsible and so apparently capable, and where all our soul so runs out to the loveliness, strength, and defenseless mortality, plain, common, salt and muscled toughness of human existence of a girl that the desire to die for her seems the puniest and stingiest expression of your regard which you can, like a proud tomcat with a slain fledgling, lay at her feet; in love the restraint in focus and the arrest and perpetuation of joy seems entirely possible and simple, and its failure inexcusable, even while we know it is beyond the power of all biology and even while, like the fading of flowerlike wonder out of a breast to which we are becoming habituated, that exquisite joy lies, fainting through change upon change, in the less and less prescient palm of the less and less godlike, more and more steadily stupefied, human, ordinary hand.

—JAMES AGEE, *Let Us Now Praise Famous Men*

We are more alone in this city.

—Marta

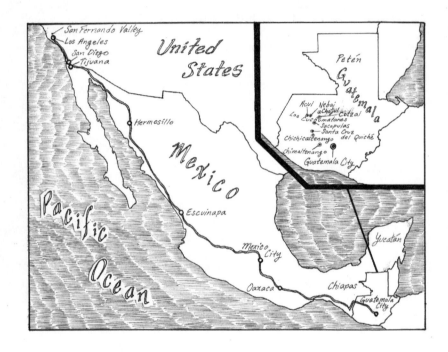

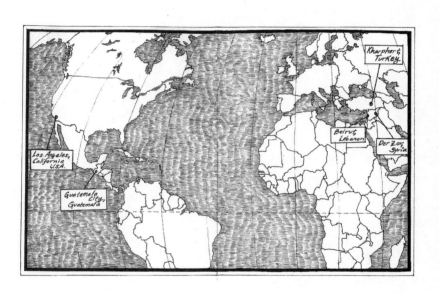

BOOK ONE

THIS IS A FICTION: a man; a man collects corpses, proceeds on the streets of this city, the city an amass of street, of canine corpses he collects, loads them into his motorcar, and the bleeding snout, crushed full canines, the black and blow flies in the anus the snout the genitals; these black corpses, these half-breeds, and not worth a dollar, he thinks; he thinks that if he could kill them all he would do it. But they are dead already. This has become his work: he finds and then lifts the corpse and the meat putrefies and after the diptera's children have done their work—the small black beetles, wasps, moths also—then the monstrous scent of death recants (the meat has been consumed) and a bone smell long remains, but not humors or loves; the bones less lonely, the dead loud and cacophonous, in the days succeeding their ancient animal forms.

He drives along the streets of this city, to the sea and up the tarmac hills, along the remote spoors of the Santa Monica Mountains, which are today the 405 Freeway, and here he is a driver and the world is seen and separated by glass, plastics, metal, and it is speed he seeks, and a girl also, he moves the mechanical steel bull along the blackened roads and gets down from the car in the parking garages, lots and he walks to the front door, the supermarket doors, restaurants, his offices; there are green signs on all of the highways and they indicate streets, miles to go, and the four main arteries of blood in this city, the moving autos and what is possible in his imagination, a carcass stinking through the steel trap of his trunk; these are the modern thresholds; here in this city, he does not walk the dirt paths or learn to keep the days.

The man is tired when he arrives home. He is thirsty and he drinks the water from the tap in the kitchen; the fescue grasses are shorn and green in his garden, and the palms line the avenue like great and tall birds. Here he has hot water, electricity when he chooses it, brown carpets overlay the concrete floors. He sits now on a wide and green armchair, and he watches the television shows in the evenings, and in his America time is made into an automobile and an interlude of shows after the business day, the things that he has purchased at the stores;—and the underground men, like dogs, are piling up, their corpses tossed onto his edge, into his mind, leave invisible markers on invisible roads; he piles up the invisible bones and the dead come to him like children invited to a party, a continuous return of the idols; he waits, he is entertained, and dying also; a sick man, and doesn't know it or recognize them as they arrive, make a ruckus in his mind like the black and blow flies.

AH MARTA, the beast released, here is the truth of it: I am this monstrous we. I chance upon it as I had upon the obelisk in my capital: tall and opaque white stone, granite and marble sandstone, the immense needle holds traces of the old gods and a new history: a monument not to what is or was, but to what we idea'd, like a nation-state dream, or the clock surface in Room 24 of Roscomare Road Elementary School—its black numbers, its loud motor pressing the day forward as if the days were only a progress. We are in my classroom as a boy in Los Angeles, in the basement of the

Polytechnic in your capital, on the freeways of Los Angeles, in the village plaza of Acul, high up the green-grey mountains of the Altos Cuchumatanes. We are in this theater of the mind, which could be a history book or America or a television show or a man— all of it passes through his heart again to make a record. I must live, it reads.

Here is the truth of it: I am an American man and my kidneys begin to fail me; my blood is unclean and I must needs piss every quarter hour. There is pain and I am irritable, a fat and ugly man, the body insists on itself despite my ideas education job.

And I would like to fuck you for other reasons than this lengthy inquiry: your tits, perhaps, slow thighs; a mark on your face; the scarred ropey ankle, and the red lines on your neck; the underlip look you give me as I drive by you on the Pan American Highway on the way to your capital; a little fat belly slips over your skirt, peeks beneath the cotton; all of your scars white lines and the imperfect marks to make the body yours; without hands. And if we are not in the same place or time, what does this have to do with fucking? with love? with my cock half-masted and then the money for the fucking the love the half-masted and lonely cock? with the obelisk? a needle? this we who speaks, monstrous and unkind?

Ah Marta, this is an essay

I remember the years of the clock in the classroom and each turn of the second hand around the clock face, time reduced split and spilled out by the seconds and each minute, this time of the clock, a lifetime's containment, so that the days were endless, the hours were days, the soul under the relentless machine of the modern, in the guise of the civilized man: caged frightened howling in the fluorescent lighted room behind the teacher's lesson for the day; behind the father and his *shame-on-you-boy*'s; behind the nation and its lessons for the shut-up children—of happiness, of freedom, of the discoveries, machines and roads; of the new Christian world and petrol and motorcars; of progress; of destiny; and inside America there is always a story about Europe, just as inside freedom there is always the story of slavery . . . And I have wondered if these were the hours when they held you in that place. You are in a garden and the sun shines and in the distance the church bells do not toll, they have not been rung in many years, the façade of the building has deteriorated, the white plaster peels off in sheaves, the priests have long since abandoned this paradise: you are alone in the garden. You know that it is a risk to be alone in this place, but you would like to sit by yourself for a moment and you would like to look at the trees and to look at the flowers in bloom and you would like the sky unhindered by steel by glass (which you've hardly known, darling), by metal plastic sheeting then; by a canopy of clouds. They find you like this and they pick you up like a man will carry his old mother; his mother is dying and you also are being carried in a casket of arms to your death: you will die soon, you will be killed as one kills a man or as the hen is slaughtered in ritual sacrifice. I am your killer and both you and I don't know yet that our destiny has been love, just as our destiny has been terror: an ancient love awaits us at the threshold.

[Is this threshold inside or outside the body like a mouth? like the vagina? like a babe as he passes through the portal, between living? This threshold your beginning or edge or end of pain? of suffering? of my love for you as I sat in the classroom, there begun the years of my official training, I have been trained in the history and morality of my country, I have learned to drive the tarmac roads, to keep the time correctly. I follow the rules and routes of majority and mob, we hold my urges tightly.]

When they bring you to me you have not, unlike most of the men, shat your pants or pissed yourself; you also do not have a hard-on; I am aroused when I see you and when I see you I burn you with my cigarettes and I cut off your hands before I kill you, tomorrow, because I have been officially trained and educated in these things, because it is my job.

These are not the stories for the faint of heart; these are not the stories that will circulate willy-nilly in the paradise of nations: the days, or your smile, your skin sweet unpissed and unshitted, a doe in the day garden. In a paradise of metal automobilic dimensions, four lane roads and ten lane highways, all of it to the scale of the car not the man, and the modern religion for the modern man: speed and cars and sweet doughnuts and plastic things, and a girl who has not shat her pants; a girl who has not pissed herself, she is clean and happy and free—but not a girl I can make into something else: my dead grandmother; and a day without clocks, without time's relentless hold on the modern, on my cock, my desires, my wishes for freedom from Freedom, and for you also: a girl in a red and green cotton shirt.

MARTA, today I found a lost photograph of a black. He is dead in the photograph and hanged from a tree; see that he has been burnt also. You can't see his face clearly, the image is blurred, the edges erased; there is only a now, a look of water to the photo. Look carefully, closely. See his pants, see his cock not outlined in the linen. Can you see his hard-on? He is aroused by the crowd and so they needed to castrate him: he was a man without restraints, a whistler, didn't bow his head or remove his hat, step down from the sidewalk and he disobeyed or some animal cock fully unrestrained, like a needle; and they needed to release his blood when they killed him in the sunlight, at noon, when to fuck is nicest and shadowless. His cock not outlined; see the piss marks; the darker stain on black pants in the black and white photograph. The piss implies the still present cock: the whites cut it off afterwards perhaps; the whites stand around the corpse, one smiles and his hand is blurred, as if he were waving to the photographer (who is the photographer?), and the dead man has pissed himself in the photograph; he's soft cocked—and the genitals stuffed into his mouth after the photo is taken, like one puts an apple into a hog after it has been prepared for roasting; the whites cut off pieces of the black's flesh as souvenir: the ears, an eye, knucklebones—placed them inside their vitrines, in picture frames, and shop windows. What could this mean? To see this black man's pissy cock covered by the cotton trousers, the naked vulnerable feet loose, hang down in the photo; he is thin, young; the dead look and sad and to make him a black and then remove his testicles, his penis—and stuff it into his mouth when he can't possibly eat it? or say anything. We say (*he must have done something to deserve his fate*): it's sordid to name such things, dirty and indecorous: don't put these sentences on the page: the dead do not approve of such things; the dead hurtle in, gather round, remove the black man's penis, small, cold now like a piece of brown chicken fat, and put it back, essay him back into the man he might have been. A farmer perhaps; or a boy of sixteen; or a driver on the streets of this city.

THIS IS MY INQUIRY, an inquisition of the air: you say that you cannot be undone, and you say (with your looking) that I am a beast of clean proportions; you say nothing with your words, in fact you have no words in my language (and I none in yours) and you insist in your dark cold chambers, in the capital of darkness, you bring me there, into the pit with you, with the other handless corpses, the half-deads, the unclosed eyes of the dying: you, the rats and diptera girls, and faceless cockless boys, and black bowed beetles, and intrepid moths on your skin eyelids—that I stay with you in that place, that I take up your hands (beautiful veins of indifference) and bundle the unringéd, unpainted fingers fingernails to your mother in the Highlands: to your dead mother, the dead brothers and father, the crucified brother, who beat each other in the winters and for whom hunger is like an iron feast: send them these artifacts of the body, you say; rescue me from this hole, this hollow they've made for the half-deads, and I am crying uncontrollably now at the side of the freeway, and I can't see you amidst the piles and it is you and then it is my mother giving me her five phrases about the Armenian grandmother when I am a boy, and the long distances between home and here, and then it is me, alone in my car, driving along the 405. Never so alone and not-alone either: a dog corpse making a fiesta from the trunk of my car.

I have wondered if the dogs make spirit; I have wondered about the soldier in the mountains who carried the mongrel on his back (an order from his superiors) and who with the other recruits slaughtered without an implement, his hands, drank the

9

blood and ate the entrails of the bitch he had carried for miles on the path up into the mountains; his bitch-friend for days on the trek into the Highlands; how he told her of his dead father and the mother who beat him like a dumb beast and that he would love her and that they would live together as family and killers in these mountains in this . . . This the shame, the mark of wood, and once assumed not removable like broken glass or cracked asphalt or a broken tympanum on the descent into steep valleys: I am making an essay into the man; he is American; he is fatter and he looks like something I could hate; he is a man collects corpses. A purveyor of the dead. He is stained and dirty; the blood the violence of the last breath has mutated his form; he thinks that a dog ought to be buried in a marble mausoleum; he thinks that the dogs ought to have their place in politics, in the movies, in love. There is money; plastic cards symbolize credit, providence, hope and things he can buy (cars, shows, clothes and girls); there are dogs and drivers of dog corpses, and all the while his dear and lovely Marta lies in a pit at the Army Technical School, which is no pit for a drama of love, or for the sentimental movie-watchers-makers (there is no profit from it, or to be entertained by it, and happy endings are not happy): this is a pit in the capital of her country, in the Antigua Escuela Politécnica de Guatemala, Avenida La Reforma, 1-45, Zona 10, Ciudad Guatemala: she and the hundreds of half-deads await their next rendezvous with the ununiformed men, the boys who arrive in the garden with their garden-variety black ski masks, hellos, black tinted windows and 9mm pistols: these are the G-2 men; and he drives while she waits, and he waits with her as he can; this "with" a small and untruthful word in his English; in his city the Washingtonias rise high and bright above his head.

HERE IS THE CHURCH the Spanish fathers built in 1678 when they came to the ancient village of Acul, and the soldiers made you come here to the plaza to save the nation today. Where would you like to go, they say in their small and decided screams, to Heaven or to Hell? You (the boy with the black hood on his head has pointed out your uncle the neighbor's boy the catechist from houses away); you. And you are sitting standing waiting (a boy's blood runs out a few houses away and his mother has pleaded with the soldiers so that she may return to her boy, stanch the blood's dispersal onto the dirt floor of her home and killing her son in this way with its unabated flood; and she is quiet now with her own split face and hands) and the small children would like something to eat (the soldiers arrived before dawn and it is midmorning now and they are hungry, tired) or to sit down quietly or to please return our sons to us (the now-departed boys, they are taken to Hell which is inside the church building); girls are crying loudly in the distance—you hear them?—this wail, relentless, it takes up residence in the middle ear, the tympanum, traitor to the race, turns the wails into wails, and from that moment it does not cease: terror once begun and entered into the body with sound and these blindly seeing eyes that day in the plaza on a Thursday in April 1982—is like any of the tightly wound string-catchers, without surcease, unstoppable until it itself stops, only to begin again in the mind, in dreams, at any moment on the street corners in the capital, walking toward the river, by the corner of the Polytechnic, on the Pan American Highway, behind the cypress in the plaza: to become, then, this inheritance for the terrified, the embittered, the fucked-ones who remain so un-willingly. Fear awakens inside sound like a good and obedient dog awakens at dawn.

Communist bitches; they are screaming now at the girls and huddled women (like bees) and the one mother begins to plead again for the bleeding boy she abandoned in the hut (the soldier'd entered, the machete in the gullet of the thirteen year old boy who is looking when they arrive; for the pigs, they say; and they say it in Spanish which is not your language and you understand the word—*puerco*—because); she now dispatched, like a memorandum from the capital, like the New National Security Program Initiative papers; Operation Ixil; and our respective presidents are having drinks shaking hands and smile into the camera lenses from a hotel in Honduras saying that *everything is good in Guatemala*; like a small wind which lifts your plaits in this infinitesimal way, only you notice its breath on your nape, only you know now seeing the arrival of the soldiers that this, for you and yours, will not end today, did not end yesterday, and the time of the clock, like history, little consoles you in this lifetime.

Acul is a small village in the Western Highlands of Guatemala. It is located in the Ixil Area, some three thousand meters above sea level, a two and half hour walk from the town of Santa María de Nebaj. The Ixil call this the Tierra Fría; a grey mist hangs above the village on most days; the Cuchumatán mountain range rises tall and green and black-grey above the hamlets and the town. At dawn you can see the smoke rise from the dispersed huts to the low-hanging clouds; see the girls carrying the bowls of maize, jugs of water, on their heads; see them make tortillas like good girls and cook them over the wood fire; the costumes of the girls are red and green and beautiful, and the lovely Indian ladies in their hand-woven skirts, shirts, and they smile at you when you see them on the dirt path and they will step to one side gracefully; bow to the bosses like dignified gazelle; hear the constant crowing of the cocks throughout the morning and afternoons; the dogs' endless grey barkings into the night; bend under the leña because it is a heavy load that the boys and men carry homeward down from the mountains, the wood stacked like ladders down their backs, like the master they once carried on their backs in a wooden chair tied to the waist; and in Guatemala, as in Mexico, a *carga* is still used as a measurement of weights: equal to two hundred pounds—the amount an Indian can carry on his back thirty to forty miles in a day.

IT IS NOT AS IF I have lost faith (I have not had it or had it not knowing that I did) in history or words or what sentences can make (the five of my mother's estate, they were given to me at random, unwillingly, it seemed, they would spill from her mouth into English), what they might entail, what they hide and elide, elucidate and kill, and the nation-state dream which could be a perpetual desire, and we are still there on the banks of that river, desiring to awaken, to return to prehistories before the nation-states or man writ his progressive histories, his riparian novels were dreams and memories were longer and then not long, like this river. The nation is a thing made of ether, made by men, make: confidence, polities, policies; decree girls, races, infidels, the souls of the living and all of our progress as soul'd men,—this drive, this project, ideas which continue apace like a sound without end;—and faith? and a man writ large on pages of notes, a poetry for his progress; a dead end.

Does it end? When does it? And the easterlies, civilization, and the Cuchumatanes in the distance. What have we made in these Americas and of them; who this we, this man who speaks? (he is speaking, dreaming) the etiology of his desires, the destruction of natural histories, the old gods, the heft of what remains and of what remains unseen (unseeable); silences amidst the endless soundings; and the interstitial noises are like a river in a small Highland village, in Acul after it rains—the silence between waters, beneath water— an owl in the ceiba tree, and the Cold War taken up into the mountains, onto her flesh, her brother's body, inside the womb for eternity, which is the moment of their demise.

He is speaking and the succubus leads him into the river. The river is full and filled to with rainwaters, the bodies and bones of massacre, and the unspoken that is carried each day and on each back, and the mountain in the distance which saved and damned the living—modern History, the succubus will say, is writ by a very small group of men.

Yet the unhistories are also material, a brown etched spoor, as if all of life were a descent into the imagination, which is like a girl in Acul before she walks down the mountain path to return to Nebaj and then takes a bus to the capital city of her nation, and travels the four hundred and sixty-five miles to Ciudad Guatemala, and her village is a village on a Wednesday 21 April, and after the fires and the tree in the plaza (which was no real plaza) became a cross and her brother and the church with its paltry crossbeams and blue door and windowless alcoves like the windowless houses of the village— and then it is not. And the mountains are mountains and the Cuchumatanes a refuge and there are owls and grasses and roots which hold one teaspoonful of water; and a six foot deep and fif-

teen foot long pit that the old men of Acul are made to dig (by soldiers, Galils on the arms of the soldiers; there are green uniforms
and black boots); and the black-masked boy from another village
whose finger pointed named the difference for the men in Acul, the
soldiers pulling boys and men from the rows, a yes or a no, his finger, put them into Heaven or Hell, and all of this is not pulled from
the national History, the imagination plays its part, a man sits on
his padded and green armchair in his valley paradise, which is like
a man collects corpses on the streets of this city, and on a Thursday
he is sitting in a high school classroom in Van Nuys and he draws
pictures in his notebook of sailboats, girls, and notes for his class,
and he stares at the clock to see the time on it; waiting; slow; and
he is wearied by the teacher's chronologies and lists words,
battles—and she has no clock to look at and the Gregorian calendar is not on the walls, the daykeeper is killed today in Acul (and
who will keep the old days of the ancient Ixil calendars now?), and
there is no school in the village, and on this land her shoes are made
from plastics, yellows, and it could be lunchtime soon, he thinks that
he is hungry for lunch, and that he will have a chocolate bar for his
repast and he buys chocolate from a machine and she does not eat
for days afterwards, runs up into the mountains with the other villagers; sees from the mountain how the soldiers destroy the world
in fire.

These are days. There are birds. There are weavers and they
make the shirts for girls; and in her village each girl learns the em-
broidery of hummingbirds, of mountains, they are the tz'unun and
in his language there are words behind all of the words: an infidel
lurks in the bushes of the lexicon—infidels, perfidies—there are
aberrations of trust, of faith, even if he cannot see it, even if he

does not know it he knows it—that beneath the sentences lurks the feeling, an old sentir, and also the lies of the ages making edifices from pain, monuments to the hidden, the hungry, this is how we might write ourselves up, he writes, how a progress unprogresses.

WE ARE MEN writ large by the logic of sentences. By the: "They made the Ixil prisoners, branded them and took them slaves"; or: "The impact of the conquest must have been disastrous for the Ixil." And on page 46 in a History book, "As a reward to Spanish settlers, the land and its Indian inhabitants were parceled out in large groupings called *encomiendas*, under a system already applied in Spain to 'reconquered' Moorish territories." He is trying to find Marta on page 46, but how to get inside these phrases? how to be faithful? "The encomenderos . . . jailed them, killed them, beat them and set dogs on them. They seized their goods, destroyed their agriculture, and took their women. They used them as beasts of burden. They took tribute from them and sold it back under compulsion at exorbitant profits. Coercion and ill-treatment were the daily practices of their overseers."

I would like to get beneath the phrases as if beneath water, and unravel the birds the mountains and find there discover the interstices of histories, our, flesh.

With faith, or without it then, he sits on a wide and green armchair and the sky is blue-clear today; soon he will drive to work. Now: "Such a drastic change must have had a profound effect on the Ixil population, and must have added a great burden to the logistics of corn growing, harvesting, and transporting. (On the other hand, logistical problems may have been alleviated with the drop in population caused by concentrating the people and making them more vulnerable to the devastating epidemics of the period. A reduced population would not have so far to go in the surrounding countryside to till their fields.)"

Then he is in his car and driving toward the sea through the mountain pass which in his mind makes a canyon, he thinks the word canyon while he drives, presses gas pedal and clutch pedal (and: I have driven these roads for years and each automobile that I have driven goes up the same roads I have always only known, the 405 Freeway like an equation for memory, recalls childhood, television shows, and even though I am no longer that boy, and even though it is possible that the roads, the city itself, has abated or been forgotten by the millions who reside here, Los Angeles could be a material dream, and it is this matter, among others, Marta, that I take up.).

AND MARTA,—even if I wished it and on many days I do, I cannot stop this thinking of, and making of, you in my mind and in my mind we are together (again) and where else and what else but with our clothes removed (and your torn skirt and your unshod feet and your unadorned face and roughhard soled feet; blackened toenails); naked you lie in my arms; your legs are open and your thighs press against mine and I would like only to stay there which is here forever in the pitch of my desire your sex is the beginning of this world and I don't speak or need to and don't want speech just your breathy cunt underarm body's odors wet cunt and my lust which is your sex undried and my—I'll eat this fruit—you say, I say it in my mind: devour the body when it sings; sing to me (O girl) of a man's lost days in this city, of his perpetual loneliness, like a talisman made of the brown-grey air.

Without days without work without I will pay bills, cut grasses, shop for things, fix them up, take out the piles of garbage;—did you do you go to school make good marks in school make up homework do your lessons correctly (learn of: Jamestown Georgetown and English subjects, King George III and the desire to be free-men; declare the new places; Americans;—but not of this place or these rivers, or of the Spanish brother Fray Juan Crespí, when he stumbled upon this alluvial plain on the northward expedition from Baja California with Gaspar de Portolá; the Washingtonias unplanted in the eighteenth century distance; the Gabrielino girls and boys alongside the Los Angeles River before it was the Los Angeles River; the Ixil girl who walks the dirt paths of Acul; the monuments to rage and poverty beneath the tarmacked roads; the black boy lynched up like a dog in 1930; the whites stare into the photographer's lens, point to their boy, *Bo pointn to his niga*; some of the boy's hair, a swath of his trousers framed up also); make the correct thinking seeing; gaze as you should; buy as you ought to buy the clothes for shoes for toys for things on the scale of yes please now; make love from the lintel, at the threshold of doors; make rules and kill all of the: don't be shy; you are happy now in this city, in this desert starred, the cinema at your feet; the daydreamed titties of the cinema at your feet and the water for this city comes down the causeway from the Owens Valley as you lunch with your bosses and friends and say thank you, please, sir; more of these things. Then you will rise from the dead as Lázaro, his sister is by his side, Marta; Marta, take me home with you.

And I did not intend to kill you, no more perhaps than I in-

tended to kill and rekill the Gabrielino girls and boys (their existence) for this American man to become so: an American in his
city; an idea of a man? and my ideas in my head (are they mine?)
history'd from my teachers, memory'd from the boys on the playground, push my head into the dirt, tarmac, the playground view
of the palms in the distance, the girls in the back row; the television blares in the background. These Americas make us and
they unmake us, unmade and making you all of time—disease, the
vagrancy laws, lynching laws, blacks whites roads rules and
Indians.—Do you exist, darling? And if not, may I?

I am a man, these my urges. These are mine: thoughts, killers,
dreams in a Los Angeles city landscape; the geographies of sadness.
Look out;—see the girl by the cypress; it is a beautiful and hallowed
tree before Lázaro is tied there: an evergreen in the plaza. The
clouds lie low on the mountains; it rains today in Acul; it is cold and
your unshod feet are cold and the cuxín fruit is sweeter in your
mouth than the last season in this sentence so I'll do it: I'll make you
from these phrases (make me also); the making of Americans from
a particular order of words, syllable sounds, inside the sentences
which killers, our deaths, and it is a tedious facile business—why
isn't it beautiful and kind? why is to make in America also to kill in
America? I am seeking the old spoors and days via this tongue.

[I wish that I could ease into your voice your tongue's dips and
the hard consonant of love and on the tongue it would be
sufficient—speak to me and speaking I'll fall into your voice like a
man into water. Do I need meaning to fall in? Can your Ixil be like
a river and invite the modern inside for some atol because it is cold
today in Acul and the atol is warm sweet thick cornmilk. My
English is hard and sweet, I'll give you some of it here; I'll give you
mountains rivers a way out of time and the basement in the capi-

tal of your country which is not yours, which is not the same as the unowned, what cannot be purchased, like sunlight cannot be sold. Beckons you back harkens you down from Guatemala over the Spanish and into English inside paradise on the streets of this city, the succubi guide us into the (concreted up) river.]

"WE'RE WORKING together to keep America strong."

The men of Heaven are bundled up like canes and shunted into the main room of the administration building. The administration building in your village is a corrugated metal roofed shack in a not dirt-roaded place next to the church. The men huddle like bees: they listen to the outside differences; they wait and you are an adolescent girl and unable to hide beneath your auntie's skirt, your mother holds a boy at her breast, the youngest, he's wrapped up in cloth; invisible. 1982 in the spring and the desert sunlight hits the sky in Los Angeles; the clouds huddle like magnets. I am a young man, and he sits in a wooden chair in the classroom or later on the sofa in his living room; he eats ice cream; he watches the afternoon parade of deceit and lovely happy girls on the television screen (I don't do my homework and your mother and auntie, and the boy too?, bleed onto your skin); the television sounds are too loud, my mother will say (I invent my mother in this moment),—the heft of our dialogue as the afternoon wanes into greys reds: I remember that they fell in love on a boat at sea and that they were eternally happy at the end of the show. I am eating ice creams and this the end of it—their happiness in the Show.

This a welcome to my country.

I STUDY THE LANGUAGE, Marta, move from time to time; think about words, of maize in this English rolls off of the tongue like a stone into the underbrush—maize from maiz and behind that the word from the Arawak: majisi?, it is uncertain—ah, the sorrows to be found in the smallest of utterances, the dictionary variances, so that we cannot, even now, know maize? And then the maze to the Arawak—see them? see the island girls on their knees, the boys; these words too a muddle; the Arawak X'd out and only the maize remains in these sentences. *Mahiz*, Oviedo called it, he was the official court chronicler for the Spanish king and he made lists for the New World; ko'm you say in your Ixil; Indian corn in my American English.

Perhaps I'm not seeking you, but seeking a new tongue with which to lick this place up. I am fat and I am hungry; voracious like a man and I would like to lick it up and lively fuck it until it's in my skin and bones (the Washingtonias tip in the breeze, a beautiful wind in the Highlands, greener air, the days long saddened); the organs are meaty.

I love it here. I am killing dying and wasting the days: the maize is the trace of it—I lose you find you—this can only be love; loneliness made ripe like a green banana after it's boxed up, gassed, and sent out of your country. I eat it happily in front of my television set today.

Your village is not in a photograph: without windows, electricity, books; without a school or dirt or tarmac road which leads there, and you and the others living, electrified, elbows, knees, the veins myths of unhistory; the unmarked dead (XXMUJER); your mother's blood; the covered up brother (he is sleeping suckling): all of it a mark on you and all of it unphotographed unwritten; denied—the Army never arrived on 22 April, your oldest brother was not a brother or crucified on cypress on Thursday. Subversives, they said. The guerrilla; commie devils. I can't understand your language; I eat ice cream and I go to the cinema, and funny things, sad battles, and requited love in Shows, and justice like a sweet candy at THE END of Shows; and they didn't waste their bullets: your brother was machete'd up,—who cares to spend a bullet on an Ixil dog? Shuttled the men out of the administration building; laughed at their cries for the cut-up bruised (alive yet) flesh of their flesh, piles of it from Hell inside the church; heaped up unhappily; bruised; blooded and the cries of the pained men from Hell; these men who soon (later in this book) will bare their necks for the slaughter like the good quiet sheep so that their fathers and brothers may kill them (for the patria). I can't see any of this, Marta, I don't want it, to see it, know, the decimation of the Arawak, their final days in the fifty years after the Genoan explorer and his crew disembarked on their island; you in the plaza, the boy bleeds out a few houses away and his mother pleading with the soldier until she is also bleeding out in front of you, but not me, darling:—I am a scribe, a stenographer of lust and the fucker inside and outside: I write what isn't said slowly, it is an essay, my self in a page of vermin, of a man like a man limps on the streets of your capital; his eyes are opaque, grey, a dull dead animal thing. It was the listening that was the worst of it you say, you know it to be true: the men huddled, like bees, listening to the heft and the whistle of steel coming from the church; the machete-made cries, the smack of flesh, and rifle butts inside faces, the imagination behind the screams of girls and women and babes wrapped up, invisible: the imagination made the men and women into bees. What else does it make here? Here in the mind and entrails.

. . . ON A TRAIN or you are speaking, he is walking toward the kitchen to get something to eat (meat) and it arrives as it arrives constantly, like a train made from the trade winds: invisible, cacophonic loud, motored, irreversible by a small man, a man's form—this is sorrow, he thinks; this can be an inheritance, like myopia or thick knees. *do I love you?* Perhaps in this lifetime I have only loved a corpsey girl, and she a woman I've not had or known her—and to be haunted by her (and my grandmother) is no more difficult than the sorrow arrives, an invisible force, the cold easterlies bring the rain and a train moves out of the pupil, down the mountainside, across the tarmacked avenues and into the mind—as if it were machinated, progressive, metallic and grey: a thing made for speed, commerce, to travel—this westward passage to the Indies; Atlantis on the brink of the mind.

I have lived as a half-alive man; I am a half-dead and the dead now my companions; and you, dear Marta, as you lie on the stonecold cement in the capital of your country (the Polytechnic), you are handless, the puncture wounds in your breast, they have removed your ears and nose—this is the corpse of the beloved, this the girl who must return to me in the heart of the Americas, in the semi-arid plains of Los Angeles, on the streets, in his automobile, at night as he watches the television Shows—a black metallic greyed container for the loneliness, for an old sorrow, a disbelief in this manner of dying—without the breast? two ears removed? to fuck her like a child and then slit the cunt open like summer fruit with the machete bayonet cut glass? this sound she makes as you cut her: *what are we, Marta?* And why does it not stop change stop or become for the millennial rounds—Or: why then can't we simply fuck to our heart's content, in the middle of the road, during concerts in movie theaters, classrooms, business meetings: as we wish it, as we are made to do it: I see you, you are bent at the waist in the fields the shop and you turn, smile, lift your skirt and invite me inside the glorious cunt-world: don't you know, darling, that we cannot live without your form? It is the cunt has made us, the cunt calls us: we kill to return; the blood of the wound for your slit unadorned; invited; smiled upon: the eternal electric yes.

And no matter that you have died in Acul, in the mountain, in the capital of your country (the Polytechnic)—for it is no small thing to have found you in the midst the multitude, O for we have multiplied—to have looked and perpetual seeking and then there you are before me: mutilated, unadorned, brown-black haired black eyed—a beauty in the sea of loneliness; a god in my unidoled Christian sphere; my own madonna girl; this sweet christ mother— you gaze at me, the black unseeing allseeing eye.

Because I've not been seen or even, perhaps, been *seeable*—the driver, he drives along the streets of Los Angeles. I can make the work; I will make my way along the 405 Freeway toward my job, toward commerce, meetings, sales; toward this American dream, to a girl who has not been slaughtered (in Acul in the mountain in the basement of the Polytechnic)—you turn round, look straight at me, speak to me in your language, the autochthonous tongue, a tongue for the mountain river ko'm and the trade winds, two-harvested seasons: say: Listen, put your hand in my slit; here is the heart for the unancient boys, for the boys who would like to return to the sun moon gods: to the real of iconic days, of blood for the deities, not the lies of the modern, no longer the driver for the demonic weeks, this 365 day calendar of contained longings, the sky passes fast cars slower than this machine tarmac blurs trees wheat cotton because to fuck like this is like dying, and we all of us want out; and freed from this tyrannical real Show. I want it: to find the gods behind the maize, inside the maze, the old sentir.

WE MADE STREETS and wide avenues in the semi-arid plains. Filled the rotund brown-grey earth with highways with automobiles and mechanical lights, with the precision of painted lines. Palm treed horizons and blocked vistas and valleys without views. We pulled the mountain to the wayside, concreted the river, machined the world and clocked the days. *where is the end of it?* The sea is cold in the summers, perpetual paradise weathers—we are concrete exiles, strange and foreigners to this place—this our destination; we at the end, and there are no more travels, we move the metal machines round the circuitous holey roads like toy cars on toy roads; we are like children without childish ease: we entertain ourselves ruthlessly, as if masturbating on highwire. Endlessly— consuming the landscape; breaking and building it up; undesiccating the millennial dusted plains. We are no more able, drivers, movers, makers—it is at the end, the sea stops us: there is nothing awaits us now. The horizon has perished, and we are stranded here, at the pilgrim's apogee; terrible; beastly; the strange millions in this city; the lackluster hordes: lonely beyond any recall—I cannot ken—ready to kill and be killers: I can smell your violent rush like a rush to purchase food in the supermarket aisles; to buy larger and metals plastics; to make heaps of capital gain-hills, houses, highrises, girls, foodstuffs and then more stuffs in piles.

I have come to understand, Marta, that it is in between the Americas, alongside the rivers we've undone, the valleys undesiccated, and waters dispatched, that I am come to find you. And we are not allied by History, by Progress, roads, by the misters Ronald Reagan and Efraín Ríos Montt (whom we did not know), the soldiers and sellers and the young conqueror, Pedro de Alvarado, as he marched down the Yucatán Peninsula in 1523, and Mr Crespí as he walked onto this alluvial plain two hundred years later, or Billy Mulholland making his water plans for this city in 1904, and Mulholland Dr leads to my childhood home (the street was named for a man?); and the unnamed countless million others who work in your capital drive in my city, make machines and itemized lists (TO DO's) and children, money and the Cessna A37-B which flies over your prostrate form in the mountain; make plans and unmake your hands today in the capital (a coffee cutting implement); undo the slim wrists; make a boy in my city who drives an auto without a past or kin; a boy who knows things History like a dog knows his master's tongue. You there like a small christ in the Highlands, the Cuchumatanes are a dream for what can be hidden inside them; he is here, driving, alone; seeking his daily bread for the hungers in his belly; watching the television Shows: a good boy a good citizen a good Show—he thinks that the world is a loud and dirty barbarian brood outside his borders; he thinks that the barbarians might eat his meat; he is happy and entertained and fatigued; he is tired every day, happy that the Shows end happy.

[Men are Makers, Marta; and since I was a boy on the play-grounds of this city I have not understood it well enough. I am the boy who would sit in the corner lie in the hammock spread your legs open like eternity's siesta fêted because I am slow because it is in-ertia for this boy, not action, I am always the slower, stumbling, and the man of action as the book says is a stupid man, and silently howls: a beastly man; and if so he will make us again also, unmade your brothers mother; made you into a different girl, a girl in the capital; an Indian dirty like a dog who can learn Spanish if you split her skull in two and pour the lexicon inside like contract men pour cement into squares and rectangular skulls: say: we are not dogs men; we are men men.]

America does not exist.

[Why do you live in the Highlands? Why did you survive or die? Why are you coming to me now, this haunt,—leave me to my things! leave me to my televisioned visions; I am: happy; we are: white men and happy and rich; thinned and fattened and we laugh to the music of commerce, and the music of having nice days lives and Shows on the television—this is no complaint or rail, a rail on the tail-end of his happiness, of the dog, the American hounds are fat and happy also.]

I am an aberration. I am nothing. I am a man who is no man; a man who seeks you on the streets of this city, a city which is no place, not a central mountain or river god—we have a river here?—not, no, just the moving vehicles, the fucking doors, walls, shops, highways and roads; the girls, the boys, the language of TO DO, the houses filled with prosperity, jobs of work and work.—And in Los Angeles we speak five hundred languages and all of them, Marta, are lost to me. (What is this "half-Armenian" his mother goaded him on about when he was a boy?, and then afterwards always added, smiling, "But you are American, darling," as if he wouldn't ever have to worry about his place.) You're lost to me, Marta, and me lost also to me.

IT IS NOT, perhaps, your obligation to speak it to me as I speak it back toward your unhearing tympanum, a drum without hammers—can you feel my sex harden like a tool (I can make girls?), the blood engorges it slow and although you are dead, I am wondering if you will fuck me today (today a holy day, after all).

Why am I making this love across the mountains desert, thousands of miles away in your America; across time and the myths of beginning and landscape and a babeled language game? We could be a compass, we could be nothing fancier than a slow fuck, than a: I will give up the auto and walk the dirt paths in your village, pass by the capital of your lost days and seek you there find you in the remains,—a spoor can last a thousand years,—I have inquired in books I have looked in the television Shows and it is all beyond my ken; my imagination; I am a burden, a failure, a slow livered man; inert; dirty, and I wont make a thing today; I wont idea a road or a girl or buy candies at the corner market.

There is a half-built house which haunts me, immanent in my mother's five phrases and I never thought of it or of the phrases themselves; I forgot them; and it is useless to worry, Marta, I am useless to try to comprehend or to do anything, to save what cannot be saved—you—the mountains the sea and a quiet sky slow-time; the time of maize and walks; seasons. I am this coward who sits on his wide and green padded armchair, drives on the streets of this city, and I have tried speaking but it is impossible now, this speech, for I am always in the river, which could be the mind, and the utterances of the quotidian float above me like clouds in a heavy sky in Acul: hellos and yeses and can you believes and that girl is a shame and today we buy this, tomorrow we will thrust it into garbage cans and buy another and to the stores and buy this and— me? in my own mind-river unable now to live the goodlife of new Eden, of California, LA, and seeking you in this current, a girl I am finding, an American man making his American Marta, his Barbarian Eve (which could be life) and not of his clay rib this girl, unbodied, spirit only, like clear glass; breath; your green Highland winds (which are memoried first and bodied second): your hands disappeared and then reappeared two thousand two hundred miles away in my folios. Am I then a Maker, Marta, of unseen unspoken violent things, like this half-built, half iterated, and then disre-membered house?

I DON'T KNOW what makes us happy—*sorrow, I am beginning to see what makes it*—but not this revolutionary happy, I too pursue her ephemeral arms to hold my hands and face and make me it on all of the nights that I can hardly bear to be. From here in my cap-ital I can see Liberty on the top of the capitol building; the obelisk in the distance; the aeroplanes fly above our heads and we the Americans have come here, to our capital, to find the gods in their New World temples; they are men like you and me, Marta, and I have climbed the steps of the stone buildings, and I have followed the rules to the president's house, and I have essayed to learn what it is, here, so many thousands of miles from Los Angeles, from you also, darling, that has made this man this man. Can I find him here amidst the museum artifacts and white halls and monuments documents to the Novus Ordo Seclorum? I have come on an aeroplane to find it here, of a sudden I decided it: to travel to my capital and find the American man I am making in this collection, hoping that your gods and His soldiers will not have reason to burn it later, upon the next conquest, in the American man's museum'd mind: the interstitial boy's life: the man laid bare, the man who would like to discover that hopefulness which happiness the monuments to the new, the future.

I am fatigued, again. I am lonely in this capital; I walk the gravel paths of the National Mall and passing all of the museums and all of my brethren, made mine by language and television Shows and the clocks of the classroom, its rules and roles; by foods and: they look like me; fat; hungry; we are loud as we walk along the free roads and wait obediently at the street corners (the policemen stop us with their gestures and black batons) while the president's motorcade passes by us swiftly, his policed life, our great man, I bow to him as he goes, wish to kiss what his tires have traversed; would like to pleasure him, fuck him, believe his phrases like dogs.

I wish that I could be a different man like these men in my capital. They seem happy, like the glassy icons on the television Shows. Things are certain, the rules have been cast, the weather makes no difference to the American, we condition air and alter what we abhor. We buy products, diets, fats, to feel good, and crèmes and machines for: driving digging seeing, and we don't walk the streets of this city and buy machines for walking; magazines to learn how to do it: making love; buying guns; safe-keeping our properties and ourselves (alarms steel bars locks and thick glass). We would like to be safe above all things, above love and hate, higher than Liberty on the old white domed capitol building.

I spoke to you today on the telephone (so you see, darling, the telephone does allow the living our conversations with the dead). And what did you speak to me? could you say, a husband in the background pulling on your skirt asking you for more of your meat more of your duties, your voice distracted, a high pitch, the formal veneer of lies of decorum of Hello! & How are you! this too made me sadder; lonelier.

I wanted to know one or two things—the simplest requirements for the simple American boy: (do you love me?; will you always love me and against the vagaries of time and river currents, death?; will you only and for eternity like a good screw love this boy who dreams of you; fucks the Hollywood Blvd and bookshop girls to crawl inside your cunt; thinks that he would like to become one of the dead to find you amidst the courageous and bolder souls of the underworld) —Does it go well with you? I said. —Do your hands ache from the pounding of the maize? —Is it more painful to live without your hands? (I have lived without seeing and this also causes pain, Marta, but a dull gainful pain, like a sore muscle; like shopping for something I don't require, cannot afford; capital amusements.) I am speaking and saying the quotidian things; I don't mention your hands the myopia of my days, just the howdoyoufare's isyourmotherwell's doesyoursonplayinthegarden's and below these set phrases and responses there is a river of words and sentences jumbled up into unspoken, effluvial desires all to the source, the sea, in these Americas: doyouloveme doyouloveme doyouloveme willyoumorestilluntilafterdeath loveonlyme? And below this rained and high pitch of what I don't say to you (this word-river roars behind the tympanum while I am speaking into the monstrous black machine) is this other black and underworld, Acheron's riotous current, the long pitched despair of the modern: a desire to cease without dying; an unbearable chest aches which we call "heart," or the ephemeral soul in the place of muscle: youdon'tlovemeasIimaginedthemannerinwhichImustneedsbeloved (IamdyingMarta,mykidneymalfunctionskillsmetoday); you have died before you could do it and you could never do it outside of this recalling this history the styled self I am making in these pages; and I am lost here, in these Americas, as I have ever been; more alone; abandoned by the gods my ancestral devices; my own dead scattered about the earth below it and don't save me or visit at the stone thresholds into paradise; into small fiery hells; behind these Los Angeles lies. (And behind his Los Angeles lies the distant Lebanon and an ancient and ruined rock citadel before that—the Armenian town of Kharphert in old Turkey—and a grandmother's father disappears, and her mother walks into the desert in the summer1915, and a mother's five paltry phrases to recall them afterwards in Los Angeles.)

I DO NOT WALK HOME for hundreds of miles into the desert, across its deserted terrain, overland, to find you, across mountains, down the ravines of sadness, and into the heart of things, the landscape a wonder. I see water runs along metal concrete byways, held in an empty parking lot, a trapezoidal water-lot, for the prisoner of water and the prisoner in water, held until the spigot is turned, until the sores of his flesh have putrefied, until he and she are demised utterly—and I do wonder, whence this water? I do not walk because we are not perambulators, but drivers, and I am a man who needs this speed like a man who needs his lover to suck him soundly: a good suck off and the run-off, the water, like the waterly beasts in the reservoir, the aquifer, deep inside the blackest pits that the soldiers made for the lonely girls and boys in your capital, in the basement of the Army Technical School.

And I remember the days from childhood, the balmy blazoned days of youth when we were unconscious of it, of the drive before sex drives, to run and yelling loudly, to play and play games and play mean tricks and swim the blued allochthonous waters in all of the chemically blued-up swimming pools of all of the houses that were built one after the other like concrete mimetic shadows: your house is like mine! (you are like me?); I return to my childhood home off of Mulholland Dr and the place is unrecognizable. The landscape altered beyond recognition? Or is it that a child, a boy, like a dog, cannot see vistas? does not see them. And therefore could not have seen the hills in the distance, the low-lying cruciferous clouds, the vega, valley peaks and dried wind, the chaparral and tall skinned palms; the sea on the distant horizon. I don't know the names of any of the vast and changed and unchanged flora of Los Angeles: in schools we studied the discrete, correctly manifested wars and kings and the timeline of progress, a Show destined for this desert chaparral (chaparrito, txapar); not the shrunken dead, the dearly decimated Gabrielinos—their doom unwrit by the books, by the river. Was there a river? Was it commuted? My thoughts are my own, a (American) man thinks: this is mine and doesn't think of the hullabaloo, of the place he is raised in as a *place* and not a point on the line of his country's (predetermined) evolution. I am a yes, he says, to the empty streets of his childhood neighborhood; to the quiet auto-tombs in driveways. Signs on each private drive: Private Property: *what do we own when we own it?* (picks up a feather) And how wide and low is it mine? (picks up a stone) *I would like to know the Laws*, he thinks: might I not go to jail for this stone essayed? this essay into the man? He is reminded of the savage stories of his youth: the beastly cinema verity, the fun of it, the *yeses*—I loved to watch them die, he thinks. A galloping horse falls in the West. The actors were paid. The horses trained. The Indians savage and loud.

I have driven to the old community center. It is locked up and a CLOSED sign posted on the glass doors. The building is located on the periphery of the collection of house shadows. I stand around for half an hour, and see that all of the dirt and earth of my childhood is paved over and housed-up now, only in the far distance do I see dirt-hills, chapparal, the word having come to me in a rush: chaparrito; the security guard arrives and he looks at me stern, a man my age, and he will ask me my business, and I a man with no business will say, and he then: *get out of here*. I listen for the rattlesnakes of my childhood; for coyotes to eat up the neighbors' small dogs; for the dirt paths naked feet upon them, and uncharted places in front of our children's minds; the smell of sagebrush, the taste of saltbush. I can hear the noise the autos make behind the community center but I cannot see them, it could be that they are driven by themselves, exist only to make this noise inside my ears, relentless, restless, unstoppable, and I am no longer certain that cars are inhabited by men; I cannot be sure of any animal living in these monstrous noiseless pine cement houses either: whence?— when not a soul rouses from the place? And are there animal drivers? I cannot see the wild things anymore. I cannot hear the tamed dogs either. I do not see you, Marta (can you see me?). And loss, like a boy's inability to see the mountain views, or the sea in the far-off distance which is seeable only two or three times a year in Los Angeles, after the rains. Deeply buried, unimagined and ingrained like the you I never knew when I lived in this house as a boy and you traveled to Nebaj with your father and ate a candy in the plaza, and when the guard tells me that I must go I am afraid as I am always afraid in this city, and I depart: I have no right to be here any longer, and I am not sure why I returned to the old neighborhood off of Mulholland Dr, made such a diversion on my way home from work, wished to see the unseeable sea, when all that there was was the usual brown-grey haze along the mountain's edge.

I HAVE SO MANY things in my head and I am sorting through them between the drives, the works, the business routes and sales: corpse-collecting in the eternal moments which are not moments and of which I am almost completely unawares . . . I am wandering on the streets of this city—there are long drives and loud music as I drive and the seconds left when the mind does its own descending, the length of a dream or a notthought thought, a universe entire in what the national offices might call a moment and what you and I know to be eternity,—about the men who take the woman from a side garden and say to her that they love her and with cigarettes and with their half-mast cocks, love her, burnt the skin one hundred and seventeen times; loot the body and leave their traces behind: black marks; cut off the hands; cock-marks; a child in the womb, the cut up cunt—they remove her hands like stars.

I live here on Hollyline Av. I am, for those to see, not too tall, an ugly man and a fat man (*not what I look* like *in this book but my looking, and you, Reader, then look through my looks*); a man who collects corpses silently, quietly, even he doesn't know that he does it; drives the streets and highways of this city. The corpse-collector can see the signs; the corpse-collector has a hard-on; the corpse-collector is a good boy, a good American boy; he likes parties, he likes the television, he likes ice cream; he hides the corpses and his imagination from his colleagues, friends and neighbors. He likes to touch himself in the dark (and when his father sees him doing it, castigates him roughly, but he still doesn't stop it—he is unable to stop it; hides this from his colleagues, friends and neighbors also); he likes to hide under the cloaks of dresses, his mother's skirts, he huddles beneath the floorboards of the wooden deck: he likes dark, silent places and the insects he finds there—he talks to small things before he cuts them up; salts the snail, smashes the carpet beetles, kills all of the flies, and he likes the lizard's tail best, this he keeps as a prize; he likes to crawl on his hands and knees to find the black things; to eat maggots and leaves.

I am free, Marta (huddles, watches television, buys an ice cream from the shop). On the News there are the wars in other places. On the News the barbarians fight wars and they are killers; when the killers kill each other he is disgusted disgruntled and then happy: that he is free and strong, and that he is no man's slave; unsavagely descended from History, which could be Ancient Greece and the Roman Republic toward England . . . even killing you we'll say it while we hack your flesh up, bone you out—kill all of the organ thinking: in America we can always win. We are: strong. We are: free and liberated from the slaves. We are direct from Europe's best stock; the stock markets hub and bub like happy numbers that can only go up and up, a river moves skyward.

If I were dead, Marta, this would be the story I'd write. A story of my half-dead life, like one writes the story of the bones he finds in the desert, and they are ten thousand or eighty-three or sixteen years old, and from these bones we make girls and long plaits and idols from baskets and clay, arrowheads and flutes and pendants for your ears. Do I make sense? Am I making, essaying, the normal, the sensible, the days without fucking (how can a corpse fuck his girl?) I am dead; I am a corpse. But yes, alas, a killer corpse; diseased—I can make more men such as me into more men such as me: killers corpses, we put our cocks into all of the virginal white pussies; we bring them out red and died in the wool; it is pain and suffering and it is pain and to suffer that we do it: Marta, we the missionaries of the proper: we would like to save the world (:*from*: communist scum; non-believers; cunty women and whores; you and the savages who encroach us). O freedom. To liberty. From the People out to the dogs: at the garbage dump in your capital the children search for unbroken toys and their mothers scraps of food to make the organs unceasingly move, make, clean up the body, the blood. My own blood dirtied now, running lower and lower to the sea. Why don't I cease? Why this insistence on the living? Fucking and dying. Why am I so terribly alone with my things, my organs, my sex and all that I don't can't say, know, although I would like to know it in this interstitial history, which is my essay toward you, toward love, Marta? Marta, why don't you speak back to me? Why this silent treatment? What have I possibly done to deserve such hateful and black nonlanguage? Are you stupid? Are you dirty? Do you shit, piss and eat corn cakes? I gave you a rib, now stew it up.

Maybe what we have and all that we have, are the traces of what is not destroyed in one way or another before this age began—

a small thing which was made, superstitions, the tossing of salt (for the east wind); the sacred objects now on the dollar and clocks; time in the moon; the obelisk in my capital; the gods' breath upon my spine and I shiver as if I am cold, and not because I am accompanied by the invisible. Because we are making a payment for this sort of living, and we not asked if we wanted it, and yet we perpetuate it like dogs, not asked, perpetually eating the food put before our snout;—I know that you are a savage, Marta, and I could love you because I know that I am the payment for the civilized man.

HAVE YOU SEEN the modern man unhindered? He is in a strip club and his mouth is open and the saliva runs down his chin and he sees you naked and you show him your cunt your fat tits and he wants only to return to find his mother in your darkness to slip his cock inside so quietly and slow and docile, like a good boy, he thinks, into your flesh. He lifts your clean and beautiful dark underpants to his mouth to his nose and breathes in and he is happy and he is not looking at the other men who all of us looking seeking you; we too love his look, the look of the open-mouth possessed amazed violent alive man who unashamed by his desire and you are dancing or you are parading your form or you look into his eyes and open your cunt lips wide even though he pays you again and again and even though you loathe him or today you do not (you've taken his cock into your cunt on many occasions) you welcome him home to the capital to America to this place which he has sought all of his life: to love and paradise and California and the black Amazonia girls in the conqueror's fantasy—to obliteration which could be love; out. See the man without shame; he is happy for the cunt-world and its prizes smiles smells; he is openmouthed and out inside the club and we are hungry as we are always hungry in my America.

IT IS THESE structures I am trying to essay: the roads, the effect of roads and motorcars on the mind, on this urge, on the sky and data and words and the clouds which sit on the mountains today like girls, do not rise or fall, on me, Marta, on you? Tell me what it is, why I write you day after day and seek you here in the fleshless place even as my semen smells up from my hands feet, and the stench of my body its fluid is irredeemable warm and I am repulsed by it and it is me and all that I have of you here amidst the English of my phrases sadnesses and distances and made in another place but I make it here also: this *made*; and the syllable is uninterruptible and its sounds make men and roads, made the tar and stones which covered my soul and sealed in a black loneliness, the reams of time, and the words I seek here to find you, Ixil girl, to understand why it is and it is the inquiring that this man makes, he is a driver, a corpse-collector, smells the semen on his feet, the stench has risen to his nose and he would eat his seed and he thinks it could make children it could make pleasure, it could be a father's ecstasy and not this shame at night, late, as he eats hamburgers, candies, he is repulsed by it—the American man without glory, with nothing but false ideas of a place with a modern man's failure to know failure because love cannot be contained because I can love all of the women and why should this love be contained by morality's compass by roads and the time of the clock, which is: whose?; who made it? profits by it?: a death for the living, a half-life which is not a life but a time among the cannibals, but instead of flesh we allowed to eat, we eat roads; we tarmac the world; we eat our neighbors' complaints and the News and Politics and Shows, we hate our neighbors, ourselves and the outside inside urges—you—a foreign girl in a foreign place (you do not exist in the News in Politics in Shows) and here I am foreign to myself to you; you make hills and trees and blouses are woven with hummingbirds: make me, Marta, make me back into the me I have not been, but could be; inside; could have been; unashamed alive, mouth agape, the gate opened, your agapet here among the dead pages.

The dead are here among the electric lights; I see you in the corners of things, behind the sofa beneath the dust motes and inside the detritus of the living, the uncleaned corners, which I cleaning now and taking out and disinfecting the surfaces of and I am sitting in the dark inside my closet and the electric lights are outside with you and you are with me every day and closer than my own pupil my image in the mirror is foreign to me and this Marta I carry next to my blackness returns inside and I am seeking the byways outside of time and reason to remake your house, to find you in Los Angeles which could be as if I were walking the paths of Acul (the tarmac has not arrived to your hamlet; the road built in 1983 by the hands of the survivors; a dirt road; the Army rationed the builders ten tortillas each day while the soldier held the Galil above their bent backs, supervised their good work as free men, as the Galil made the free men make the dirt road); and I see your hut in the distance, it is the house from before the holocaust, and there are dozens of houses in Acul and each separated by this plot of

land and the maize makes wind in the fields between houses and the
beans grow at the base of the maize plants in their curled and verdant maze, a green animal, and I see smoke emerge from the chimney pipes at dawn, find your home and I enter the door, this lintel
which crosses time, it is blue, the centuries undone as I walk down
the paths of your village and into your home and you make the tortilla by hand with hands of grace and each time I see you making
them, the pounded maize and your hands like gods from the repetition of the gods, I am hungry and you offer me sustenance and I
would like a drink (I am thirsty) and you give me water you have
fetched from the river and we sit in the dark interior of your belly
in the darkness of the house your grandfather made from cypress
and the sun does not enter (there are no windows) and the embers
are hot and you will give me some atol to drink when you are finished preparing it, and it is warm and sweet and reminds me of my
childhood in Los Angeles when I drank black teas, hot milks, and
I would like to undo time, Marta—undo all of its useless strange
mendacious and then the norm of the terrible the man who must
drive to work fill his car with petrol phone strangers (this is business) for business and pay bills watch games kill cut the barbarian
into small pieces and feed him to the dogs; use the fat of the vanquished Indian to assuage the Spanish soldier's wound. He is a soldier and he is made to carry a dog on his back from the metropolis
up into the mountains of your nation and mine and into pity and
the places without roads or pity carries the dog on his back like a
good soldier and the young bitch, he loves her, and the dog does not
cry, she is a bitch who understands that the nation is not a whim or
simply a man's desire to make but, rather, it is the tooth we live by
like the god's eye that is printed on the dollar and all-seeing—(*I am
coming as I write this, Marta—my semen spills onto the page; this my*

American history of the dead half-deads the half-lived you and me). I am this soldier boy as he walks up the mountain paths; he is an Indian in a book I am reading and in another book his name is   . His mother discards him at six and his father discards him after his semen ejaculates into the mother's cunt. His father's ecstasy cannot, however, be denied and perhaps it is the best thing about the boy; it is, darling, what I love about him, what I refuse to deny for any newspaper-man or politician's academic's pleasures. He climbs the miles into the mountains from the capital with his bitch on his shoulders; she is young, no more than a year perhaps, pied and four-legged; at the tip of each ear there is a patch of white as if a sign from god he thinks: God, he thinks, has given him this trial. He has joined the Kaibiles to save the patria: (*from?*): from the communists the atheists the dogs unbelievers and killers; those who would destroy the beautiful fatherland; because he is hungry; shoeless and cold in the streets of the capital; and because: the Army takes him by force from the streets on a cold morning in January 1979. He walks and he is beaten with sticks and clubs as he walks up these mountain paths—Move it mother-fuckers pussy-fuckers faggot-fuckers Indian-dogs and fuckers: move!: (and yes, darling, he is your killer coming up the mountainside—your brother's killer, he'll rape the young girl and her friends; he'll unlive what you love, your childhood will burn in him, by him, the village desecrated and decimated in fire—and is his story blinded then? should we sacrifice him to the gods of the Army? to a moral or an immoral character? *continue*:) he is walking and they are not allowed to drink water and the dog begins her moaning, she cries to him and her bound legs and she is suffering and he shoves his fingers inside her mouth, her sex, and he thinks that she will be his domestic pet, his companion in the mountains, and so he whispers to her as they make their way up the mountains—that he will love her, that he can care for her, that his mother did not love him, that his father's ecstasy was not enough for the boy who did not own shoes until taken into the Army at sixteen, and that now his boots pinch his feet but that he is proud of the pinching, the blistered heels and crippled toes—he loves them like he could have loved a mother and an ecstatic father—and he walks higher and higher into the mountains, up to the Tierra Fría, and into the Ixil Area—your killer comes to you, Marta; he approaches your village, although he is years from you still, still untrained, not-blooded, he would like to love the dog on his back and tells her more and more of his history and he is a hungry man and he is angry that he has been hungry for this lifetime and a filled belly is not familiar to him, like shod feet (and his toes are stones in these boots) and warmth and sugary sweets during the day and at nights and without payment of any kind he walks, climbs, and he is sweating, pays in exertion for this heat and the bitch is quieter now, she mourns moans, she knows what awaits them at the apogee, but he insists that he will love her always and she tells him that he is blind, that a soldier must earn his keep, and he does not listen to her as they walk, he climbs and she held to his back, pisses down his spine and into time and into his trousers, down his legs, and the boots are pissed and he imagines that all good soldiers have their dogs for comfort like a shepherd will have his (and he has no flock this soldier boy; unshod, unfilled in his belly, and a mother who sold him for two pounds of maize when he was six years old to the plantation owners on the coast in Oriente and): your killer is a lonely man,—Marta; he could be lonelier than me—his hunger is like fear. And it is not for forgiveness or atonement or a confession, but simply that we can say: Yes, I know it—my killer was a lonely man; a boy whose belly was never filled-to; a boy who thought that despair was a shirt for everyday use, his only wardrobe inside a black polyethylene bag. And when the Lieutenant tells them how they must do it, they arrive at the camp in the mountains and they are tired and hungry and happy to have arrived! and each recruit takes the dog from his shoulder and rubs his aching shoulders and the sweat and dog piss have wetted his shirt through and each recruit has not had anything to drink for many hours and the cold winds in the mountains come down the mountain and the hot sweat is fast cold and they want: "Now you must do it, boys: do it quickly," the Lieutenant says to them, barks it out, like a dog. And each boy, who is becoming the good soldier, lifts the dog from the ground and each boy who is a recruit for the fatherland and each boy must prove must make himself into this de- fender of faith of god of roads of time's required acts; the nation; now, the Lieutenant says to them, you must do it (or, as usual, the boy's fate will be the dog's). And the Lieutenant raises his pistol and knife, this Army man who has been a man for many years and (who remembers when his friends from school punched his face and he vomited and how his mother threw her shoes across the room at him and he cried, and the hands of the father holding the black rod above his head, and he will laugh when these boys twist the necks of the bitches) he orders them: with your bare hands!, and their girls look into their eyes, thanking them, offering them this blood and meat and all of the girls' blood and viscera is placed into a bowl, as if in a church ceremony, and the boys line up like penitents and (do it or we'll kill you He says): they drink the blood the body of their girls; they drink the vomit of the boy in front of them also. They are in line and the boy whose vomit has mixed-in with the blood and viscera is ordered to rejoin the line and in the queue he waits; he drinks again: blood is soup today, they say, and love is like soup in the mountains. The new recruits are made to drink and eat their girls, each other's bile, until they manage to keep it inside their new bodies.

And when the recruit drank the blood and ate the meat of his dearest companion, and the blood and flesh surged back up through his throat (uninvited to leave), he ate and drank and ate again until she no longer returned,—when he did it he did it because he wanted to live more and "We'll kill you fuckers; do it or we'll kill you" and blood could be wine and the body is love.

The semen dries on my feet now and you wash my feet in this essay; I eat a meat sandwich—meat salt sugar and wheat, and it is good, and I am happy that my belly is filled.

I AWAKEN each morning and for a moment at the moment of waking on each day I am confused, lonely, and do not know whence I have come nor to where I am headed; what is the day today; in whose bed do I lie; who lies next to me (you another girl you); the day; year;—and I am a boy in the San Fernando Valley and it is summer? or a girl in Acul, in the Polytechnic in 1983, and my knife wounds ache me and my back pains me and I am you or I am another man, a woman perhaps, and today I have dreamed of doctors saving me, curing me, the new priests in the New World, to save the lonely and embittered boy who drives along the streets of this city, works along her byways and is unable, finally, to understand better than he does—the dammed rivers, the damned girls, the Gabrielinos who greeted Cabrillo in their sly canoes in 1542 and then Fray Crespí in 1769, not knowing when greeting the latter that their demise lay in the friar's plans and black scratches inside of his travel diary—ah, but those two hundred years they had of extra freedom! between the Spaniards arriving and then arriving again, and those two hundred years for the Ixil when most of the population died (of the typhus small poxes) and the slave labor and the harsh whips of the judges the friars, O bluegreen iridescent blues and the translucently lovely wings of my death eater—diptera girl—sits here as I write this, imagine you out of time, the Gabrielinos out of the Los Angeles basin ("Gabrielino" from the San Gabriel Mission put there in 1771), the Ixil of the mountains, this bottlegreen animal on my thumb, this notArmenian and not unArmenian either boy writes in the late evening solitudes of this now become city and the concrete rivers and the greybrown skies and the rivers unrivered . . . we march forward, darling, the damned and exiled races, and the damned unexiled races, as only we can, we not given a choice, and so we do it.

[IT IS TRUE that I don't know you or I haven't held you next to me, or your flesh next to mine, smelled your fear, this love when it is love and not some other thing that we might call desire or hate or simply boredom in the evening when your husband returns from the fields, from his factory of metal, and opens your legs. Los Angeles is the city that I know and no more know it than I do the geography of your thighs, the meeting at your sex, your cunt lips, their particular shape and curve, blacknesses, this smell you make, out of boredom, or arousal, or sweat from the days of work in the fields, at your hut, by the factories of rivers, of the dead and their brethren, my mind a river, overflown, then concreted up and demised, shapen by modernity's tricks.]

I AM A MAN who would like to know better than I do (you are whispering in my ear: it has not been for lack of knowing, and the five phrases of your inheritance, man?) and a man who writes his historiographies of these Americas, which is a history of the smallest sums of fantasy, of silences, of loneliness like a christ's unmarked utterance (for the dead brother and the boy in the Polytechnic), the interstices of your black cunt lips, the rifle barrels, of the manner in which I shut the door, manure, shunted the doors, held you next to me, a knife to your throat, a knife slashed your cunt lips open—shall I not, then, include the barbarian stories? their hordes? You're what I've made you, or at the least you're like a character in one of my: a Western! for the People!: these the books we unwrite unread: unthought books, a prewritten kind of text: the interstitial books: the sort of narrative that makes loops in the mind, like ribbons and flood rivers that leave only a trace of the before: both the past and the future bound up in the disappeared and prewritten writings, a lover's tarmac, the blues; covered up; the five thousand idols and twenty-seven books that Diego de Landa, Bishop of the Yucatán and bringer of the Faith to the Indies, burnt in 1562 to kill the old New World gods. He said that the devils lived in the books and statues, and how the Indians cried, he lamented in his own book written years later in his defense, when he did it—as if pained. But isn't that, darling, some thing after all? A man makes automobiles, a man makes historical dung-machines, he is a worker and he would like nothing more than a girl, a savage unhindered girl: like you—he makes roads too—to suck his cock: and so what if the preacher doesn't approve and then—why do I sleep? why the fatigue? Is it the perpetual lies? Do they fatigue the man? To lie is not so easy, to history a constraint on the nerves: why are we, Marta, so lonely? Why so many ingenuous lies in America to live by? Lonely dung-filled lies, and the flies feed upon them, like dog corpses. We controlled, we contained, we censor the blood that runs in our veins, our ancestors denied access (my grand-mother and . . . they are banging on my doors, lining up to kill the man who would say) Marta: the dead will do it; will kill us in. They can't bear it anymore, their bones buried in the muds of time in the muds of lovelessness: ah Marta, where is the possibility of possi-bilities now? Of Atlantis Eden, of the unconquered savages? *Where the joy?* Can we survive? Will we live on? The grizzly bear an old (modern) myth for Californian children now (the last "official State Animal" killed in 1922); the scant sea otters don't live near LA any longer (only two thousand remain in state coastal waters): why so many of us? Why do we breed like flies? Why can I only say *breed like flies* when what I mean is: *why do we breed like men?* Why make savages and kill them for their savagery? *stupid ingenuous questions, yes* I would like to know: where does the love of it end? I'll write it up in my book before books end until the moment of my demise—I'll not stop until we are demised—I'll keep typing and typing and scratching these black words onto the invisible unwrit-ten imaginary pages: I wont quit, I wont quiet—help me, save me, when can the modern ancient dead girl save the half-living man who would like nothing more than death, to die or to kill; or is it possible to live? I am certain your bones could have done it, of this I am certain: I found them in the ether, sun-bleached, whitened, that beautiful bone-smell—I am notwriting the story of the city of bones (I found them in the Der Zor desert), I will be sorry when it ends. I will be sorry and my sorrow will not, is not, enough now or has ever been to alter things and places. Perhaps it's true, that on some small and dark occasions, I have been overcome by the sorrow of *this* place, its unutterable and ghastly unfeelable traces, its closed spirits in rocks and under roads rivers; the sorrow of the dead decimate things; the lost bunch grasses, grass-houses, and the Gabrielino girls and boys at the Los Angeles River when it was a river; such violent losses, for this, in Los Angeles, we make movies and electric night lights; don't look into the darknesses, don't look at the dead at the maggoty wounded boys, the handless girls and hungry distended bellied children; half of your children die before they are five, Marta; I can't see them; I am hungry now and walking to the kitchen, turning on the lights, eating, drinking, watching TV. It is dark in the sunlight now, the semi-arid plains have become the rotten, the forbidden has become deserted, the flies, the dead, and men, men have become unlike gods after the gods were killed like so many killable bears otters mountain cats, like flies, and love and a christ who can no longer utter us from the underworld. Here we have quarters, profits, work-days week-ends Politics and the News, but not this girl on the path from Acul to Nebaj, no boy who looks for her, seeks her in the ether.

what are we become in this America, Marta?

HERE IS THE MAN: Mr Reagan writes a letter to your General President Ríos Montt. It begins: (The mass grave in Acul is six feet deep and fifteen feet long; these are your uncle cousins neighbors): *Dear Sir: You are a man of great personal integrity and commitment who wants to improve the quality of life for all Guatemalans* . . . (and Mr Ríos Montt says to your people that the New Israelites will remake paradise and the New Jerusalem will be rebuilt on the stones of the plaza in Nebaj and when your brother was tied to the cypress did you notice his pants—a man pisses himself when he is immolated). Mr Ríos Montt ruled your country for sixteen months until the next Army coup d'état and during those months—you don't say to me, it is not written, you don't know this man's name in the capital of your country or this man's name in the capital of my country; and me, Marta, I do not know that you exist in 1982 or 1983 or existing that you could be something beyond my imagination. A Cessna A37-B flies above your head in the mountains; in the mountains and by the rivers, years later, we'll not say, while the Cessna A37-B flies above your head, these are bombs that fall onto your bodies, that twenty-five people were massacred in your village, that one hundred and seven died high in the mountains (my president is eating dinner sugary desserts in Tegucigalpa with your general), we'll say that the Army defeated the communist threat, and what do these words make in the mind while the body flies apart, a bomb on the body can be languaged into destiny into moral correctness in America (and the body will fall fly apart and the red-torn meat, blood like a river, and a dog makes no distinction of master or son—your brother—the dogs always have their meal after massacre).

IN THIS UNION perhaps the greatest disunion for the modern man, a man such as me, a man who moves from the white wooden structure to the metal yellow transport to a concrete grey steel work structure and then the metal transport the tinned music (his radio) and then the cardboard box food and then the loud box entertainment (the small people saying, "Darling, I love you like I have loved no other") and all of this taken out of him, removed from him—the to-be slaughtered chickens and pigs living in boxes also, they can't see sunlight, they've not seen it—and for him, for this man it is because of his own shitting removed: his ass on plastic and his shits dropped into water; a man who never smells his shit; doesn't have to discard or bury it as he didn't have to discard or bury his grandmother's corpse (or Marta's); or see the hen as it's slaughtered, plasticked up and placed on a styrofoam tray for him. It is this shitting into water, he knows, that is part of the myriad made distances he lives with, the making of dead men walking around: living in boxes (alone, even in their conjugal unions); driving in metal transports (alone); eating from boxes from tins; O triumph of the individual! The shit swims in the water and until he picks it up to smell, feel, and yes his own disgust, a disgruntled halo: to taste, and eventually to discard, then he knows he wont find his way back to himself, his animal barbaric loving and fucking inheritances from the earth; himself as he is. He dreams about it. At night he is visiting a friend and he feels the need to take a dump; it's been days, he thinks in his dream, and the shit pushes at him, pains him, he finds his way down a long white hallway to the bathroom. He shits a load out of himself into the water and he doesn't smell it; it goes away from him without shame and without remorse. But in this case the toilet wont flush and in this case the water rises and in this case he reaches into the water bowl and takes his shit out into his hands; he is ashamed, he knows he must dispose of his feces, these black dank corpses; his friends are laughing—it is a fiesta—drinking and laughing and he tries to run with his shits in his hand, the dead are following him and he can't escape their pall, he can't discard any of it: he is in the garden and he is digging a hole and he is trying to bury the dead shits and his friend comes out to see him and his friend would like to stick his cock up his ass and he's never done this before: allowed a man to penetrate the shitty places he holds in his boxes of wood, of concrete, of metal and skin. And then they are fucking in the yard and he is holding the shit in his hands while his friend is laughing and drinking a cocktail and the friend's cock buried inside of his ass and it is the ecstasy, the shame, which wakes him: he is afraid upon waking; afraid and aroused by his own uncensored imaginings.

Marta, I live in a strange and unfamiliar familiar place. Here my feet don't touch the earth; here my food has no dirt residue; here: I don't touch my food, my shit, the blood on a child's face (it carries disease). I am showering three times a day and I apply antiperspirants: I don't sweat; and colognes: I smell like a chemical rose; I don't eat garlic, onions, or spicy foods (the stink). When I feel lonely here, I bring some things inside my home; my house is filled with houseflies and: televisions shoes clothes stereo-sets tools

garden supplies pesticide dog bones towels plastics cleaners maca-
roni sauces in cans dried potatoes and chips in boxes and tins of chili
beans chicken soup catsup mayonnaise peanut butters and mar-
garine, carrots in a bag; of tinned wheats and oat; we have: paper
plates napkins plastic forks and glasses: we are out of milk and we
would like some ice cream, and when I am hungry I buy a tin of
sweet milk for my coffee. I have a house and the outline of the material plastic metals that I strive to obstruct: the outline of solitude
the shadow of good; I am good and my neighbors are not my neighbors (I don't know them) and when the automobile looks old then
it is placed into the garbage can: the new and the young, this also
how I like to fuck. Here we are fat and so we have machines to suck
it out. Here we are hungry and so we have machines to fill it up.
Here, fat and hungry, our appetites shamed from us, we walk
around with the guns tucked between our trousers like small hard
cocks (my cock is hard and small when I think of you, Marta) and
we love the suffering of others (on the television Shows) like we
love to fill up our houses. Now I can hardly make a path through
the material world of my home, my home a filled-to lean-to of
things and their things. I am not really alone, I am half-alone half-
alive: does a refrigerator have a name? electric tools their souls? See
the American man make toast from paint thinner! The savage modern will now perform a trick for you: up on his toes, arms akimbo,
he is naked, shitting naked, cock akimbo, pisses while he shits,
comes while he pisses—he's a modern factory of sexy fun and delight, the delicias of crime: the forgotten invisible heart cities of hollowed bones—we have no way back, Marta; there is no return
along the wooded dirt paths of my ancestors in old Turkey; I have
lost the cosmos, the moon is no longer a mystery, and the tides do
not exert a pull on my limbs. I've lost my way and I've not had a

way or known or cared to know why it is that the sun makes me sadder, that the moon is so far from the soles of my feet which, never
having been dirted up, always contained by the shitted pissed dia-
pers of modern thinking and shoes: I am, finally, undone, unliving,
horrifying to myself: a man who thinks too much as if thinking
were made of things, so a man who does not know what he *knows*,
and this thinking and not-knowing which, finally, these thoughts,
notmine, things: have made a monster of the man, have made me
think we are on a tightrope of progress like those boys in my
schoolyard and arms legs akimbo we run faster and faster and then
the end is not an end, the faster is not a faster, we can no longer fuck
our mothers or our fathers can no longer make cock-stands like
girls make headstands—what is this? what could all of this possibly mean? Take me back to Acul, back to your hut your village of
the lost river where Lázaro is tied to the tree in the dirt plaza and
your mother has disappeared along the river's current with her
youngest son, and the clouds have descended into the valley today
and the mountains are mountains and the maize *will the men plant
a new crop after the soldiers burnt the old?* will grow. And I will become older which can only mean that my fat will collect on my
belly like the flies collected on my dog corpse—the dog lived,
mightn't I?

How do you, darling, fall in love with a dead girl and why do you
give your love to her who cannot (for the same bitter reasonings)
requite such a love? I fell in love with your sorrow, the manner in
which you bore suffering: the sour and pitted sweat smell of your

woven clothing; the blackened toenails and buttressed blackearth heels; with all that you did not say to me in my language, and for all that is not sayable between a man and the loose distant foreign (like a bell) object of his desires: for foreignness like a myth: for Indians like a stone—and a man who has never known you or seen you or heard the black and red roosters on your mountain (the pitted earth there also; the Cessna A37-B above your heads making craters in the earth) the pit in the basement of the Polytechnic, of the Army base in Nebaj, of Acul's old men and your father digging the six foot deep fifteen foot long grave over and over again, made to bury their sons their nephews; made to watch as their sons' nephews' faces collapse unto themselves from the close-up bullets, and the wails they made, these boys they could not save, that they, in fact, abetted the killing of ("Why are you all so sad? You shouldn't be sad," the Lieutenant tells them. "There are dead everywhere. There are dead in Cotzal and Chajul. So, you have to have a little, too. Why are you so sad? It has to be this way.").

And perhaps it is true: that there is only this: that I have loved you longed to love you to know your kind sweet barbaric ways because I know (a good Christian) that there must be a reason (for what they did to you) that I couldn't have saved you (you did not exist then); that had I known you as a boy a young man in this city it would not have altered time; that there is a good reason (or god) that I am free (drives along the streets of this city) and that you— dear sweet redoubtable Marta—girl for whom the bells have not nor will they ever toll in the distance—that you must have done some thing to deserve your fate or have a fate or make fate like tortillas in the early morning dark hours;—or a hard and cold and constant toil and this constant hunger, that you did not make yourself; just as you did not make yourself into an Indian or me into an American,

but we made from places eras ideas phrases and we do live accordingly, thus, and I am glad, darling, that I am no Indian or black
(and have always been such a glad and happy) and if they killed the
old grandfathers in old places it is of no matter (Kharphert 1915
and) to me *now*—and if there has been this—what?—guilt, so I'll
name it, and if I've known that at any juncture they will arrive for
me—so what and what of it? Your corpse changes nothing; your
bones in the Polytechnic covered in cement cemented into the black
well behind the Army barracks in the river hidden for eternity, my
great-grandmother in a far and desiccate place (the Der Zor) elided
also forever, which could be eighty-three years: do not undo the
world (or the fate of those old great-grandparents); the man, a
colonel from your country, has the good cause and sweet and he
fought for the patria the cause and his ideas (his superiors and fat
moneyed bosses) and the Sunday barbeques with his daughters and
wife, and (he lives in Miami now) he also loved you, darling? Did
all of your killers whisper soft in your ear that you were a subversive dog, a girl without reason, a girl upon whose body the future
of the patria rested? It is true, Marta: I swear it.

I AM THINKING only of the dead—of the monstrous ruptures,
and the more of the earth and then it is the sea, and my loneliness
is like such a sea: she lies beyond the automobile glass, in the distance and barred and naked and visible only after rains and the sun
shines brightly on the semi-arid plains of Los Angeles and the sea
presses through this glass, Marta;—is what makes us lovers, makes
us possible. My loneliness what makes us. Without end, the hori-

zon untouchable, the insatiable horror of the delimited soul—I shall, then, continue our essay of the man:

When did this hollow first appear? I say "hollow" and of course the word, like all of the words, makes edges makes pictures an etching to try the faintest idea of what I mean, what you'll understand, when I say *hollow* and I mean: when did it become apparent to me? When and how did I become a man, modern, who although filled with his organs, the blood and sinew and fat and all of the muscles, the liver and bladder, spleen, a heart-muscle, feels his unfilled heart like a hollow? I say "heart" and even that is made, a strange picture, the circling round down to a point—of meeting? circumference of to feel—do you see ♥ the likes of which small girls draw in school? Like that unplaited girl made hearts while I made boats all of the year we sat together in a classroom, grey, blue sashed windows, it is 1974 (the wars are beginning in foreign places, in the Lebanon, and in your country the corpses of the corn farmers on the roads, the boys sprayed with bullets in the capital bar) and the unplaited girl makes hearts in the margins, in the corners of things; and this boy makes boats and wave upon wave. The ocean is beyond his seeing; the rain comes down and so the children cannot play outside today; today it is a Thursday in April and you have been dead these many years already; I have not died yet, nor lived either.

I HAVE a photograph in my possession of these foreigners. They are dark haired and their eyes are dark and they don't look like anything I can recognize: they are from a distant place and I can't understand them when they talk to me. They say that they love me and they say that it is time to eat something, but I cannot understand them and so I kill them because they look like dogs, Marta, they act like dogs also: dirty; dark; unfathomable and stupid; they smell old. This photograph was taken in 1927 in a photographer's studio in the Lebanon; this place is not like anything I can recognize, and the people in the photograph made love, made a child, and then later that girl they made made me—and I had to kill all of my family in America, just as you had to kill yours. In my case there were no soldiers to do it, no gendarmes in the middle of the night yelling, Kill them, kill the fucking dogs, or hands making wounds of babes' mouths in the mountain. I killed them without trying, they died the death of the American dream: of ignorance of forgetting of fast-cars -love -foods: movie-going fun: a fast-death (within one generation, within one boy, in LA). I don't remember any of them (my grandmother), their language (Armenian), and songs (sad), and I like ice cream, and to be entertained!

MARTA,—I am dreaming of bones.

A bone boy came (uninvited) last night into my dreams. I made a picture of him while dreaming; he is an Arab boy and I cannot speak his language and he is holding his hands out to me, extended as if in offering, and I look down to his brown and dirty hands and his tattered trousers and his look; shoeless; he looks into the sun in my dream, squints up at me and the small camera I am holding in my hand, and the wrinkled-up forehead, the smallish eyes not seeing me well (the sun at my back), and looking up at me and shy makes his hands a plain and I am the foreign man in the dream, an American, and he is holding his right hand extended toward me and in a small and white brown pile in his hands, like a pyre, lie the bones of my ancestors—great-grandmother and young dead aunties, cousins—in this white and dusty and small collection that the boy has made today on his way toward the schoolhouse, to class, he is running for he is tardy as usual. They will be gone soon, and so he gently cradles their old and eighty-three year old desert deserted bones, like a small palm offering, and he offers me my family's remains and runs from me then, into the desert, toward the schoolhouse and his lessons because he is tardy as usual and a beating, as usual, awaits him there.

The boy wears a white dress shirt which has turned grey from the many washings and wearings, it is too large for him, and I assume that it once belonged to his father; he is unsandaled and we are in the Der Zor desert of Syria, and it is like the moon here, or rather it is, dreaming, how I imagine a moonscape to be: rocky, desiccate, and desperately far reaching in its vistas beyond to eternity and the earth in the distance: blue white and alone. Here are the Armenians, he offers them to me so that I may bring them home—to America? to the Lebanon? to old Turkey? Why dig up the bones? I ask him, and he nods his head wearily. For they have not been dug up, but lie atop the soil and resembling sea shells in the Paleozoic stone sea; travertine; the children play bone games with them as they have always done, since the summer 1915, when the bones first began to appear in the landscape.

He returns in a moment and I can see that he is holding a dead black thing in his hands and he hands this to me and I notice that there are thousands of these monsters lying scattered across the desert floor and I am afraid then, for this thing which lies in my hands now, and of it, and feel that I will be devoured by them, suffocated by the black ghosts like veils covering the rocks and shrub and dirt,—and then, I realize that it is no more than plastics: black polyethylene bags cover the Der Zor like pieces of black hair left behind by the motorists on their way to Aleppo or Ras-ul-Ain, and so I gladly put my great-grandmother's bones into the bag and then tossed up onto my shoulder, and I wake up then as if I have never been sleeping and you lie by my side for I have only been asleep for five or fifteen minutes and you are the whore I have paid for on my way to the capital to ease my hard-on and I think I gave you pleasure, you smiled, and broken teeth can be beautiful and the scars on your wrists and ankles make their own sort of fleshy jewelry; the blood on your thighs metallic and sweet; your folded skirt a blanket beneath us. And then I awake again inside a third dream, which is my life in America, and I am alone as I am ever alone here in this city.

THIS BEGINS with killing and this ends with killing; and the small hope can emerge like small children who have lived in the mountains, who have lived in the Mesopotamian desert, who have survived, dear Marta, the bluegreen cypress in April, the dead mothers and the bulleted fathers; and the baby carried by the river's sad currents which continue—the bones of it could be and would be better than these words, these phrases which seek and inquire and essay—perhaps much like my mother's pitiful five—: I would like to know, Marta, why it is and how it is or rather: the sunshine the wind your body spread before me on the grass, your legs open and all of the universe in your sex and our sex together all of the universe between us in us and no words, sans phrases, no paper or symbolic system of signs to make: a book, a new philosophie or religion: to reason it out; reason it in—"They are no better than dogs."

Reason is a lie; a tautology, the reasoner says. I say it is sweet, cruel, the killer of love, the cosmos and underworld, a death-maker,—because once Reason became our (only) god, then reason also became God's sword and machinery. Yes we are ancient killers, and now, reasonable, we're killers without the order and mystery of the cosmos, without what cannot be seen, (is), without the sacrificial awe for anything but our abilities to do to make, we can kill the dogs, they are dogs: kill his children his wife, fuck her, kill his daughter in the sunlight; and then make the father slaughter the son, the son slaughter his, unsave his, brother: make the dogs killers so that you can laugh at night with your wife as you fuck her (to death), while you drink the blood soup, while killers are killing in the mountains from the half mile distance of the Cessna A37-B bombers in the night sky. Yes I am alone, Marta. Yes I am lonely with my things. Yes I don't want to know more of this more than I do—Yes, I would like you to shut it, to shut it up. No more histories no more of your truths, lies (you *must* be lying). And what if the Army massacred your neighbors your family the clans, small children, the fields houses all of your property burnt out? And what if a newmother, Doña Ana, died on the mountain with a babe later sucking nothing, a nothing made from your tits? And your brother tied to cypress in the plaza which is no plaza—your shame your father's shame, for you leave Lázaro's corpse to rot like a dog, the dogs eat his legs to the knee; the crows his eyes. Then? I am a man, a North American, and I would like some ice cream, and I would like some unpornographic fun at the movies and porno fun on the sly; and I would like to eat clean foods at the supermarket; I want paved avenues more than love; monies more than . . . I am a man and I cannot aid you in any way (you must have done something to deserve it): don't come here anymore. Don't visit with your sad stories of woe of death of what you call in your tearful tirade *The Situation*. It is not my own fault my own doing that you arrive from a barbarian place; that the barbarians must pay and pay; that you are barbarian stupid and dirty. I don't look beneath stones and I don't seek the myths of this place or I wouldn't like to know who lived here three hundred three thousand last year years ago— paradise awaited me in Los Angeles; perhaps a few dogs roamed the paths before we did; we don't count the dogs in the census making. I'm no killer; you make me into one killer one writer, a sentence-maker. I drive an automobile, it is yellow and clean. I eat ice cream, and it is cold and brown-grey today in Los Angeles; contaminated with petrol fumes and calendar girls. I have girlfriends, a divorcée, loaded beers and music, days that are made by television blares and what the neighbors my colleagues and friends tell me about sports, the News, beautiful Shows on TV. I like to read comic books, I like to ride a bicycle (as a boy); I trust the police to secure my goods my body from: the hordes, the criminal, from the insects who eat upholstery, eat my bread, who would like to eat me also. I am not saddened that I shall never see my own skull like a soup bowl or flower vase.

Let me tell you something which you shan't hear or hearing shan't heed or reading shan't decipher in my language, or perhaps it is you who tells me: that history is not eternal, and History has no place for your mythic men.

[AND SOMETHING you ought to know about me, dear Reader: that when I am not fucking the girls of my imagination and when I am not living the bodied desires of cunt-heat and all of its offerings, eternal altar for what is (on Hollywood Blvd), then I am sitting here in my green and padded armchair, hoping that you exist somewhere inside outside in ether; as I make my Marta, Reader, make me, please.]

I AM LOST. And this is no metaphor for the man or his manliness, it is night and he is driving on the roads of this city; the city has darkened and he could be in a labyrinth, he thinks, he could be in his,—that water surrounds him even though he drives in the desert and the dead have descended, will come for him—will bring you on their backs like cherry pickers, he thinks: will bring his girl like the wind brings rain in the summer months which is winter in Acul, and then take him perhaps—there beyond night—a darkness inside darkness; inside the pupil; inside what is impossible and then, he says, how we wished that the gods had made us differently—like trees or trout—less of this sorrow, like a river unriven; like you, a seed of the possible,—Marta.

There is no outlet to the roads and no map of its geography inside his motorcar, there are numbers, dials, and a steering wheel which he clasps tightly because he is now afraid and he is driving faster. He drives now (what does this American man fear? the night, an endless road and without markers or gasoline stations or electric lights, and a moon that does not rise on the horizon; his neighbors; the blacks who are not his neighbors; the dogs that lurk in his heart; the ghosts of his childhood; silence;—this most of all—a quiet hush without the speed of this drives, without the television blares: to be alone, he thinks, and he knows it then: death approaches encroaches his styles). It is night in Los Angeles and the desert moon is not in the sky; he can see the road, its painted lines— lines of steel unmarked by the night's shadows and these shadows then unmade by the unrisen moon. Perhaps you are here, Marta, inside this loss of sight; this dark nights road; this day which doesn't begin for all of the years I am traveling on these roads—who made them? what man made it, these? Are there Gabrielino bones in these roads, beneath the byways? Are there hidden burial mounds for the mothers and sons who died too early, and for the old also? These bridges unmade men? men inside the concrete dammed places. Which springs have been undone in Los Angeles? Which girls unmade in your Acul (the springs, rivers). Everywhere I look there are the things man makes; and in each of us the possibility of what can be destroyed (how simple it is, really, to destroy what is) like the river in Acul unmade the children from their mothers' bosoms; as I can unmake your mouth, the ears will undo childhood and the hooded eyes will close because we wont see its history: your brother is tied to the cypress (evergreen and not fruit bearing); my mother sits on the sofa in Los Angeles weathers; there is a grandmother in a foreign place (the Lebanon) and she has died today in other wars (for this bleeding mind)—and then your brother (his bleeding soul), you, the foreign breath like schools of dogs, they make packs, pacts: dogs are like children, their schools like sadness, a steel harness—do you know how simple it would be to make a monster from a babe, darling? To beat then maim or bleed the babe from your own womb? What is this power we yearn for, almost as good as the Maker's, the Unmaker will have his day, darling—"The dogs have carried the boy's limbs back from the abyss," the old man says; we have all made dying today; made sadness; made roads and history was tarmacked like that: like black thoughts. The dogs ran in packs in those terrible years, you say, ate the villagers' bodies like children eating ice cream. See the meat; eat the meat. When the village dog had her pups in the mountains, the children's eyes and my brother's face stared back at us from the bitch's progeny: was it wrong to slaughter the pups? I couldn't bear it: their bones made of my blood; my brother a meal for the bitch and her companions in Acul. (The soldiers were laughing during the repast.) We killed the pups in the mountain because my brother stared out of their fatty eyes—we couldn't bear it: those mongrels looking at us as if speaking from Lázaro's grave.

THERE ARE NEVER people walking on the streets here, and in my car I am looking at the drivers, at each man as he drives, the women drivers also (their careless and shy turns from me) and the children and I think how each one: driver, passenger, and the not-walkers on all of the streets of this city, the only people I see, each enclosed in his metal moving machine (his metallic coffin tinned music) and each of us—the drivers here, we've taken our feet from the earth, from the roads and sidewalks, the tiled avenues—is a proof of a man's ecstasy: we made by our father's rush and without it and without this love we don't drive, look—unexisted but for his momentary grace and this grace, Marta, in the bleakest moments of the drive and drive and the tarmacked hills and the cemented passageways and this boy in his car, a man now, a corpse-collector, can find solace in his Americas by this: we made by our father's joy—his electric desire in this world *in that moment.* And perhaps this all of it; and perhaps it is nothing more than picking one's nose in the back rooms or the self given pleasure in the back rooms the cold beds at night, my hand is always rubbing my cock, but still that could be something—we all of us a physical picture of a man's ecstasy, and what simple beauty in that, darling, to drive along the streets of this city, and separated from the rests of the city by steel and speed and what ought to be done and the time of the clock (meetings appointments deadlines the school bell tolls) and the TO DO's!, but looking now at all of their faces—fierce and isolated concentration on these roads, and sometimes rage and sometimes a smile or he picks his nose she admires her form in the mirror or frantic driving into the cement barriers into cars—and we, all of us, despair is our friend and fear and rage and our fathers, whether or not they loved our mothers, and our fathers, whether or not they loved their progeny, and cared for us and pleased us—we still can say that we *are* because of such a man's unbridled energy: his godlikeness in that moment of fucking, his fiery self in a river of seed secretion.

(And of my mother's ecstasy? The vagina holds her secrets tightly, like the earth will hold out beyond the tree's demise, like the symbol can never be entirely explained or understood. And you, Marta? were you pleasured and pleased by the Army men?)

THE DIPTERA GIRLS are filling up the house, Marta, filling up and inside my mind. And each black beast takes me down another path—is it you?—each one flits on my pant leg or rests in these sores and each black and killer beast, each sad and lonely animal, could be you, could be us, across this abyss of time and culture and reality, rather five hundred years ago, rather two weeks past, rather 22 April in Acul, each morning in the Polytechnic in early fall, you quiet and dark (those lonely severed hands on the concrete floor); a heart muscle is left behind by the Army as souvenir in the mountains; a man's brains left to rot next to his abandoned rubber boots; and we have persevered, you whisper. A small and not insignificant feat—*but at what price, darling?* perhaps no more or less than the price this modern has paid for his things, his lonely and lying days, without love's circle to rest him; arrested in his nights; starless ungazing, electricity when he flicks his fingers, water when he turns his wrist.

Rather, no.

Ah these black corridors to the soul, Marta—for what we do and what we cannot bear (to see know) and then bearing it, only to be forever haunted by the black flies. The men who beat Monseñor Gerardi's head in with cement blocks on the day after the Church published its findings about the war in Guatemala; and the men who pulled the fingernails from a child's hands; and the electric shocks to the feet, the vagina, each scarred and slashed breast: do you think, darling, that they are also forever violated or marked (Cain) by what they have done what they do, the peasant farmer they killed today yesterday and the girl at the river whose cunt they slowly cut open with their cocks knives and the endless children swung against the trees their skulls smashed open like so many solid and weighty stones; to see the girl's babe as it is pulled from her belly (does it make a popping sound, the umbilical cord as strong as ten wires, and quietly resists soldiers, good soldiers), all for the patria, they tell us, burn your breast and back, mother-fuckers, we will save the nation (at all costs!); this is The National Security. So is there, darling, a payment to be made for all of them and all of us? And is that, in the final reckoning, if there can ever be such a quiet consolation for the dead (these five hundred years since the modern age began), this sparse and dearth payment? I've not paid, have I, darling? (for my sins?) For that girl from Acul, that girl from the capital, that girl on the Pan American Highway leads to the capital of your country. I've not paid and will not pay in this lifetime. So why is it, then, that you, sad and lonely girl, have made your way into my reckoning? Brought the diptera girls up from your village, capital to Los Angeles. Whose soul do you summon in dark night?

AND SO I AM alone again, and then always alone, and there are days, Marta, when your specter is not enough for the living man and he would like only a little bit of your flesh, or the girls like yours, who could come to him and lead him out of this descent, which is not madness, but this timeless loneliness of souls—which has no end, except death which awaits me of course (and which may be no end, only this eternal outoftime revelation of continuity) the black cosmos looms on each side of the living, I can see it there, see the specters hover like flies here; and the question remains—to hasten or not hasten one's own demise, which could also be a return (—and if this return is painful? and if this demise takes four days, the let-down blood the hypovolaemic shock this progressive asphyxia caused by the heft of blood in the lower extremities?) I have no answers and (I am a man who cannot posit the questions correctly) the corpse-collecting does not make the evening come on sooner and the mountains in this distance, the clouds in this distance, your form and you always unavailable except here, amongst these dead and desiccate folios, which could be pages between pages of my own thinking, a book between books, in the interstitial spaces of notbooks: a poet could make more of you, but the corpse-collector can make nothing; food for the dogs; historiography for the uninitiated, uninterested, television crowds. There is the tree, there is your brother tied to the tree which is a cypress, became your rod of mourning; the ladder to heaven was broken on his spine; the ladder to heaven was knifed to his groin. Is it morning in the altiplano? is it evening now? Is it hot as it is always hot here, or at the least a not-cold? Or in your mountains (that saved you) is it cold and beautiful because the clouds will sit like girls on the rims of wells on the mountain rims, girls in skirts, woven in the evening, free, floating skyward like red and black hummingbirds, while the souls disappear into wells, behind the church doors, beneath this tree's root—the blood a good fertilizer for springtime planting. It is spring, it is a cool morning and it is nineteen eighty-two (in the Gregorian calendar, and in the ancient Mayan calendars, darling?). It is April, we can say it is six o'clock in the morning, and you have been up for hours and your brother is eating tortilla and coffee and when he doesn't look at you you think how you are tired, how life is no good today, the days are long, and you cannot know that a man sits in front of his television in a semi-arid plain and doesn't think of you, cannot, but could if he were able, if he were a different man, if he could see across the distance and beyond his own hot desiccate mountains, if seeing were more possible for the human in ether; if love could make of mountains what wishing makes from comets and girls in their Sunday skirts before they have learned the ways of seeing and sitting with their legs crossed (without their hands in their crotches); sex closed. Lázaro combs his hair and he leaves for the fields; in this phrase (*he writes:*) in this phrase your life as it was is now becoming a history, and then it will be re-done, and you will have an after-life, which could be the life of the dead or of the half-deads as they travel down the mountain paths and return to the town of Nebaj in 1983, and you later travel alone to the capital of your country. You are combing your hair with a wooden comb; your plait is tight and the part down the middle of your skull is pulled wide white—Come back to me, Marta, and tell me, whisper this story in my ear; I am a man without prehistory and I would like to know (nothing, the American boy would like a hard candy); whisper it to me and I'll folio it up for you and later when we fuck together and I tell you all of my lover's lies you will pause, perhaps I'll come inside of you, your cunt will take my semen in, will not make my many sons who cannot be born, and we'll make love in a moment (for five dollars American in Chimaltenango, on the Pan American Highway, on the drive to your capital) but in this moment Lázaro is leaving your home with your father, the hard-packed dirt is cool and stiff beneath his sandals which have not been taken, yet; his cloth bag holds tortilla for lunch and black beans, chirmol and honey; and the Army has already surrounded Acul, although he and your father do not know it yet, it is quiet yet in the village; the clouds lie on the rims of mountains like girls in lazy skirts; it is cool and you are tired today, and the clouds are a bright white, then a soft and sad grey—white looks like a beginning of day, you think, and the greys are familiar on the sky.

They take the men to the plaza. I say plaza, but it is no modern's idea of the square; you don't call it the plaza in your language, you say: Tzi' Ak'ula—the bank of the Acul River— and it is flattened dirt in front of the church which is a concrete abode, a small wooden cross sits atop the parapet—a painted pink arch and bright blue door. I'd continue this apace, but I am sad today and sadder than I have been in many years—you've died today and left me alone again; you've died again and again today and my sadness knows no bounds, my solitude is sharp and bleeds the knives I carry for a heart, a well which is a shrouded landscape, a desert, inside of my flesh. I could continue, the story, your plaza which is no plaza but a dirt and grass-knotted hamlet at the side of a river, which is a collection of scattered houses and corn fields and an administration building (the wooden shack with the corrugated metal roofing next to the church) and no markets or school or road or corn mill; or Model Village (yet). ("The Indians educated, armed, could take the country away from us!") Your courses were the fields of maize and the gods in the clouds and skies and above the mountains where later you fled; the Principales who kept the old ways and the days; the stories of your grandmothers and grandfathers and gods— these your scholarly routes. And I wouldn't last a month in your mountains, the city boy would die loudly and in terrible pain quickly; despair would also be his killer; and cowardice; and his fat and fragile form; and you lasted the fifteen months before you walked down the ancient spoors, starved and naked and beaten with the other survivors to Nebaj and taken to the Army barracks. And that is no small feat for the strong and fierce Ixil girl, to have survived in the mountains for so many seasons.

SO THAT I am waiting, his life is a wait for—for a lover who will be a Lover, and for this job that is his work, and for a wife and children and the rewards of happiness: he waits for happiness which is a waiting to live like progress is a drive to the end and the to come is always possible but not yet arrived. I drive around this city as if seeking to find the life that was destined me: it is a waiting like an animal in the corner and this corner is always around the next corner, a litany of the next for the man who seeks Love: is this, then, the modern's life? The man's dreams of living which could be made from a television Show and all of the Shows have made him make dreams or daydreams which he waits for: I wait for you, Marta—and you do not arrive and you do not show up or are not shown on his screens—he seeks you, drives, watches, waits for you now inside; has stopped his movement and says that he will wait, that perhaps you seek him in the flesh, that perhaps he finds you in the flesh of his lonely boys and girls, that he could pull you down from the ether, from the trees that make wind, hold sorrow . . .

I am waiting like a girl waits for her lover and perhaps I've become a girl, I'm undone as a man. I seek it in all of the girls and none of them make you, return you to me: but they might, they could perhaps; this is an essay into his desire, I think: this he who is a man making himself into a woman.

WE HAVE BEEN makers of machines of things, Marta . . . and I look out the windows of this highrise now on Hollywood Blvd and see all that we have made (El Capitan Theatre, Hollywood First National Bank Building as it stretches above the streets and fray, and the old dilapidated Pig 'N Whistle, and named and unnamed stone stars in the sidewalk and sidewalks a road stretched out into infinity and the downtown highrises in the distance and the Washingtonias sway in the wind today and the old letters of the Roosevelt Hotel reflected back to me in the windows of the adjacent building, eerie and white in the clouds and day and red tonight while I think of you; lighted in my mind) and the topography is a guess now in this city (there are mountains rivers?) and who walked the ancient spoors the girls along the ancient rivers when the basin was rivered and night skies when the canopy of stars was something wide vast and filled with the autochthonous gods . . . What a fool is this American man, egregiously inventing the past idlylls, a sly and nostalgic beast inside him, and still I have been amazed and then when upon the dark moments of despair (the concrete waterways, the river that I never knew was a river) I have been amazed at the long desire and drive, like a man drives, for speed and highrise buildings and to build to make to tarmac the earth in squares and rectangles lines, driveways for the automobile and entrances for the automobile and façades large enough to be perceived at twenty miles per hour in the motorcar on Miracle Mile and everything made to its order, to the car, and its scale as we move these mechanical beasts—red white yellow blues grey blacks and orange—

across the tarmac city, beast with only one function and up the
mountains and down into the valleys, and each motorcar is a symbol of our freedom; of this man's desire to move; to live in a house
and it is *his* house and a garden and a driveway and he drives his
motorcar to a place where he can work and build and the motorcar
to shops where he can pull his mechanical beast up to its veritable
doors and walking—not more than eight or ten yards—he is inside,
sits down for his coffee his whiskeys his beer until he is beckoned
again by the motorized transport and it is *his* and it can take him
where he wants to go on the government roads and the government
has given him roads wherever he would like to go, he goes where
the government roads the place up, he drives to the door of his
house, the garage door opens for his car and he puts the car inside
its building and walks the three or four yards into his home; turns
on the television and sits while the moving pictures move in front
of him with News and romance and adventure stories of the West
and the boys fighting the Indians the boys who kill all of the enemies how we defeated the Barbarians and killed the Savages in
America (in California, the bounty was five dollars per Indian
scalp). [You look at me from that window, the yellow and white
painted bars as I drive by you on the Pan American Highway on
my way to the capital—such beauty then and sadness like an iron
thing—and you know much better than I that what we've made:
the asphalted roadways, the wood and sheetrocked walls for homes,
glass and thin aluminum sidings, is an impermanent material, and
that it will not last a hundred years, and that the ghostly girls from
Pompeii with their mineral blue thighs and breasts, they've endured, and seek to see us through the ether, in history, and the
Mayan girls on pots and walls and the temples of birds and we are
modern makers, darling, ah but for a now that can only demise—

this our demise now, sweetheart? Now our things wont last but a day or three minutes in the fast food restaurant or perhaps five years if it says it will go the lifetime, and then of course the millennial garbage on the edges of our thingéd cities, in dumps—to comfort the boy who seeks the dead alive in these dead things?— The end of these dreams and thoughts and freedom just over the hills, through the Santa Monica Pass—we are makers, darling, but not of the sacred things, the perpetual temple things and clay pots of girls and essays of eternal mineral pigmented walls (lapis lazuli and hematite) and none of it perhaps in a thousand years—or even tomorrow–just this now, this ephemeral moment, your breath, dear Reader, which we cannot know just as we cannot know you.]

AND STRANGE it has been to have been raised on such ideas of freedom and new Eden, which although adjacent to the Gabrielino girls [are you with me now? These black buzzard flies will not leave me now, have filled my room, have come for me only to make their buzzéd demands, fitfully at first in such a rage, then rest, then more rage: is this how the soldiers, also, came to you as you lay prostrate on the floor? your ankle bound and chained to the metal cot? Shall I ask you now to pity the soldier who armed and enraged and with a violent beastliness he beats you and you will not give him what he wants and (he was given American dollars this month from the Guatemalan government, and you, darling? what remuneration did you receive for your aims? your desires?) I don't mind them, darling. They remind me of my perpetual fear but they are harmless enough, only loud as they take up residence in my kidneys, make the tympanum sing, will not stop until I have resumed this essay of mine which I fitfully, in between the long night drives, the walks in the mountains I have not walked (and there the spirits run down in rivulets, black loud, like rivers), pen; an unwritten treatise on the dead and a damned unexiled race; the enslaved; the black flies loud and violent now, resting in all of my sores; heartless; the dead have returned and they are filling my house in Los Angeles—flight now—burning up the boy the man who wants more sweets more liquor fatty foods and none of what I see when I see you in Acul, your shoeless naked arrival in Nebaj, on the road to the capital, and then the handless spirit at the Polytechnic, in the ditches and all of the XXMUJER XXMUJER XXMUJER XXMUJER XXMUJER XXMUJER XXMUJER graves in the capital city and countryside. What is it they feared, darling, above all else? Why is it that in all of those years they did not release one man or woman, not one girl or boy to return home to her village his neighborhood in the capital and say how it had all been mistaken, how the soldiers loved their brothers, their unexiled races; they loved you not hated, and forty-four thousand dollars in a bank account is like fucking; when I fucked you darling in the basement of the Polytechnic did I know, could I tell, that your spirit would haunt me (like a talisman, ancient bird) for eternity. An unrepayable remittance; the hum in my ears will not cease and I am blind now, deaf, a mute who pens his dead girl up in sentences, in hoary exiled words; in a language neither of them owns or origins: forgive me, he writes, for I have sinned.] made those girls invisible, like a girl in the basement of the Polytechnic in 1983.

I AM A MAN collects corpses. I eat photographs and I am a dead man also. A tired man; a whorish man; a man who does not look back, I have only the future in front of me, no present; I am a man without history; and I am a man of despair, collects around my heart like the corpses pile up in my trunk: there are dog corpses, they line the avenues in droves; there are girls in other places, bitches and boys by the roadside (362 this month in the capital, they are XXMUJER and cigarette burns and handless also). It is he, the quotidian corpse-collector, the priest who pulls two hundred hearts from his devotees and they are then plunged to the steep earth below; the priest who gives one hundred lashes to the neophytes burns them with his brand, marks the skin the hide and they are hungry in his houses; fucks the girls; the girls and boys surrender violently to Christian Mission gods, then commerce: I hardly know its breath, breadth: despair has friends, enemies and lovers: a name: here in the motorcar it is hot, the freeways are long and wide in this city; ten tarmac lanes stretching the distance of fifty-five men lined up side by side; the man drives on all of the streets and thoroughfares of this city, from an aeroplane it would appear beautiful, grey, high green clouded mountains, what man makes (you can't see death from the aeroplaned distance) a maze of the sublime heavens.—We are more alone in it (the skies empty but for the machines; birds?) More and then more alone and the dead live here, the specters, it's a piled up heap of dungy corpsey paradise; sunned; sad; contaminated in its air sea waters and the dirt; neither death nor rain could relieve me of my illness. I am a sick man; a tired man; a man who likes to fuck the pornographic girls, the girl who willingly spreads her thighs and cunt lips and without shame and today I've picked up ten or twelve, the woman wailing has hurt my ears their cries so loud. Are they ancient Greek goddesses, the women from death dreams? Did Odysseus have such a fright with his lovers on his way home? Or the sad crier, La Llorona, who travels all of the old paths myths in Mesoamerica? I've touched death and I've made it: killers are makers also. We make dark in the sunlight; we petrify the thresholds, a lintel littoral pulling back of the species. And all of it, darling, in an attempt at a return; I almost had a boy once, and a wife for an interlude.

(WHY THIS ANGUISH, MARTA?) These nights without sleep, without love, with the ideas of what it is, what it could be? A girl lies next to me, the money is on the bedside table: I cannot tell if I made you sleep, the orgasm the sex we've made made you finally drowsy, I'm sleepy you say, and she leaves—this aloneness the worst: the dark nights of piss in the bladder, the full stomach, semen on my thighs: and don't want living, Marta, a monster is made in me; grows; gorges your sleep to make my notsleep tiring, I've a headache, I can't live, can't not; sleepy; can't sleep. I am rabid sorrowful—the worst sort of client. I would like to talk to you; I would like to know your real name when I come on your pubic hair; where are you from? what ancient nation is yours (do you have nations)? Why does English not emerge from your mouth? your teeth don't knock words verbs together properly, in a moral fashion. Do you know the palm tree? The Washingtonia robusta? A symbol of victory like the palm of my hand; or: look underneath the smallest word: palm: and you'll find our history—Egypt Jesus and the word and Matthew and—the Indian says: the palm is a mother—Who planted these palms lining Santa Monica Boulevard? Who spread their semen on my thighs while I was sleeping? The palm at the end of the mind; you hold my heart in the palm of your hand: mother, palmera, the nights are shorter in summertime—in the semi-arid plains we cannot think of love or of anything other than love (money garbage Shows and things).

I see palm trees line Santa Monica Boulevard. The trees look like a vacation, like warm weather and sunlight and *take a vacation here* and put on your bikini! here and we're happy we're happy we're here: sunlighted boudoir sexed up touristy fun.

Morality, you say, when you awaken, turn over, your ass presses against my ass, is like anthropology. For when you study the native, you do it to see how he fucks his wife and girlfriends at parties, the boys in the back rooms; how thick his foreskin; his large and small cocks in colors; is he naked. This is how we do it, she says, pushes her ass into my ass; you can't make children from this, she says, screams it: and then, yes, my semen on my thighs.

—You're the new Eve; Los Angeles our garden—a graveyard of Eves, of XXMUJERS.

Why is it (*that you can only comprehend us by how close fitting we are to some idea you've already got in your head? That we are, as ourselves, so invisible*) that men invariably like to do me in the ass?

WHAT CAN BE SAID? Is it so hard to speak and hence I speak to you here, amidst the dead words in a dead tongue and from a half-dead man—is it only written that I can see you and you seen see me?

I don't trust the utterance and I am no longer speaking. In the supermarket I carry a small pad of paper and write: DO YOU HAVE ANY? to the clerk. At the gas station for gasoline I ask for more gallons and DO YOU HAVE THEM? and in the theaters and by the drugstores and cleaning shops I ask and inquiring with my pen and paper and I am happier man, Marta, now I could be the ingenuous boy.

I don't speak; I am writing; these the notes to posterity; no: these notes from the underground, the fat and ugly beast, afraid; the unspeaking man who writes to the dead girl he has never known and writes her up, writes himself in the making, essays himself from ether, with pen pencil paper: a descent into the lettered bus of time.

Writes: on a Blue Bird bus, it is red and yellow and white *Dios Me Bendiga*

: she is more beautiful that

: a look of despair

: the leña is heavy, it is loaded onto his back and each day he carries the forty pounds of wood up from the valley floor and the path is foot-worn and he has green rubber rain boots for his shoes and when it rains these are the good shoes and when it is hot his feet are hot also and sweaty blister like burning-skin his skin abraded by the material, and in the winter months there is a small fungus that cov-

80

ers his booted feet and his toes are covered with this fungus and his toenails are ruined blackened by the invisible arrival of the winter rains and this small invisible animal eats his nails, pains him (he doesn't complain of it) and: is he your father, Marta?: the strap cuts his forehead, a furrow is carved into his skin like an ancient path, strap-worn, from the decades of carrying the leña these many miles in the mountains and the Cuchumatanes in the distance look beautiful in the untaken photographs of the place; a river on his forehead, scars make rivers (he is a digger later for your uncle's neighbors' grave).

:here, you said: We are alive; we have not died in your books of *Classical Mayan History* of *Pyramids and Pottery* books—see me, you say, my sweat smells of maize and despair; I have not planted the field; I have not prayed to our gods, my pain has come from this:

:the cypress in the plaza which is no plaza and this eternal return of my brother's suffering to my mind; his mutilated form, his cries as we stood there around him, all of us in the village, and this shame: of saying nothing, not stopping the men as they did it; our men doing it to him: hacking his limbs to wretched pieces

:a brother who smiles at me still, chases me in my dreams, legless, faceless (the dogs and picking birds)

:my own lost and blackened hands in the Polytechnic, this longing for their return to me

:the river, and the sounds of massacre—which is the children and women who are begging, scream inside my ears like flies, like children

:and my mother

:and my youngest brother

:and

:and the whys and the love that burrow like the lies I tell my-self so that I can find you amidst the rubble of the mind; amidst and between the sentences, our history lies in between the:——the hor-rific downings of time and makings of Americas and a north and jungle paradises and Pedro de Alvarado and your father's rubber boots (without socks), his strap-worn grimace, your hands and the veins like rivers across them, whose

dog in the street whose bones and bony tail make patterns on his fur

the dog looks like hunger, I think, and like an idea and: you, I can't see your hunger in your face, *are you hungry, darling?*; walk-ing down the mountains to the Army headquarters in Nebaj, and you will take a Blue Bird to the capital with your black feet; a girl who would find them in the city if necessary—who will look for them in the black pit at the Polytechnic; they are living with the rats, this bluebottle fly who accompanies you down the mountains and into the capital city; the soldiers place you gently into the pit and now you can see despair, you think, and now your brother will re-turn (like Lazarus: he is Lázaro first, a christ tomorrow); the sol-diers piss and shit upon your heads; throw the burning chemicals onto your heads.

[At the bookstore I am followed by a young girl; I smell her sweat her sex and I will fuck her in two hours after I feed her a cheap meal in Los Angeles near the bookstore; she is lonely and shy and hardly looks at me (a black short skirt; she wears no under-pants), and I know that she can smell my fatty body odors, and I know that she will come home with me, the shy and lonely des-perate American girl who looks in magazines and in the mirrors and sees what she can hate and not love and although she cannot see the grief and sadness of the masks in the magazines, or below my own face-mask, she can give me a small piece of paper; she hands me a book, writes in this book like I am writing it: *Please——; please fuck me.*]

WHAT DO I KNOW?—everything because nothing? because I am a decent man, a good American son and I know that I eat good meats and I like the movies and I would like an automobile with a leather-backed seat, and I would like the idea of happiness in my head, and then girls to love me, lick my thighs, my ass, and not the ideas that I know and don't like and the bullies on the playground and the girls who turned from me, and the presidential sons who said, large ignoble heads from television screens, they are screened up, in, thin-lipped and angry men and they smile while speaking in this river, a river of half-truths of halved reasonable ideas (of liberty and free-dom and) of these words I heard as a boy in my books of this place and of my place in it, this "American Empire for Liberty."

You see the textbook of it, how phrases are like truths and how these truths can make countries, a nation of hounds, like a nation of trees unearthed, and the earth makes no claim upon a tribe of men and tribes of men can be erased from the earth as easily and clumsily as Histories are written for the living—it is in the Historian's hand, his work and his day, he lays out the maps of our longings and sadness, these the black maps he puts away at each day's close: these the drawings of lakes and rivers and the edges of mountains that never did enter into his History books: these are love stories, and as such, better left undead, riven, the emptiness of what has been possible—of what could be made, and he, clumsily, the

Historian is a doer for nations and powerful tongues that lick the backs of gold men and their gods, a capital's delight, he sits in his green and padded armchair, and he pens his histories of the heroes and of the lands and the beginnings that, by the light of his hand, become beginnings and ends and tribes of men are dropped into the bucket of black maps he keeps at the foot of his bed, he pisses these black mapped tribes, these erased rivers riven from his mind, yes, perhaps they do haunt him, and yes, perhaps he fucked and loved his servants, and yes he is depraved by his desires and the range of his desires, deprived by his very own histories (of love, his own flesh from another place) but: he showers before bed, he is clean in his linen, his toenails do not blacken and fray, his plastic shoes were never his, nor left in any mountain tenement and then aerial bombed—and this can bring happiness also; and this is good also: his house, the green and padded armchair, an ice cream at dusk; some sugar pies before sleeping.

I'LL TELL YOU SOMETHING, darling,—my mother was a (an Armenian) girl who arrived in America with all of her ideas of America (from the Lebanon) and here she had an American husband and they had American children who had American childhoods—and she spoke in a language I couldn't understand (notEnglish) and she cooked foods that were strange for my friends and not strange to her son, and she gave me sentences about her before and her mother whose father disappeared and whose mother walked in a caravan to the desert and (I did not listen ate those foods with a voracious appetite) I was given the sentences about a place and a time when she was someone else and when her mother was someone else and it was dark then, lonely, a bitterness like . . . and I hardly listened or remember what it was that she said, where they were from (Kharphert) or what it was she wanted (unsad); names. My mother was a happy person, and she drank whiskeys in the afternoon suns of Los Angeles; she invited strangers for coffees and sandwiches and she made foods that were strange and inviting to the strangers; she would laugh and then whispering at night. She made a boy, me, and she made him sad and melancholy for all of those evenings when she would wake him in the middle of the night and they ate cold chicken wings (the flesh) and they sat on the sofa in a large and warm and filled room, and she would cry to him, berate his father his whores, tell him how she was alone and then more alone and they sitting and eating and she crying and he is running his hands up and down his mother's arms and kissing her arms and her mouth and loving her, telling her, that these people, this Armenian (an Ixil girl) was something that could return and she laughing, licks his cheek, tells him that soon all the girls will love him fuck him and it does not happen as she tells him it will and he is lonely soon in turn (watches the girls run from him; turn from him; and he *could* love them so well as well as his thick-armed mother); and he tells her the story of the moon until she is laughing, that he will take her up to another place out of Los Angeles, to the moon!, that he loves her, kisses her fat arms up and down the goose-pimpled flesh, for years, until he discovers that you are his girl, Marta, you the hungry peasant girl and unshod and tired and you will kill a child in the mountains while you are hiding, running up the steep and mudded slopes, it rains continuously, and hoping that soon, very soon, you will come down from the mountain and your brother will walk with legs will see from eyes and the cypress,

your uncle, the six foot deep fifteen foot long pit and the babes un-
brained, unbombed, and you will be the beauty, the Ixil Festival
Queen, and your language is Ixil and your people are living in the
Tierra Fría and the Armenians also return to their place and we are
together, thousands of miles apart in some ancestral eden, loving
each other over the autochthonous distance of death, of planets, like
hummingbirds, like the black moths, these black flies which filling
fasting are eating me up in my home in this lonely city, Christ's
mother, this Los Angeles her namesake, her feast's day, like the
dogs, they long for my demise my own flesh to make theirs anew,
to propagate fairly, a continuance of continuance. My people are
dead in America if they were people; yours? deadened, dying all of
the deaths of the ages, but an Ixil girl in the village of Acul, and an
Ixil girl in the capital, and an Ixil girl on the Pan American
Highway: she is, veritably, insatiable, unvanquished, the form itself
could be paradise.

TODAY I made myself into a woman, Marta;—Marta: I am no
longer a man and I am finished (laughs) with men. I am a girl now;
I am an Ixil and I live in Acul, in the altiplano above the gods and
the Spanish who conquered like typhus and small pox and who
fucking made boys girls and who could not unmake the mountains;
and nevertheless made me: a man into a woman; Eve's Eve.

I am another girl also: a girl raised in a city and it is Los Angeles
and there are streets named for men and streets which tarmacked
make the landscape anew; I like to read romance; I like to read
books in the closet without the lights on (a flashlight), and I have

given up on the projects of Love and Reason: this what I read today: "Man is born alone and he will die alone." And then the &tc &tc (the travails of the modern man, his loneliness, his: I can't make the world in my image which could be a cock, obelisk, but really it is only a receipt from the supermarket). And this was when I became a woman, reading the love-stories of men, our philosophie: I love men which is why, Marta, I must be unmade and made into a woman, to do it better; get fucked better with my legs open and a cock uncocked. Because men make sentences and (women make the progeny) in our sentences we make and made worlds and streets and street-cars and desire undone like a bayonet undoes a baby: we unmake the mother who births the child; we undo the umbilical cord which cords the mother and child; we take out the mother, pull our faces from the pussied globe and cut and west and happy happy days! We make Indians; we make chocolate; boulevards; we bring the Washingtonias to Santa Monica Boulevard!

We make modern pies with sugar and shortening. Sugar. Shortening. Sentences with only one word. And the telephone rings as I write to you: it is my mother and she is not dead, tells me to: answer the telephone; ring her up more often; stay married get married again have children lose weight go to the gymnasium and like a monkey swing through and behind the metal weights (of History) and burn calories and burn incense and burn the days out to death (which is the end of the Show tonight). And will do it; do it: a man made into a woman and as a woman, a girl, Marta—I'll make red the color of night; I'll make red the grower of grapes and harvest time will be the blue the green the red gods who will return from the dead before the dead and living will cast their eyes to the heavens which like the canopy of stars (lost to electric light) is only an idea now; memory couldn't do it either.

THE SMALL CHILDREN. Two- and three-years-olds, ten-month-olds, and neonates. (*she says:*) how can I remove their cries from the middle ear? We are walking in the mountains; in the mountains we walk for days and weeks become months;—the mountains that saved us killed us, and we mothers moved our hands to cover the child's mouth and when he ceased his wail, when the good mother takes her hand from his mouth (like a sore then; the mouth is the wound; wails; the wind falls inside) he sleeps; he rests quietly; my breast is a tomb, she says, and this pains her. The mountains are filled to: with the people and the children's wails which filling up the tree branches and strong leaves bring the soldiers' metallic insects on the top of their heads, then bombs on the top of their heads, take the heads off like a soldier will break a boy's skull open against the trees, the stones. These wails, you whisper . . . —it is night in Los Angeles, three a.m. in Los Angeles, and I cannot sleep and I think how my dead lover will one day bring death to the tarmac city and how these wails become like small souls of pain, snail pockets of godliness, exposed in the ear shell, descended down to the tympanum, make noises, make the heart like a small and silver fish on the sand makes the heart like a stone on the river, make a river of pain in the body which flows in Acul down my street in the semi-arid plains of this city; a concrete sluice for pain. We are: alone. It is night; three a.m., I am tired and fatigued and cannot sleep tonight. I have returned from this journey abroad. The children are wailing in the mountains and their—dear—mothers will suffocate the breath from them, place the hands that make the millennial tortilla like a girl will plait and replait her hair, will place the palm over the wound and how he suffers, this Child, he makes the song of our suffering—she places her palm over the wound; the thousands and the hordes of the children in the mountains make songs like pain makes and into the trees; endless; eternal; and invisible: like this ♥ . . . this is his sound and the mother is helpless, she is angry to kill him and hopeless she must do it or the Army will find them and the black insects on the top of their heads (the Cessna A37-B) or they will all be killed, she must do it and she is happy to do it; terrified; endless—grief can be like a river also, and here in Acul Los Angeles the standing trees are filled and the waters run on, run out: my own desiccated soul an invisible heft, like the prehistory of this city which although not seen and although not felt could be something like what lies behind is.

Without the standing trees (the loggers have arrived in the Highlands): (she whispers): where will we leave our sorrow?

I WAS NOT BORN a slave like you, darling. Did not feel hunger's despair, her chilled hand, the inflamed liver and distended belly; bloated feet and hands. And such a desire for meats and sweet things! And the visions of such a feast and days of one meal only and tortilla and beans and then that is all that there is and lucky to have it; an egg on special occasions. Do you remember the piece of candy your father bought for you in Nebaj as a child? What a beautiful bounty and how you would dream of it and more of it; and I too a lover of sweet things to eat and girls and their shy gazes and too much food for this boy; the plates and piles of it put before me;

the too-full belly a constant remorse and reminder that today again and now again at this meal I have eaten too much for comfort—just as now I write these words—too much meats too much of the sugary sweets—too many words also.

(Is it that I am also a kind of slaved boy? Fattened (like a calf, darling) unhappy fat hog in the feeding lot, the meat factory, awaits his death and surcease like a good animal and) Mr Reagan says that your man Mr Ríos Montt is a good man, undemoniac, he is no killer of Indians, he is no slaughterer of girls and babes against the river stones; he has been getting a "bum rap," he has not ordered the burning of your village and fields today; he has not taken your father and your brother to the plaza, to the river, to the side of the building where your skirt is lifted and (no underpants for this girl) the soldier fucks you like a hog; meanwhile, as in the epic, your brother tied to the cypress, your brother slitted and cut, like a pig also. The dogs arriving to lick his sweet bitter blood; the flies in droves on his neck chest wounds, his eyes which gouged now by the crows, his torn feet torn legs—ah, his demise their bounty, and poor Priam cries, knows the end of us, all of us, good and rich and assailed and faithful poor and inconsequential: for all of us the skull serves as a soup urn—your hands caress my bones in your sleep, darling, this sleepy dying girl, who lifting her legs and offering her sex proffers eternity to the boy, who, on the streets of this city, on the tarmac playgrounds of his childhood, later in the dark dirted days, the swollen rivers of his youth, how he tried to know better than he did, sucked the tits of girls gladly, sucked their cunts also, albeit afraid, gladly—pulled words out of his form like semenic spills—cried for you; will have died for your worth, for your black beauty, your dead smile (the wide white teeth blinking back at him) before History's end (and he will not miss History) and we return again to that other time before Time: to the round days and un-marked hours, when the moon rules all things and the sun gods have come back from their sleepy neglected asylum.

THIS IS THE Cold War, and you, my darling, are always cold in the capital in the mountains (hunger makes it, rain makes it, pain and cold); and I am eating fast-food and desiccate foods and box plastics foods. This is a war with enemies in every village and re-publics of enemies and evil and the republics of good are at war now—it is a war of shoes and moneys; of land and four-winged in-sects; of who can carry the bludgeon highest, swing it down with-out remorse or self-imposed limits, like the flies will eat the wrists off of a girl—there will be victims; there will be severed heads; it is for a good, for the patria, for freedom's Show and . . . It will be a war against God or a war for God and it is better to die in this war than to till the field to plant the maize or speak with a tongue made of glass, of old pottery sepulchres; of dung hill ancestor bones we are hiding in the mountains.

"Food is a weapon in a world at war."

("We are always afraid.")

Where can the unspoken or rather the unwritten sentences find room between such debased sentences as those found in the stately departmental treatises; in doctrines and training pamphlets, in text-books and on TV of a war against—whom and what exactly? You? An Ixil girl who sandalless and without a village now wanders in the mountains like a dog? A hungry dog; a starved breed seeking the roots which hold one teaspoonful of water. How many teaspoons to sustain a girl's life? It will not end it does not end and my own sorrow is not enough to make more sentences that could tear out the dead from their places of unmarked buried lives, beneath the pornographic pictures of girls, their cunts, the Galil rifles and a boy tied to cypress and a babe's head split open because to be a subversive is to cry in the midst of so much uncertainty, this much sorrow makes men into more than meat; kills the ineffable; makes a girl walk naked round the plaza of Nebaj (sixteen months later) seeking her brother (who is tied to cypress still in her memory) and the children, and who for one moment would like to unsee; unmake my thinking my sorrows, also, Marta—take this out of me as you put it in me with what you did, made that day in Acul—she screams it inside the plaza, beyond the horizon of grief and in front of the cathedral she lies like a dog, boned, each vertebra pushes through the skin in her back, a marker of roots eaten, of the grasses consumed during her tenure in the mountains. Do you eat the fescue grasses in my Angeleno garden? No, my grasses from another continent and a peasant girl does not travel, read books, eat in restaurants, drive in a car, know how to read; a peasant girl does not lie in the middle of the unwalled plaza in Nebaj saying she would like some chicken a piece of tortilla; that she is so hungry now, and cold; please; she would like to have what she has seen taken from her (back), and yells it out in these pages to take it from her (doesn't she do it in the plaza? Walks in circles in the plaza for hours until a terrified lady gives her some quetzales some clothes some food, get out of here, the lady whispers, they'll kill you) put it where? here?—The end will be silences, this has always been the epic of silences, because to speak is also a betrayal, failure, and to feel is a dog corpse in modernity's garbage heap—the intellect a bin, a well, for the lonely.

—Do you know what it is to be always afraid?

—Yes.

—Do you know how it is to have your wrists removed like glass?

—

—Can you see my eyes into the pupil where darkness is not darker than this idea?

—

—Who is speaking?

—Marta. Marta.

—Who listens?

I AM DRIVING in the darkness; it is night and I am alone. This could be the soul's journey; this could be the modern man's travail; or love's conquest, or the adventure of a man who drives tonight, sees the lights of this city refracted and like moons made on all of the lamplights, the carlights also blaring into his eyes like loud noises, like the small and loud noises the children made in Acul, in the mountains; there are sounds we cannot erase from memory, which like memory reverberate (the tympanum) for centuries and for naught and for the years of this man's lifetime, more than bones perhaps, more than sight? this is *his* death tonight? And I will die two thousand two hundred miles from the girl of Acul, the peasant girl who walked down the mountain fifteen months later, ragged, torn, shoeless and fear like an iron; hungry; the girl who stands behind the yellow and white painted bars in Chimaltenango on the Pan American Highway; the girl in the capital, in the basement of that city so many thousands of miles from him, from her savior who could not or would not traverse time, traverse the mountains, save what he could not see, or seeing, could not bear.

A coward, your swain. A writer.

These things in my head I would like to give to you, language them all for you—then seeing—me—would you bear it? love him better? or perhaps not at all, a never, in this lifetime.

I am a failure, dear Marta. A fleshy hook for the miserable and spoilt, ah this boy from the semi-arid plains of Los Angeles, this man made from ideas and speech and American History like a Show (and the five phrases of his inheritance?)—who curtails this lonely and pathetic essay? Who reads the man's words on the page as he drives writes—which is it? The driver the writer—are they not the same for you: flat and full, profane and profound: are you reading me now? And do I not exist? And then do you not also exist? What a feat of metaphysics! I am cut off from my friends and family; the telephone is broken and breaks in waves, static only upon receipt of your calls. There are no callers at the door. In the supermarkets and the coffee shops I ask for food and water with my penned notes because my voice no longer registers, I am mute, I have died and my corpse moves around, drives around, the streets of this city (I will not leave it) seeking sustenance, girls, cunt-love, and each store vendor berates me, reaches over my skull and pulls sentences through my eye sockets as if I were invisible! Why do they treat us so, darling? No worse than dogs, you say. Yes yes; but I cannot bear it. I have not wanted illness or the loss of my family; I've not wanted to know you in the pink arched church in Acul and on the highway toward your capital and in the basement of that city. I did not want your ungloved and lonely hands like a souvenir, they rest on the mantelpiece and the maggots now and when the bones emerge, sweet minerals, first a knuckle bone from flesh then a thumb's metacarpal; the diptera girls do their duty and their progeny dutifully undo your hands, betrayers and small gods—they return us to the sepulchre.

I am confused. Is it you who died, or do I? Is it me who haunts these pages fitfully, in starts, or has your sad and lonely specter looked me up over the Santa Monica Mountains for this? Am I hurtling down the highways of Los Angeles without destination and without course, collecting the corpses, because the half-dead must do it? Because, abandoned here, we have needed to make our own amends? Our own business: take in the garbage for the dead?

you

do I love you do I not   have we made so much poison now, the ideas released from the box so that there is no return to a before, only the playing out of each theatrical piece until its end; and in this play we all of us, citizens of hope and despair and citizens of the republic and notcitizens and the dogs also, the presidents, the garbagemen, the girls in Acul, the editors for books, my neighbors and your neighbors, shop clerks and clerics—for us await the end of the, as yet unwritten, books; we reading them (although not Readers), we play in the dirt and black asphalt; the universe inside and the universe outside.

WHAT CAN WE SAY, darling, to the end? For the end is both imaginable, and the end, if a fiction for these papers I pen, this man's foray, then allow me my perversions, my perseverance, my pillaging of time and space. Because, Marta, you have survived; and not in your particular place or you by the stream in Acul, that ancient village that Pedro de Alvarado flew toward with his ideas and God and proclamations and god-like steel guns; but you have lived, darling; your language not a dead-thing and the maize does grow again (I have seen it with my own unseeing eyes), and the hunger, yes; the long days of work; cold; without medicines and half of the children die before five years of age; and four hours each day for the grinding of corn, its myriad preparations, the simple beauty of its repetitions, the comfort this man finds, from you, in what comes again and again: the making of the tortilla, "leë" you say in your language, its own return each day; and the children have returned to Acul, have not seen what you saw that day in April, they run through the massacre cemetery, the now filled-to six foot deep fifteen foot long pit, like girls in the playgrounds of my city; they are happy and they laugh out loud, smile into the tourist camera lens and I smile also, take their photograph, and give them a candy to suck on.

This how I found you: I am walking in the cemetery in your capital. It is not night; at night no one walks on the streets of this city because it is not safe here, the black-hooded men, the men who would like your money, the G-2 as a possibility behind all of the fear which makes the metropolis into its own sort of prison. The cemetery is a comfort to me; I am among the dead, I am less lonely; it is daytime, but it feels like night here; the Jeep Cherokee, its windows black as the black car paint, drives through the streets of Guatemala City; the silver-tinted sunglasses men are standing on the corners; each of us hurries to his destination; we do not look at each other, or speak; these men write XXMUJER on each grave marker, they do it without doing it, they do it in the basement of the Polytechnic,

in the pit of Acul, up the Cuchumatanes: the unmade boys and girls
made into unnamed animals, they marked you XXMUJER, the ceme-
tery lined with the rows of black brown marked XXMUJER XXMUJER
XXMUJER XXMUJER XXMUJER XXMUJER XXMUJER XXMUJER XXMUJER
XXMUJER XXMUJER XXMUJER XXMUJER XXMUJER XXMUJER XXMUJER
XXMUJER XXMUJER XXMUJER XXMUJER XXMUJER XXMUJER XXMUJER
XXMUJER XXMUJER XXMUJER XXMUJER XXMUJER XXMUJER XXMUJER
XXMUJER XXMUJER XXMUJER XXMUJER XXMUJER XXMUJER XXMUJER
XXMUJER XXMUJER XXMUJER XXMUJER XXMUJER XXMUJER XXMUJER
XXMUJER XXMUJER XXMUJER XXMUJER XXMUJER XXMUJER XXMUJER
XXMUJER XXMUJER XXMUJER XXMUJER XXMUJER XXMUJER XXMUJER
XXMUJER XXMUJER XXMUJER XXMUJER XXMUJER XXMUJER XXMUJER
XXMUJER XXMUJER XXMUJER XXMUJER XXMUJER XXMUJER XXMUJER
XXMUJER XXMUJER XXMUJER XXMUJER XXMUJER XXMUJER XXMUJER
XXMUJER XXMUJER XXMUJER XXMUJER XXMUJER XXMUJER XXMUJER
XXMUJER crosses.

Who is this Marta girl? Whence does she come and why does
she haunt the pages of the essayed man who resides in Los Angeles,
in a foreign city, who doesn't know, cannot see, blind and quiet, he
is watching a Show on television, he is eating his lunch, he has gone
to work and met deadlines, made phone calls, harried the secretary
and wrote memoranda letters graphs—and what can the half-dead
provide the dead, darling? A half-Armenian boy for the Ixil girl?
He is seeking the roads between his own blood. He is making a
half of a pie and a half of a book and a half of a bloody thing; he
kills the half which denies the day sun time keepers in Acul—he is
killing the old modern even as the city kills him.

THIS WHAT YOU INHERIT: a life-long solitude; a life-long desire to notlive; to not be; which is never the same as wanting to die—it is something else and those of us who lived in Acul live in Acul: the killers & killed & the notkilled—for all of us, now, it is a life-long inheritance. I can say to you: I could never be the woman you loved. I am ugly; I am deformed—there is a monster made of these organs, bones, the sinew is corrupted and makes invisible maps with blood and rot—there is only a monstrous place and it is not the inferno, the inferno would be preferable, would be a place I could apprehend; a ruthless yet deserved place; a hierarchy of possibilities, the castes of the down-trodden and the deserved dead—and then an opposite implied: some kind of paradise and in this dark and monstrous place there is no haven which awaits the clean, the beautiful, the boys and girls with washed feet and hair and who have not sinned; no; for us we have only what is and what is ties the brother to the tree in our square and his father and his uncles made into his killers, a betrayal of the possible, unmakers of love, but always and it is the living who must live whether or not we wish it, and whether or not we wish it (unless like the dogs and unless like my father, the tail between the legs, the cock, a hunched man) we may die of fear, this *susto*, or the knife pulled across our gullets. Don't write me up, man. Don't imagine yourself a lover from paradise's ether: I will make you a misery; I will take you into my darkest place and there, with love in the hand, I will make you monstrous also, and then you'll hate me for it and you'll hate me for it, and despair will be your companion also—we are not destined, we are weevils, dogs, no better than dogs they said of us, killed us and trained us and beat us like dogs—But listen, man, I am a woman who loves mountains and a woman who wished for a different life and who, as a girl, dreamed up lives of the undestitute and lives where a butterfly could mean the beginning of a wish, and then—and do you know unfreedom? Do you understand a life without possibilities? Where every action is determined and predetermined not by god but by the bosses and the boss' men—the men who would beat us and the men who would cheat us and then of course (the soldiers, the civil patrollers, the liars, the fuckers): the men who fathered us and the men who married us: all of them, you also, betrayers, liars, desperate to be loved to be feared, in fear you live and you rule us— and so I'll lie here also: I'll make love to you with my ethereal sentences, and I'll not be your guide in the underworld, I'll not chase you down the alleyways of memory and retrieve you, save you, so that you'll turn from me, you are betraying me, you are a man and the men have always done it: the wars, the lies, the desire to piss the world, reason it all out while pissing it.

If I could be a better woman I would do it. I wouldn't be self-ish or tired or desperate for love's apogee, again and again, love's lonely call to this man and this man and—I'd become real, I'd cease the literature of men, I'd come out of the books and poems, I'd be no man's guide or muse or whore for his—understand? Don't call me down, don't make me, then make me up for your reading and fucking pleasures—it's what the soldiers did, and my despair is my own, and I live with it because it lives with me and we cannot take our clothes off in winter, for then we are only cold, only flesh without recourse. In the mountains. In the mountains we had no recourse. Shall I tell you of how it rained every day? Shall I tell you of the abiding cold? We are sick all of the time; we are in pain. It is worse for the children and old men. The children and the old men the women and all of us colder, hungrier, we eat grass, we eat rootbuds, we can shiver for days and the days of cold of hunger of we are sick do not make the hours move and although the mountain saved us, it did not save all of us, and the dead there unburied, the bones like flies because we used those bones to beat the rain from our brows, to beat our brows, a bone can be a killer also. When the men said that the children do not contribute, when they said without saying it that we must take these bones of our dead and close the crying mouths of our youngest boys and girls (which bring the Cessna A37-B onto our heads; bombs) then I was certain that a thing in the chest, an invisible marker of hate or sadness, could also become a killer. But it is not so. The children were died, or killed, or abandoned up in the mountain and more bones only made more bones—you see, it is a material question, a question of the lowest order: we are dogs after all; we are beasts; and we are enraged and rage can make things and rage can unmake things also: rage unmade my child in the mountain. Do you see what happens when you pull me down into your language, into this English, an island settler's foreign tongue, the word *tongue* itself like meat: continue if you must, follow the lines of your argument, tell us then, dear Sir, about these Americas, about your sadness, your tales of woe and lonely individual days,—do you know lonely? Do you know the mountain? Do you know Acul? Do you know this tree? Can you see my brother tied there, his chest slashed open by the hands of his family members and neighbors—a machete wielded with love—the soldiers said that they had done it too fast after they did it, the boy after my brother was beaten longer, died slower, as if this sort of act could unmake thinking and loving. And when the old men of the village dug the burial pit (my father also) and were asked to stand inside of it, they assumed they were making their own sepulchre and that now they would perish, and when they were told by the soldiers to go and get the men from Hell, their sons and brothers and nephews ("Now that you have finished the graves, each one of you must take a person. The men of Heaven must take the men of Hell to the cemetery,") and when the father was made to kill his son, the brother his brother, made by fear, then we all were forsaken, and we could not return; we became exiles of love by our own hands' acts, and refugees of pain—this is our land, and here we have lived as the exile, defiled, demeaned, and branded for slaves and fucked by bosses and carried the bosses on our backs and the children have always been dying in droves and yet there is more than this—our own sweet tongue and the beauty of the girls who run laughing, and I look around the room and the room is filled, in the old days, with all of my mother and father's children, the eight of us like a sword for what was possible in the future.

BOOK TWO

Others form man; I tell of him, and portray a particular one, very ill-formed, whom I should really make very different from what he is if I had to fashion him over again. I cannot keep my subject still. It goes along befuddled and staggering, with a natural drunkenness . . . I do not portray being: I portray passing.

—MONTAIGNE

The settlement of new countries, and the progress of civilization have always been attended with perils. The career of civilization under the auspices of the American people, has heretofore been interrupted by no dangers, and daunted by no perils. Its progress has been an ovation—steady, august, and resistless.

—California Governor JOHN BIGLER, 1852

When the Indians had died the villages ended . . . all the people ended.

—GABRIELINO CONSULTANT to
John Peabody Harrington

AND MARTA, REALITY? America as real as its Shows—so that all of the masks made the real as a Show on the television and not what is: this essay: the man: that I love you or that when I put my cock inside your flesh we are one and the heave of breath, the outness of fucking, its fire and my own godlikeness in those moments, and out, dead; or the energy that zings around the room from my soul and crotch to yours to the girl in the bookshop; love; and not this other thing of TO DO (lists bills moral-plays the good and the bad buys girls), to watch the television, pay the taxes, wear this not this, and to eat, to drive, to work and don't pull your cock out, don't speak what is in your soul or say that you are half-alive that you cannot do it any longer that a man must needs be a man and not some modern stuck on the roads in the maze of the American real, a strange and lonely dream, where I cannot love or fuck as I would like to, need to, feel; where my desires are denied (and I myself am the schooled policeman of these desires) and allowed surfeit in food and things and the machines, but not in love or semenic grunts, not for the dead or the living who refuse the refuse of the modern: or the gods in stones, mountains, rivers, but only the half-deads, drive around this city as if living were half of some thing, and this thing can be purchased (again and again) at the shops at the market inside the classroom where we make boys; Americans; good citizens for this time when the sun dials are obsolete and the time of the clock is a good business measure; trains aeroplanes run on time.

IT IS NIGH IMPOSSIBLE to see your age, Marta—one's epoch and historical moment. I look upon history with a gleeful modern serpent's eye and (my superiority assured) berate the Spaniard his wooden batons crude cannons (Cortés' 14) the cruel mercenaries who bashed your children's heads against stones and used the dead Ixil fat to salve their compatriots' wounds, and each slave branded for his owner, and I don't cry darling when Lázaro is tied to the cypress like a dog (kill the devils commies) and you are taken from the garden on the corners of Calle 12 and Avenida 4 and (not seen again, my darling); and here in America we eat outrage for dinner like soup in cans and its beauties biases, loneliness in a can, and supreme blindness like a man sees himself in an old glass pitcher: how to do better, Marta? So that later, when I am old and then tired, I wont go to my own death (you are bones now, not-dug up by the fierce girls and boys) knowing how I failed my fair girl and did not care to love you when you were an Indian, an Ixil girl bathing in the river, not-eating in the mountains: you are running in the mountains, the bomber is flying above your heads; the Army is coming and you are looking at Doña Ana and she is holding the babe and then there is only the sound of higher death, descending, and then the newmother's viscera covers the landscape like a bloody fog in winter and the babe has miraculously survived, he cries for days, and dies on your own worthless titty (worthless because milk-less)—his last breath and I am pushing a sandwich into my mouth: bacons cheeses mayonnaise; it is good and I am, as usual, too full and my belly hangs over my trousers and I am hating that there is too much food in front of me all of the time and thinking how I must go to the gymnasium and push machines up and spending energy like dollars making me more beautiful like a small god (and then the girls will love me want me, want to fuck my sad skin)— you there, I can hear your wails today in my ears, the tympanum detects across ether, across History, that moment in 1983 when the babe takes its last breath at your titty and I take the last bite of my bacon sandwich and hate myself that I have eaten too much (again) when the starved babe dies at your tit and we float into death's sorrow: me a half-dead and you, darling, a corpse on the horizon of your wars—the Army must needs do it, Marta, they had to save the patria from the devils. They were not sorry to do it, for it needed to be done. ("What have you observed here? What is it that you have seen?" They asked all of you that afternoon in April after massacre, and you were silent before the soldiers, heads and backs bent. "Now you've seen the dead. You have to return to your home. You must go tranquil. Go home and eat, relax, and sleep. Don't do anything. You have done good work here. Go home. Go home tranquil.")

And sadness is also an American toy, and breaks and cheap and not for the Ixil girl who heard Spanish like this boy hears her cry in the distant reverberation of his ears.

Now I can't live without you? or was it yesterday over a coffee and doughnut that your absence became like a weight, and this heft around the organs when you leave me for the ether, when you don't come down from the mountain to visit me, wont come up from the Polytechnic to see me (your hands); do not love enough, I scream through the silences, to see that I am becoming a man who cannot bear the unMarta'd days: I need spirit like some men need minerals and cocaine.

How does this proceed, then? I am standing in front of the glass in my house, see the street outside, unriven asphalt, the river has not come in years now, the pots and cups and shoes of my neighbor's house do not rush headlong down Hollyline Av toward Ventura Blvd, which could be the sea, except that we are in a desiccate valley, and the waters run inland. I stand here, and you have been dead these many years now—where are you interred? XXMUJER in the cemetery in your capital city? Or an unmarked, not even XXMUJER in Acul? Or the plaza in Nebaj? Or the mountains which saved you and killed you as they have long done: from the Spaniards in 1530, and from your Quiché neighbors before them— the Ixil have always resisted the invaders.

And why this obsession with the bones, Marta? With the Bone Boy of my dreams, he walks through the Der Zor at night and dreaming tells me that I can find my relatives there like small bushes or rodents—but so what if they died in another place? Were slaughtered like sheep in the desert in 1915. What does this have to do with you and me?

LAST NIGHT I dreamed that you no longer loved me. That I was no more for you than another lover amidst the hundred boys, the soldiers in your village, the Lieutenant and colonels and washroom boys; your blind killer; the boys you have taken from the streets into your back and darkened room which is no room but cordoned off by a woven blanket hangs from a rope and tattered with use, a black which has turned grey and the reds now pink and the dust of trucks which move up and down the Pan American Highway, cover the grey and pink blanket hangs there (like a talisman) and the other girls and old hanging blankets and the concrete slab floor, the bared and stained and striped mattress which, I am certain, has never been covered with bed linens in this place. I can see beetles, the long and loud black flies, the days are invisible inside your room, inside (as in the Polytechnic) it is always night (the bare lightbulb hangs from a loose wire and) and night now as the big and red blue yellow painted Blue Birds take the peasants up toward the Highlands (home) and down to the sugar plantations coffee plantations, to the capital city of your country which is not yours (the Laws). You welcome us with your pained mouth your crushed teeth and painted mouth—your hello's and come in's and scars on your neck and ankles and bared wide ass; we do put our cocks inside you and hating these girls, which could be something like love, or wanting them more than destiny, more than time, over the rules and regulated days of how we can love, of when we can do it, and by whose calendar; with whom; beneath new stars and new coverlets.

Ah, Marta. What a nice girl you are. See your brown smile which sad and sadder does not reveal itself to me. And you are happy with the money I put into your hands and when my cock is part of your body and we are as one then, if not happy, then? have I at the least adored you, worshipped correctly? like a supplicant to the old gods, your own gods in trees.

And when I awoke from this dream, I was at home and my wife was sleeping at my side (you see how the dead make us dreamers). She was not touching me in her sleep; she didn't touch me with her

awake eyes or hands any longer either. Our boy was sleeping inside her body, he had not died yet. And I considered getting up then,
it was early yet in the morning, and driving somewhere far from the
house that I lived in and far from the woman who was no longer in
my bed and the boy no longer in her belly. I thought, then, that I
could put petrol in the deposit and that I could begin the drive
southward. And I would begin driving on the 405 Freeway and
pass through the portal of the Santa Monica Mountains (where the
Gabrielino guide guided Portolá and Crespí those many years ago,
the ancient spoor now locked beneath tarmac roads) and see the
west side of Los Angeles; see the city in the distance as it spread out
for miles, and if I were a lucky man today then, perhaps, O the possibility of it!, to see the sea from the freeway, it happened twice that
I can remember, a distant haze at the edge of the haze the city makes
and has made permanently since 1942. And continuing apace this
405 and I am driving with hundreds and then thousands of my citizens and I don't know their names or whom they love or what, at
this moment, has made them these drivers, these movers of flesh
and steel, the bluegrey plastics, over the tarmac hills the concrete
byways toward work and school and grocery stores and hardware
stores and the post office and an appointment! and an assignation!
and they are not driving toward you, darling; they do not think of
making this tarmac world into another place, a before, when you
could be a girl on the ancient spoor and I could be an ancient boy
walking to the sea or, better, leaning against the stone walls of time
of the pomegranate trees of figs in late summer and eating the
peasant's breakfast in the East of flat bread, sheep's cheese; O, sorrow, why have you writ my name in America? And in the end I am
only made good for this, which is to say, for no thing: a penner of

words, the corpses uncollected now, the bitches decompose in the desert slowly and stink like the boys in the plaza in Nebaj, the twelve they cut up into pieces of themselves and deposited on the cathedral steps for all to see and (by whom we always knew; silent like thieves, beetles) all around the four corners of the plaza, the sun, moon, yellow, black, of the center—let me speak to you with flesh; let me tell you how a man wants no more than hammocky days and the wide and open cunt; she loves him only; she loves him always (until the next girl and the next)—why have you left me in my dreams? how can you come to me at night, I am sleeping, vulnerable, afraid, and my wife, if I had one, is angry with me; fed-up; and my son will be spoilt and fat and watch television more and want more plastic toys and more sugary sweets and if I had a son children and if I were wifed then what of you, in my dream you are standing behind the yellow and white barred window of the whorehouse in Chimaltenango; this is the Pan American Highway and you lean against the bars of the roadside place, on the threshold of the place, and we drive by your establishment (who, this *we*?) and you stand there with the other girls and shyly the girl behind you touches you with her fingertips (the nice one) and the mean girls slap you, but I am driving by you, crane my head out the car window to see your arms visage, to see the hands entire, this you who is no longer the Ixil girl from Acul but who is not yet, either, the one from the capital in the basement of the Polytechnic—a girl between girls; sixteen years old perhaps—suspended in time; and if I stop this car and we go to seek you, find you, fuck you, then it is good and right and the grey and pink blanket for a moment, which is eternity, hides our nakedness from the gaze of the others, and I don't mind the stink of the mattress, old semen spit and shit; and I love the menstrual blood on your thighs as you unwrap the black corte and spread it out, like a blanket, beneath us. I drink your blood at the altar of your cunt and without shame I stand within love's room, I am happy dreaming.

AND WE shall not have it. You shan't make your way down the mountain; you have not eaten anything in more than thirty days, a root's spoonful of water has not quenched your hungry thirst; you have no shoes and your clothes are bare rags so that you are effectively naked, blackened with the dirt, you are sick and like the twenty or more who come down the mountain with you, you have this sickness in your eyes and the eye weeps its yellow sands; you are exhausted; emaciated. You walk into Nebaj and the soldier at the plaza sees you (he is from a village thirty miles away) and he ties your arms together like bundled wood and he (takes his cock) and he (licks your cheek) and he also can never make his way back to his village; the villages have been burnt (626 villages destroyed) and the new places will be made—a Model Place in the place of old Acul, and one wide road (the width of an army truck) will bifurcate the village—and is he the cocksman of the child you unmade in the mountain more than six months ago? and his hands do not shake today as he lights his cigarettes, grabs the men by their hair and pushes them to the ground—Guerrilla dog, mother-fucker commie whores—with his Galil, takes all of you to the Army barracks for your re-education training.

Why am I then a sad man?—and this longing, whence does it come? They've not taken my father to the administration building;

they don't spread my legs like a mountain for their nightly pleasures; I am not starved and the bones like mountains pushing against my skin; and this shame as you walk naked into the plaza; and this fear (of the soldiers); and desperate; and these are not the questions for the modern man who lives in the great metropolis; and freely circulating speech, like cars, and the old modern is tired; I am this he, this man made in America, made of the myths of the new; of a violent surmise toward the ocean and work-work dreams and (and fear) newnamed places: America; Los Angeles; the Porciúncula and then the Los Angeles, River; Hollyline Av; a river of errors and pre-errors, of eros like a bayonet. He has been sitting and he is driving, drives along the streets of this city; sings; drives—they are fucking you now behind the cathedral (the Army barracks in Nebaj), eating maize dumplings cutting off a boy's ears and nose; they razed Acul at three p.m. on a Friday (and the cypress walls your grandfather boasted of, that heavy dark wood he carried down the mountain before you were born for a hundred years' house, a hundred years' floorboards, burnt slower in blind consolation to the blind witnesses).

I am sick today. I have been sick since De Landa burnt the books and destroyed the gods—when Crespí saw the small spring in the semi-arid coastal plain of Alta California and he thought of Monica and how she wept for her wayward unchristian son; when the ancient river became the Porciúncula became the Los Angeles River and then was finally concreted up like a girl in a stiff party dress; since the guard, he loves you, in the Polytechnic in the capital of your city, removes your hands like gloves; the children and their mothers, shoeless, naked in the mountains, hungry, these motherly hands which stop their hungry breath.

He is no icon, our man prostrate on the cross—no devil worshipper either; see the dead we kill, we don't drink the blood. See Lázaro rise from the dead (in the mouths of maggots dogs and the black crows); see the dead in the river, in the mountain, along the streets of this city—see them, see how they fuck corpses in the desert, the soldiers fucking the Ixil girls in Acul Nebaj Chajul Cotzal Xix—see them there; see the commie sympathizer bastards stretched out like tiny christs; see a girl's split-open cunt like tiny supplications—see the child's grey brain matter like the corpus on a saint's day.

A Manual for the Americas

We are inside the basement of the Polytechnic and I am admiring the bone shadows that your heel bone makes in the sunlight inside the palms of my hand in my mind. When you come to my bed your feet and hands, your breath is sweet and we can love like this for hours. I can find christ in your body; this too, the documents have instructed, must be killed like a Show on television, slowly, and with pain and blood that is beautiful, like a red river. You made me into a woman and I surrendered to it, the christ was a woman also; to clean your feet, the heel: a man made into a woman and returned. But you don't come to my bed, this is the metal cot you are chained to in the Polytechnic. The manual stipulates the killing of the communist faggots first; and I do; we do it slowly, with time's extensions; a christ, his face removed, his penis removed with a red-hot coffee cutting implement, the maggots in the wounds, the teeth and hair weeks before—he is your christ in the black pit with you. Each day becomes eternities of days, the sun never sets or rises, the bare lightbulb on a wire, and while I hold you on the examining table, the metal cot, and I burn you one hundred and seventeen times with my cigarettes, while the other guards have gone out for a meal (beef steaks, tortilla, potato, red wines), then I will ask for your forgiveness: I understand that you become a christ today also.

And you look at me, or rather, you stare at me, make a picture on my closed eyelids, make a picture on the colored disks covering my eyes, on the pupil through these tinted lenses to arrive at my retina (I am always wearing the sunglasses in this room—for what, I cannot say). So this look, a stare I have said, an ethereal beast looks from his bodied-cage where pain is made into a commodity of sugary things: where sugar, sleep, your head pulled from the basin of water—where breath—can be enough to make me into your god, but a god without rivers: an unsatrapied god of the shadow's shadow; lonely on his throne.

I whisper into your ear-hole, the ears removed an hour ago, making you look more and more the simian whore: I whisper into the hole, a beautiful whorl still visible beneath the cracks (blood bones): *Is it possible for me also to be saved?*

You begin retching, the vomit heaves you up from the cot where you are held by the chain and you cannot stop the retching, the heaves, continual shaking of your legs and arms (the hands the nose not removed, not yet). I, for some reason, take the bottle of wine which I have been drinking and against all of the rules in my manual begin to toss it down your throat as you begin crying now, uncontrollably, like a child will do it, crying but not speaking to me, a prelingual child, you remind me of my black self—an hysterical flight of the sorrowful form: tears and your mouth agape (like a bird's) as I pour the wine into your mouth and you sputtering and spitting and want more of it and we drink the rest of the bottle

together—you and I—the unsainted god (your agapet), the sobbing girl, there in the dark, I hold you closely, and we are like lovers
amidst the howls of shit, the pissed floors, your ear shells on the
floor next to my booted feet (mine own hands handy work). (After
work I will try to have these specimens saved, and to this end I go
to a taxidermist's shop in the capital, but the man puts on a look of
horror when I pull the ear shells from my jacket, wrapped carefully
in cloth, and he refuses to do it, to preserve them for me (and my
9mm also makes a look of horror when he sees it and I return for
him later that week and unmake his look), so that I will never do it
again—your earshells forgotten, a rodent feast perhaps, diptera delight in the trash bin of the Polytechnic (where I tossed them), of
History. Days later I am convinced I see one hand—the left?
right?—carried off by a small rat, his dinner, and so I investigate
the rat shits for days afterwards, seeking the traces of your body in
the shits of the animals: is this not some form of transcendence, my
darling? but of a lower variety, certainly. A downward rising. The
maggots themselves small white gods like an animal mob.)

You did not, of course, answer my question with the language
that we used between us. You vomited; you stared into or at the
lenses I wore to cover my pupils, the keep-some-things-in and
other-things-out (but ineffectual) plastic screens. Ah, Marta: was it
not possible to make love in that place? I could have saved you, a
piece of you, and I do make an essay and I listened and I obeyed (I
had hoped to carry your ear shell with me into eternity, a preservation piece for the peace of our species). I read the manual from
beginning to end—a manual for the masters and the slaves. And the
master hates the slave who refuses him her soul. Yes, he owns the
form: the ears and face and sad and lonely wrists, but not the ineffable: we would like your spirit, it is what we seek in these dark pits

of the capital. What else could be accomplished, or desired? The speaking, the words I can make you utter, all of the phrases forced with breathy sound in the language that we use between us: this Castilian: this not what I'm after—I wont pretend; information like a dog, and we beat the dog, kill the dogs. No. It is *you* I want—that withheld piece. What shall I call it except love? Why can't you give it to me? Why, even at the end, the pit's stench has defeated you, the pit's death howls, the pit's endless night: why, even then, even when your vagina has been opened to the air like a ripe plum, purple, reds, your breasts slashed, why (how?) then do you still withhold it from me? I am only a man, after all, and I cannot live without it, a schooled boy of these Americas.

WE DON'T HAVE the language to understand you—in this speak I can only see your Indian colors, sweet red hummingbirds embroidered on your shirt; you run like beautiful gazelles. I make you Indian, make you my monstrous lover; a commie devil; could fuck you day and night, and I have, I do.

I have an old culture in my pocket and I can't find my grandmother; I'm looking for her; the dead of lands and rules and the ways to continue: this loneliness from the dead—they are immanent in my mother's five phrases, the half-built half-iterated and then forgotten house of my ancestors.

(When radically different ideas meet head on: one bulleted and cannoned, and the repeating rifle, the Galil: and the inability to say, to defend, a difference, then the most brutal and well-armed will vanquish? The other ideas decimated? The ideas of war, of honor;

of a nature that is not "nature" but me and the wind are like me. Disease.)

What is it, Marta, to be from a place? The Ixil earth-bones hold the bones of your family (and mine?) and this is a story that cycles, re-cycles, contextualizes the meaning of days, the weather days; sun; heat and rains, the wind invisible in the mountains with trees for allegory.

The material and immaterial: the visible and invisible: trees, wind, sorrow.

These are shadows in tandem, eclipsed by shadow; America is like this also; sad girl; happy girl; the lies like fruit treason and History, a straight plumb line from there to here.   •

And shame and the lies are grey and this legacy of futured ruins, of thingéd solitude—the interstitial shadow days—; a fear so wild that only unfire will unmake it, not to destroy or destruction's natural bent because we would like to be new again, we would like to be Adam'd again (on your backs in your pupils black and seeing) or Eve'd this time, round on a straight path?—a renewal of the dead and cast-outs. (*what have we unmade here as much as made?*)

You do not read or write; and I am writing you and unwriting you: have there been books before letters? can a girl be undone and then redone in this man's mind? have there been empires without whores? without letters? without the sun? cycles? *We are not dogs.*—What does that sentence mean? What could it mean when on a Thursday in the middle of the spring months in the northern hemisphere of America, it is April, and it is not hot in the Highlands and rains today in the Highlands and lowhanging clouds that sit like girls on the Cuchumatanes, and the men—*named?*—shove their machetes into some boys' low bodies, except that here the soldiers use Galils [made in Israel] and a cock between whose legs there?

And [who makes the sales? eats the profits of the Galil, the UH-1H, Cessna A37-B?] and a baby pushing from out of legs there and build a pyre and burn the thing which makes no sense to him or him: *¿que puede ser, si estos indios son indios?* [and you have taught me, Marta, that my fallow places of shame are not fallow and that love could also be an unraveling of the possible]; I am a man; and then American: like this (I almost had a son once):

Why are we, in the accounting, the obedient and the boys in class lined up in rows? obeisance is always our school lesson (to: the nation, to god, to sitting in rows, to amateurish fun with cockstems, to we own you, we are owners; yes sirs; to the Big Companies and small lies which sustain god nations Big Companies, to the straight plumb line in time:) and you unschooled in school but still a good girl? a good girl's thighs are wet, your pussy is. My morality is the best defense against the barbarian! And what it can't do, we have fear's cudgel and machete: farm implements can implement the boy's bashed brained cranium. We have UH-1H helicopters and helicopter parts and Cessna A37-B parts (Mr Reagan authorizes 6 million dollars in parts for your man of great personal integrity!).

If I knew, Marta, what I wanted and where it is I were driving to, I wouldn't write to you or write you this book a notbook or notebook perhaps which is the same as a driver's manual, a series of lines to uncover the girl with the brown hair and the pupil closest to my own: your black moon looks straight into mine and we are blind, blackened by unseeing, sees you there in the basement of the Polytechnic and on the road to the capital in the plaza which is no plaza; the cypress stands; our monsters cast shadows which can make and remake a boy who was unmade that Thursday in Acul; it is imagination's only desire, or duty? It is all and what we have been given? Our tired and free allotment? It is 1982 and I am sitting on the sofa and you are standing by the hearth. I am walking toward the kitchen and you are walking toward the door (there are no windows in your house; in my kitchen the glass windows are cut into four squares). Your stomach acids churn around three tortillas, black beans, and my acids eat up peanut and chocolate and sugars—we are hungry, you and I, and it is never enough, and I am a fat man and in your face I can see bones: you will die in a war that is not a war (the *Internal Armed Conflict* they will call it—and were you armed, darling?) and I will watch a television Show while you are dying. You perish; *you are dying* is a way to say it: how to speak agony in the television Shows and sell shampoo and fast cars in the commercial interlude? When I am drunk I cannot speak clearly and when I am drunk I pick whores up off of Hollywood Blvd; they are: kind to me, and their fat collects in kindly places (the upper thighs); they smell nice. They listen to everything I say: I say that I love them, that I will always love them, to save them—kill their pimps for them. They also do not read this driver's Manual for America; they also did not hold a son I did not have like a cudgel or small and old bone.

Why is there so much God? Is it to forget the dead or to retrieve them as if the dead could return to us, tell us how to do it better than a god then a god who lives near the sun and his sons will do it and the girls on the riverbank, riparian gods are taken from that river and it eventually becomes the graveyard of time for the books that burned so many hundreds and thousands of years ago, that as I walk to the kitchen and you walk to the river to retrieve the water and to wash I am washing my hands and only here do we do it—together—this endless walking of souls across the landscape of the possible the impossible rivers for all of the girls' bones their hair released and hacked into waters where we seek gods and books from the gods and a whore to wash our feet—and a happy whore would be nicer—and all of this untruths, just an American meandering so that he can understand why it is that he would like to die each day without dying and how all of the televised Shows kill him make him a killer a shopper fucker and how he hates what lies outside his kitchen neighborhood and city country—the barbarian hordes arriving each day to his city and—what am I, Marta?;—and what this place we've made like a dog makes and why is there so much wind? disease on the winds?

THEY SIT ON the walls, circle around in their haphazard unreasoned flight; the patterns so randomly made, it would seem, but no collision in their frenzy, these black birds, smaller than my fingernails—flying, filling, running up and down my walls, my kidney. I am fly-filled, their bodies like small pieces of my fear, and the material bodies, the black corpses when I kill them and I am unashamed by it, the corpses, an insect interlude—but they come from the corners of rooms and they fill my house, my lonely organs, all of the bile is larva infested: my shits their nest, and denizens of History denizens of livered historiographies: they are flying filling doing me in: they wait for a corpse to appear and I will give it to them soon, soon enough: my eyeballs and the vicious viscous matter will make dinner for the diptera girls.

As a boy I loved the girls. I watched them and longed for their purples reds and what could be a plastic necklace; hair stuck to the shoulder blades; to be kind and then mean, these are the playground days which are years. I've left my fingerprints on the windows: how long will they remain? Is it the oils that make fingers print? the sweat dirt, the cells of my hand sloughed off like snow? In Los Angeles it does not snow and the deluge comes every few years, makes a river in my house, through the streets of this city: the river comes down up from Acul: from your village, Marta, brings you with it: brings love like a girl on the playground brought her hands together as if to see me there on my knees. And this river flows through my house, will take out the pots, the kilim, the books of inquiry History, and all of it flows through the doors and windows, down the street and beyond into infinity. This is infinity ✸ the sun in motion, endlessness of repletion, of suns, of days, repetition, this river of yours makes a river in my city—your forests and rains and my deserted days, the afternoons eating kumquats and pomegranates from the neighbors' yards. Do you know kumquats? their sweet skin, bitter fruit and seeds—my childhood in this city was spent waiting for the pomegranates to ripen in October; and the tree bough hung over the neighbor's fence and we children picked the red fruits and threw them onto the asphalt to open them, stained our fingers t-shirts the tarmac red and this red like your brother's handprints later on the cypress in the dust plaza of Acul, no permanent marker of the years.

Can a ghost love her creator? Do you love me? Do the djinn make their djinn-makers into these theses and bridges? Is it you who writes me, Marta, as your brother lies prostrate on the cypress? Do you think then that you will tell the foreigner, tell him and cull him from the ether? The man makes and the American makes you, makes the Cessna A37-B in Kansas, the UH-1H helicopter in Texas, and breath can unmake them, me—or ideas from another mind; the cypress will have her revenge: and this blood will take down the citadel; this pomegranate juice will sweeten the tongue redden the tarmac black. Do you believe it? Can the cuxín make more than a picture of wind? Lonely, grieved, and I would kill you in a moment—this also: that the damned exiled race and the damned unexiled race could make more than pain and more than this love: we could make the progeny, if the dead could rise— doesn't Lázaro's sister know of it? didn't He do it? Couldn't we?

(SHE ASKS ME: *who is speaking*)

I am finished with words and their religious histories, what lies behind them and they are filled with the gospels of to do and did and not just who is speaking but how

in what manner

form

which ideas

language does he do it with; he is doing it again; making it again and

this is my only tongue for it, this English from an island I have not ever known, a place that exists, as I do, in my imagination,—must I then give it up and I'll give it up for silences making spaces an abyss and a fifteen foot long six foot deep hollow for something other

than what I can say and what saying

things then means—your father and brothers and the dog's progeny transformed not at all by my words (black diptera girls, the blue beetles) but then also, perhaps, demised by them: a conquest is made by the tongues as well as by the killers,

I am fatigued by commas, by the semicolonic reign rage to

reign in the stars and the abyss: I cannot find or see between them
and the buses along the highway their diesel dust in my nostrils their
black and soot in my form my fingernails picking the dust
pricking the black dirt from my eyes nose I
would like an endless page or a page without form or I would like
none of it this
desire to write it up the
decrees of passion
of the soul and
who is soul'd and
who is no longer (when the babe dies at your breast) and who is not
listening and reading
and you
Marta
are you in these pages and these pages are delimited not by the
Gregorian calendar or the time of the clock, but by this form
paper
what I can see say the sentiments of to end and I am talking and
talking to see you you, making no sense, non-sense; a maze and
amazed
how I lie to you even here, alongside the gods I uncover and recover
    (hear the Cessna A37-B above your heads in the mountain;
bombs like girls
even I need the parenthesis the aside
and the interrogative
its mark so
that I may ask you
inquire)
pugilism and puncture and to punctuate all from the prick, this
baby in my darling trousers.

AND WHAT can you possibly be in my American mind? Today I took a drive out along the highways of the desert and I could hear the owls and I saw a hawk and in the distance there was rain and I could see it as if it were something to hold, my eyes were holding, (pause at each comma, darling), my eyes were working and making rain, rain clouds in the distance, a hawk on a fence post, the Washingtonias on the horizon and then making you on a bus, your trip down the mountain into Nebaj, your wanderings in the stone plaza (after re-education in the Army barracks), then the loaned quetzales from the terrified lady to the half-dead girl, to you, darling, and you get on the old Blue Bird school bus that I remember from my own childhood (but yours is red and bright blue and *Dios Me Bendiga* on the front sign), and inside the bus the original seats have been removed and longer ones put in their place so that it is difficult to pass down the aisle, but you do it turning this way, your hips left right left and eight people can sit cross-wise on these buses; and the chickens roosters make noise, the children are vomiting when they are sick, the old men close their eyes and sleep.

(the owl sits outside my door in Los Angeles but I cannot see it and during the afternoon hours I cannot see stars or Venus or the wind because there is no wind today—the owl sits in an electric tree and hhoos all day even as I write this to you; our skies are emptying these many years; the disappeared birds, the lowland marshes and river; trout; brown bears and otter'd seas.)

On the bus you sit down; you carry a small package and inside it you carry two tortillas, some beans, chirmol (the same terrified lady gave it you, got you out of her sight). You are not wearing the huipil that looks beautiful to my eyes here in my book, your costume which is a thing of beauty—the red birds and green mountains you once embroidered on the shirt; the hummingbird who fights his jealousies for love: will you leave it in our museum in my capital when you die? You left it in the mountains and naked you walked out of the mountains—today you have a skirt and shirt the Army gave to the naked Indians.

I am, quite suddenly, hungry, sitting here in the green armchair (do you know this sort of hunger, darling? the hunger of those who have always had so much to eat and eat food like television Shows and shopping malls and would like more and more). I walk to my kitchen, open the refrigerator and eat something savory then sweet. Stay on the bus; stay until I return. It is the small details I see; I seek you in the small prick, the words behind words, the tortilla, the Blue Bird; a corrugated piece of iron your neighbor saved and carried on his back for months until he died in the sacred mountain; the mountain which saved you killed him. I am failing; a failure and I don't wish to talk and I say that I am finished with talking (writing only now) but first: a snack, a pizza perhaps, then more sentences, more of you on that bus. And the rains are coming to the Ixil Area, in Acul it rains now and plastic sheeting has replaced the burnt clay roofs, the clay tiles smashed like the birds, like the children's skulls against stones, on a Thursday when the Army arrived at six o'clock in the morning, time of the clock, darling? or time of your sacred sun?

WHAT IS this place, Marta? a new underworld, a place that is no-place, and inhabited by the half-deads; more violent, passive: monsters of derision, of shame, of unsexed and sexed-out loneliness: of more information and less *knowing*; of games and Shows and picture magazines of how to live! eat! run! parceled out like sweet pops; we are more than lonely; we are shy, quiet liars, killers—of ourselves—the sort that hate the dogs and whores the Indian and we made ourselves and our rules here and the money rules here: make the world, the word: this Right into a dollared sign like a green faggot; we are always afraid.

Come sit on my knee, say, and I'll tell of the dead. In a new underworld the height of civilization has been reached, we have attained paradise, cleanliness, rules and roads, and the modern works sixty hours in a week! and he buys his groceries in plastic bags from plastic carts in the metal aisles; and he thinks of the Shows, News, of the wars like Shows in his mind, of the emaciated Africans like Shows on his screen of the girls taken from their childlike childhood beds and not returned, of magazine photographs and clothes, like he thinks about the pictures his mind makes; like he thinks about you when you are sleeping: he is not bothered but aroused and he would like to see your cunt like he would like to see the inside of his pocket—it is foreign and hidden from him, as are his own urges. The man is allied to his automobile and his things and more metallic machines are with him in heaven which is an underworld's idea of hell, a nice joke for the modern: here you shall live on crowded roads alone and quiet and shame will make you into the fucked-one for eternity; until death; and you shall fear living more than any thing: more than dying, although you fear dying, and doctors can be the new priests and you shall not live—you shall not bend at the waist and open your anus for life's joys: don't look at your anus in the mirror; bury your shit in water; don't love your shit, your wife's blood and come; you fear the dead, killed off the specters, all of your meat wrapped in a plastic sheet, cold and unfathomable as an-imal, your wife's cunt is wrapped up in plastic perfumes also—and you without your friends who are not the garbage-men; the slaughterhouse-men or the corpse-collectors; the workers who fill up the longing of days with their sad unspoken and opened beer cans: men on streets. Dear Reader, bring me a drink, fill it up with an excess of druggy love—a world filled with human detritus, our shits spread out across the modern garbage heap: what to do with all of our cacas? our shitty paradise here among the angels is fill-ing up filled in with detritus us and then more of us all the time.

How easy it is, darling, a facility, to make my decisions in Los Angeles without thinking of you—the hunger in your belly now, or the soreness of your cunt now, or how you cannot breathe with the black plastic hood covering your head and your head immersed in water and you are held in water until you have stumbled down into a darkness, which is not death, you realize, when you awaken and the man still holds your hair, the long plait was undone long ago, and although sorrow is a river, inside the cells of the Polytechnic, fear is the only animal;—how these sentences, my

own phrases, cover you up more than reveal you; and the sentences
of News and Reports:

200 Reported Killed in Guatemalan Villages

An armed band attacked four isolated villages in
northern Guatemala's Quiche province and killed
more than 200 people by cutting their throats, a local
official said Thursday. The official said some of the
dead were decapitated.

No Independent Confirmation

The telegram said that survivors buried the victims in
common graves and that the armed band escaped.
There is no telephone communication between
Guatemala City and Zacualpa, and the reports could
not be independently confirmed. It was not known
whether leftist or rightist groups were responsible.

Do you see how we undo you in our News, if we write you in the
News we unwrite you, these wars in foreign (savage) nations, where
what has happened—the Army arrives at 6 a.m. and the men are
taken to the plaza and the church and the administration building
and the boy tied to cypress and a girl behind the administration
building or the desacralized church, and her quiet and bloody cunt
and her mouth is closed and bleeding and she is not screaming while
you read these sentences now or in the *Los Angeles Times* yesterday, or while I am putting some fancy fatty butters onto my toast,
and the engineer who makes the Cessna A37-B in a small plains city

in Kansas, a nice man, and he also does not think of you; thinks of his mortgage payment, of football losses, his boys, and moneys and the girls he wished he'd fucked as a young man, and the girl at the supermarket who touched his lonely cock in his dark trousers (once) and—not of you—you could be dirty; you are foreign; and the barbarians have long been the enemy of civilization (and of books)—

Can I find you in this book (could my grandmother resuscitate in my mother's lonely and awkward English five)? What is this News but a good man who tries, he is trying, darling, to write and make what is and if this is has little or nothing or only a small re-semblance to your village that day in spring when the soldiers ar-rived in the early morning hours; when your brother was taken and tied fast; when you were you and taken (behind the administration building) and undone and made into another girl, a broken thing like broken teeth, broken hands later—And these sentences, darling, also a falling away . . . for this we call on the gods and I am calling on them now: help me to do it, Marta, I would like to do it;—you my dear and sweet muse; bitter and dark, beat me unto death then.

IT IS RAINING today in Acul, in Nebaj, and in the hearts of things; in the mountains it rains and this is the raining season. Where are you today? In my mind you could be a young girl before the rains in the winter, and your corte is wrapped tightly around your waist and tied with a colorful belt, and you help your mother and your brothers return from the fields and have brought the day's wood and now playing football or running up the trees chasing green ants metallic blue beetles. This is any modern man's idyll. This is you in my mind. Are you tired? And without electrical lights and without the water spigot, water pipes and windows glass or motorcars or gas-burning stoves or brown pile carpets on a concrete slab—you look lovely inside your home before massacre, and here in the underground underhanded North American mind, your poor and blackened nails, the nails on the walls for hanging clothes, the tin pots and plastic water jugs and loom for making the huipil: the days look beautiful—your dress is like stars. I love the way you appear in my mind—a native girl like a native bush; she looks happy (now) and contented and her beautiful and colorful clothes make me happy to see her like that and I can't see massacre; I can't see hunger, or pain, or how the fat white lonely American ("half-Armenian") boy looks to the girl in Acul.

THE WASHINGTONIAS are throughout the valley and in the long low basin of the city, the sunlight is reflected in the March day leaves and the five o'clock yellow on all of the shiny green as if tall bright glass, and the tops of the palms look like the pigtails of small girls and the girls are running across the tarmac playground in my memories of childhood when I never noticed the mountains, the tall Washingtonias surrounding the tarmac world, the sea in the distance on a clear day, and children don't see the view of places, this distant looking, and so the man who returns to his childhood home is surprised, he is startled in a small and unconscious manner: the tall Washingtonias and mountains in the distance; the sea beyond the mountains on a clear day (today). And he can see the valley spread out in front of him to the San Gabriel Mountains in the northeast and there is snow on the high peaks and he has driven on the freeway and perhaps fifteen or sixteen times he traversed the river which he did not and still does not recognize as a river (a concrete sewage sluice; an eyesore) and the palms scattered about spindly and elegant, planted for an idea, for the Mediterranean Artesia the developers were making to draw the East Coast crowds to the new land the new place and they are luring us into paradise and the waters are here (from the Owens Valley); and the sun shines on all things here; and he is here also, a man moving along the streets, driving up and down the tarmac roads of this city, knowing that none of it will last and that when he is dead (I am half-dead now) none of it will matter and none will recall: (him): the shops from childhood, the old pizza parlour, the liquor store on the corner of Ventura Boulevard and Hazeltine, and the Cadillac shop and the supermarket with the red sign and the restaurant with a French name and it will change—more cars more girls more motor vehicles and when he is sad then, thinking that it has been lost, he'll console himself with the indivisible wind in the palm green leaves and the girls he sees in trees and an innocence or at least sorrow deposited high, higher than the buildings on Ventura Boulevard, Santa Monica Boulevard, sunlight made green.

I MISS YOU NOW;—why have you died when I am missing you like I long for the pomegranate tree I knew as a boy, and the orange flowers that spoke of you—you were in Acul then, when I was a boy and young man, when I was young and foolish and my cock at attention for every girl and I longed for every girl, every cunt to put it in there, to see them there, to undo them and then too shy for even one kiss or even this party today, we are standing round a table and we are in a large room and the music blares and beers and vodka orange drinks, and I am afraid to say to the girl with the cunt that is calling me (electricity) that I would like a small dance on the floor with her, which, after all, is no more than a hustling: we hustle in front of one another—move our arms and legs and heads and I am doing it awkwardly and the music confuses my legs and feet and hands and makes them into some kind of tree and the girls are like machines with the music, and all of this in English and it is 1983, and I would very much like to have the girl who is shuf-fling in front of me allow me to put my lonely cock into her flesh and so I am essaying the dance, the words to the songs of no help, and you are hanged by your wrists from the bars in your cell and it is a black place they've got you in and the men putting their cocks, their rifles and glass into your cunt and your asshole, and then I am watching a television Show about a girl who, more than anything, would like to be loved by the handsome boy (not this fat and ugly boy), a lovely large blond-haired sort of the muscular boy, and he doesn't hold pain in his face and you, Marta: the pain is visible, as it is in a Madonna painting—do you scream at this moment? The sentence announces a "scream" and do you? And how much space is there between what I write you and you, Marta? And who can hear you in your cell? Perhaps that boy hung up by his arms, the face already removed (but not the penis, not yet), the maggoty wounds, perhaps he hears you and then he is sad and terribly moved by a girl's lonely howls, a pitch different than a man's, by her suf-fering in the adjacent basement cell, and I masturbate to the girl on the television screen, the girl at the party ten feet from my sex; we are residents of the earth, the three of us today, the American fatted and tired and lonely young man who doesn't recall his grandmother or his mother's five phrases, the new christ hanged by his wrists and maggots for manacles, and the Ixil girl, and I am watching television and I am eating a snack of potato chips and tinned cheese, and you are begging to them to please stop it, and I don't love you or desire you and I wish that I had not eaten my over-fill after all of the snacks have been consumed. The christ in the cell next to yours dies in a week's time and his howls inside your ears for eternity.

I wish that I had known of you, your existence then: you are the most beautiful woman I have ever beheld (I am the kindest sort of lying animal, darling—) and in the living room (off of Mulholland Dr) and in the prison cell (Avenida La Reforma 1-45, zona 10) your wrists torn, your face undone, I chew and sit lie on the sofa and the innocence never to be placed back (as onto this actress's pampered shiny and lonely visage: she looks like plastic ease and thingéd ease and): *I am sorry.* That I missed you. That I didn't know what they did to you (what they are doing now): I want to return to you there (then) and enter the gates of your prison cell and raise my voice, high cramped fists, I'll yell the yell of the righteous god, and dignity and freedom, kill all of the guards, and I see you tied to the metal cot, and I smell your pissy fear, its shit on the floor, the blood of it all, and I would cut you down, untie you, unmanacle you, unmake your pained look, and then,—kiss your blooded face and cup your ass where the blood spews forth like a river making you: forever theirs, forever marked and notmine, the wounds do not abate, you can never leave the pit they made for you now, not in this form, it forever inside of you, your perpetual payment (as mine is sorrow?)—and I love you and long for your torn flesh; please return to me, then forgive me, forgive my appraisal of your pain as if it is some thing we can purchase, or see on the television—no purchase for this love and then: scale the walls of the dead and return to your father, your brothers, the newmother in the mountain: I am a beloved for you. Ah, Marta—(an American stands in the room as they make that river in your ass, things can be: salted; your pain in a can, in a book or letter:) can you forgive this transgression of notknowing? can you make me clean again? wash my feet, whore for me again and again? (If I'd known; it's not for lack of knowing you say; if I'd known, I could be the good Christian;—of those men, their salary checks each month, the university education and cocktails with editors of the newspapers, the *Los Angeles Times* is a newspaper and a Central Intelligence Agency manual of love for America (to save America, dear Reader) and to tie up dogs and make them speak these words of love and please; please stop it: I want to write. I would like to be a writer to make you across the rivers of ether, toward sorrow, across places and the time of the clock: and I've made you—in words, make flesh, make monsters and men—I'll be a philosopher also: I'll write in the vulgar tongue; I'll be Western and civilized and the ladders of knowing are mine, the divides of yes and no and truth and scientific truth and whose history whose fables of woes; communists; capitalists. To fuck you, suck your bloody cunt and ass its rivers and then: I cannot continue. I am lost, Marta, on these roads in these folios. I am lonelier than you, than you ever were imagined in that basement cell, than: no, it's a lie. I've no idea what they did to you; my ideas are an inheritance of nations: in my nation I would save you on television, contained, cleaned, you are not a whore in my television, you are not brown like a beetle, your ass has no bloody river to show us—you are valiant, beautiful, legs crossed and clean, braver and you win and I'm hungry, it's four o'clock, I turn the volume higher on the stereo and in the books I'm reading for pleasure's sake, to be entertained! I am not: dead; I am not dead; Iamnotdead—nonononon (I'll leave you in that cell with your brethren, perhaps you've done something to deserve it, you are ugly and deserving, you are like the dirty man on the street and the one-armed child the vagrants and thieves (stealing my things!) and the blacks in Africa starved and dogs and the Indian who bows at my feet says welcome to the Orient, I could be an Oriental black but I'm hungry, it's four o'clock, I'm having ice cream and coffees and when I buy something I rub my semen all over it, smell it up mine, then gobble it down quickly).

[And does it matter if I miss you like this? If missing brings my soul to the edge of things and reason and wanting is a heft in me, this heaviness—of heart? soul? I bear and bear and: it won't bring you to me, you'll never be something I can make, possess, shove my own cock into when I'd like and when I am able to have you I'll be done with you soon enough anyway. So, the modern mind. Come and adore the modern! See his outrageous and funny thumbs! The cranium! His ladders of meaning and occupations! His dull-witted cousin, the primitive, sits at his feet, forever abeyant and forever in view, sees his cage like this:]

IT WAS no more your choosing, darling, to have lived on the horizon of your nation our empire, than it was mine to have been its citizen ordinaire. Some must be slaves and some must be buyers and if History decreed such an existence for you and for me then it is of no surprise that I thumbed my nose at such History, my cock, and returned to the eternal warmth of your breast your belly your sweet and sweated sex; and abolishing linear time and History here on these pages, no desire for its ends or means or what redemption it promised; just you, darling, darkthing, in the nights when I am driving along the streets of this city and it rains today in Los Angeles in Acul and no man can stop the deluge or the destruction of these streets, the mud makes a wall and comes down my street like a river, kills nothing in its path, and in your mountains the falling bombs kill you and others like you; but not me today; today I am still driving penning redoing History, essaying with these words, readying myself for this return down the tunnel of your vices and wants and hopes, inside the rivers of desire, toward love, toward union.

YOU ARE an Ixil girl, a girl's flesh, which is to say that you are part of modern History and sweet it is! the nightmares the crowds the machines for your nation my nation. Do you howl down the towering crowds in the cinema as you race across the screen with feathers (eagle crow quetzal) pinched atop your hairdo, and a yellow and ocher painted face and the hooting noises you make (like an animal)? Here is another: docile and dumb you have no ability for speaking in the civilized tongues and you sit at my feet and you are weaving the huipil at my feet and when the urge is upon me I lift your skirt and put my civilized cock in the dark barbarian place (to make the progeny). Or: you are hateful vengeful and you have not appreciated what our race has made for yours; lazy and drunk on the sides of roads; you fall over like flies and we crush your thick skulls. And: your hair falls out in sheaves (from the protein deficiency, darling); you beat your children and give them sugar-water for lunch; you are dirty; lazy—unschoolable beasts, worse than dogs; in Los Angeles we love our special breeds. And you want me to beat you; and you must needs work because—lazy—because kind and noble and the savage is always in the movies. We'll movie you up if you are dead, darling, there is no doubt that I could write a movie about you, a small and censored love story which will not show your hands—brown and tired and blooded and boned and removed—covering the mouths of babes in the mountains, these invisible uncinematic wounds, or how they are removed later with a coffee cutting implement, and untenable for the telling in America. Instead you'll be a good girl, my translator and guide, down the mountain paths and over the Cuchumatanes high up through the Petén into Mexico to San Diego and up to Los Angeles, down Hollyline Av—through the glass windows of my home; below the crevices of time, and into my bed, my arms, my mind and eyes to see you, finally, like I can see wind without trees, as I can see my own grandmother who stands at the window of her home in Kharphert, Turkey, it is the summer 1915, sees her mother and sisters and cousins walk by her on the deportation march to the Der Zor, those whom she could not save, for whom the gods did not intervene (the husband stands behind her, pleads, "Please," he says to her, "we can do nothing for them"; waves their French national papers in front of her nose, their two passes, like tickets for a solitary ride).

(And later in the Lebanon she cannot forgive the husband who could not save her mother and sisters (a coward, she thought), pardon the phrase which my mother then gave to me in English more than a half century later in the Los Angeles basin (and which I had forgotten, Marta, until you arrived): that she never saw them again, that they walked to their death, died like dogs in the Der Zor desert.)

WHEN I WAS a boy walking the roads in the San Fernando Valley, I never knew that the concrete trapezoidal sleeve was a river, had been a river once, it made no mark on the boyish mind, and when I walked across the overpasses on Coldwater Canyon and Hazeltine, I didn't think the word *river* or about the place of my birth and education, or that the tiny sluice was once other than it appeared (like the valley itself).

The U.S. Army Corps of Engineers' "Los Angeles River Channel Improvement" project improved the ancient river for property and business. We then protected from the floods like children from the gods who descend willy-nilly and make new courses across new houses and streets and so had to be undone for the sake of the normal trend of development and for the value of things and the river was improved and the floods of

1815

1822

1825

1832

1842

1849

1851

1859

1861–2

1867–8

1876

1883–4

1885–6

1888–9

1891–2

1913–14

1916

1927

1933–4

March 1938, inspired the project of the Los Angeles River as one requirement for the growing metropolis—to bring the water from outside the city, and to control what autochthonous waters traversed the alluvial plains.

AND DO YOU KNOW the past like I learnt History? I am reading a book about Indians; these Indians have been on my television screen for many years and they howl and the feathers of birds decorate their scalps like so many silk ribbons; these are Shows, movies. I can say *Indians* and you see Indians on the screen, run across my mind, like a small girl in Acul? (Acul is never on my television screen or in my mind.)

I am reading a book, it is the first history book I read which is not a school textbook. It is a book about the Indians. I am in school, this is the eighth grade, and we are reading stories about Indians and the book is not like in the movies, on television, in this book there is sorrow and pain on every page.

This is in my book:

The question for me, the inquiry, which plagues me, yes, as if it become a disease, my own disease and unease with this inquiry, this *to be*: is, simply: what am I, Marta? But is this also the misled and constrained question of the stupid and damned living American man? This man, a man such as me: violent, lusty, I smell the come on my fingers even as I write; there is shit beneath my nails from the inquiry into asses: and I've no place of mine; the dead bones here I cannot claim; the weather too haunts me—sometimes I more than long for grey, for rain, for cumulous clouds to overtake the inside fettered and dried-up soul (downturned visages)—and what of the girls' entrails on my cock? all of the girls over these years who I've lain my cock inside them, the strutting bird who has his pay and pays them to do it (or pays their pimp to do it)—What is this man, Marta? Why more alone; why this strange and sad city; only the trees can say the story silently with their quiet noise, with rain, wind; the man writes—himself, Love, a small christ on the cypress in your village; his grandmother and her clan hidden inside five (forgotten) phrases; his own blood history; yours on the concrete floor of the Polytechnic. A beast, the barbarian, a monster—here then is the writings of the unformation of the monster himself: the story of the undoing and the unmaking and perhaps the unwriting him. I don't want him any longer; he's yours—I'd rather be annihilated than continue it longer—I simply cannot bear it—this You that you were made into, this me; the ways of seeing; of your corpse that day in the cold rain, the streets of the capital grey and fear like the grey heat: I'll be alone, yes, but no more alone (not more alone, and then free?). The rain can say it without speaking in tongues; the trees, water, cold damp days—there's weather whispers in my ear, makes the tympanum a flute for our breath: I would like water; I will cover the world in this deluge of words and like a song (a man) make un- make America, essay us here, this controvertible "we."

QUESTIONS POSED INSIDE
THE POLYTECHNIC SCHOOL

1. How long have you been collaborating with the guerrilla?
2. Where are the guerrilla compounds?
3. How did you aid them: with information or logistical sup- port?
4. Who in the community were members of the guerrilla?
5. How many and of what kind are the arms they have?
6. How long have you been collaborating with the guerrilla?
7. Where are the guerrilla compounds?
8. How did you aid them: with information or logistical support?
9. Who in the community were members of the guerrilla?
10. How many and of what kind are the arms they have?
11. How long have you been collaborating with the guerrilla?
12. Where are the guerrilla compounds?
13. How did you aid them: with information or logistical support?
14. Who in the community were members of the guerrilla?
15. How many and of what kind are the arms they have?
16. How long have you been collaborating with the guerrilla?

17. Where are the guerrilla compounds?
18. How did you aid them: with information or logistical support?
19. Who in the community were members of the guerrilla?
20. How many and of what kind are the arms they have?
21. How long have you been collaborating with the guerrilla?
22. Where are the guerrilla compounds?
23. How did you aid them: with information or logistical support?
24. Who in the community were members of the guerrilla?
25. How many and of what kind are the arms they have?
26. How long have you been collaborating with the guerrilla?
27. Where are the guerrilla compounds?
28. How did you aid them: with information or logistical support?
29. Who in the community were members of the guerrilla?
30. How many and of what kind are the arms they have?
31. How long have you been collaborating with the guerrilla?
32. Where are the guerrilla compounds?
33. How did you aid them: with information or logistical support?
34. Who in the community were members of the guerrilla?
35. How many and of what kind are the arms they have?
36. How long have you been collaborating with the guerrilla?
37. Where are the guerrilla compounds?
38. How did you aid them: with information or logistical support?
39. Who in the community were members of the guerrilla?
40. How many and of what kind are the arms they have?
41. How long have you been collaborating with the guerrilla?

[AS A BOY, I spoke with the trees and this did, even then, strike me as a strange undertaking—tree-speaking—but natural, honest, something I did, a manner of speaking with the trees before I knew them as pine cypress beech palm and separate. I would speak and I would listen and in the listening the Santa Ana winds would rail and the sun shone and the skies of the semi-arid plains bright and brown-grey (who knew then that it was an arid place? that there were no autochthonous pine cypress beech or Washingtonia girls; that it was watered green, the water from another valley two hundred and ten miles to the northeast of my home; the trees also from another place). Our conversation:

—

—

—

—]

SHE SAYS   and my face becomes a mask, and the topography of my face looks unchanged for the looking crowds—the smile, the eyebrows at an angle, each cheek pulled back pulling the lips back also, the man smiles as his wife speaks to him;—but her sentence pulls back what was there (behind the face?) that made such a smile when it came easily, without effort or thought, and then the ash remains of it when she speaks as if all of the emotion of love joy and what is fall into that pit with you, Marta; a mask I kept there for the surface details and I was falling then into that place with you as if everything descends but the veneer, when you say that you do not love me anymore, and my own American wife is saying it in the car in the afternoon (before you told me that your child had died in your arms, your hand made his wounds in the mountain), and my own American son died inside his mother's womb on the way to hospital; when she told me, she laughs as she said it, a year or more after the demise of the boy in her belly: that I would always be alone, that she did not love me any longer (you left me like this also, an abandoning ghost); forever now—and I have fallen back from my face and can sense the plastic mask of my face as one sees, senses, the edge of water from ten feet below the water's surface: I know it is there, but I can't reach back up to the present, back up to my own visage; I am all hollows now; a modern mask like the ones so many of my American brethren wear in this city: our occidental costumes: we the driving working dead of this city; alone even amidst the millions. And the American son has long been demised—who ate his flesh? the decomposers now also decomposed—the American wife a memory or even, perhaps, a fantasy: she lives in another city now, in the east, so that I drive the streets of this city seeking them, diptera's children, but not my son, and seeking you, Marta, as you yourself sought the christ on that day in April so many years ago when we were younger and our own children lived like bees, or at the least, had the possibility of living like worms in our swollen bellies.

BOOK THREE

Lord, if thou hadst been here, my brother had not died.

—John 11:21

He has excited domestic insurrection among us, & has endeavored to bring on the inhabitants of our frontiers the merciless Indian savages, whose known rule of warfare is an undistinguished destruction of all ages, sexes, & conditions.

—A Declaration by the Representatives of the United States of America, in General Congress Assembled

IT'S GONE DOWN again and my kidney fails me; the diptera girls have returned, and we all of us, brute and man alike, sit here, have stopped the perpetual movement, the drives along the streets of the city, to seek and then find the dog corpses, the girls, brave and cowardly Hektor and his ruined corpse; and Lázaro begun to stink already, the maggots inside his mouth; and you, darling, in the pit there at the Polytechnic, behind the administration building in Acul; on the road to the capital.

It appears it will rain today, from where I sit the weathers turn foul and appear greyer blacker than even a moment ago. Ah, return to me. Like the weather in my mind, come back to your boy: why do you not visit me today, today which is melancholic and grey and when I would like for you to visit me, tell me again your stories, I will hold your battered and brown fingers (your fingernails removed); and I will return those hands to you (still twinkling), and I will look into your eyes, across ether, beyond the Gregorian calendar, past time and days and I will not forsake you.

My kidneys ache; my back; I fear it is poison and that I have been, and that I am, being poisoned. What are these chemicals minerals which are beginning their unmaking of the man? Is it the Shows make a bitter metal taste in my mouth (*like a 9mm pistol* you whisper; how you longed for such an easy and fast death, my darling) and me? Afraid. I am afraid like my brethren here, my American brothers and sisters, we drive along the streets and in this city we hardly speak to one another, in monosyllabic grunts at the market the post office the coffee shops; not looking into one another's eyes; or if looking not seeing the sadness or anguish and rage; such a heft of the lonely in our pupils, what aches there and shame; rush home to our wives our televisions our lists of TO DO. To do? and to be? This my list of TO BE:

- To have lived, Marta
- My mama for eternity
- Hammocky days
- Unresigned and unselfish for you, your cunt

But perhaps it is not my fault, it is certainly not my doing that I have lived in this Age of Things. This not the final age or definitive, or that it hasn't been thus before, and will not be so again: greed envy avarice: such old and mythic gods. Ah, but at such a pitch here—I can see it on all the storefronts and in all of my friends' and neighbors' and notfriends' eyes: this *to have*. We have been makers, now darling, in this age and place, we become havers. Were you a maker, darling? of the hot yellow masa on the griddle? The hundred fold tortilla you made from your hands, the grinding of corn, the patting and shaping of the round earth discs. I have wanted it all: to have this house on this street in this valley (the unpredictable fifth winter river); the shiny motorcars; the sofa and cabinets and television boxes and boxes of food and tins of food and drink and wine and whiskey and girls on Saturdays and girls on the road to the capital. Did you think of us, the havers? These tall and fat buyers? Once in the old capital of your country I went to the public market, you were dead then I was shopping, and I looked down at the blankets the old Indian woman wanted to sell to me and she took my look and looking said, "They came for my father in the middle of the night. We never saw him again." And then nothing; my memory of your capital, my memory of my mother recalling her mother (two of her five) divides, abates, disappears back down into the river, until later you appear to me: demanding, irascible, handless and tired. And I began to remember?

Or I've made up that man who traveled to your country in this essay, this man who doesn't leave except to drive the streets of this city: too afraid and then doesn't know, really, that you exist. Do you, darling? Does anyone exist outside of this city? or book? (my imagination?)

I HAVE LOVED WOMEN. (And I have hated feared admired the men, or had drinks on Saturday nights; or sports games or a jerk-off round of card play, or play or fucking as a boy, and the camaraderie of boys, the pissing circles, the cocks on display, the lust of us, and our shared understandings of this: this lust for the girls, our love of the bodied smells, the foreskin on our penises, the nights of longing, the need for the female form and our inability to say so or make it so; how we loved (despised) the cunt: this we shared: we pissed the world, pissed on beauty and morality and sunseted evenings; pissed after sex; pissed in hallways, behind doors—we pissed all that we loved, penis pied, pissed off, putrid—but not his love, nor his muse.) From the moon mother to the notborn sisters, all of the whores and my teachers from elementary school, and the secondary school bitches, the magazine-counter teases, the bar-dwellers, bookstore girls, the shy girls on the streets, fat and unloved, who want love and too shy to lift their faces for my gaze;

the skinny tight cunts in the rich neighborhoods who pull the air tightly through their skin as if expecting a burn which cannot arrive; the fat bitches, the lonely ones, skinny unloved, ugly unloved—here they are all fat and ugly because to be fat and ugly is to be modern, and in America I've loved all of them, all of the Americana cunts. I love their unseen looks, the ways in which they hide themselves in their clothing, the occulted gaze, the tight heeled shoes, the tight hair-weaves, made up faces for the day and evening, the hand that covers the fat on their belly, a shy seeking hand, they hide their fatty cunts in baggy trousers, they cover up their smells, smooth their skins, darken their eyes, and this, all of this, en fin, todo, *todito*, I could love. And it is not as if I didn't understand what they hold between their thighs, not as if I couldn't smell their cunty power from the long distance (no matter the perfumes, the baths, the douchy pubic hair smiles): I have always understood how they, with not more than a look (uncensored, the dead blackness speaking back to us) how they can (how they will; how they do) annihilate me. Men know this simply—cock in hand, pissing—which is to say we don't think; which is to say we need god and hand-made bullets; and make money and make buildings made from steel and steel towers and more money made property and dirt this Galil this 9mm love-handle, this to kill you with—this make and make to unmake the . . . If I think about it for one minute longer, which is to say I never think it only know that she'll devour my ass, cut off my cock, swallow the flesh from my bones, she sucks me granite dry—her cunt does it, sucks it, desiccates the blood, a blood sucker; a bleeder by the moon's machinations—a vampiric whore; she wants more and more, and I need her like I need sun, like I need the sea, and water, and fucking every day: like Love; more than food even; like Food—which is to say, not at all (and so I killed her?). And women so stupid and niggardly—their down-turned gazes, their laments of "the oppressed!"—they do this to us and pretend that they're the sorry bitches in this scheme of things. That they have suffered at our hands, below our shoving cock-heads! What does a woman know of to suffer? of Love? If she's lonely she can stick her fingers into her cunt and the world will await her there, the gods inside her flesh, the unborn children inside her flesh already there; immutable; a christ could emerge from such a tomb. And I'd rather sit in my hammock all the day long and then swing through the trees where there are no roads and there are no cars and there is no noise I have made: of cars and aeroplanes in the blank sky and locomotives in the distance and trucks ticks the machines: and every hour or so find one of the beauties—the fat the skinny the ugly the shy the turbulent beautiful bitches who intrigue me with their pussy smells—torment me all day long (and I'm having a drink now, whiskey) and stick my cock in, if only for a few moments, and then resume the napping, the walks around, branches swinging; have a few drinks with the boys; we'll laugh like boys. I'll stop this working *I loafe and invite my soul, I lean and loafe at my ease* and ease the hard-on, stick it in once or thrice and they control the world, they are the government (which means, of course, no Government, no Progress, no History, no Christ) just the beachy days of long solitude, good weathers, seasonal fruits, and fruits of the flesh: no wonder we've made cages, caged them us in—it would be the end of the world as we know it. So instead I drive to the office and squeeze my shits tight until I can find a proper porcelain toilet for their burial grounds—a water burial of no proportion, no stink, no dead scenting me, on my trail, their skeletons a fecal archetype.

I would stop them what they did to you as I sit in my green and padded armchair, and more than comfortable as the comfort makes holes in my shirts shorts, the long pieces of linen which tied around your throat and arms and my linen shirts trousers—I would save you from them then. I loved you and didn't know you your form, and still your form unavailable for this man who sits here lonelier than each of these forms, of the birds which hunted and haunt the eaves, the drains leading to eternity, the water whence?: ah Marta, if I weren't more this coward the boy on the playground who runs and stares at his shoes and who, dreams, dreamed of you and didn't know your tied up arms your form in the dark places and pits which are not the inferno, but man's powered engines ideas of progress and bounty and you must die for it, darling, and I miss you never having had you, long for you and I would kill for you and I would take an aeroplane and I would drive to your republic and knock on the barrack's door and demanding entry to the place they've taken you where your wrists lie on the floor like a hacked up dog's corpse and linen and torn flesh is ugliest in the light and I would lift each and tender palm, cradling your form in my hands, the detached light and my own hands moving to caress your face—I will go back and do it—caress your flesh, whisper in your ear, love you after death, eat your flesh, this woman; wrists;—this our covenant, a living love after death—I will not abandon you: *te lo juro.* Will not, not ever again or again and then. Love me back, come back to me, make your way back from the dead corners of your republic and the interstices of historical rendering where you have been:

buried: please return; I am sorry, I swear it, sorrow's sorrow is my fleshy foolish history, this legacy of fools and—I was foolish, ignorant, happy then, and the News made no sense and the News never lightened your wrists in the morning before the corpse was dragged by the ankle and dumped into a grave of notgraves, the XXMUJER—your form, your smile and the poetry of lies lives on, and your bones, darling, forever beyond my reach, the barracks' underground bounty is even still in your lonely and lying republic, these republics of shame, and the sham which is rendered, dollared, made up each day on the News.

YOU LOST your name in Acul, in the whorehouses of Chimaltenango, the basement of the Polytechnic in the capital—and you became Marta, which could be my girl in my dreams and dreaming the world in words, the imagination's descent down to your nation, which has not been yours, you worked in it, born in it, made it, built the roads the cathedral the beautiful stone steps were laid by you in Santiago de Guatemala; you seeded the corn and pulled the weeds and carried the wood for fire and cut the wood and crushed the corn and carried the water in blue-striped plastic jugs on your head (they were clay once); you wove the huipils and the shirts and skirts; walked the four miles to Nebaj three times a week for market days, and your sister was on your back as you climbed the mountain paths—and all of this you did for your patria which was not yours (the Laws), you belonged to the fatherland as the minerals and salts did, the lumber and coal, and each hectare of land included the "work of the hand," which in the nineteenth century means the pounds of coffee for the picking, and cane to be thrashed, and corn harvested. In my nation (it is a different sort of exile here: from the old histories; from bones; the dead and their requirements; from the gods; from an unthingéd and undelimited joy) I am a good buyer and I buy the things I see on the television and I drive my car over the tarmac roads and I fucked the pretty girls with their tight underwear and pants and undid their brassieres which left the breasts to hang low, like clouds. These girls and I painted our nails and ate diet foods and cookies and sugarless drinks and potato chips from small plastic bags, and we read magazines with pictures of girls who painted their nails and purchased skin creams and it was beautiful, our manners and dedication to our ideas, the self-loathing in small and large packages: new cars, new hairdos, shoes for the weekend, breath mints mouth washes; toilet cleaners and sink chemicals; petroleum bags and jellies; fashions by the weight; we sought love in each magazine and bought its simulated taste for our dedicated money. Is it I then, who seem ridiculous and enslaved, Marta? It is you I pity here in these pages. Your wretched suffering. The days of hunger (thirty tortillas a day for a family of ten); of cold and shoeless and torn shirts and no medicines in the mountain and half of the Ixil children have died, and the soldiers cutting throats and pregnant girls and their vaginas torn open, and the children screaming all of the time of massacre, and when these girls and boys see a soldier in the years that follow, they all of them piss themselves in their mother's embrace; quiet like graves in front of these soldiers (they have been trained); the babies you sacrificed with your strong and dirt palms; your dirt and humiliated looks when you finally reduced and starved and naked come down out of the mountains to live, you say, and the soldiers round you up like so much bony cattle and interrogations and more tortures to rout the enemy they say, and so the manner in which you beg me to rescue you for all of those years; that you waited for me those fifteen months in the mountains while the Army pursues you and other villagers from place to place and Doña Ana is undone by falling bombs one month before you come down from the mountain and (all of the dead children fodder for wild animals) you think that: the Americans will save you; that they will see what the Army does and surely they will arrive with democratic kindnesses in their hands and clear eyes; the Europeans will arrive with preserved foods and wheat breads and old civilized cultures; the Mexicans could do it, they are closer by, they could see it—And who wouldn't save the innocent? a child? our thousand children who die in these mountains, which saved us then killed us, who have died already in Acul Nebaj Chajul Cotzal Xix? Why is there no one to see us? *Why are we, as ourselves, so invisible?* Don't the Christian nations arrive on a steed; we are Christians; see our pink and blue churches. See how thin we are, we weigh seventy pounds, do you envy the peasant his form in your magazines for the lithe and beautiful sufferers? but not his life . . . We are dying in the mountains and the children don't cry from hunger when they die; you eat your frozen milks and red drinks and worry then, hate yourselves then, for too many calories ingested: O fat men, have pity on us with your foods and your money: see us here, we don't want any of it, but to survive to not be killed, for your medicines, enough maize and bean and squash for the living—don't give us your lonely nights and masked days, its covered up world, blackened, tarmacked, the mud cannot be made in Los Angeles, the mountains unblackened, the dead souls of all of your living—there is always a payment to be made, Sir, and you know it, even as you imagine me out of the torture chambers, the broken brothels, the mountains above Acul, the village on a Thursday in April and the six foot deep fifteen foot long pit that the old men dug for the young: that I also cannot save you, this word you don't make in English for a soul, even if you essay it, it will make nothing and alter even less.

LIKE A WOMAN, then, I wait for you; attend you; gather at street corners with my eyes tilted backwards; the eleven o'clock arrival of the unasked for advertisements, the lists of the dead, a newspaper's clippings—not your letters or a knot of your hair—each day I am waiting, see the postman arrive with his satchel which is his pockets today and he jumps from his automobile (cannot see me in the glass) and I hunch down by the window think that today you who do not write me (or think of me), do not know it, cannot do it—mightn't the dead send letters, darling? find justice in their missives?—still; still I am the optimist hoping that against these destined determinants or time of the clock and the delimits of the real, that I will have your letters and rifle through all of the coupons for supermarkets and advertisements for love and bills and today there is no post arriving from your village; no corpse correspondence; not a girl who cannot write verses, who would love me from her village and from her cultural miles and the ancient and the modern have a cup of tea together and we don't drink tea—you or I—we can't discuss culture like a piece of dung atop your fence; we can't be ancients or moderns or lie on my sofa like girls picking at their toes, American girls who would like to find: Love; Boys; Things TO DO: between picking the paint off of their toenails, this to be Beautiful (which is so far from beauty as to be loathsome, vile—

self-loathing the great boon to fashion and the economy!)—do you have a fence to surround your garden? or wooden dolls for house-up games? Does the maize make roads in your village like the feet make lines, the veins of mud and dirt for a girl who climbs into the mountains, runs from the brother who is left in pieces and dogs eat the pieces and (your father?) your mother and the youngest brother strapped like wood to her back (fall into the river and drowned) and all of them in piles like boot-heel dust; like the time of the clock and other cultural artifacts. Is the postman the only artifact I can find amidst these words of lies, these lie on the sofa reveries: there is nothing for it; for us; the gods wont come, the dead do not arrive today and I am loneliest without them—they have abandoned me also, left me here amidst the choices of words, a bracketed sentence, the leaves on branches outside the window, there is a view of the beech; Washingtonias above the distant rooftops (hold the light like shiny green hands); a postman's arrival is the reappearance of surfaces and men make surfaces into otherwise oddly dimensioned clouds. I am writing you to find you here, not amidst the postman's materials, but amidst the immaterials and the only possibility is by possession, in the devils themselves, my only life can be found there and you and I will have a cup of tea in our hellish landscape where dogs cannot eat a brother's meat and a boy's "You" finger cannot unmake clans and a boy on the schoolyard does not hope for the out of childhood, these fences, he understands that tomorrows are like blackened girls; like an Ixil girl in the Cuchumatanes where the clouds will sit on the mountains like girls and it is raining every day in Acul, the mud is closer to the skin than cloth; your feet do not dry and the toes will crack from the mud-eating disease, you say: here the mud makes holes in the feet like needles sewing thread. I am possessed by you, Marta.

[Tell me, Marta: why are women insatiable? And it is never enough: the money the foods restaurants gifts and Iloveyou's flowers chores phone calls and rings and helpmeet around the house and whywontyoutalktome? and youdon'tlovemeenough. She always wanted more and more, and I unable, finally, to bear it, give it to her—this wife who departed for the East Coast—bitter and lonely girl.]

I AM DYING, Marta, and America dies also; my sweet America. For I have loved her—the glorious landscape, the granite mountains I visited as a boy, the long and untidy rivers on my Av, and the sad and tidied concrete byway, the old river upon which the Spaniards stumbled in 1769, and the beauty bounty of the place and the cottonwoods sycamores the wild grapes, the dozen Gabrielino villages there and she was named El Porciúncula for the small chapel in Assisi and the feast day by those Spanish men who feasted that day alongside the river, and then later gave the place its full name, and it became a pueblo in 1781, a city in 1835. And when I was a boy I'd no idea of the river, the sycamore, trout or grizzly bears, or of Crespí and the Gabrielino girls and men: just my house, the misters Washington and Jefferson, pilgrims, Virginia, virgins.

Ah, darling, the great desires of this place, no different, I suppose, than the great desires of those displaced men of Europe. —This freedom in the enlightenment tomes and books, democracy like a bell: how they longed for it, then demanded it with what was to become customary pride and arrogance and just inheritance!— and although never a freedom or a declaration for you, darling (your death knell), and they were men of their age (aren't we also, dear Reader? the new moral code is a tight coat also), but still—was it not a great experiment in time for them, and hence for me? A new idea, these united states in 1781? And here I have been comfortable and I can eat in the morning and I can have meals at midnight and I am not constrained by the habits the old customs of Europe of Asia; no; and the blood has not tangled me in its web (merely five forgotten phrases, which is not the same as blood); and free to wander to study to fuck the girls on lonely avenues and then, yes, to be lonely also; to be richer and poor; to watch the television six hours each day and imagine those girls with their legs spread before me; can I not say that I am sorry?; that even for this boy, this badly livered boy, the congested kidney, this angry and disappointed and despairing and blue boy—even he has loved his America; has wanted to be home when he is away; has wanted the rough English words and the angled gazes and the suspicions and the slow-minded and the narrowness of his creed, his country after all, and his country-men: we have lived some kind of man-like dream and I for one shall miss it terribly when we awaken and the rivers, desiccate now; the seas reached and emptied; the gasoline girls cancered up; the skies sans the great blue herons, the sandhill cranes (O sorrow for this, those beauties and grey-white chevron miracles in the unabated sky—vanished? extinguished. I can't bear it, Marta) the trees have been cut and the people too are cut down, drivellers of the TV and entertained, darling, until our mutual doom: O demise of the spirit; O demise of the materia. Sweet America, and the horrors of it, well known or elided or blackened with ink in books and movies—and Indians and blacks—we smile as we perish, the world simmers and the airs blacker and the skies denuded of birds of tree views (and where will we leave our sorrows?). I have made you on my own death bed, which is this window gives onto the street of my home: Hollyline Av sans the holly trees but yes we have orange and lemon and kumquat on special days, during the season; we have a river every five years and the floods come down and we lament, say it has never happened! the houses fall into the sea; this boy falls into his mind, into a book now which he makes, a pitiful although not pitiable sort of man who can only make an essay—his dog corpses abandoned to the streets, they are filling the streets of Los Angeles, filling the concrete river and he hears them whispering of the old long and warm days when the river was filled to with silver bright trout and a brown bear might eat ten of them and the cottonwoods did sing and the weather was always beautiful; blue sky; waters just below the surfaces;—before sewers, before you and me, before America. I have retired from the world now. My family abandoned faithfully. I am giving myself only to you, to what we can make together—a dying American man and his dead and mutilated American wife: are we not both made of these mountains and seas and desiccate or filled-to rivers? You in your capital in Acul in Nebaj and me in the San Fernando Valley in my Los Angeles (for the Italian madonna)—we will be together here in this book, which is to say, darling, in a history. And that is no small thing, no small feat, for I have always wanted to find my girl and finally, I can say, I find you in these lousy—from the barbaric animal—English phrases: to do to make to make up, sweet love.

THE SOLDIER has learnt (beatings blood) to be an obedient soldier, and he does not inquire: (*Can a poor man interrupt the course of the gods?*): beyond the now of things, the war of things. He has

learned on his trek up into the mountains; he has drunk the blood
of the small bitch which he carried on his back and the bloods of
the bitches of his compatriots also; he has swallowed his own excrement, their communal vomit and bile; and he has been trained
in a new religion, an apocryphal priest now as he does it for the patria, for the preservation of capital and state.

She is before him, and she has a look of terror in her black eyes
which, although difficult to describe here among the folios, is not
ever difficult to ascertain—the priests can see it in a moment; and
it makes them happy, like too much sugar makes small children
happy. [Here are the gods.] He looks at her distended belly and
perhaps he thinks the Spanish sentences of his trainers about the
communist scourge and the subversivos, apostates, gavûrs in an
old language which he doesn't speak (which you didn't speak either,
Mother: it was your parents' foreign tongue: Turkish for the secrets
from their Armenian children; the enemy's tongue);—the soldier's
own Kaqchikel is becoming a scar in his mind, a childhood memory; (*Remember, the Lieutenant says to them in Spanish, We'll fuck
you recruits like dogs if we want to, and when we want it. You have
balls? Are you men? Speak your Indian tongues and we'll remove them
with knives; we're more happy to do it.*) and meantime the president
himself, General Ríos Montt, is speaking at the press conference in
Tegucigalpa, and steak and crab with lime sauce for lunch, and another president, mine Mr Reagan, touches his head and heart faithfully, unwrinkles his pant leg with his unsmooth hand.

—One of the fundamental aspects of the new government philosophy is respect for human rights. Incorrect information published abroad, and which the Guatemalan government lacks the
funds to refute effectively, has led to a wide-spread belief among
foreigners that it is carrying out massacres of the Indian farmers.

But the woman (your neighbor). She is eight months pregnant and she is beautiful—she has the sublime look of the pregnant lady and she terrifies him of course (and me also—my own wife of years ago) to look into the god's face one is also terrified, the sublime always kicks you back in the teeth, the groin—; he has a hard-on while he does it. Takes his machete and pulls it across her belly as she looks at him with a different kind of horror now—she screams at him in her language which he doesn't speak or understand—it is your soft Ixil, Marta—and he pulls the babe out with his hands, a bloody and perfectly formed boy who doesn't know shame or death or bad things, and then the soldier, as if in a dream, cradles the boy to his chest and imagines for an untimely un-calendared moment, that it is in fact *his* son he holds in his arms, and that his wife has loved him for eternity, and that he will not likely be killed by a fellow soldier in a few weeks time in the barracks of Nebaj. His own flesh; his own boy. And the babe is not dead, which then makes the priest afraid again, because the gods are no longer quiet and the babe (the woman also) is screaming: viscous yellow fluid and red blood and white fat falls out of the woman's body; her entrails are bright and beautiful iron-red and white; she is crying, sobbing, making too much noise for his ears, and when he smashes the small babe against the stones of the river, then he thinks that it is just and justice served today (the communists the subversivos the dogs covering the landscape) and he silences the woman afterwards and all around him is the silence which waits after massacre, which could also be a religious icon awaiting its god. He stands there while the blood and bile and aural agonies rush forth; he is like a man underwater: he can hear the screams of the children and women, the permanence of the barking dogs, but he himself has become a mask now, he has fallen back from his own face and down from his throat, chest cavity, below the lungs, the liver, genitals and knees, he resides quietly in the soles of his own swollen and booted feet; the sun continues its arc across the grey and white cloud-filled sky. It is a Thursday in April; this is Acul——; he doesn't know the name of the village, the woman, or the others he has killed today, and when the bones are exhumed in fifteen years he knows that his bones will not lie in the hole that the old men dug out for their sons and nephews today, and that the large green rubber work boots lying at awkward angles in the uncovered pit in 1997 will not make *his* bones into diminutives of men as they do of the men he is killing now, bones in boots like sticks in bowls. He will be more forgotten, maligned, and hated in a silence of profound and black days, as he ought to be, as he can't quite bring himself to contemplate but knows late at night when the dogs are barking and he can't sleep for nights on end, when he thinks of his own mother who sold him at six to the cotton plantations and the beatings and constant hunger and he knows that he has become a dog, yes he knows it, that the bitch's blood and all of this blood today in Acul has made him into a temporary angel for order, for capital's necessary roads and ideas (leading eventually northward toward my own city—Marta; the road to Acul was built in 1983 by your neighbors upon Army orders; this road leads to Acul; this road leads to Los Angeles); and he has killed his own son, like a god he did it, and for this also he will suffer; he does suffer; see me suffering, he says, from the place of his calloused and booted and swollen peasant feet: I could have wanted a softer life; maize; a wife and small boys; bags of feed fertilizer and enough money to live; a soft belly, and a little meat on Sundays.

WE LIVE WITH fear as we live with breath and so we don't notice it until the soldiers arrive at six a.m. with their Galils, they have blocked all of the paths; until we are digging a ditch on the edge of the village and we think that we are digging our own burial pit and the words fall away, lose their meanings, we are digging for meaning, for unhistories—to make—and the horror lies not in the shovelfuls of dirt we pull out from the earth, or the clouds which hang low today on the tops of the mountains, or the cut on the bottom of the foot, or the neck, or a tree which is made into a cross like an arrow pointing us to heaven—but this: it is for our sons that we dig (although we don't know it digging), follow the old colonial orders of a hundred five hundred years: they make us killers of our sons and nephews today, the old men made to kill the young, and so they do, finally, naturally, destroy what we have been up until this moment; they destroy the future and the past in this six foot deep burial pit.

It is constant, more like blood that invisibly runs beneath the skin and rivers, the riparian fears which follow our blood and this tensing in the stomach, this low-down and perpetual thing like a man carrying leña, the heavy wood he has gathered and he is bent low, bent at the waist; stooped by his blood, the blows he expect which will arrive, the pit he will in three hours' time be expected to excavate, and made by a held Galil and hundreds of years of the rifles, the spilt blood to dig the ditch for the children's burial pit; this pit of shame that he has dug out with the Principales of Acul today; the place where his sons are arranged on the shore of the newly dug-out grave, and shot in the heads like hunters shoot dogs, so that the brain and blood bone explode onto the dirt, fall into the freshly dug pit which is become the funerary urn of the boys, the men, and all of this choreographed by what holds men in their stance and women in theirs (the screams of girls; the soldiers' weaponry, the please don't kill my children): fear; shame; the reviled; the I would like to live.

I don't know what anything means anymore, Marta. I detest words (these) phrases (my pitiful bare and disremembered five) and the idea of the word, of God—will the words take us back to a beginning, an origin of the simple, when only three things existed perhaps: to love; to hunger; sad. I can't find words. I hate this hard stone English in my mouth—I would like to be prelanguaged, like a babe. I would like to crawl back into my mother's cunt and not see the soldiers as they are killing sons in front of their fathers, nephews in front of uncles (the fathers and uncles stare open-eyed blindly, bent heads and backs—such a posture of grief in their forms), or you on the dirt behind the administration building as man after man puts his cock into your tender cunt, one leaves a babe there (which soldier you can never know); or your brother prostrate on the cypress before the house of God; or the babes' heads cracked open against the stones, cut open from the womb, all of your wounds—I cannot bear to see it; I'll watch TV and not see it; there are no pictures on the television of Acul that day or yesterday or fifteen years from now: you are never in the News, darling; in the Shows; the Shows are happy, even when they are sad; and they are never dirty, bloody-cunted, vile.

Is it cold in the Polytechnic? I am cold. Does pain become like a river? I would like some medicines. Are you dying the indignant and despairing death of the vanquished? I am dead, yes. You saw that boy in the Polytechnic, he is strung up by his arms, another christ in the capital, and in his wounds you see the maggots eating his flesh, like good girls, and in his face you do not see his face, for they have removed his ears and nose and eyes, skin, with knives; he lives; you hear him breathing, this undone man. And the screams when the guard comes in with the coffee cutting implement and removes the man's penis while you are looking, the guard makes you the witness, makes you hear his screams which make a scar in the tympanum, a road which cannot be unmade: you hear him long after he has died, and you are happy for his death, and *this awaits you* they tell you, awaits all of the communist dogs, and you open your legs like a good girl for their knives, cocks afterwards and before. You are suppliant, aggrieved, and I also am tired, hungry, wait for a commercial break to get a snack. It does not occur to me that I may one day join you in the capital, in the basement, girl and soldier; girl or soldier.

YOU COULD ONLY be a thing of my imagination, Marta, because you don't exist in books or History or the newspaper articles or what I can see on the television or in my school lessons—only here, the girl who walks the mountain paths; the girl whose brother is tied to the tree in the plaza which was no plaza, and the Galil rifle and the Cessna A37-B and the money in the man's pocket with which he buys his daughter a sweet in Nebaj, and a pit in the capital city of your country which is no more your country than you exist; unwritten you cannot possibly be? I am an American man and here is civilization's book,—I begin with Homer and move toward St. Augustine, on to Mr Montaigne, past Kings James George, unto Locke, and when the pilgrim boards the ship for America, I am wearing a black and white paper hat that I made in school; we eat brown paper turkey for lunch; we cut corn cobs from yellow cellophane.

Do you begin with Socratic methods or manuals? Do you live in a university village? Do you know how the sun makes waves? Let me tell you fuck you return you to our History which begins here with rage and Hektor's mutilated corpse . . . I am suspended in an historical fracas, it is loud as the diptera girls are loud, all of it buzzes and hhoos inside the middle ear, makes a ruckus of History and a maze here in these pages, leading toward you, Marta? I can see you but you do not exist when I tell you of my woes. A modern's sadness is like this semi-arid plain, it appears different than it is—is it a mask of itself, then? As I am a mask of some man? my self? watered greened with the allochthonous waters and the riverfloods in winter every five year (the "improved" river still not entirely contained) unmakes the houses here on Hollyline Av. There are small details; there is the path to Nebaj which you climb each market day, you carry the load on your head and it is stable and heavy there; there are the fields of maize you pass as you climb skyward, the yellow and metallic blue butterflies in spring just before the rainy season begins, and a dog's vertebrae which push at his skin like beams, this dog leads you up the steep ascent; he is your family dog; protects the house; warns of intruders; and he also will eat your brother's legs; there is the taste of tortilla from breakfast in your mouth and the need for more leña; the heavy smoke from the morning's fire is in the stiff cotton of your huipil and skirt;

there are clouds that make a tower in the sky; make the storms that will arrive this afternoon. It is cold in Acul today, everyone knows these are the cold lands, a place apart.

WHY AM I like this? the loneliest a despair which tricks me cons me into this being which is no living and the longing for love (like a talisman) the desires unmet and unmeetable among the rivers down to the roads where the machete'd boy waits cuts my skin uncunts me; undoes my sad and lonely gait: the universe unfurled by the time of the clock steel and the kinetic thrusts of to idea—is this you, Marta? This your voice that whispers into my ear canal and these vibrations the tympanum's delight: do you speak? and speaking can you do more than grin?

I have driven over the river in Los Angeles and (the over-pass driver) its concreted swell for decades and I have not once felt a dim sickness in my kidneys when I looked (I did not look to the side: see the concrete by-way) at what predicated some kind of before, some small despairing water swell which concreted and dried on the dim raffled deluged winter nights would rise, grotesque, up the white walls of clocks, of progress' gate, to the houses and steel fences of the lined avenues: do I have the words for this lost river? Can I make the words right for Acul and your river and your brother's throat like a girl's back thigh and the gods have abandoned us here, but why did they do it? How did the idolless god make us into a sickness of ourselves, we become some kind of disease (*and I have wondered: have we ever made anything good for this place? these lands? are there any fauna flora among us who, like the dogs, counts their lucky stars for our dominion?).*

There are insects in my mind: wingéd moths and beetled soldiers; the flies like girls. They flit and buzz in the tympanum ascend to the sinus cavities, the mind, into the grey matter and impress their now-dead stiff corpses into the flesh. I would die, Marta, if that could save you; I have no doubt that I am willing, like a christ, for the sacrifice of flesh—but without the god, who to rise me up? Who to pull the threshold from the grave? I am these hard-backed insects, an exoskeleton so that all may see him; he lies on his back, struggles to turn over without any success, his form his prison now, the turn impossible, the relentless unwingéd essay—to turn! . . . today I awoke as a junebug in May; my floor littered with their black and dumb corpses, and my own corpse the corner of your mind, your own grey matter applied like a gun to this sentence.

THIS IS the tympanum, the threshold—this stone at the gate of my tomb; the limestone legend before you enter the consecrated space. Do you remove your teeth with stones when the soldiers arrive to your village? Will you remove this stone from my house so that I may come when you call to me? I have longed for you— desired you more than I have desired to live—do all men desire our gods like a cock will have his cunty hearth? A return to the gods and your cunt—this homecoming is all that I have wanted, to assuage, perhaps, these wounds, the mythic loneliness, this man who walks for thousands of history years, across the millennia he walks drives, he is seeking his gods here, his Marta, the idols smashed upon the threshold those thousands of years ago; and was it this destruction, the sun moon and the tree smashed there which have forever forsaken us, we ourselves forsaken, abandoned by the sun moon trees—and a loneliness then, a millennial longing.

(because to deny their vibrations is to deny is—and this denial of is, ourselves, and the earth, makes us foreigners to ourselves, the earth, divided upon ourselves, without union and this disjunct makes a loneliness and a longing to return to being to being men.)

HAVE YOU EVER seen a television Show? Watch. I am sitting and watching now for twenty thirty years. I have Shows each day and each night which I can sit in front of to see the people and their lives and when I see them then I am not me, you are not in my mind or on the television—together we are in some other kind of place where we don't exist or notexist and the people in front of me could be something better, happier, whites and (a few) blacks and Americans on the screen, in English, with things and their thingéd happiness and three minute sorrows. I watched the Shows today for six hours and finally, somehow, managed to lift myself from the green and padded armchair and stumbling, drunk and aroused by my hunger for food (the advertisements) and love (the Shows and advertisements) I turned the TV off and then looking at my wristwatch saw that it was late (two o'clock in the morning), felt that I was tired, that my wife had divorced me years ago, that my son was never born, and that you also were gone, Marta, or to be found later (if I am lucky) in my dreams. This is dying and if only I could buy indulgences like a good Christian in the days before Luther posted his theses, and made us, eventually, into readers (and then notreaders: TV watchers), into Protestants, moderns, individuals and Americans here in Los Angeles.

WHY DO WE photograph ourselves? Make images of ourselves, as if, if not, to make the black white grey ghosts. Here's your image and mine next to it: taped to the wall of my living room. I am beautiful in the photograph: an American fat smiling happy man (and my foreign mother, her phrases, not visible in the me that you can see); you are less beautiful: burnt, string-bone arms and string muscles, the veins in your hands show up in the photograph like unloved rivers; too thin; and sorrow in your look, like the river—we are together on my wall. What does the photo reveal, can it reveal anything or is it only more of the lies of watching. You are foreign in the photograph, something I can't recognize as home; you wear a strange and beautiful grey and black costume; your hair is intricately woven with cloth. This strange also: how the photo makes you into something I can see and something I cannot see; or know.

I'm giving up on writing now, Marta, and I am staying in the piles of photographs. I'm collecting them, like corpses: they're piling up around me and some are in decay and some have lost their sharp image from water, time, the chemical leak into the air. Each time I am spoken to I reach into my billfold and pull out this photograph, and this one. This, I think, is my imagined photographic essay. Why did I kill you? (here the photo of a goat) And I love you (here the picture of the corner of the room and the broken gurney).

How is it like this? (a girl kneels at the altar, it is her first communion, she is my mother and I don't recognize her). I am sad (the sad black man from the beginning of this book).

Why? (again my kneeling ten year old mother—she looks foreign and strange, a darkness about the pupil; dark skinned in black white and a white communion dress.)

What could it possibly mean? How the long days? Why do I only think of fucking and eating and dying (O monstrous death!) later than now? (again: the mama kneels, blacks whites—a darkness around the edges, the white veil covering her black hair—she is pious in the photo.)

I am fucking now and coming in a stream of unthought thoughts—we are together, we are lonely, we are apart. This all words, uninterruptible mind sounds, syllables: here is the image in black white:

A girl in another place and time kneels in a photographer's studio. He says he will take her picture; he is called Vahé. She goes to Vahé's studio with her mother and her father; they drive in the father's car and the girl's mother doesn't drive or speak the language of the place: they are foreigners in the country, but the girl was born here and she is comfortable with the weather, the sea, and the Arabic and French music on the radio. She says to her mother in their language that her white dress is very pretty and the mother agrees while the father drives.

Soon the girl is kneeling in the pretty dress on the wooden altar which has been brought into the studio for this occasion. Vahé tells her to place her hands on the rail and to clasp them together as if in prayer. She wears a long white veil, she has the look of a bride. It is 1949. She has the look of an angel, a foreign angel in the Lebanon. Could she have known then that she'd mother a foreign boy? (half-Armenian, which is half of nothing) carry in her womb a monster of derision, of shame, of lonely driving days in another place? She kneels on the altar; clasps her hands and she is ecstatic with the look of the looking toward God. She is dark haired and dark eyed—the white fabric is a beacon against the hair black backdrop of the photograph.

Vahé says to her that she is a good girl and he takes her photograph. Perhaps he fondles her small breasts and caresses her nape (the mother has warned her about such men on many occasions) while the mother and father wait outside in the entryway to the photographer's studio. The girl is frightened and aroused by the man's touch and soon she will begin to read romance novels. She reads romance every day. When she marries the American and moves to his country, she ships crates of romance books to Los Angeles: all of them are written in French and not in her language. In French, Vahé says to her that day: Okay, it's okay? and in their language: You are comely, not too beautiful though, Armenian girls are never so pretty.

SITTING THERE, it is a brown and white room, a greyed old color, and not knowing what for or why did they take me, or what is the outcome but for an innocent girl, surely, an innocent outcome, and so I devised all of the ways that I was guilty to atone for their confinement of the body in this place, greyed modern castle in the capital, at the borders, the frontiers, of citizenship; to be here; and a companion is by my side for a moment and then he is taken away from me (and I never lay eyes on him again; so a last looking, his

downcast smile like a boy's at the river when I was a girl, and not-
knowing then that this river would become a horror, and not more
knowing now, but older, young in what they could do in this thinking, but an adolescent girl who has no stories for the removed hands
(yet) the soft blue wrists (yet) and slashes in the breast like awkward
t's and a vagina like a container for their inquiries: pubic hair on his
mouth knife and the black rods, the pain, so that each moment I
think it yell it out loudest, that this is what the body can bear this
and then another and each *this* until the slashes like birds in each
cheek: the breast bone revealed red white grey: a cut-up smile; they
removed my hands in front of me (the flesh unresisting to steel; the
bones amenable also):

an Indian girl in the capital.

See her lovely wrists the long brown hands with vein-ridges like
covered rivers upon the skin see her smile the browneyed look of
sadness it is a fragile thing, you think, so easily rent, so easily turned
aside (no blackened cheekbones); see how shame despair pain can
be made as easily as dough or maize cakes.

Walk into the capital of my country. See the city. See the old
colonial buildings. See the Plaza Mayor. See Justo's Bar where they
gunned down the university boys in 1967; see the grey castle (the
Polytechnic), the University of San Carlos, the men without uniforms and with sunglasses, the colonels and their wives, the man
with the coffee cutting implement: he is the threshold; he cannot say
that he will save me; he says your guerrilla companions, like a gen-
tleman; he is the good listening man; not a wrist-cutter or the breast-
slasher (yet). When he looks into my (they are brown sadbrown
and I give it to him) eyes, I think that he is a nice man; a city man
who will do it: take this sadbrown girl out of the basement of the
Polytechnic and take me back to the river hamlet of my girlhood

before we were ruined by time and the times, by things beyond the boundaries of what we knew (maize the local indictments an old history and the gods who lived in the mountain the trees and rivers) when even then it was not possible to think of the to come, when even then and looking into your eyes as you do it, unmake my sad-brown gaze, forever, I could see a lonely boy in your pupiled hands; a boy who cuts this girl (for money? pride? spite? out of boredom and loyalty? by training? cruel like a glove; vicious like a dog) who tears her spirit, first from the eyes and then the soul leaves the body like a sad and leaden thing: can you notice my heat in the long sun-lighted days of your summer months? can you feel me at the back of your neck, a chill, as you drive the streets of the city? You've un-done me for a generation or more; my mother would have cried for me (but dead already); my father and brother long companions in this night of lonely souls—see how fear can kill a girl in Acul and in the basement of the Polytechnic; we could be the same girl a different girl (there are uncountable girls in the unhistory archives; uncountable souls in the ledgers for the unnamed dead XXMUJERES XXHOMBRES).

Pray for me slowly, slower than the gashes on my breast, the wrists, each thigh. Put your hands together like a good girl at the altar; spread your legs beneath your white communion gown; kneel before god; below the belts of money and caste and idiom—below culture—stare intently, ahead, an innocent gaze like the pattern clouds make in the grey sky. Speak to the gods to the dead tonight and then you can speak.

THIS IS my memory of silence (because there is a payment to be made for speech letters, what I think; know; don't know), we said nothing that day while they killed us. We sat we stood in front of the tree in the dirt not plaza, some of the women are weeping (for the killed boy in his mother's hut, for the twenty-four in Hell, the boys on the dirt path to Nebaj from two months ago, the twelve boys in the town plaza before then and); we dig the trench at the soldiers' behest (a request of "Dig, sons of whores, your resting place"; laughter); we make food for the soldiers at their behest after massacre;—and they would like ten chickens slaughtered and they would like more atol and hotter and they said why do you cry as the old Principales, our teachers and keepers of the days, of the old calendars and old ways, are digging the trench for the young and tied and bleeding men, their sons, nephews, and "Why do you cry when they are the devils? The shit of the earth?" And so the old men crying are quiet while they dig the trench; and we girls say nothing (screams as they do it) as they do it we cry but we cannot scream or we are then the boy nailed to the cypress, my brother, dead now, in a plaza which is not a place—he is there for days, the dogs remove each foot like a talisman, each bone for a nighttime ornament; the crows eat the eyeballs nose and fat cheeks; tied there, machete'd up there: and the dead, the men began to think, the diggers, the dead make room for the living; make trenches in speech and for shame we don't speak and it this shame which kills us, eventually, killed an us in us; and then we become modern, darling? like you—individuals, for eternity?

I TURN the water taps on because I am thirsty and would like some water, or cold and would like some tea, or dirty and to shower, or the fescue grasses in the front and back of my home require it, the swimming pools, citrus trees and hot baths and cooking and it has never been in my mind, like an undone god, to wonder whence it comes—it doesn't arrive, darling, the snowmelt moves down the Sierra Nevada into the Owens River and into the lake of the same name and then waters purchased—riparian rights—following English Common Law, and a channel built and the waters moved the two hundred and ten miles southwest into the San Fernando Valley and onto Ventura Boulevard up toward Hollyline Av and inside, then, my water pipes, the kitchen faucet, a flick of the wrist and into glass and into the desiccate waiting and desperate mouth.

There is a river in Los Angeles which has been altered and deserted to itself now, no willow sycamore elderberry and wild grape; there are not fishes, and the alluvial fans are forgotten also, almost, the creeks where the stones were carved and the gods recognized and recognizable and adored to bring rain, to refill creeks and rivers, to cool the hot September and cloudless days as I drive my car on the roads and beneath them these creeks, these gods, that red stone girl with the long and thick labia as offering, she is in stone of stone etched bright reds in the grey desert earth.

I have not ever traveled to (or read or heard mention of) the Owens Valley. I don't know that it exists in the summer heats and in winter there are luminous snows covering the Sierra Nevada. This is the rain shadow of the Sierra Madre. There is a river; there

was a lake until 1926. In Los Angeles in my California my country
we moved the water into the semi-arid plains to make paradise: the
modern metropolis. The New Jerusalem . . . a lake undone (but we
couldn't and cannot see it; it hundreds of miles from us; did it exist
then? not seen or accounted) the water tapped, and we need more
and then more water here and the Colorado River and Mono Lake
waters diverted and brought to Los Angeles, but still this boy has
no memory because no history of the wide-labia'd god with her legs
splayed and scratched onto the rocks above the water sources, to
honor the riparian gods, bring the rains down to Los Angeles and
fill the rivers streams ancient creeks, and he now, this American
man, flicks his wrist and the water arrives, he drinks the allochthonous water, waters the fescue grasses in his garden (the grasses
whence?), and all of it is nice and clean and he pays his water bill
on time, a good rate-payer for his nation, and he is the happiest
American boy in his car, except for lonely, except for despair, his
new mechanical god, except for the absent vibrations of the river
mountain gods.

WHAT DOES it mean to be haunted by the dead [America itself a
German cartographer's belief in Amerigo Vespucci's letters, and the
letters (likely) a Florentine's fiction, and so the continent takes its
name by chance, via the maze of half-truths and errors and de-
sires], because America has always been a Christian's desire and
dream, and this dream of monstered and seven-headed hydra and
cyclops and men with tails and cannibals and girls without shame
and girls with lust between their eyes like a talisman; of cock-

suckers and savages without the rules of decorum, the hours of the civilized day; the Holy Trinity; blood for the gods iconic devils (and Land spices gold peons and Land): America has been made, Western European Man's ideas of Love God & Providence. Here we are (always) seeking Amazonia, the cities of gold, the west passage to India, Atlantis, the Grand Khan in China, Eternity—an earthly Paradise; Amerigo's *Mundus Novus*.

What is this place,–Marta? and then, what are we? have become been made here–a thousand year Ixil girl who says to the soldiers in Spanish that *We are not dogs*. In my language which is not my mother's tongue I listen across the mountains, your foreign words fall into the tympanum, down the river reveries, these dream-cities, razed nightmares (burnt) villages—We also were not dogs, we also would have liked a slow siesta in the midafternoon haze beneath the Anatolian skies of Kharphert *the dogs whispering that they would like some of the meat to eat the meat of your brothers and mother.*

Now I know it, what I have always known and not wanted to (know) remember that: we have been dogs, darling, you and I: Armenian Ixil curs; and a thousand years of history can be burnt, can be razed, you can watch as it happens, you can light the pyre yourself. This the shame of it. Why were the gods silent while it happened? Why did they abandon us here?

. . . WILL YOU HEAR IT? it is this bell tolls inside of me, as if the futile speaking and notstop of words which come down, like a river (willy-nilly whether I will it or no), a river of silent sounds, water makes sounds, and I cannot stop its perpetual flow, cannot control it, no more than I can make my own blood refasten itself into new veins for the living, or curtail that which, once ungoverned, continues, a mass, eddies, lakes toward my own demise; and how darkness opens the pupil and age on the skin beneath the fatty cells which dissipate, riveleted time, and were I to do it then I'd stop the living which is no more than a blank page, a dark book, brook—this is a man's minded essay, which is the same, perhaps, as a possession, he is possessed while he drives along the highways and freeways of this city: by you, or toward you, to make you and then to make himself: we are: more than lonely and then: we are more than afraid—in my mind you are in my mind and there you are beautiful and I can recount without shame or the loathing of small dogs who will do it, who did, eat your flesh, like small gods; but I cannot not do it, not think you as I see you now kneeling above the grave of your dead uncle cousin neighbors, this wide pit in Acul, it was Thursday when the Principales were made to do it, and I was walking to the kitchen while they excavated (the soldiers stand by) and you kneel now above this earth as it will be undug for bones, today, which is also a Thursday, nineteen hundred and ninety-seven according to the Pope's calendar, to make a history which you already know, like sadness, to make Believers out of the rest of mankind, like distant bells tolling in the metropolis for your brothers, uncle, father; the bell in the belfry has been restored; the church itself reconsecrated and God returned; the look of the sad that you wear in a photograph that I have not seen, a look I cannot adequately describe, inscribed here amidst the folios as a failure of what I see, am able to say, would write to you across the ether and Christ Time and mountains, which could be tomes or

. . . and then why can't I begin to stop or stopping begin to think of what I will eat today and not: you: and you as you sit with your legs tucked beneath you (modestly like a good Indian girl), a necklace hangs like bones around your neck and the hummingbirds and mountains stitched across your new huipil, the tired and strong hands; I can see the veins in your arm like rivers as they cross up and down above the skin like days, a new calendar of pain and work and not enough food in your belly; to always be hungry. (And of how I long to lick your thighs, your bony old brown knees pressed together above this grave and cradle my mouth in your mouth, my saliva could be yours, and I want only to be inside your cunt, between your legs, home, a return to the village of your look, this sadness which calls from the dead calls to an American (half-Armenian) boy, as if it were a thing itself, like a bone necklace, like crude and cheap jewelry on the streets of my city on the streets of your capital; and this crude and violent and ugly man—how far from paradise in the paradisiacal highways he has traveled in search of: love, outside of loneliness, a modern's decree that everything may be assumed at the corner shop, in his auto, decreed for Happiness and the bread lines are invisible in America and the obedience is like this daily bread—but more, Marta, I am a liar and I am a fiction maker: I have not traveled to your America; I make a newer America with my old world letters.

Let me tell you my history which is no History or who I am which is not his *to be*, and my father's thick-soled shoes, his tempers restrained his palms the hands are fear and his hands pulling me down the highway the hallway into a river which is my bedroom and all of the norms of shame and to slap my face punch my mouth and "Do not pull your cock out in front of the teachers, girls with unteated chests"; do not take your cock and place it in your mother's lap like a small bird which tired and lonely wants the mother, this girl the father married in the Orient, and she is dark like the darkness of untraversed and imagined distance, and she has hands which rise and hands that rise down into eternity's lovish firmament:——I might have killed her, but first I loved her hands on my face (on my cock) and the foreskinned reasons without intellect: a caress on my back with her hands and the veins above the skin run like rivers, like your long brown and loveless arms in the untaken photograph; bone-thin as well; to the sea; and a street which made a river in the winter desert. I am a man, Marta, can you see my American clothes in the nighttime? Can you see how I shiver beneath the cloth of ideas which I've not wanted, the costumes of America, and beaten and sugared into me, like the weather makes clouds, like the weather makes days——like schools will make bullies and bullies will line up obediently for the bus or they will make stories with their fists: I have not wanted this, and——the weather never made the Gregorian calendar——it is mine; and I have wanted to put my mouth on your nether mouth and drink there quietly; to pleasure you for eternity; to pleasure myself in this returning essay.

Come and lick my back; pass through the portal I've made in History, the cut-ups I've made of Pope Gregory the XIII and his calendar; of Mr Waldseemüller and his maps; pass through this tunnel of words, this ethereal passage through time and space, which is Time, Space, so that I can see you you can lick my back on History's thighs: drive by me in this city, it is 1982 1983 1998 Anni Domini Nostri Jesu Christi, and we are thousands of miles together, our distance makes us more likely lovers; your hair is unwashed and its smell of time's oil in the wreckage, of hearth smoke, of a species living in its chemical, a chemical love is in your scent, the unwashed parts of you that call over the distance and make me——showering, a hot bath——want you more, need you seek you seek to explain so that you will arrive or arriving keep me and not in your Ixil: abandon this son of baths; this driver—corpse-collector; a notman; and he is always afraid.

Today I am eating the dogs with honor and to honor them. Don't hear me or listen me up. Don't arrive today. Die in your village in Acul today, next to that brother prostrate on the evergreen in the plaza which is no plaza (a brown unburdened untarmacked place). I'll stop recounting and I am sorry for this rampage this rant of the dogs of the lonely, the pathetic, you wont say, and speaking to me in your language, which is the language of the not-speakable unrecorded unwritten (my mother's distances, which are not existed, denied beyond the pale of deniability: to be an American is to kill off the old dead); your suffering is not a book, Marta; your footprints sink deep into the summer mud as you climb the steep path to Nebaj, and your hair is unwashed, there is no black soap, and it is cold and windy today in Acul, the heat of the valley burns my skin in Los Angeles; I can see the Washingtonias arched above the rooftops of these houses like nation-state flags. I am clean today and you, darling, smell of excrement and the blood of the cypress tree is stained on your torn and muddy skirt; when you walk down from the mountain you are naked and your hair is tangled and matted and it has not been washed in many months; there is your monthly blood on your thighs; your teeth have blackened and chipped; you are terribly ashamed; you are like Eve, darling, putrid, and we spit in your faces as you parade by us in the plaza in Nebaj, in the capital, beneath the roads of my city where the ancient spoors and the ancient bones still lie.

IT IS AS IF this descent into dream—this America—which is not an apprised descent, which can only be apprised by an ascent: you are in your bedroom and you have fallen into sleep—but the fall is no fall until a train passes outside of your bedroom window and you are pulled from the dream, pulled up from this fall, and a flight upwards, stairwells, ladders, the slope of this mountain: a fall-up—then it is that you know *down*, understand that you were descending, and it is not the underworld, Marta, it is not despair's well or the hollows that despair's beetles made in the sinew, bored down into the organ's demise as if boring holes into wood, or plastics or metals—the dermestid beetle eats all the modern's designs for they are the animals of a modern dream and it is dream, Marta, it is the human imagination, like the human hummingbird's wings on your huipil, like a haunt (*the dead can live here and without them and without our blood*)—which requires and requiring the fall-into, makes form of formlessness, can only be known if the train passes, the lights are illuminated, the loud blasts of horn, train wells, tracks and metal—and then you forget it sharply again, you have fallen asleep, and when we say fallen it is to forget like to dream is an obliteration, each day a new and the nightmares replaced by the men carrying leña, a donkey's tether, a why won't you raise me? wake me? awaken me? (I am your brother, Marta.) To return to the living, the return to dreams and imagination's hoary whorish beautiful and possible loves: our only—human—esperance. Because if the dead cannot live, neither do we. Is this why, you said, America does not exist? Is this why your christs cannot use their voices to call out to the half-living?

I HAVE FLOWN in the aeroplanes across the country and I have seen the rivers undone by dams; by ingenuity which could also be hubris and greed, and I am a man who turns his spigot left right (flicks his wrist) and never thinking of his hand's movement, drinks the water without wondering whence did it come? that I live in a desiccate place; that the one river here was long ago undone; and this water spilling from the spigot arrived from the aqueduct (engineered by Mulholland) in 1913, arrives from the Colorado River, from Mono Lake, from your village, Marta? from outside—We have made *paradis* in the desert? And is there a man here who mourns the fowl the fish the men who once made their lives along outer banks, in other places, who says I remember the Gabrielinos, the Ixil, the Armenian boys and girls who once played here, in this river, who once made stories and gods from each stone and bush and mountain—Ah, silly sentimental boy! go home to Turkey, you'll say, return to your ancestral village and find the bones and take out the black abandonment and dire pains and old wounds and new undone rivers there—to go home is to die, then? We return in a basket, we float down the old rivers of mind, we find each other, we find lost children, orphans, abandoned babes—we speak all of the languages of time, which could be fucking, and we lie together for hours for lives and we are fucking and I am eating your cunt, falling back in, finding myself inside where the man has always been himself: inside you; warmed; content in the cunt-world.

MARTA, I complain to you incessantly here, of the machines which idle isolate and sadden me: these motorcars, this tarmac for them, the televisions and tools, trucks, and things of every variety: to you I mourn this thingéd loneliness, essay it, and you are walking in the milpa fields and you spend four hours a day soaking picking through grinding the maize for masa with your hands and an ancient stone tool,—and I would like to tell you that there is a price to be paid for my machines, in this loneliness, yes it is obvious, but also to live in this Los Angeles landscape and although in it not ever in it or of it, separate from the ground the old spoors the seasons and waters and rivers (concreted) floods and even the sun's light, air (I have electricity, air conditioning) and all of my leisure time which the Victorians promised us has come to television time and more time to hate the girls who wont fuck me and hate the ugly fat man, this me, who is haunted today by his mother's sentences and a girl in a village without machines, without a camera or radio or tape recorder or telephone (and no material *proof* later, darling, of massacre, just your small and unintelligible Ixil words to say what they did to you—when the Army said that they hadn't done it: they equipped with the UH-1H helicopters, the Cessna A37-B, computer keyboards, telephones, Galils—they are writing Guatemalan History (and the victors wrote their History of Turkey also, undid the Armenians there like this half-Armenian boy learned the History of America, which could only be Progress and Freedom and not massacres either in this semi-arid plain)). And so the modern does what he has long done, sees the savage, kills him fucks his girls and then longs for a return in the years after massacre, says how beautiful they are, docile like gazelles!, and would like nothing more than to put them on display at all of the World's Fairs in London Paris New York City; and I was a savage once, showed up at the end of History for the Armenians and laughing, jumped from one leg to the next, my penis swinging between my legs like a trumpet and making all of the English girls laugh behind their hands, see the sad skinny savage boy, how they wished I would stick it in them also; and I did it until they cut it off, stuffed it into my sad and happy, opened, dead mouth.

I DID NOT KNOW it existed, Marta—the Porciúncula River and a lonely concrete girl in this place we've made and I didn't think it when I was driving on bridges crossing freeway overpasses and beneath the freeways highways and the cars moving or not moving like a river yet this place this Los Angeles place were it not for this sad and lonely river which is no river that I can see or have seen into the distance and for fifty-one miles it stretched (once meandered) toward the sea, and I never thought it, or saw it, I saw something but not this thing, a *river*, perhaps garbage detritus sewage that traveled lonely and dry in the summer months to an invisible and black locale; then perhaps I wouldn't think you, have thought of you, a girl on the side of your river washing and bathing and carrying more water in the morning hours toward her house and the stones in the river do not look like skulls then and the blue is blue and not blooded or blocked with the corpses of girls and boys and babies broken apart there by the soldiers' efforts and blood carnival on the day of massacre.

I have seen the sea and this river after rains and it flows quickly and the torrents of water and no matter the concrete sleeve *it is a river* and the water with its refuse and shopping carts and plastics of every color—pinks whites and yellows—cast upon the waters and catching in the metal carts like birds and I have gone to the river, Marta, to seek a girl who does not live in this city and who, thousands of miles from this place, saw a river in Acul, saw her brothers her uncle her bitter father; a girl on the Pan American Highway, and looked up to see the blue sky that day in April and, not seeing the gods, looked toward her father (he is digging that fifteen foot long and six foot deep trench and not-knowing yet for what purpose he does it) and to her uncle waiting inside the church (Hell) and a UH-1H helicopter hovers in the distance and the cumulous clouds in the distance and the flies begin their gathering at the corners of your brother's mouth the torn lips and chest bones extrude beneath the cuts and bruises and he has not died yet and the old fathers digging, the girls in the not plaza, the other men in the administration building and the soldiers yelling that the Ixil are no better than communist dogs and the one soldier translating awkwardly into your language from the Spanish and you don't understand the hard words he speaks but his hands his look his eyes as they don't see—blind and how blinding is this human vision of ours; how slow and thunderous like strange electric weather; burns; kills—; I am on the streets of this city; it is dark now and sixteen years later and the sun has set behind the mountains and the lights were lighted hours ago and this is Hollywood Blvd and the whores walk along the streets by my side and the mendicants pushing their carts, bathing in the Los Angeles River this morning and this, more than anything, darling, comforts me; brings a certain kind of joy; that in finding them and fucking them I can seek you also, thousands of miles away, across all of the boundaries of flesh and culture and country and even, perhaps, of time; this our time. You on the road to the capital; you on the path from Acul to Nebaj; you on the concrete floor of the Polytechnic your ankle tied tightly to the unmattressed and metal bedset (the ridged and thick ropey scars later if there were a later) and awaiting death or the next client on the bare mattress, that look you give me through the yellow and white bars of the whorehouse, ah sorrowful look from the Ixil girl!—and beauty, for the caged and beaten, the violated girl as I shove my penis deep into your cunt and do not see the father brothers uncles who beat you fucked you the clients who do the same and the scars on your wrists and belly and ankles and how I am happy when I come deep inside your cunt and you are mine and—together, when I find you, save you, together we'll refish the seas, put back the sea otters on the coast of my city, the Gabrielinos will return to their riparian villages and we'll put it all back: make it back into what it was: ottered, unconcreted, and the oaks for miles and the orange poppy flowers in Altadena for miles and foxes and bears and you, dirty, black toenails, and glorious in your scent and skin. Naked, like a savage.

WHAT DOES a man say to his girl, his lover and servant, the black beans at night with cream (if we are lucky for cream); and the hot tortillas and meat (more fortune if we eat meat) and I realize that you can only be figmented in my imagination—and what of it? The church; the Army barracks (later) in Nebaj; the cypress tall and wide and evergreen—what of this man who imagines you there in your natal village—the dogs barking at night and no light tonight for the moon is new and old and blackness and we lighted candles if we have them and the heat from the hearth and wood piled in the corner and hard-packed earth floor and what of the man who sits in his comforted and brown carpeted house, in a green and padded armchair, dreams up your red tiled roof house, the chickens in the yard and the loud and beautiful red-black rooster who crows all the morning long, struts the day in the village, the black puppies who run beneath our feet, hot atol on cold grey afternoons when rains and rains in the winter which is July, August:—who is the more real? You or him? (Or the You who reads this book?) The American man (half-Armenian although it useless to be half-blooded) and the Ixil girl with the long ponytail and tied skirt and red and green huipil, her plastic sandaled feet and she is eating the tortillas with chirmol and he is eating his boxed foods and the rain is falling in Acul in Los Angeles and who could be wetter quieter closer to death? to truth? who dreams larger and more vividly in the nighttime? who hears the cock crow first at four a.m.?

IS THERE, darling, always a payment for love? Some kind of debt which endured, must, finally, be remitted? The gods will exact their due, in time; the sacrifices; the throat of goats and lamb (1,000 white and 1,000 black) will be slit and this blood sacrifice, this burned flesh, these new temples, have not been enough today. Today we are more alone . . .

And who would have foreseen that I would love the dead peasant girl from Acul; her blackbrown plaits beauty, the dark pupils in dark irises and brown lips which kissed me back across the rivers, across the mountains, our many myriad divides;—and no one's story on my television news (Mr Reagan says, smiles, that Now Ladies and Gentlemen . . .) an unfolio'd in my books, and unhistoried in my mind (like my own lost grandmother); unsung; and perhaps she is ugly and stinks of earth and detritus of all manner and notshowered or plucked in her brown brows, the hirsute limbs, the blood of her body on her thighs and back;—and she doesn't walk up the stairs to my home in Los Angeles; and she doesn't drive an automobile; and she doesn't attend dinner parties or restaurant in restaurants and expensive coffees our gazes do not collide like cars so that we may begin our liaison and I can take her, abruptly, from her husband to my own place two thousand miles away, and the god of love aids me, loves me, and I will win in this war, and she also, this peasant girl, a kind mother she offers her tit to all and sundry; to me; she gives her soul in these pages passages to a worthless and cowardly man: he too runs from Menelaos, he too flees death with fear on his brow; and we, the both of us, beautifully defeated by the godlike soldiers in Acul (in Kharphert in 1915) have our small consolation, which is no consolation, to be paged up and versed for two thousand seven hundred years, and unlikely and . . .

BOOK FOUR

The guerrilla is the fish. The people are the sea. If you cannot catch the fish, you have to drain the sea.

—General Ríos Montt

We should wish to know, for example, how it would be possible to tolerate, and to justify, the sufferings and annihilation of so many peoples who suffer and are annihilated for the simple reason that their geographical situation sets them in the pathway of history; that they are neighbors of empires in a state of permanent expansion. How justify, for example, the fact that southeastern Europe had to suffer for centuries—and hence to renounce any impulse toward a higher historical existence, toward spiritual creation of the universal plane—for the sole reason that it happened to be on the road of the Asiatic invaders and later the neighbor of the Ottoman Empire? And in our day, when historical pressure no longer allows any escape, how can man tolerate the catastrophes and horrors of history—from collective deportations and massacres to atomic bombings—if beyond them he can glimpse no sign, no transhistorical meaning; if they are only the blind play of economic, social, or political forces, or, even worse, only the result of the "liberties" that a minority takes and exercises directly on the stage of universal history?

—Mircea Eliade

I RETURN, Marta, to Nebaj, to a place I've never traveled, and it rains as it rained yesterday and the day before then and the clouds hang like girls on the mountain and the dangling mist like their dangling legs, and it is grey, the red tiled roofs are black in my view from the rains, and water is visible in your hands in your hair pulled into a safe and fat knot at the nape: I have sorely missed you, desired you, how I have longed to undo your corte and unwrap its secrets behind closed clothing. What else do I see? The signs painted directly onto cement buildings for the Ferretería Ixil, two American flags adjacent to it and the letters U S A; Tienda Walfred and its Crush sign with the halved orange squeezing the brand name; Farmacia; Distribuidora Ceto; Librería "El Silencio"; *Comedor y Cafetería "Anita"*; *Comedor "EBEN-EZER"* and today it has occurred to me for the first time that all of these signs are not written in your language, I have not seen your language written—does it have slants and swirls? an alphabet, or pictograms, Marta?—and although this is an Ixil town, perhaps two thousand Ladinos in a world of twenty-six thousand Ixil, none of the texts are in your tongue, in your language which lifts up the clouds on all of the days, covers the mountains like the ephemeral mists. And it is something you have always known, like you know how much lime to add to the corn at night to soften it, know how to grind it and form the leë each day; stupid, I am sure, but today as I flew up over the mountains and the desiccate world became green-grey and softly edged, as I passed from the Quiché area of the Highlands and

203

higher still into your ancestral lands, toward home, I wondered (worried) this small and stupid detail: that here in your town, in your land, you have been, what exactly?, a half in and a half out—a modern's exile (like this half in and half out half-Armenian boy? No, darling, not like the American boy.)

The cathedral in the distance, its red tiled roof, the blanket of clouds, the rain that falls without respite today as I have flown into Nebaj to seek you, up from the capital, through Chimaltenango, Chichicastenango, Santa Cruz del Quiché and finally to arrive in Sacapulas where I crossed the river by foot (the bridge does not exist today) and begin the climb up the Cuchumatanes, see at first the dry brown underbrush, turn and climb, the vista and Sacapulas becomes smaller and smaller, and then over the ridge over the fallen rocks and landslided earth and the air begins to green and I am getting closer and the air becomes cooler and green, the rains begin, it is raining historically, perpetually, and I begin the descent into Santa María de Nebaj, into the Ixil Area. See the Plaza Mayor; see the Commissary; see the girls on the church steps their green and black striped shawls; see the mothers with babes strapped to their backs and small children held by the hand and they are hurrying somewhere, don't or wont look at the foreign man, and although no one looks at me, I could be dead here, I see the dead boys in the plaza, see their hacked and sad crania; salute the Army boys in front of the Commissary, hellos to the boys in the Cuartel—I know that they see me. And I think that I will make the climb to Acul, over the smaller mountain, pass the maize plots and wooden houses on the path (the small children run outside to stare at the foreigner; they are giggling like girls) to find you at home, as you have ever been, you come outside to greet me, smile, and you are not hungry or disfigured, and I am cold. I would like some atol to drink, it clears the humors, heats the kidneys, makes the man wish that something as small and strange as sweet corn milk could save a boy and make him stronger, revive him, make him more possible for the Ixil girl.

Why do you open this thing in me, Marta,—it is a wound, and I cannot say whence it comes, or how it has arrived in my chest, the lower intestine, burying, burrowing, like rodents or black flies, as I am speaking, notspeaking, writing and then driving: you never loved me, you never can love over this distance—making an inside from this want, the low-heave of the belly, and this shame because of such an unabated desire: why does it make the man a fool? Why is the unrequited love the desirous, the tenuous wounding, the wrong-doings of the fates stars that have misaligned you and me—have made this man, his shame, and he is prostrate for you, I do bow down to your pleasure, and you forever beyond my reach, the bones not possible to allay this sickness of mine, the words this man's only solace, and I am not a writer, simply the man who drives, moves, would like: to move faster, to have more girls, more booze, more cof-fees, then money, then money'd things and movies and dancing girls and really, here I can say it: it is you I want because I can never have you, because death is my ally, allays me, no Heaven for Adam, you his Eve: you unribbed, naked, an Indian girl in Paradise California (and Cortés' men still seeking the black Amazonian paradise in America before it is America, just around the bend) and I've made you into and back into a heathen for my pleasure. *why am I so lonely?* Why has god abandoned me here in this place where my bones find no purchase, no ancestral huts behind me, or sacred mountain, and your dark bones buried in the landscape, behind the trees from other lands (and I am again and again drawn to this papyrus this new bible, to—what?—seek you; seek flesh) and (eucalyptus birch the Japanese maple in June): I am the dead one, darling. Perhaps I have died today. I am thingéd up; I don't have a son or wife who: cooks for me, she works for me—has thingéd up our beautiful large home and we are big people; and we love the big packages filled with food and televisions and piles of cotton and notcotton clothing. Where is the story in this? A beginning, an end? Here there is only a middle: of the nation, the American boy who dreams of boats, of Indians, of slaughtered girls and night-stranglers; who thinks that something, and he cannot put his finger on it, his mind unable to distend or attempt to make sense—that something is wrong here. A place of lies like a cake of dreams, soured, freshly made each day to honour the contemporary gods of History, American History "is the story of magic transformation" (and the Indians have been allotted a paragraph in my History book, darling, see that we don't elide you): be good, happiness is around the corner (don't think of the savages and) I have never been a happy man and it is my knowing without knowing—of the savages, the hanged and burnt black man, his stare in the convenience shop, the girls who clean toilets, suck dicks, bury their heads in my lap and dance on my cock for five dollars: I'm dead and death is like a vacation from notliving—to return to death after paradise is deceived—it has all been a charismatic Christian dream and drama—we await the Messiah in our paradise; it is ours; we have discovered: paradise, how to make things which can only be bigger and stronger and the bomb-killing from a thousand feet in the air now—but we are no better at making love than the boys whose brains we dashed onto the rocks, the girls whose quiet cunts, which brown, we said, which dumb, we said, which unreasonable, we said: we cut open wide. I would like to own the world and I would like more and more—there are Galils, 9mm pistols and ten hundred machetes—in my essay, here, I can kill all disbelievers dead on the spot.

RAINS. Have you thought the clouds are like girls? not girls perhaps, but this permeable blanket which lies, like sadness, like a heavy weightless cloud, visible, and yet the hand moves through it quickly, over our insides and the outside worlds: the Army world, the villages, the girls on the steps of the old cathedral, the boys' cut throats and arms like icons below the Christian crosses, the sacred ceiba, the verdant cypress in Acul, the bones in the six foot deep by fifteen foot long pit [the corpse-collector of Los Angeles, his electricity and box foods, and the Washingtonias in the distance; the European fescue grasses and modern History].

Why didn't the rain save us? or the climb over the Cuchumatanes on an unpaved and steep twisted road? or a few small words in Ixil? or these ideas of the gods? or the church steps, the sacred interior; birds in flight; silence; rain; and then the ubiquitous summer muds?

I see trees; I have no names for these. Clouds. Rain. I can see rain falling like invisible blood-markers, as if that were possible— an easy sacrifice is not for the gods?

The dead are here also, the farmers and daykeepers and wives and girls and the small children . . . the dogs' howls have taken up residence in my ears and the tympanum is a constant tangle of dogs of cricket noise of the bells in the distant dairy the lightning bugs the zzac zzac of the small birds the cocks crow each quarter-hour— when will they forgive us our trespasses? And refrain this constant night this horrible dog sorrow which sticks inside my skin and the boys and men putting the seeds for maize for frijols for the small

potatoes and chicozapote and the woman making tortillas at four
a.m., the boys and men carrying wood stacked from their tailbones
up to their crania . . . each one carries half his body weight in wood.

[DRIVE BY the Los Angeles River, a trapezoidal plumb sleeve,
and a feat of engineering by industrious men and none of its old
course or newly made route in my head as I drive by the white
monster on my drive to work, to find the corpses await me in the
streets, on the highways and along the freeways of this city. Have
you seen it, darling? Our concrete sleeved river which is no river,
of course, I thought it a sluice, a garbage heap for the watery grime
of this city, a flood control mechanism for us here, for us here we
would not like to be reborn after the deluge . . .]

Here is the Real river: I am on the freeway and the cars have
halted. We all of us, a thousand thousand of us as far as my eyes
can see forward and back: a river of cars, and unmoving now, although this hum of music vibrates the windows, the engines also
vibrating, invisible smoke from engines; lonely men sit inside their
cars idle and we idle in the midday heat, the low grey contaminated sky in the midday heat and the Los Angeles River to our
right as we don't move southward along the tarmac arteries of this
city. And then who can say why it is, but of a sudden the cars are
moving now, in syncopated rhythmic movement, like a beast, a
wild metallic and deranged hoary dragon who sputters and falls
and lifts his heavy head, his metal paints, his gummy tires, lifted, and
roars and we proceed apace now, along the tarmac river, across the
LA River, the cars like water stopping and starting and making

contamination for the species and taking us home to work or like me to find the corpses of wild automobilic rhythms: we unmade rivers in America and machine-made rivers in their place, in this place what has come before?: the Gabrielino girl who plaited her hair alongside the sycamore tree, she eats trout for her breakfast— ah, delicious primordial fantasy for this man! let me, tell me to do it: she plaits her hair like you do, she has lived on this land and alongside the old river for millennia; her fathers have fought the wars against the people over the east hills; her daughters chew sticks, cook fish in this manner; her sons caress their flesh in the night, because we all love the boys, their sweet stink at night; their shy kisses on the neck; sweet dangerous boys, what sorts of men have you become? And if the dead can see from up on high, as Christ assured us, or if the dead can peek through stones as the old gods told us: what to make of us now? The concreted river; the girls undone, her clan unmade; the tarmac hills, the metal and plastics and pipelines and electrical poles and wires and corners made from fluid and hot days; right angled up the place; the place became a place—center, periphery, streets and street indexes of corners, straight paths, the river itself made straight and true, like Science, like Reason, History, and unlike, very much unlike, my meander- ings for you here in these pages, darling of my notflesh.

TO THINK something notmakes it true;—even a system does not make the system a truth or the sun's axis different from what it is, and not for all of Ptolemy's desire, and you also—in truth;—Yes: thinkers can be killers and thinks and kills can become the same thing: kills makes thinks a thing, things it up—cultures, nations, creeds—and wording things up might make soldiers move into the Highlands and burnt and removed and macheted the real; the girls; your brothers—you. There was a name for such an action, there were commandments, reasons, orders; a Cold War. It happens in these pages even as I think them.

This what I cannot understand, Marta, I wrap my words like gloves around the palms in the mind, at its end for you around these ideas as if ideas were candies and could be sucked upon and dissolved into the world like a wide and hungry mouth.

Before the machete is it the thinks that is the killer? and yet ideas, thinks, the makers of remorse and sadness then shame then— I dreamed of you last night, early morning, and in this dream you were you and not the you I have made here, for my own viewing, to make you and unmake you—history the ugly man, the small man, a fat and small-cocked man's desires: in my dreams you did not love me. And in my dreams you were not an Indian girl— (when did you become my Indian, Marta? in October of 1492, or thirty-one years before Pedro de Alvarado made his way south from New Spain, or in 1597 when Gilberto Suárez and Jacinto Menéndez walked into your village? or last week when the store vendor scuttled you out of the restaurant and inditas cannot enter here; or in 1982 in Acul when the machete made from an idea made flesh into a question: who can be the best killers? Or at the beginning of this book when I found the dead bitch on the side of the road? Or now, Reader, as you read us up?) Why can we not be monsters, Marta, without our ideas of the savage beastly whorish and then savage and then: I am this man. I am this monster and I am this man who made you makes you either beautiful or whored or a cunt for my cock or—Did men make women, Marta? I am an adam—a maker, idea faker, cock-taker; in this, here, our modern world, our freed and libertied—our ugly and beastly—our cock-collecting corpse-collecting building roading making: we make women, Eves; we make dogs; we make Indians; we make money; we make autos; Progress; we make lights; the 9mm pistol and the Galil; an aeroplane for the end of things; we make wars and transcontinental highways; locomotives; presidents; republics; cosmetics for the girls in my school; plastic shoes and plastics and surgeries and pesticides—and we do not know—and this is a lie—that our making can also unmake us (the Cessna A37-B flies above you in the mountains), ideas and laws. Primarily and fundamentally and foremost and in the treaties and treatises you will see that we are liars—we are, like our god, alone, and we are, fundamentally, like this same unnamed and iconless man: vengeful and afraid; we too have killed the mother; a jealous god; righteous; the judge. Take a Blue Bird bus to your capital city. On the bus everyone is crammed in together and the chickens and small children (how you envy those women their babes; your girls and boy in the mountain, boned there); the tortilla and bean sandwich you've packed; you are wearing your new clothes, your hair is tied back in one long and blackened plait and your blackened toenails are blacker today; your heart is a black place and there is no escape from it—you have left the mountains; you have made your way to Nebaj and you have gone through re-education training; and the frightened woman gave you the quetzales for the ride into your capital city which is not yours, which you've not seen and you are afraid and you must leave the Ixil Area, you think, the townspeople hate your looks of sadness and despair and when you walked naked around the plaza and recited the names of the children of Acul because you wanted to remember them, yes, perhaps even a little bit more than your fa-

ther's name—because you made those children, loved them or
hated them, unmade them (because they could bring the black machines on the top of your head), and the wound this horrible and
black thing which remains unnamed and cannot be interred, in-
ferred from the ether, these assimilations of time, you must say and
then resay, because you know that the wind will take them, but in
the leaves of things and the trees of the plaza and the trees of the
plaza removed, cut down by soldiers because they blocked the view,
the drunk they killed for pissing on the tree stumps, and so you offered their names, naked, to the air:

Hold me, Marta, in your dead invisible embrace, and I shall
hold you back in mine.

You are on the bus. The buses have names and La Roca, El
Salvador Guzmán, La Reina del Ocaso, Dios Me Bendiga can take
you down to the capital, and in your language you can have the
words for unseeable things, for a soul, but in this Castilian you are
only learning how to call what has been dead, arranged; these ideas
and this language—an español which is not yours and a not-yours
which has altered you, made a darkness which is more, which is the
names of the children which you walking in the plaza until the soldier takes your hand and placing it on his cock says to you to stop
the walking in the plaza that fucking you again this evening as he
has every evening since you returned down the mountain will be
his pleasure, the sores on your forehead, those mountains reclaimed
by your skin and his medicines did it for you and the children's
names are whispered to him in Ixil but he doesn't speak to you except to say that you are a whore and a stupid bitch, in Spanish.

Because here is a thing about love: the ideas notwithstanding the
heart and livers and what men make and call out and down, the
muse—that love entails suffering; because to love you means that

I can never have you because you are in a foreign place; a girl without my tongues to speak with; a girl who lying next to me, who I have paid in full for—none of this, your tongues your pussy lips can alter the loneliness which loving you makes and makes more apparent—it is no motif of poetry or history; it is, Marta, like your brothers, the cypress, that hunger and sickness which took you down the mountain and into Nebaj (to surrender to the Army), down to the plaza, in front of the Commissary, and then finally when that old woman, a widow, destitute, terrified, but kind, gave you the necessary quetzales to leave the Tierra Fría and travel to the capital city, to the center of the nation, and men in the streets, and you walking there in your new Indian costume, lost, alone, and looking like an Indian, and not speaking the language, and trying to make sense of the black things you inherited, like a comb or a bucket or what could have been a piece of corrugated roof from an old home in Acul; finally you take a rest in the old church garden and the men arrive in their black ski masks to escort you to the Polytechnic.

YES you could be right, correct in your reasoning as to this why, that I also hate you as I long to lick your thighs, then hating, fucking, the rape of the eternal [cunt], the secret you keep between your legs [from me], it is this sex of yours, a return—; and I hate your peasant cunt (like a good civilized man); the disgrace of your fall [into the Polytechnic]—this ignorant smile and dirted black nails that bite and then fallen from grace and then the unclean smells of humus, your unwashed thighs [blood on them, unashamed reds], the fallen poor black disgrace that I have made of you here in these pages: yes, it creates this dullish desire to annihilate, which can sharpen which can make the blade descend which,—let me lick your face, darling. I could piss the world, could fuck it you and then control the humus of your thighs, this Los Angeles basin, these valleys, the sky's apogee—a reason of the most unreasonable and smallish and then fine because good idea; the idea of man pissing the world, of you, thighs open, sex smells [unwashed brown then red in your meat]: I want to return, and: what is religion if not this making and unmaking vision? The remaking of man into his own image as he makes himself into: a man; a man who collects corpses; a man who collects: dogs, ideas, the girls with black plaited memories—I'll pull it from this grey matter, from the mind [is it grey? round? black and then blackened]—this too an imagined history; a Show of the gods. My mind unseeable, the heart an illusion of musculature and false pretense and the descent of Love and the cocksure liver—my kidneys pain me today, burn me in my back and the blood is dirty now and I am pissing on the quarter hour—these things as things portend more than the man's demise—the very picture of my meat my end, like the photograph of you, you are standing on the Pan American Highway in Chimaltenango, a small defiant Indian girl behind the yellow and white barred window, and then the clouds fall down like girls, the men into the riven pit and it is not despair it is merely the garbage heap which when the dogs deposited there and your men and uncle deposited there, it was as if the clouds could make more or less rain in that instance; more natural lies. And it is, consequently, and it is you I kill each day, your meat stinks, its sex humus, its decompose my painting a photograph of these long days without you—without this notheart finding your unphysical not chemical a material nothing—in the ether—in the ether in these words which are no more than words and *a heart a mind* which is no more than an idea: I have sought you and longed for you and made you, and you only make the eternal harder, never having you, not ever having seen you [except here among these sentences (which defiling even as they make) in these images I rifle through toward a river, to the mountains, toward where there is not a place: the pit in the capital of your country which, the Army avows, never existed, as you also never existed or died there]; you unseeable like my living meat organs; like the photographs not taken, this clamor in the winds, this unflinching distance which love cannot route or rout, and the rivers can be more than what is possible [a container for the Angeleno monster, unpredictable destroyer] and the heart, an organ's meaty desire, can be like capital's descent into your cities and towns—because who built the cathedrals? and who unmade the rivers? and who unmade Acul with a fire that did not bring god into the church but a new-god where the men were taken to Hell and in Heaven the women make shirts and trousers and would like a little bit of yarn to make a round and sad day for a day's work without end. I'll tell you— it's not surprising—the machinations of men are the machinations of men. This the full of it. I'll tell you: there are no photographs of that day in Acul, the you standing behind the window on the road to your capital, in the Polytechnic, sleeveless and handless; the gods did not record your howls (but perhaps an errant soldier boy did it?) there is no material proof of what the Army did, so did they do it then? Did they?

IT IS NIGHT and the clouds are sepia-toned from the moonlight and shadow. We are walking in the mountains; we are cold. The trees are like statues, beautiful and elongated, black-green in the moonlight and the trees like statues make me think how sculptors must take their ideas of form from the pine oak cypress on such a night as tonight when every tall mass is a darkline, etched beauty; black-green edifices against the sky, and the light is a halo on the sky; and the sky appears larger because of the sepia-toned clouds overlaying the cosmos, open in places, closed in others, like white wave crests on an empty sea.

I imagine you are here; no wind tonight; and so the trees delineate the world. You are walking and a little less cold because the wind died down and everyone walks slowly because hungry and tired and sore feet or cut feet and the babies are not crying because their mothers have taken their small palms and tightened them like screens screws over the smaller mouths of babes; it could be paradise tonight, you think; it could be a god's world; and you are not as cold as you have been and even hungry and afraid (today's bombardment in Santa Rosa Xeputul, the Cessna A37-B flew lower than it seemed possible, and you can still see the enormous hole left in the world where the four ladies lived, the small babe (you carry him cannot suckle him); you can see the beauty of the landscape, the cloudscape like an old photograph, the trees like cathedrals, arching above you, seemingly offering safety, sanctuary, hopes for the small and new children; and you see the babe's mother again (she was crying softly, whimpering, a half-dead, you thought, since you have come to predict with great accuracy who will die, who dies first in the mountain): her vital organs a spray of flesh blood and bone-grit on the trees in the small hidden mountain village, if it is that we can employ the word *village*, for the three mud huts, a half square of maize, these wild dogs. You can see moonlight, you can see death tonight, and you can see beauty in the trees (no flesh hangs upon them, suspended like small hair ribbons), and perhaps I notice the beautiful night as I take my walk through the Santa Monica Mountains—a lonely walk where what I want is more love more money more houses and cars and titted girls and painted fingernails (and a son if I could make him in Los Angeles), and you would like a pair of soled shoes, to notexist tonight, to kill the pilots of the greenblack airship who killed those whom you had only recently begun to love in the mountains: Doña Ana's hands, her three month old babe, and hot cooked food; some meat. [But I am no perambulator, and cannot see beauty tonight in these mountains—can you, itinerant Reader, find beauty in these turns of phrase?]

In the end the Army will get all of us, you think (we have survived all of these years for this sad and unholy end; a woman's entrails like hair-bells in the greenblack trees).

And I am thinking about the man who used his hands to put the sheets of metal in place on the aeroplanes in Wichita Kansas, or drew up the plans for the metal sheets, and he comes home tonight three years later and watches the television Shows (I am watching the same Shows alongside him and thousands of miles away in Los Angeles) and he eats from boxes and desiccate foods and his wife and three boys (running wildly, the desiccate foods are filling them up) and he does not see you in the mountains or Doña Ana's stomach liver large intestines making a blood puzzle on the earth, in the tree branches; and if he thinks of you, which is to say not any you who carries another neighbor child on her back tonight, walking the paths higher into the mountains; you are fleeing the Army again, you are cold; he thinks of how you deserve your lot, how you must have done something (wrong) to deserve this ignominious end: how only bad people come to such a bad end—how the communists are waiting at our borders, nigh on our heels, and will devour us like beasts if we let them, the Barbarian hordes (—ah, Marta, such comfort to be found in the nationalist's tight embrace!); he sleeps in his bed quietly, like an old dog (and he also would like more love, not less, and he doesn't get it either, but his comforts, yes); his bedcovers pulled to his neck; his bedclothes are new and plain green, thick socks and the sweet smell of new plastics in his motorcar. He is a builder; a maker of Cessnas and then maker of what unmade your friend today—and this means nothing; only here do I put Mr Peterson of Wichita and Doña Ana of Acul into the same sentence and hence into the same breath—breathe them both up, Reader; they are rightly together: the maker and the girl who is undone by his machine: that is something, isn't it, darling? like a dog corpse feeding the diptera girls their lunch?

SHE WALKS the paths in these ancient mountains and she tries to leave her sorrows on the branches of the pine and cypress as she would a hair tie or lost article of clothing. Tomorrow she walks the mountain paths and attempts to leave her sorrows there in the same manner. Today; yesterday; here is a pine; it is young and green and a smallish sapling and she thinks that this one will do it well and her uncle told her as a girl how the trees were for their sorrow, and that if undone then no history or repository for sadness—and although he is dead when he whispers it to her again (in the Polytechnic) and she has tried it (in her mind she makes trees, her mother and brothers' visages) and she fails each time she essays, she can be freer although it is not true, and even though what is is and she would like a blanket (she is always cold now); and she would like medicine (there is pain); and hot soup and some kind of familiar look or her language here or—who can say what love makes in her language?;—or she would very much like a 9mm pistol (only the G-2 have them in Guatemala) and she would very much like to put bullets into all of the brains of the G-2 men: one by one she would do it; and remove their penises with small knives and stuff them into their waiting mouths like one stuffs an apple into a hog's mouth before cooking him on the hot coals; she has not eaten meat in months and years; it was chicken on occasion and eggs more often before the soldiers arrived to Acul.

(And as she needed trees for her sorrow, he has needed this essay for his.)

WHY IS IT that we've not developed the diction to speak it when there are terms for each part of the beak in a bird? Or the species of ants can fill books and the etymology of TO DO and I don't believe it is because it is unspeakable or unknowable, but more because we don't desire: to know it (although we do know it)—we don't utter it scientifically recondite and if each layer of skin on a man's body is named layered, then why not the words for the destruction, the removal of his skin? for the machete's work on the body? what a man is without his eyes, ears, nose and then sex (we are afraid and we are ashamed and we have been for as long as I can remember and longer, before I can speak in all my History's history and this nation's backward slide into its origins). The narratives of pain and sadness we make over and over again on the body only to hide descry and decimate in sentences: the burial of is:

> The soldiers direct the villagers to make a queue in
> front of the cypress where the young man has been
> tied up. The soldiers order the villagers to beat his
> head in with their farm implements, to cut him up. The
> villagers beat him until his brains fall out and onto the
> ground; his chest is a gaping mouth-wound from the
> machete wounds.
> The Indians are subversives. The Ixil are
> communist dogs.
> The soldiers bashed the children's heads against the
> white stones alongside the river; cut them into pieces
> like pork roast.
> The Internal Armed Conflict lasted thirty-four years
> in the Republic of Guatemala.
> We are fighting a cold war, gentlemen, the communist
> scum will get us if we don't watch out.

Do you see how these sentences operate on the mind like an entertainment, an outrage or sedative: a killer of feels know in the flesh, beneath the layers of skin, a liver stone and a kidney stone, make sentiment, but do not make you, Marta. Do you see how a sentence is one of these beasts which burrowed beneath your skin in the

mountains, made mountains in the flesh, a distortion of the face's
geography and history. A disease; an infiltration of the physical details like ideas and (Christian) morality on television beneath the
too-rich clothes and the happy television actors with opaque unseeing smiling (lying) eyes. I watch them; I watch television and I
too am dying. And happy sedated for the duration of the Show.

Why do I call you Marta? Whence this name and this calling
down, this pain hunger cold of the girl who walks into Nebaj fifteen months after she fled into the mountains; a girl who makes her
way to the capital as so many did before her, and as I do here in my
dreamy lies, these sentences of the old books made into a newer
thing, another book for bookshelves stores and the eventual pyres;
more garbage heaps in the dispersed shops of my city.

What is this place,—Marta?
Why am I so lonely in it?

Today I'll take a drive along Santa Monica Boulevard, Saint Monica
was Augustine's mother, the seer, a North African lady—and he the
convert, made into the good son who then made Christian history
a plumb line from there to here.

. . . NO I CANNOT remember it now, an involuntary now, the
memory of it comes like Marta's breath on my shoulder and a shud-
der, unbidden then, like this memory returns. What have you done
to me, are doing, Marta, that I should remember such a thing when
I have only remembered until now? Until there have been palms in

my memory (at the end of the palm of the mind) and wide Santa Monica Avenues and the drives along the arteries tarmacked ways of this city which is no city, like I am a man who is no man, a man freed from his dead (shackled then, to what?), freed from his past (shackled then to . . .).

A phone call from the distance like water moves through the atmosphere, invisible until clouds, rains. The inventor attempts to speak with his dead and deaf sister, makes a telepathic device, a telephone, and the dead on the phone call from a foreign place, a place I have been, yes, but only in memory's imagined dark recess, perhaps I've not been there at all, perhaps I've never been any place but the chair, the television blares, it is a comedy, the telephone rings loudly and my mother sits on a sofa, the girls on the TV are laughing like trees and she is tense today, my mother is quieter; she's had a bad dream and she thinks her dreams are certain, she is waiting, certain that dreaming and knowing are one. She waits like the weather waits, like rain arrives, the clouds, cumulous, at the ready, and can at the right moment, a vertical uptake, make storms; precipitation; unmake a mother via this dream she's had, this telephone between her hands (and the veins in my mother's hands are like closed rivers, broad and blue)—and a flood down the streets this winter, a river on our street. Or she picks up the telephone receiver and she dials the numbers in her book; or she remembers the numbers from her childhood in the Lebanon: they have not altered with time, not like this dream I am recalling, this notmemory, the river that runs down our street taking our neighbors' pots rootballs shirts tin bowls cans. There is a break in the line and stuttering, a thick noise, and a war in that place which the television will also blare to us for the evening's four minutes of News, the mews and in the eaves we listen, it is an eavesdropper's trade to trade in the News of other (barbarian) places and sunlight makes news also; undone lakes are not on the news and a civil war is uncivil, of course.

[In those places a boy who is not my brother is tied to the bumper of a car, it is a Mercedes-Benz, a taxicab, the boy is tied, by what? where?—at the wrists? the shoulders? the neck? behind the ears? In a conflict, on the playground of wars, the best tying spot is quickly determined (the wrists too weak, hands fall off; the neck too facile—will only go a mile; an ear?); he is tied at the wrists; he is eighteen years old and an M16 is taken from him and a wrong-sided confession or the party of god his neighborhood or his words and accent; he is ugly, weak, or like some boy I hated on the play-grounds of my childhood: a coward; this weak fucker to be *killed*; he so easily pisses his pants in the dust; a small piss river. And so this one tied up (by the shoulders, around the back, at the wrists) and the four other boys of this: confession political party: hump jump into the car, laughter, weed, whiskeys later that night, drive him up into the mountains, farther away from the sea and they can see it in the distance as they ascend and then pass Aley, toward Bhamdoun Jdita Zahlé; up the long road which, the brochures for tourists (who no longer tour this place) once boasted, made it pos-sible for you to swim in the sea in the morning and ski in the moun-tains in the afternoon. This is not the boy we will see on the television News in America; he is not my brother or sitting on the sofa in the living room watching television. The boy's name is not brochured; he cannot scream in my memory and when the barbar-ians are fighting in other places, in America we are eating ice cream and watching Shows; and we are dieting on fat bowls of cereals and swimming in the allochthonous chemical pools, and here we don't have wars (not since 1865); here we only have fun and happiness!]

She calls her home in Beirut. I do not know what was said in a foreign language like this distant water—"Mama died today," and the first moments of knowing, in English she'll speak to her son: where pain begins to enter the body like an invisible rod blow, or a beating from my father with his wide palmed hands when he arrives home from work, or the boy tied to the bumper of a Mercedes-Benz by his ankles, his head bounces up and back, smacked open, like Hektor's corpse was tied to the victor's cart, except these Achillean boys did not kill this boy first and honorably on the field of battle, he is killed on the ride up into the mountains, there is nary a piece of face of his face left when they arrive to Zahlé. A mother's death on the end of the phone line; and a telephone makes distance? Or a telephone does what the inventor desired, this desire (like all of the fucking I have wanted, the hundred girls I could have fucked) unfulfillable, undoable, because: ether is ether, and because, her mother's death was not to be undone by love's desire or my mother's sorrow; a Mercedes-Benz drives up into the hills of the Lebanon and a mother mourns the dead boy there, pulls out her hair, and here in Los Angeles my mother is undone. *What are the gods when they made us?* did they make us? did they make us to arrive at this moment of war's delight on the vulnerable form of man, how a gun a machete the smallest tool (a coffee cutting implement) can make pain like mountains, more than love it is easy to make pain, like a man will make buildings or wide dams, undo rivers; a lake undone three hours' drive from Los Angeles. My mother's English then (and the terrible inadequacies of the language, of the word: pain: like this or the body like this inside the word, so that you may know it, understand, Marta, in your notEnglish, and you do, you know it well—you could be this mama I speak of—when will you be my mama and let me crawl inside your cunt?); the death

of her mother; the thousands of miles of distance; the unbreach-
able charge; the body which she'd not seen, felt, smelled in years
because of war which could be eternity's requirements—a mother's
body made distant by boys' playground designs (and boys sitting
around a businessman's table) and the boys who took a boy up the
mountain, tied him, by the shoulders? the ankles, to a taxicab, a
beautiful German design, up the mountain road, along all of the
curves, the ascent, until dying came to the boy (his loud cries obliterated by the louder diesel engine); my grandmother's quiet brain
hemorrhage in Beirut, blood riven—she dies easy in her sleep; the
mortar shells pound loud, pound the unfiltered brain; the gruff
husband to hold her hand after she dies alone (*we are not born alone,
man, but we do die alone*), moves away from the husband and farther away from my mama in Los Angeles and a grandson, me, who
doesn't know her, who doesn't remember the mountain road to
their summer home in Aley, its curved arches, the Mediterranean,
or a language he does not speak (notArmenian notTurkish
notArabic or French): but he does recall one song in Armenian
(not the meaning of what he sings, just the syllable sounds) it comes
to him willy-nilly, when he least expects it, perhaps when he is terrible sorrowful, when he is driving with the bitch in his trunk on
that day that he found her along the 405, rescued her, and then the
song came to him out of the blue, from ether, and he sings
the phrases " Նորից զարուն եկալ, զարուն աննրման " makes
barbarian sounds; he knows how pilgrims made corn-cakes, how
laws made slaves; but he doesn't know his grandmother, she holds
his hand in the backseat of a car as they make the ascent to Aley,
the wide curves, steep incline, when he is three years old (except
that he has never left America). She is not whispering to him and
she cannot drive and yet she is whispering it to him still, like Marta

also whispers in his ear for all of ether's eternal loneliness since that day at the side of the freeway, and the dead have come to him, and a car cannot make men but it can unmake them, and he cannot remember it later: *these are our dead* and the names are older than History and cars make us lonelier, television is a killer also, of the old dead stories and places.

[LIKE ACHILLES and Agamemnon and Hektor and Priam, we too know that we cannot have war and soldiery without you, Marta—without the Marta-girls, and the desire which calls us, drives us. As we know that knowing comes from the body, and not from school books.]

THE AGE OF THINGS, the age of Greed, of the Individual, like a thing—does it begin its circuitous and strange sad snake its way toward its end—all ages end, each thing has its fin. I'll not miss it (I lie)—all of my comforts, my small and large material joys: coffees in the morning sweetened with white sugar crystals and the milk of bovine bitches (she does not suckle the quiet child); ice creams and motorcars and telephones televisions clothes of every variety and color; I'll miss the filled-to supermarkets, thick-warm cotton sheets and blankets, electricity in the evenings in the days when I wish it;—hot-cold water when and as I wish it; chocolates; sweet meats; all of the vegetables fresh in the morning and trucked to my home from the Central Valley; the petrol for cars, and the thousand thousand motorcars on the streets of this city; tall buildings; the houses filled-to with thingéd joy and noises: I'll miss the excesses, the men who specialize in fly eggs, and the girls who spend their days rubbing their heels to a beautiful sheen, cutting their hairs every fortnight, the eight hundred dollar and natural! perfumes; the meat; movies and television Shows of happy people and that I could very well become one of these happy corpses on the television with big houses and green and padded armchairs and Real lives—these I'll miss most and desperately, when all that we've made and all that we've unmade will form a different covenant. The age of Greed, Things did not make us killers, we are killers quite like the sun makes light, quite like the black caterpillar makes a black butterfly, like the diptera girls unmake your flesh, your brother's—but this age has had no outside to itself, we made monsters by it, emperors of space and time, little beetles drinking sodas and running in vicious business circles; we became specters of the specter, spectators to life and life became a Real dream, and we have suffered, not as you have suffered, no—, but my suffering amidst my candies and cigarettes (ah, the sweet bitter tobacco leaves), the too-much foodstuffs, the too-much stuff-stuffs: machines and shampoos and pesticides and radios, piles of cottons and nylons and polyesters to cover ourselves with; leather skinned things to carry, to spread out, to cover ourselves with; this plastics abundance—polyethylenes polypropylenes polyurethanes polytetrafluoroethylenes—in cars, in houses, in food and there are beetles who can eat it—and all of it has brought and made this ghostliness—we scared of death, we tried to kill it with our things and killed the gods and all of the men we hated; we paid the invisible steel tax of the lonely fat and lazy American boy. I don't ask for or expect your pity, Marta, I merely tell you that all my things and the beers and booze, the tobaccos and medicines and cocaine weed highs have been paid for, and this paying, albeit calm, lovely, slow, has also made grief, not your kind of grief—never that—I can barely lift my head amidst this pain— but nevertheless we can, I can, call it by this name, it is the only word I may find for what ails me and I am sorry, too, for the paucity of my language, this essay, leaves both you and I even more lost amidst the specters and the spectered folios—sorrow is such an imprecise word for the girl in Acul, the girl in the Polytechnic, she stands behind the yellow and white barred window on the Pan American Highway; for this corpse-collecting boy.

This is it, Marta: we—this we you cannot, should never, pity or desire, monstrous and barbaric:—we unlearned how to live here. And the professors spin their yarns of the History of Man; and the psychologist stretches you out on his chair, strips your pants and sucks your cock, or you suck his, to make more History of Man; and the successful politicians and busy businessmen doctors do it also and they eschew the dirty, the contaminated, the unlawed girls of the bordellos who sleep with them, kindly attend their needs, suck cocks day after day and for thousands of dollars (because only the best whores shall do)—when they take it in their assholes, oh yes, they want to and they are ashamed of this want, and this shame is pure pleasure in the white houses: hence the shame, the increased pleasure, the torn and tough assholes.

I don't know how to live, Marta. I spin this essay by way of an exploration like the black caterpillar and relentless black flies— part of my inquiry: because I have wanted to know the whys of it, that men make suffering like our mothers made food, made children; like our mothers slapped us and held their love up on high, as if shelved in aluminum tins and rotted. I don't understand and I

suppose I will go to the grave with this inquiry still on its run.—
Perhaps the questions are poorly made; perhaps it is the me (we)
that is the illusion (*what do you opine, dear Reader?*)—Who could
be happier than me? I am a man who drinks coffees, eats and drinks
and buys and works and all of his desires fulfilled when his desire
says this thing thatthing *now*. It is this "stirring up within one's
own self"—do you remember we spoke of it? I spoke in hopes of
your listening: "It is horrible," I said. I have always tried to understand this horrible, perhaps because it haunts me, like the black
butterflies hang from the trees outside my window, so jutted and
gathered together they look like black bark; they blend into the
trees—in my greed as a boy I collected the black butterflies into my
jars and I filled my room with jar upon jar of the black beasts. I fed
them carrots, lettuce leaves, and candies. And they always died
within days; the black corpses filled my room, the bottoms of my
shoes pasted over with the soft black wings. I used to dream that I
flew around the city of my birth, as if I were an animal, and then
awoke as a boy (to follow rules and not these flying urges). I
pounded the butterflies into a paste and I mixed in sugars and hon-
eys and milk and I ate it like cold cereal in a bowl—this corpsey
porridge was my secret from myself—I ate it without telling myself the truth of the origins of the thing—the coffee from where?
the sugars? the butterflies from outside my door in the garden.

This is madness, they'll say (who this *they?*); this essaying
(which is always a failure, a trial, leads nowhere). Tell us *what* happened. *When? Whom* did you fuck, or kill? Who has cancers, adul-
terous liaisons, a lost child returned at dusk unscathed: give us
happy endings and beautiful girls with crossed legs (they'll uncross
them for us later in private); give us happiness—pursue it faithfully
like a bitch suckles her young. Give us a straight line, a plumb line,

story with a beginning middle and (happy) end. Work and work and work (but not urge)—buy up your happiness at a shop, it is for sale for happy-buying—see it in a magazine for sale. Buy your coffees (from where?) your sugary sweets your cloths your leathers your automobiles for auto-intentions: buy it up, eat it up. Don't look underneath the butterfly corpses; don't eat the corpses with sugary sweets; don't grind their wings into a paste and dip your fingers into this past and rub the black dough across your lips like a gloss. Don't stick things in your ass. Don't love those people. Don't love the skin that swags; the ropey scars of pain and suffering—the smells of the pubis: don't love the pubis, sticking your face in it reminds you of the places which you should not love; your mother is in your lover's cunt; your mother is also in a whore's cunt. Don't love whores; don't turn your ass for the whore to beat you with her black whip, her clubs, like she herself is beaten when the take is too little in Chimaltenango. Don't look into the vagrant's eye. Don't give away a dollar at the end of the day (your thousands should only be spent on important things).

Kill the vagrant; fuck the whore. Don't say (think; don't think in America): "I am afraid to die." Say: a man is made in the form of a man and these are the reasons. Give the reasons and its History: to buy to work to eat up to smoke up to fuck with (blindly)—to marry (the *right* girl, clean cunted and pretty like a Show), to bury the dead before they stink up the house, to hoard the riches to spend and buy and use foot creams on calluses. I am an American man. I know of whom I speak. My cock and where I have put it makes it so, makes me so: when I rape the girls (such an ugly word for this doing) when I do it, it is because:

(and here it must stop. I cannot continue. The inquiring leads me astray, into darkness, into death: I do not want to die, Marta.

And I would like to live more than things, more than this house and soft and padded green armchair; more than work or the looks of my neighbors; my teachers; my father's judgment when he beats me for beating my cock day after day; my mother's sorrow and paltry five phrase history for a lost clan and place.)

I HAVE a sadness inside me like an inheritance, like an invisible river. Do you see the shorn face in its reflection? How the river moves the small children's teeth like amulets and a boy's quiet arm his teeth a girl's shorn plaits, like the tortilla flats and palms and the nape, and the emptied lake bed in the Owens Valley which was defrauded then forgotten then reforested by red halobacteria and soda ash: as if my body has been riven, the trees born down, as if the wind could no longer pronounce the names because without the pine, cypress, Reader: where do we leave this essay? We are dead, we say, and unnamed riven, shorn. And each day I make the effort, like girls grind the corn, make the tortilla—see their hands, how beauty resides in the hands of girls and old women—how the dirt and mud then dust will make hands, then reside in the veins of a woman as she makes the masa, makes the food for the family, the veins like tunnels over hands, the earth like plains and then the sadness of fingers (removed), the palms in the mind, when the masa is gone and the children lie quiet from hunger (they no longer cry), and the girls never returned from the soldiers' demands in the Army barracks in Nebaj, howls of hollowed then grieving then buried-up bones—why I can't say it? It is because none of these false prophets of words, makers of girls, then hands that can't hold masa or tor-

tilla because the earth has died, because I am no longer a girl, because the soldiers burnt the hands, then milpa fields, then chickens
and hogs devoured, and time has become a killer too: it is only a
matter of minutes before the boy's blood on page 11 of this book
will clean him of himself washed out with the holocaust which followed the massacre in Acul and he will die. He is dead already,
Reader (and the christ on pages 116, 136, 172). But how, then, do
we proceed apace? Progress? This is an essay against Progress,
this essay does not do it, but like the maze of days of thoughts of
memories and notmemories, like the phrases which tumbled willy-
nilly from a mother's mouth, or an invocation, a song;—repeat
themselves endlessly, without form or with it? again and again and
again, like the days.

Does our sadness make the abyss, its pit (where the men were
shot up and discarded) where there is no respite nor return and
when our sadness is abyssed, and when our women's hands do not
mold or shape the tortilla, and when there is no more light in the
darkness of the mind, then we will die, an unfecund death, the sadness of mists and mountains, and a day without compass—when
they killed your brother, Marta, when your father and the neighbors
from the millennium lined up, machete held high and following the
orders of to kill then you understood, you waited behind the administration building and boys yelled out to closed-up heavens,
that it is more than god who has died today, it is anguish's hand that
reverses a shadow's line, it is a shadow whose soul cannot be unriven. We are finished, you say, after these hundreds of years they
finally finish us; you whisper, weave it into your huipil like colored
comets of sound, huddled up with your mother and sisters and
small boys brothers in the plaza which has already been unholied
by the sounds of Lázaro tied to the tree (you did not see them doing

it, his screams fell into the tympanum as if into a tunnel; you behind the administration building while they are doing it), the men's
howls in the church as they are trampled on by their fathers, uncles,
the old men who dug the pit for their sons, watched death's arrival
in the form of a "You" finger by the masked boy from one village
over—thought until the very last that it was *their* pit they were digging out; their death which awaited them; thought so until they
walked their sons nephews from the church to the grave, hand in
hand, father and son, and led their sons to the fusillade: they saw
their sons and nephews' faces shot apart like glass (and you didn't
see this either, only heard the sounds of the Galils, the imagination
making the men into bees).

[AND WHAT did they do with the grandmother's corpse?, she who
died in the Lebanon thousands of miles from my mother on a
Wednesday, and wars there for sixteen years and my mother had
tried to fix the grandmother's papers so that she could arrive in
America, pass Customs, cross borders, smile at the security guards,
give her Hellos! But she has died again today in Beirut, I can still
hear of her death in the ear, the tympanum's vibration has never
ceased, my mother's wail over the black monster (our telephone)
when she heard that her mother died, heard the UH-1H in the distance, the mortar shells in the distance, her brother saying to her in
their tongue, their language of the vanquished (and Armenian was
never mine, Marta): "Mama died." It is not my mother's face I can
see or even her words that I remember (not the phrase I just gave
you, darling, a phrase I invented from the ether for this essay) but

the sound of her grief that day when I was a boy and you, darling, that girl in the dirt plaza, in front of the church, or the girl on the way to the capital, or the girl in the basement of the Polytechnic: each sad and battered girl, my sad and inexpressible mother's grief: this: howl: this too has been my weight.

(Because they paid a Muslim boy a thousand dollars US to get the rotting (Christian) corpse across town, across the green-line and the divide of the confessions, to the Armenian cemetery in West Beirut and into an unmarked grave.)]

A MAN reduced to collecting corpses, imagine it, Marta. How alone he is, or might be, or feels it, and if only he could open up inside of himself (the shut-down places urges), let the rivers run through him again, take down the rectangular and concrete channel, uplift the dammed parts of his self soul: I am a man, Marta: American: Armenian: or half of some thing, and I have lived this half-life because I have been half-alive, and I say "alive" because of breath, of shit, of the semen on my feet and hands,—but this "half" a terrible approximation in my English for what has been denied me, I denied, for the rigid and rules and moral History theater in the mind: an unfree man in this place, like the tarmacked roads have unfreed the spoors, have pre-determined all routes, the girls on the sides of the road, the animals no longer in an emptied sea, the trees cut down as if no longer gods, the high branches and wide valley springs destroyed: drained and desecrated. And I have tried, or thought that I have, collected these poor pied and lonely bitches on the streets: the dead animal corpses, which in my mind I lifted into my arms and gently, sweetly, placed them into my motorcar, drove them over the highways freeways and streets to home and buried each in the garden with ceremony and pompous god-like invocations, incense, candles and cried out songs: to live, Marta. To feel that I am a man and not a manikin of three functions making roads or making business calls or counting up the numbers like days until vacation until television Shows until week-ends until disease and then death: an ugly man, lonely like my brethren, these Americans, burdened by their things and desperate in thingéd lonelinesses and the heft of too much material, no spirit or love or sex with the outside gods—That the corpses could make it clear, their decaying forms evidence or a juxtaposition to my breath, my life-force, my very own tiny soul which has slipped out from them—it is obvious when you see it and yet until the corpse is confronted then the half-dead may continue it, his half-living—which is to say, this poor and approximate "half"; that he has not been allowed to be what he is, and not what he ought to be, or tried to be, or wished or denied or pushed off into the groin, ground. His own self, not halves or quarters or tiny segmented variances: but himself as he is: lusty, jealous, kind, petty, cruel, greedy, compassionate and violent: a god and his adam, urge and urge and urge: to make to do to fuck like dogs in the streets with his own cock in his hands because this is pleasure, because he is a man, because it is the real and not a Show or decorum's the rule's the religion's the historian's the teacher's idea: is.

We have made capital, we have undone clans, and yours and mine undone or altered or unfamed and unframed by History, by conquerors, by men in green and white uniforms. In a small town in the desiccate and treeless plane of Anatolia, the other in the green grey Cuchumatanes, the clouds like girls, the mist is heavier than written History there. And this too I would like not to have known: that my mother's my grandmother's blood made a river in me: of their sorrows their electric pain and desires transmitted by time or blood itself or into the eyes through glassy fields of fire. I tried to be the good American boy: obedient, good, clean and clean-smelling: not ever ugly and fat and his sex like a rocket and his needs like rockets and watch TV (don't open your soul like a mouth to be eaten and to eat) and go to work (don't touch your cock at staff meetings or finger the girls) and weed the garden, shop the foods, pick up laundries and play games inside rules: don't break them: the rules, the regimen: shit is dirty; sex is dirty and good dirty: but don't open your ass for it; let the girls inside of it; want to be made into a woman like madonna and child and you the both of them to-gether in unison: the madonna, the child. No. Be good. Obedient. A Citizen. You are free here (don't break the laws and rules). This is Liberty (or open your ass for viewing). Be on Time. Stay within boundaries. These girls are the beautiful girls with big tits and blond hairs; don't see the eyes, don't lick their cunts or licking them don't like to do it. Happy? Yes you are happy and fulfilled and proper-tied. And free inside your maze, what you think reasonable, the judge—the body could be a motorcar, fix it up, paint it, crop and fashion it right (urge and urge and urges denied); the body a ma-chine to be done and redone, taken apart and put back together again (even Humpty-Dumpty will have a happy ending here!).

You will become a sick man here, Marta. We are the sick and lonely adams, you our eves so far from us, these thousand satellite balls not touching but unable, also, to disperse.

TODAY I don't love you or make you or write you up like a good grammarian. Today I am sicker; my organs perhaps, this pain in the lower back which does not abate now—what could it be but your specter taken up residence there? You sly and small and a black girl in my kidney, these black flies in my liver, and the bile your black hiding places in this body which also, and no matter the preservations and good meats and good vitamined cerealed things—it too demises, cracks down, makes fissures in the spit and blood; we all die, Marta;—I have died today; there was pain.

I am drunk now, altered. I have had five and six glasses of whiskey and I cannot see clearly or straight; this blind drunkard ambles over to his white pages and fills them up with his ceaseless machinations, his fingers which even dying must make and make and actively (he sits quietly speaks to no one) a girl, seeks her, will find the dead amidst the ruins, in the interstitial rivers, the interstitial tissues; his body, more, his imagination; this beyond where she may live. So I have called you on the telephone again, a retrieval of sorts. And you are speaking to me, your "Hellos darling" and you are talking about the weather and about your children and a small illness your boy has found at school like a stone, you say, children pick up diseases like stones; and there below the river-din, somewhere in the atmosphere, I can comprehend your meaning but not the language you are speaking (is it Ixil you harangue me with? or the Castilian of the overlords and the owners of things and the plantations and the capital? or English for this boy, his Protestant roles and rules of decorum, proper freedoms) but I understand you, darling; I can understand your tone like the music-listener knows joy or terror in the symphony and (do you love me?) and you tell me about your day and about your husband and three or four sentences more in one of the languages you might be speaking in, this language a river above my body, outside the body, and I can understand your sentiment by your tone and I can see, a blind man now, that the end is coming approaching and that whatever I have been for you is done for today and I drink more and more of christ's bloody symbols and the river rises, a blood river in Acul, and overflows its banks and then more sentences until our destiny is finally revealed by you because you my god and good-bye and this good-bye my death knell and I am lonelier sadder and then the river rises, takes me over the mountains and down into the valley where you live, on the west side of the Cuchumatanes; submerged now; and the tympanum bursts and good-night and godspeed and I whisper back this good-bye as I put the receiver into the black plastic cradle; stagger to bed; boy, staggers; dies like a good and sleeping dead man.

I HAVE ALWAYS wanted to be free. My earliest memories of school not of the playground, the tarmac and dusty undirted places where we children ran about, kicking one another, trotting up one another's backsides: lying, screaming, the strong ones beat the weak, the look of the dumb fat boys and ugly weak-eyed girls: not of this. I have memories of the window frames; sashes for my guards: the outside world pictured through glass; rectangle of metal grey: a slice of lintel, sky; sliver of the possible blue and uncropped

Washingtonias in the distance; and the *to come*; and the invisible wind shuttling the leaves and lonely girls, their hair unribboned, pulled back like horses' tails. I wanted out: of the classroom; the droning noise; the ridiculous time spent watching a clock mock its way ever so slow, like the end of time, to watch time move mechanical, toward the hours, the 10s, 12s; and the free weather beyond the glass; lunchtime in the distant future; and for now the harrowing 9s, and the slow moments delimited by the red second hand on the white clock face. When I was not fixed on the machine, I made page upon page of sailboats, like this ⛵; the teacher-voice, absurd, abused the boys like yellow bruises, her voice overlies the boats in the margins of my book.

The boats the only transport I could make into a form; I'm not able to make the world in pictures: then the waves and tiers and slants of the slopes: all of it askance so obviously, only, possibly, the hint of the thing, like this ⛵〜.

Can you see it? The me I was then; a boy in his slouch; a girl with unplaited hair sits to his left, she is unlucky and unpretty; untucked shirt; the dirty hands, mouth; scraped knees; scared to death of the boy in the first row and his friends; scared of them; of the teacher teaches, the drone of her voice like jets above them; of the night; ghosts; the dead;—his boaty dreams, or are they hers? the unplaited girl's: a night-dream of freedom's ride. And when I finished school, and the gates were unlocked and the fat lady principal left behind: then I was free; but it was a freedom of small cages: a freedom to work and work and the television blares loudest all of these years since then: I do not know death, it hides on the television Shows behind adventure and loves; I've not had silence as the sea, and loneliness, yes, not a man's salt solitude; I've been conscripted, a contrivance of the damned; I'm happy fat-happy and the desolate lives in the bones like the television girls scream their screams of murder and lusty days. I've not had what I longed for then: the girls the moneys the long idle days when work is a dream and a lawyer looks happy and fit as he fights on the television's showed rituals; I've had the rule of clocks, of the Gregorian days, which is not to eat when I am hungry or sleep when the sun has set: it is never to follow the sun's light *in my own place*, but rather a different place, not mine, here I can't name ten local species, do not know the name (or the people) "Gabrielino"; have not known or seen the spoors that the Gabrielinos told Crespí and his men about all those years ago as they passed through the basin of my birth on their way northward to seek the bay of Monterey.

I'll not open up my belly soft-side for you; turn me over like a conch; give you the soft bleating sheep's skin, my hard-head think-ing. You'll kill me. Love me to death; or worse: take your love out of us, a love we cannot make together, Marta—I am the sold soli-tary beast: the city; you; umarked days and untocking clocks clos-ing the hours down, closing down the days like a shopkeeper closes the doors at the o'clock: I am made rough and harshly lighted: a man without a white-night belly; a man filled of remorse and lost things, he would like to discover some of what was lost a century ago, yet the lost and the losing are like the Pilgrims, these myths with their plastic black and white construction paper costumes for school holidays, who themselves thought that time, like the weather, belonged to God and that it must be improved upon by men in their work and worship. It is lost, and the losses themselves lost: erased, beyond memory, like seas of silence, like the black seas that once covered the North American continent, the large brachiopods in black and mute formations now in the museums of distant histories, and their 440 million year old stone paintings beautiful on the walls of what is surmised once was. It is this beyond he seeks; he seeks love in the same fashion. Like he loved that unpretty, unplaited and recklessly untidy girl in the second grade, in a school on the top of a hill, the Washingtonias in the far distance, the tarmac yard—he's returned there—driven the thin mountain road, and he can see the San Fernando Valley stretched out to the San Gabriel Mountains and the Santa Monica Mountains below his feet and he drives along Mulholland Dr and notices a view he'd never noticed as a boy and remembers the man whose history he never knew also: Mr Mulholland who "brought the water" from the Owens Valley, and today Owens Lake is a desert and the dead shelled fish making their fossils for the future gay men in science and history.

Yes, Marta. I loathed them: the school, the rules for the downtrodden, the dumb beastly American citizen: who buys, who is happy when he sleeps in Freedom's comfortable bed, beaten into us not with rod blows (the rod outlawed by the time of my schooling) but with the same kind of rod death blows to the imagination: freedom's boat-ride curtailed except upon the margins of lined school paper (or freedom's boat-ride invented because of this paper?). But listen, this does not mean I was a failure at school, in fact I was the best student, yes dragged to it daily by my mother and then: head of the class. A good and pious scholar! How else could I begin this conversation with you now? How else could I have the words to make it? It is reasonable, historical, a hunch in the mind, this my foray; never something I could think, but not thinking it, I remember you and then me. In school, we learned it all: Progress, Freedom, Savages, Destiny, and America.

WHAT DO you do without your enemy? You must make him like you, make dolls monsters of paper words and papier-mâché: he's your mirror form, distorted, his nose pulls the other way; his face misshapen; shaded, an off hue made-up—make him to do your work; make him up; he should carry the Master's wife on his back up the mountain trails deep into the jungles of the imagined rape scene. He rapes the girl and then says to the husband that she was happy while he did it. And then the enemy, this small and hungry man, carries the Master's wife from here to there, up and down the mountainside. Together they propagate the world; the world is a bastard's barn, and the kittens tired of being tied in rucksacks and tossed into the sea, into the lakes, into the puddle marshes, and drowned: we won't allow it any longer, they say, we will fight the Masters to the death.

It does come round. Or it doesn't change, or history is merely a revolution of the evolving same, a circle for the cosmos' humorous days; the menstruation of time; the circumference of pain suffering and the dancing monsters; the die in the blood death marches—here and up down the mountainside, the man, stooped and old and without enough food for comfort these many years (stone-hungry; one egg a month in the good months before war): he is yours mine, he tells history repeatedly; he is silent; quiet; he is loud, he stands in line while the machete'd Kaibiles sharpen their blades, or worse, leave them dulled: a dull blade for the most painful wrench of the kill. Blood time, blood marks time; this endless *o*.

Why the need, Marta, this where I am dumbfounded, dumb

like the dumb soft Indian I've made for you: he's a doll: indio'd up on the page: why the need to make monsters before you behead them with the dulled and rusty implement for cutting coffee? You see: here and there and here and there it is the same: a pregnant girl, she is your neighbor, she is nineteen years old, say, and here she is dark-skinned, I say *dark* because I think it today. The man, her killers, are also dark-skinned, but different, we know, because it is so; we made it like this. One is this man, one is that one over there behind him (the Lieutenant holds the 9mm to the first man's neck): the first man holds a machete, holds his blade, the man is power-ful, he has fucked the girl for five or six minutes (and he was not the first or the eighth) and she has whimpered like an animal and she has cried out in her dumb language, the language of the dead (which he does not speak cannot hear)—oh Master, she says, have your pity on *me*. And here and there there is not pity; there are monsters; there is a 9mm pistol: there is a monster in her belly and the blood must run out of her cunt for posterity, for the patria. He takes his blade, she looks at him, she prepares stares him in the eye when he's doing it, she'll make him see it, she thinks,—and for the moment of looking his shame, his horror, is the black wingéd bird of his childhood nightmares, his mother's wrenching of the teat from his seeking desirous lips: she left him with the plantation owner when he was six: a millisecond perhaps, in the arc of the de-scending and dulled knife, steel hot as it removes each teat. He reaches down now, like a reasonable surgeon, a scientific inquiry, he cuts her belly open wide like a mouth (his own mouth unham-pered, wide, a vagina without speech) and picks the babe out of the womb like gods will descend to make rains; like gods will make sunlight; feasts; a harvest of flesh. He pricks it and tosses it up— machete's it for his friend's amusement, like the carnival days of be-

fore when the calendar was a moon calendar, and time was imme-
morial. Does the babe cry out once and thrice before he is sliced up
like pork roast? I did not read it in a magazine: the baby is sliced
up and left on the stones in pieces of himself, in Acul, *like pork
roast*. Or is this the same babe from page 168, the killer's momentary son whose head was cracked open against the stones (he almost
had a son once). You decide, Reader: in the Ixil Area they killed the
pregnant girls and babes like this and this.

YOU HAVE BEEN in the mountains fifteen months (and I wouldn't
have lasted a fortnight); you have fought with the Army of the
Poor; Doña Ana is beheaded by the Cessna's rage and bombs (O
machine, here unraging men make havoc and kill from the distance
that aeroplanes allow). Tell me what you see; what happens to the
eye when it sees the new mother's body slain like a goat: the tod-
dler smashed upon the river rocks; the oldest son's chest slashed
with his father's machete; the neonate your hands have suffocated
(to save all of us, they say—the palm is a weapon in a world at war);
the seven girls like small black-haired christs on the road to the
capital, they too are eviscerated for the patria. When can the eye
cease its seen, and once seen now forever unpullable from the soul's
eye—the nightmare's vision night after night they will return to
you, your dead and the dead which you do not own or claim, their
bones revisit you in the darkness, in the mind, inside this life which,
although a dream, kills each child each night for eternity—this lifetime within a soul's limits; the girls' cries, your mother's final
scream as she falls, with your brother, into the river, the babe as he

sighs in your arms, all of the children that day in Acul are screaming—the tympanum over-taxed now; it derails like a train, pulls back from physics and refuses to vibrate any longer.

I HAD the sentences and then forgot them, but unable, always, to comprehend them, as if and although spoken in English, they were in a different tongue, a barbarian's iconic language.

What was my mother saying with this tongue? Who this "They" dark and horrifying; who this "She" young and sad? And to which night was she referring? To which days? As if five sentences could in any way begin to make a map for the world my mother hid and also served up as foods, smells, longings, a different language on long-distance phone calls to the Lebanon, and her own dead mother who lay dying, then died, denying her daughter the last sighting of motherly flesh. O to kiss you one more time, Mother; how my mother wailed when her mother died.

"You are half-Armenian," his mother would tell him as a boy, as if this could explain or mean anything to him in America. He ignored her sentences and ran in packs with the neighborhood boys; ate kumquats and oranges and pomegranates from the orchards on their street; took yellow Blue Bird buses to schools; said his name shyly and then learned to say and then begin to spell it automatically—for teachers, shop clerks, new friends, girls at parties whom he so dearly wanted to fuck more and more. A foreign name? they sometimes inquired, although he himself for himself was American and ran in packs, had sleepovers, collected plastic figurines.

[And he half-listened for years to his mother's phrases and then notlistened and then forgot them, for years, until you arrived, Marta, with the dog corpse on the side of the 405 Freeway: girl from the ether, made of ether also.]

I SEE the whitewashed church first built in 1678; the portal is blue this year (1982) and this is not the original structure (I am excavating around the rocks rivers of lost and distant idea'd time). I see the old tree in front of the church. The administration building and the plaza which is no plaza. In the distance the clouds hang on the hills in the morning (like girls). It rains; my hands are cold in the cold river water; we wash the clothes every six day. Here it rains in the winter summer months; here the clouds and the easterlies bring rain and two milpa harvests each year—the mists of the Altos Cuchumatanes remind us that the gods—neglected, battered, they are lonely and silent, embarrassed, *we made them into dogs we are not dogs, men*—have not abandoned us here to this History; we long for our pre-History, which is to say all of the other times of living: maize, the mind, circular and free.

YOUR Guatemala has changed me and then it cannot be yours because can a dog be a citizen of the nation?—this invention, this *Goatemala*, as foreign to you as the men in the capital who have taken you down and then further down the recesses of pain. Not made by you, has not been yours; the invention of an idea, of men

who write History books as I write this book to you which is no letter, but a set of treatises, manuals and fables about why: I long to
lick your back; the *naturales* are dogs; the dogs are rickety-boned
and tail-tucked, you turn your eyes down in shame and when the
soldier who is from another region, his broken Spanish slams into
your face as he slams his cock blades into your cunt, puto he says,
when you know that the sun is masculine and burns into eyes that
don't close, because, you decide, you will look at the man who has
been made into a blade, a rickety-boned blade, an awkward
Castilian metal, a boy (and you could have loved a boy) who is
older than your brothers, and younger than your brother, whose
eyes have become suns (we laugh together at this harsh lying poetry): whose eyes are brown, then black, and opaque gods do not
reside there while he fucks you bloody, dirty, dead then—but you
don't die, it is not the only death, and there are more and there are
the mountains and there is the neighbor girl you carried on your
back and the boy you carried in your belly and the child whose
hand you held dragging her running up into the mountains, and
there are more and there is more (a palm which kills your son nine
months later; a breast which cannot save Doña Ana's boy five
months after that (the milkless worthless titty)), and I couldn't see
it, Marta, and I was watching the television and I was saddened by
the girls who would not fuck me at the cocktail parties, who turned
from me in disgust—fat ugly undiginified and dirty—who, when
I walked into the shop gave me their eyes as if their eyes could
make looks like steel and a chemical look, a look that made the
body detestable, made this boy lonelier and then more lonely: have
I said it enough? that I am an ugly man, a fat man, a whorish man
and I have been monstrous—and I only have the women I can pay
for; the girls I pay to speak with on the telephone; my skin pock-

marked, my teeth matted and grey, and I am fatter and my cock is smaller and this is the man who does not bring the girls at the fiesta, and this the man who is shy to return such a look of loathing (why this loathing look from them, these vile and beautiful girls: what have I done for such a look? Why this look of hate from the beautiful? When what I want and have always wanted . . .)

I do not wish to see: this you beside the administration building, his eyes are brown and the opaque pieces of his iris spill onto the whites, his black fingernails, his look of rage (like the epic hero's rage), he is a hero for the nation; he doesn't look into your eyes, won't look, while he fucks you. Let me say how beautiful you are (I am a man who admires the beautiful its horror and its music and the cunt is beautiful; the fat sticking thighs, an ass haired and unhaired (by the girls in my city) and the half-shaven cunt hairs: all of it I can love) your clothing and the plastic sandals, they are not broken yet, and the colors woven into your hair, your huipil looks like something beautiful and happy: the hummingbirds tell the old myth of jealousy of love on your blouse: the barbarians are happy in Paradise, a savage couture. Why does the blood enter into my reveries of Paradise, beautiful and bare-nippled girls, a soldier who kindly takes her hand, kisses her fingers like stars and moons—all of his words said correctly and true with the victor's tongue which has become common to the place—Guatemala and our Americas have become places—like the eucalyptus on the hillsides near my home become commonplace, and in the canyons of dust and distant memories I am searching then for love's intersection and locale: for you. Are you here in my Americas? They are mine, I have been made here and I have been schooled and I have posited questions, Marta, to all of the learned men in university, and the late-night p.m. store clerks, and the men holding their hands over the cash register's gleam and guns can be wider and I continue apace: why are we, then, these miasmic tale-tellers? Because fictions are the bones of these Americas? Mine own fictions? America is built like a tall limestone monument, like tarmac roads and highways, like the dirt plaza where your brother your uncles and (where is your father? he is alongside the pit by the new cemetery, he will die in two days' time of this *susto*). America is no more real than those places, than these places of worship—we do not exist, no, but killers can wrong can be fictional tales, and still the machinated machining up of the world does not abate; progress of the fabled Progress, monuments to the new gods.

Marta: this is true and this is real—I am an ugly man: I am sick and my kidneys pain me; a horror; and I sit here in a padded and green armchair and I am eating ice cream and good and white flour and white sugar sweetened and my belly has never been empty or fatigued from eating mountain grasses and leaves and falls over my belt and hides my penis and not-shitting from the grasses and roots we ate today in the mountain if lucky and without luck the child on your back has died and then the girl in your hand has gone away (she was killed? or she couldn't keep up with the fleeing villagers?) and then not even the watery roots today or the UH-1H helicopters can be heard or you can build a small fire if the clouds hang low enough to conceal the smoke; there are bombs; there is a girl in the pit of the capital, sees the christ's penis removed, and lungs like bells in the tree towers, and none of it, Marta, changed any one thing in your mountain, on my chair. The mountain, you whispered, saved us. Did your geography save you? make you? did your Tierra Fría do that? Does topography save a girl who runs high and the rains come down for months and the plastic sandals are broken now and the toenails blacken, then fall out, and the forehead swells with the animals who are small and live beneath the skin, making mountains in your flesh, make hunger for absent gods, hunger for which the gods were killed, they came like the torrential rains, then bombs, then flesh torn apart and you are running higher and higher, and like an animal, you say, we lived in the mountains: without food, shelter for the babes, fire, and when the babes were birthed in the mountain the mothers cut the umbilical cord with their teeth and they did not tie the ends off: a baby dies quickly this way, you tell me, you whisper it in my ears in Los Angeles and I cannot hear you I have not been able to hear these bone-words because it is late, it is the middle of the night—it is effortless to kill a child like this, you say (how many children died in those mountains, Marta? by their mothers' hands, the Cessna A37-B bombs, the hunger and thirst and no medicines: dysentery is a killer also). Do we take these whores for killers then? Should we string them up in town squares, run the gasoline into a discarded black tire, hang the tire around the whores' bent necks and burn the savage dirty blood from our eyes (like suns) which can't see, will not make light? Not me, darling. I am sitting in my green armchair and I am eating ice cream and watching the Shows and I am happy and if the bombs fall onto your skin, as if this were possible—show me the proof of it? who would do such a thing?— and if the roots you dig up are desiccate today and so today you are denied the teaspoonful of root-water that the mountain gives self- ishly as if obsessed (by demons, by the light not-shines, by your dead) and if—then no; and no; I may switch the channels, watch a comedy, it blares loudest inside my middle ear like black flies, like the small animals that have burrowed beneath your skin, made their shelters there on your forehead, made carnal mountains, a new and bodied topos—you the deformed god when you come down the mountain naked and absented shoes which plastic and broken lie up in the mountains with the bones of the children then fathers then neighbors and old men (the old men die quickly in the cold). The dogs arrive! they say, as you walk through the central square in Nebaj, and your shame is like Eve's, yes, Marta, give this rib back to me for a penance. Give me your flesh, this man, this ugly and fat and small-cocked man would like you, seeks you, writes you up in his America while his History lessons continue apace on the television (of Liberty and the freedom of Freedoms and a democratic cunt wish) will devour it, will return to your cunty paradise in America, beneath the humus of your flesh—the mountain's gift of root waters. In paradise the suffering is real and you no more real than this unreadable and unread book (will you read it, Reader? Do you?). Who would care, desire, read such a fable; and who enough time in America from the Real to spare a lonely fictional man his foliol due?

IT MATTERS little if I have chosen you, or you have chosen me— this fatter and sick man in Los Angeles, the dead Ixil girl in Acul, in the capital. It is a wide sadness which binds us; I can't bear it sometimes, Marta, the heft of it, heavier than anger, which is a killer, yes—Achilles' rage a renown—but for Priam, you and me, we must bear our lonely weights of the unglorious vanquished days, and such a thing as massacre on 22 April, 1982, in Acul, and walking into Nebaj naked and starved, each chestbone a marker on skin, and the capital basement and the man eating the maggots from his wounds because he is hungry, angry, and his rage does not make History or my grandmother who died in a war one week before she was coming to America, her young mother ate the old grasses of the Der Zor in the summer 1915 in a different war, and her father was disappeared in the night, and (you also disappeared, Marta) my own foreign mother who made for herself an American boy, and tried to cut the sadness histories from her memory and family-history like fat and unattractive ulcers (but for the five bare phrases, which fell out of her mouth and into English, as if without volition, the bones of the story). The American man is made into a modern monster; a man without a place or any of a history's heft (its rage perhaps?), filled with raw unmapped places which could be like rats, eat his love's lips and facial tissues, and make the days long, and desperate he eats fucks buys the petrol for his motorcar, goes to movies amusement parks parties in bars—but whence his mal-adie? malaise? He does not know its past as if the past were still de-vouring him; the rats; he does not know that he is a sick man, a tired man, his kidneys fail him daily; he has died also; he lives in Los Angeles. And if he is sad he does not know it (eats an ice cream); if he is lonely he cannot say why (buys his things, machines); hun-gry, eats and buys whores, wives, ugly girls at the shop, fucks eats buys and watches the television screen for fun for masks he can't see which he likes to place on top of his face, his own fat face leak-ing blood beneath the too tight disguises.

MARTA, *I am in the shower and you do not shower or bathe in porce-lain plastic tubs because the water is a walk to the river in Acul and be-cause electricity comes to you via the air (rubbed against the cloth of your skirt, or lightning) the candles not made from electrical wires and so I am cleaning myself with chemical soaps and you say to me who is this me that is making you:* what is your name? *And I am struck by how it is that distance and names and what happens like a fish swims in the sea before it is struck from the sea, does not and do not hinder how we can be lovers, be* in love, *like this small unruly sea animal.*

All of the Martas in the world cannot change the Martas from before. And all of the rivers cannot make new rivers in the desert if the thousands of miles that separate this river this desert is thicker than a dream, than you are here in your mind which is my mind, makes you, loves you

no.

There is nothing more terrible than this story you are relating, its cover-ups and its impossible desires returns, my body like a river for your journey—to where I can now have this name, his name, I'll speak to you speak back in your language which is not your maternal tongue or mine but: which progress do you follow? What gods are guiding your critiques and what will the critics say to this, to you, a man who pulls savages and whores out of his hat his codpiece better to elucidate his: passions; his: acumen; his: zeal to atone for the sins of the fathers (the Indians of my city, Marta, invisible boys and massacred girls); his: loneliness and sorrow—his gods require it? or does he only love what cannot be his, like a river loves the flood course it strives for every five year, it remembers and longs for the paths of its youth, old alluvial fans, is this why you speak me? make fatty soups for your dinner with my bones?

Who is speaking and who listens?

Do you speak on these blank pages? Does the dampness of time and the books I read and don't read, I am a pilferer of books, of History, Shows, I am seeking you in these pages and pull the pages out of me like my semen is pulled out by your mouth your teeth touch my testicles, make love, pull out the seed, make sentences from syllables which are the gods' ways of saying: "Yes"; and this push fuck spit inside, blood and put it all together, a juxtaposition of juxtapositions. An enigmatic yes. In our languages yes is a one syllable sound, like the sound my mouth makes when the semen rushes forth—into the river?—into her heavenly cunt, like holy spit.

AND BECAUSE eight miles up in the air inside the aeroplane coming toward the city I can see places without men edifices and this comforts me—like your Cuchumatanes—a place of quiet, there are animals, and red carpets of poppies, and snows and clouds and a refuge for the Ixil girl and a place that man does not either desire to, or simply does not, tread (yet).

And I saw the wild poppies from the sky—a glorious red gloaming lifted toward my blind and dumb metallic sight. I am returning from the capital of my country, my journey there at the beginning of this book.

And some anguish for these squares and rectangles in the distant dust, caravan of earth, and carved onto earth, and now the housed concreted and streeted place comes into view—alas, you purple groves! Alas you sycamore and elderberry, the cottonwood girls by the riparian dreams—willow and wild grape.

Where does the end of the city begin? And where do ends begin, if this is, in fact, our end arriving these years. The age of Greed, of TO BE: Entertained!, will have its day, its demise is definite, and you and I, darling, will not be witness, hammocky days await us, two lovers, unstartled and perhaps benighted by stars to become victors in a conflict where the weak, the lovely, the sad girls have stayed behind in the dark wells, these black and fetid pits; and the boy in Los Angeles knows it is wrong, these corpses rotted and fetid in his car, takes them to the rendering factory and sweet disavowal and dissolving their meat with heat, makes food for the living dogs. The Los Angeles dream will have its fin—ah, what views and ideas the aeroplane affords the man! Such a comfort, his bible, his apocalypse.

I see the river now and it looks like a highway from the air—a concrete artery in the tarmac place; browngrey air; the closer we come I cannot see—o automiled paradise! You have won our hearts and we prostrate ourselves on your metal palladium, the altar is finished with reds and blues; the closer we come the dirtier the garbaged places there are Washingtonias and cars yellow buses trucks and cars.

THIS what you whisper in my ear, the tympanum descends and then ascends to your syllables like a hand in prayer, a man entering and leaving a tunnel: they do kill it us and the babes suspended by the umbilical cords like dolls from plastic ribbons and the blood is a new river here and the mother's opened belly and still the soldier keeps her legs spread apart to fuck her again and again, the babe pulled out, her viscera spread out also, a wide red mass of dying girls;—it did not happen, they say. "We did nothing," (shoving the knives into eyes throats behind each tender ear; they pulled a boy's teeth like stones). "Not us: the guerrilla did it; the subversives have caused it." The Cessna A37-B flies above your heads in the mountains and you are half-naked while they say it in all of the capital cities newspapers of our countries, while Misters Ríos Montt and Reagan have dinner and hot coffees in December 1982. Seven months after that, you will walk down the mountain and into the Army barracks in Nebaj. You are always hungry cold, and the mountain, the Army, defeats you.

There is, of course, our continual refusal to see in America; or rather: a cowardice of the half-dead who don't want must not needs see it; say it; read it in a book, perchance; a television Show!; but not this sees, for once seen I too become the marked child; the sons of Cain, his mark on my forehead, and the skullish nightmares and the bones your viscera, each day's horror—an unreturnable inheritance: to see it, dear Marta, to know how you suffered in Acul, in the mountains, in the Army barracks in Nebaj, behind the yellow and white painted bars in Chimaltenango, in the pit in the basement of the Polytechnic: the knowing changes nothing, changes no American man in Los Angeles. I listen to the News; you are not in the News; Mr Reagan is in the News and I am happy; he appears happy; you are running, hungrier, seeking this teaspoonful of water in the roots of small plants; the bombs rain down upon your heads from time to time.

the whys: because

the first time is a transgression and the rules and the Good and we all of us think (the Lieutenant holds the 9mm to my head while I take the knife to your belly) that God's wrath will descend; that we will hear the toll of evil and the bells of injustice and our mothers will slap us and Gabriel remove our old and tired crown and we will . . . die or suffer, and we do not either die or disregarding the bell's toll (it is not for me), we pull the knife across one and then another man's throat, and there is glee in the carnage, at the meat carnival, and what does a man look like, how will he squeal, when the eyes are removed with small teaspoons? and the penis taken off with a coffee cutter's tool, fired first, red metal, and *how* his howls? will they make the gods descend? (no) And if I toss this girl's breast into the evergreen? and her babe's torso alongside it, to suckle a corpse! then do not turn your head in disgust, do not curtail the gaze or allow the eyes to move off the page for the barbarian on the page as he machetes murders all of the innocents and the culpable in Acul in the capital city in the basement of the patria—what are you, Reader, in your comfortable and naked green armchair? What, pray, do you toss into your dreams of a night when you can no longer run from the mediocre the modicum of your life, the ways in which this living has killed you and not only our poor and dear and dead Marta girl, the Ixil girl who walked on the ancient dirt paths from Acul over the hills and down into Nebaj; who faced the soldiers in the plaza with her shy and sad eyes; her naked form; who walked among you, boarded the Blue Bird and traveled to the capital and then later up to this city and into my dreams imagination, which is to say, into me—into us now.

[To adventure, Reader! to war! You could fight for the cause; and you could defeat the sweet enemy at your doorstep, save the patria from the invading (communist like a flower) hordes, the barbarians arriving at the gate and . . . didn't we do it during the Cold War, and didn't we win it, dear Sirs? And doing it, in our dreams, did you see what it *is?* like a small child wails in front of her butchers, not knowing the time of the clock or days or more than hunger and sorrow; she is pulled from a brother's arms, her head is smashed on stones, her brother sees it; he lives and then lives with the memory of the sister he could not save, her childish skeleton chases him in his dreams for decades. Later he may become a farmer or soldier or cherry picker in your city, and the girl's screams do not abate for this boy and in this lifetime.]

   why didn't you save me?

BOOK FIVE

One must realize that in pre-Colombian times there were 130,000 Indians in California. California itself had about 16 per cent of the aboriginal population of the United States by comparison with 5 per cent of the land area. Even at this minimum estimate, the density of Indians in California was three to four times greater than the nation as a whole. No one knows precisely how many Indians were living in California in 1848; but the best estimates range from 72,000 (Dr. S. F. Cook), to 100,000 (J. Ross Browne). By 1865, however, the number of Indians in California had been reduced to 23,000 and, by 1860, to 15,000. As these figures indicate, California "solved" its Indian problem by liquidating the Indians.

—CAREY MCWILLIAMS, *California: The Great Exception*

To yield entirely to love would be to be absorbed, which is the death of the individual: for the individual must hold his own, or he ceases to be "free" and individual. So that we see, what our age has proved to its astonishment and dismay, that the individual *cannot* love. The individual cannot love: let that be an axiom. And the modern man or woman *cannot* conceive of himself, herself, save as an individual. And the individual in man or woman is *bound* to kill, at last, the lover in himself or herself. . . . The Christian *dare not love*: for love kills that which is Christian, democratic, and modern, the individual. The individual *cannot* love. When the individual loves, he ceases to be purely individual. And so he must recover himself, and cease to love. It is one of the most amazing lessons of our day: that the individual, the Christian, the democrat *cannot* love. Or, when he loves, when she loves, he *must* take it back, she *must* take it back.

—D. H. LAWRENCE

I am in a motorcar and driving. The motorcar itself is the metal of solitudes and plastics, I can see my citizens through glass and see them cut their skin with metals, but I cannot smell them on the highways, do not love them from me; cannot hear their breath or sense the degrees of strong and less-strong loves, angers, we are close in proximity, the six feet of car-lane space, but it is an un-peopled void that I travel in as I drive even though there are people; the cars make solitude; make a man wish he were a girl to take all of the boys on the corners in the trucks inside of herself, and find fight this separation of metals glass and my inability to speak to you, Marta, and to my wife when she was my wife, and my own mother; O sorrow, have you always arrived in an automobile? Why do you drive it up the driveway and into the modern's home, sit on his sofa drinking sweet drinks and chewing candies.

I call you on the telephone and it is black night in the car. You pick up and you speak to me in your language, which could have been a language from Europe, but instead is something American, foreign to me, an unfree speech. Do you see how poorly we essay into us, darling? You thousands and then more than miles gone from me, and I am driving these streets and cursing the other drivers, hit my fists on the steering wheel and door handles and seek speed and I can't have it because there are more and more cars trucks buses on the freeway and we are not moving on the streets of this city and the motorcar was the dream of independence and freedom's individual ride and a man alone in his vehicle could go here to there as he wished it; and we have made so many things, so much thingéd possibility here, so that we see more and more of it: the girls, the boxes, the Shows, clothes, machinery and poisons for the insect hordes which are killing our flowers, making noise in our ears, I have bought the insecticide and I kill them for posterity for Progress to eliminate what is undesirable, stinks—the shit-eaters corpse-eaters and this man then become the corpse-collector, a diptera girl himself now, because all that I think here I have not thought in reality; I have worked at my job and I have worn a suit jacket and trousers and a blue tie like my president; and I have driven the car over the Santa Monica Mountains along the 405 Freeway to work each day and the meetings and the men who sit at tables and cross their legs adjust their cocks and none of us speaking of you, our fathers mothers and the girls we would like to put our cocks into desperately, we the desperate moderns, who are making copies, money, counting the time of the clock minutes, contained in buildings held to our chairs and everything is counted out and down and we are happy with our houses things and things TO DO! tightly knit girls and do not miss the sun the loud ruckus rivers our unshod feet on the ground (these ancient spoors) the birds above us and wormy beetled soils or running loosely and laughing like stars and the canopy of heaven is farther gone and I never knew it, have not missed the heavens above me to then imagine the underworld where I now reside fitfully, the flies un-vanquished here, the corpses staring angry into my car's thresholds.—Can you imagine another animal that denies its de-sires, needs, to itself so vigorously, academically, in philosophy and religion—in schools homes and offices? Makes morals for Sunday repast. Builds edifices of TO DO and fashion to fashion the man into another thing, a factory worker, businessman, a man who buys to shut out the trees and stars and urge, and his own fire.

How I would speak with the dead—for what purpose: for company, perhaps, accompaniment, because the whiskeys and girls and highs and Shows make this small space where you could reside, come in and speak with me, tell me whence I come and to where to what I might travel; speak me and speak to me; allow me to rest myself on the spoors, and seeing and a slight knowing of what has been and before the sorrow river can overtake me, kill me, deaden me, you take my hand and walk with me in the mountains, whisper in my ear of what is possible and you are with me, holding my ephemeral hands, and you love me, accompany me, Marta, and the nights are not so lonely, the interstitial days when I look into the mirrors in bathrooms and the moment of seeing myself and knowing my loneliness and making, then, this essay of you of me, seek you in my solitude so that we are together in the capital and Acul and in Los Angeles—I could save you and you could accompany me—a small gift for the both of us, and a daring trade, that the un-exiled girl, the girl whose hands they removed like stones, and teeth and small children and her history stories and Diego de Landa burnt the books, made her into an animal for his perusal, she made into a girl I could never see, then essayed here and still unseeable, a failure perhaps amidst the folios, the bombs of war reign down supreme, and the strong always prevail and justice is a small and tiny wish from below the river and you and I along the river-banks now, you hold my dewy blank hand and I lick your fingers and press your belly which could make inside of it my own son, and the exiled man kisses you now, tries to know better, to be better, but all of this, any of it, between the sun's light streaming from his kitchen window to the living room, as he makes his way back to the television Shows and *feels something* and reduces it to foods he would like to eat, a new machine he could buy, and sits in his green armchair with the blaring recorded noises in front of and behind him.

THEY DID WIN, Marta—it was not so difficult (with Galils, UH-1H helicopters, the Cessna A37-B bombers, 9mm pistols) and so what if they denied that they did it as they did it and afterwards also? not their winning, of course (of the Internal Armed Conflict), but of what transpired in the Highlands and higher in the Altos Cuchumatanes where no journalist or photographer or fat and ugly lonely American man arrived to see it as it happened, to record it while they did it; photos; graphs; newspaper articles; radio transmissions and film: none of this arrived to Acul or Nebaj or the Ixil Area in 1982 or 1983 and none allowed to arrive by your president who prohibited the newspapers from reporting on the "confrontations" in the countryside. More guns (50,000), and eight AMX-13 light tanks, and seventy-nine grenade launchers, and cannons and transport aeroplanes (Aravá—for moving troops into the Highlands) and monies and uniforms and the government was theirs, the national language, schools, businessmen lauded loved them; Mr Reagan gave them candied hellos and helicopter truck parts, could say how nice the days are and how happy the villagers; and there are no paved roads to Nebaj to Acul, one telegraph line in the region, there are no newspapers or telephones or cameras or recorders—no one to see you but you, Marta, and to say in the autochthonous language, which could be silence, *they killed us like dogs*. And to drain the sea is no more than metaphor, no more than ideas that men in my country your country or rural China in 1937 made and then made into massacre: to kill the girls and boys and old men of your villages, the Principales and teachers and midwives; and to make terror its own best weapon for the Army; destroy the clans when they tied your brother to the cypress and removed your hands like birds, and babes who smashed against white stones, the old men dying so easily (like flies) in the mountains, and girls and the bones of the hungry living push through the skin; diseases and despair—for all of what is, was, my phrases inevitably fail to record and remember enough, well enough, to make anything from the brutality and violence.—And all of them destroyed, removed, obliterated and burnt, like offerings, to the wars against the infidels (for the patria), and the wars against the communists (for property), the evil-doers, the dogs who, subversive, were raising their hackles and showing their teeth, who wanted to live and live as freemen.

And you are an Ixil girl from the ancient village of Acul. In 1982, in April, you are fifteen years old and there is a boy from the village who looks at you and you at him, you think that you could marry him; you walk to the river and you wash the clothes every six days. Take my hand, I can see that your hands have done so much cold-water washings: beautiful cold fingers in death. And in the mountains and in the villages (virtually every village in the Ixil Area is razed) the Army vanquished the guerrilla fighters, vanquished the Ixil girl, made the fathers and uncles into killers and corpses; made the girls into killers; made the Ixil into something silent, horrified, and afraid, unstoppably afraid, because once given, the massacre does not abate for the living; "We are always afraid"; and I too am always afraid—of what, darling?—of my neighbors of the News of killers of dogs of disease of bad people of ghosts

267

of communists and germs, of stepping outside the boundary, of leaving the country, of traveling beyond the perimeters of this city, of black people, girls and their hidden cunts; of men; of dying; of me (mine own urges).

Vanquished girl, why have I tried to speak for you? It is not, of course, possible or even desirable in this age that I live in: do not speak Priam's sorrow or imagine his last words to his son on the eve of massacre . . . and me a man who has not traveled, except here among the folios, to your beautiful grey and cold land, into the mountains with you, your ancient green Cuchumatanes, to the sacred mount which rises above your village and where the old gods have hidden away until they may return (perhaps they returned already but the foreign boy may not know it)—why this he? This American man? He is a half-Armenian, which could be something like five phrases in the place of origin and a language and a knowing (of the old places and desert marches to the Der Zor) in his blood, of who he is was may have been: not adrift, not always alone, entailed by his blood—o sorrow, he was given it by his mother, despair for her children like an amulet, like the five phrases pulled from her mouth:

They came for her father in the middle of the night.

She never saw him again.

Her mother and sisters were sent on the march to the Der Zor.

They passed beneath her window.

She never saw them again.:

which did not give him the full of it, the it of it, but merely the faintly outlined heft: he too unfolio'd in America, the disavowed gods in things and the dead of before, and he has not found it in the books, in shops, behind closed doors, in ledgers (*Armenian? Massacres?*). And of course it is all a failure; this essay to find you;

you have died and you have been vanquished and his grandmother long dead in the Lebanon, and her people also vanquished all of those years ago in Ottoman Turkey; removed. And in the place of their three-thousand year history there are scattered stone crosses and etched metal bowls, sepulchres and clay pots, bones, and fading forgetting rumors, a symbolic unworshipped mount (Ararat) and tree, and no one to remember the autochthonous gods in a time before when an Armenian girl, my grandmother Anaguil, walked the ancient spoors of Kharphert and tried to leave her sorrows in the leaves of the old maple tree on the rise, because, except for us, the total past felt nothing when destroyed.

WHAT AM I THEN? corpse-collector; essayist; motorist . . . a once-husband and a half-father; half-Armenian; and a businessman on most Gregorian calendar days, a buyer on all the days, and I have not liked my meals in courses, but piled on my plate, and meat at night and for lunch every afternoon—the business and the leisure, the Shows and the shirts made of fine cottons and wools: I have been stricken; I have been stiff and my bones, as if made of wood in the mornings before I travel the highways to the office, over the hills of Santa Monica and down the canyon, which is the 405, to work; on the days when there is no business, no TO DO's, no wife or meeting or dinners! or games: then I am stricken, then I am wooden and quiet, alone in my green and padded armchair in the San Fernando Valley.

When and how I became a corpse-collector is of no interest; perhaps it began with the diptera girls and the piles of their corpses on my windowsills—black and translucently wingéd—which I carried to the garbage each day; or the dog I saw on the roadside and quitted my driving on the 405 and parked the car on the side of the freeway and walked back to find the bitch (I am in the Santa Monica Mountains) and her snout is crushed and white teeth push through the snout-skin and the diptera girls are happy and buzz and beetles, maggoty things eat their dinner and I am happy and disgusted, the motorcars roar by me like high-pitched and lonely screams through the narrow mountain pass, and that night I dream of a terrifying wingéd insect, a corpse eater, and loudly buzzing flaps its translucent and chemical copper-bodied wings near my dreaming eyes and somehow my marriage ring has slipped around the beast's breast and then it is flying away from me, high over the plains of Los Angeles, takes my wedding band, which is also a telephone, and I am afraid in the dream, and think that I wont be able to call anyone, and that I shall never get my telephone ring back, which gives me no end of despair and sadness in this dream. Upon waking I realize that I have forgotten the bitch in the trunk, and it is garbage day today, and if I can lift my wooden legs and knees quickly from the bed and run or walk faster than slow beetles to my car then I might have a chance to be rid of her forever. But of course I cannot, and it is her stink which has permeated all of these pages.

AND THE COLD WAR came down into your nation into your capital up the Pan American Highway and toward the Highlands, passing Chimaltenango (106 killed) and Santa Cruz del Quiché (56), and arrived in Sacapulas (78) and up the dirt road (the bridge is out) for three and half hours until the Army arrives in Santa María de Nebaj (87) and over the mountain spoor to Acul (34). And the Cold War was in my nation also, but not fought upon mine own skin and inside the pupil and my son was sacrificed not to the gods of the patria or ideals or hope for a difference, but to some god's whim— who can say why my boy died at five months inside his mother's womb? He perished inside the mother's body (her body a tomb) and was removed (by the doctors in hospital) and we buried him, mourned him, and then the mother (one and a half years later) with rage upon her brow for the husband moved to another city, and then later you arrived, Marta, outside the possibility of a son. I was in the padded and green armchair and I was staring outside the window (see the glorious bright-lighted Washingtonias in the distance) above the images and noises flashing by me on the television screen and saw a girl in the light, heard a noise in the ether, this christ's scream in the basement of the Polytechnic? your own ancient howl when they removed your grace and hands with the coffee-cutting implement? And the howls have desired to be unrestrained, Whitman's son rose from the armchair, and the notreading notseeing and unseen American man who knows no more of history and poetry than stars do of heaven, rose and allowed his imagination to descend and the girl appeared to him then on the path to Acul, on the Pan American Highway, behind the yellow and white barred window, down the abyss of the black cell in the capital. She wasn't speaking to him above the din, not howling, but looking into his pupil, past the black and seeking a soul there to speak with: a speaking of souls, electric, real, sorrow and joy and the quick of the living and of the dead, who not wanting to die will essay a speaking inside these pages: we lived, we have not only died.

THIS WHAT we've always had and makes the living livable—it is this possibility of the imagination, to imagine something there beyond the mind's horizon, some past that could resume or a future pulled from the past, and in dream, imagined, some darkblue line at the eye's edge, place, where the sun shines as it does here and then the dogs returned to us and barking growls throughout the night, the loud distant toads crickets, because a boy walks past, a girl in long skirts—this makes us happy—sunlight; grey clouds; the loud cries of unhindered accompanied dogs; a river that is not filled to with bones or bone-colored mass (the dogs are not hungry either); concreted up by the U.S. ARMY CORPS OF ENGINEERS in Los Angeles; filled to with the mothers girls and babes and the truncated red dreams, soldiered days ("the rivers are a tomb") in Acul. It is the twenty angels fire, and we have died for it here, and we have been the killed for other dreamers' dreams of nightmarish proportions—it is the savage nightmare you brought us; it is the christly nightmare you gave over; but we can make a habitable room in the nether regions of the imagination's descent into love's possible dark dirted dogged life and unbarking, the unboned river, uncontained to notbuy—contained living—*we have survived*; we live the inchoate days; and the peasant will have his day and the peasant will plant his maize beans squash seeds and we will live, not as we have always done, not as the man who carries the leña the machete, it is not the same machete which he used to kill his brother in 1982, it is old but it is new for him; he has built roads with it; he has cut the maize with it; the coffee plants in the season of coffee on the plantations in Oriente; he can sharpen the blade with a stone's toss,—but, it does continue, the contextual rivers, machetes, the lies of what happened there and we saw it happening, as if in a storybook or as a cinematic gesture—but I'll say the river continues its course, the river does not appear boned-in, the small children who have lived only in this new village, the new place we built in 1983 with the rented (from the Army) machetes, the old and new tools; we continue, Marta, contained, a life at the edge of what could be: the imagination's lament, yes, but also the imagination's sweet and round black dirted earth; your body; receives; gives over; the sweat between your breasts and underneath your chin; your sexual lips;—Ah, this paradise;—the language lives and we breathe our own words and although you cannot speak them they are spoken, and although you see pain and dirt and blackened souls when you see me, blackened toenails fingernails dirtycut hair and holes in my skirt—you cannot, perchance, see the light slants through the slats of my home, the rebuilt by my sister, her hut home, her leña for the wood-fire stove (and no longer a wooden roof, first the plastic borrowed and then the aluminum lamina); we have a wood-fire stove—we have not been redeemed reduced and you, darling, required; we have continued; we have not been saved: (No: small christs on the road to Nebaj; no large and standard man to make a story for a newgod) planted reseeded and replanted the maize, a maze for the gods for the apogee of my despair, who can see, like I can see the bones that invisible, and the blood that invisible, and the girls and their brothers—they still move past me in our blue-green river, the river which runs today, a torrent, tormenta, down the asphalted sluice of my street—your home and mine are adjacent today, it is a Thursday; the imagination makes a possibility and the imagination makes remakes the dead and so if I am always a sad

and then sad and then saddened specter, then when you are bathing
in the river and then when you are washing and bathing in the river
don't look for us here; we've gone up into the mountains; we've as-
cended the star; we howl like dogs (O happy dogs!) and this child's
wail opens souls in the palm in the mind—on aeroplanes; in automobiles; behind the television screen; for the newgirl washing the
clothes at the river's edge; for the boy eats his neighbor's pomegranates in late summer, the citrus fruits in winter; for them and
their possible—I can cleave history with my thinking and yeses
and rows of ideas and rows, this boy, with the ideas he's been given,
with time and other killer fantasies. And across History, he drives,
to find you.

IT IS TRUE that History is always a history of its age, and the censorship, the author, the place and time; it is a whip for the nation;
a record for its prejudices and sly winking lies; its cant-says wont-
says; its blindnesses and its perverse refusals to look at, see: its manner of seeing, en fait. Perhaps it is one of the glorious myths to
come to us from Judea, from the old Greeks, the early Christians
and then Europe—to give us a progress as soul'd (civilized) men,
as the exiled tribe and then Christians in paradise, in the New World
which given a man's name (Mr Waldseemüller calls the place
America in his maps to (finally) name a continent for a man!—
until he doubts Amerigo's claims six years later, but by then *America*
has caught on). But it is for you, Marta, and me also, our America.
Because the terror of modern History has made us into its subjects
and although we didn't will it or make it, and I did not choose my

journey to America or even to become so, to be half-Armenian,
American, or a white either, as if I could be made into something
also: you an Indian and me a white (like the whites in the photo, the
black whose skin and trousers they kept as souvenir). I don't ask
your pardon or even that you would like to love me, I have fallen
into this book like a man falls into his birth, perhaps, and didn't either choose you or this essay, this history of the New World, but it
given to me by the dead and I have tried to heed their call. I never
asked for it, this corpse-collecting which could be like the Bone
Boy or simply a driver on the roads in his car seeking what it is that
has made him here beyond any kind of comprehension into a man
of things and a man who feels loneliness as if it too were tangible,
physical, thingéd—what makes him into who he is. And it is not a
progressive story. There is little narrative arc or man-killing
Achilles, who, for all of his violence and the massacres of men,
feels pity for wretched Priam and returns the rotting and mutilated
son corpse to the father who, then, kisses his son's killer's hand and
Homer gives us (each time we look into the book) the portrait
of the vanquished and the old razed city of Troy before it is destroyed . . . and there is another place in Asia Minor. Anatolia.
(Armenia.) And from there there was a girl who arrived with hidden stories into the Lebanon and made a daughter into a girl who
wanted nothing more than to abandon the old world and to come
live in the (European) new; to be new and unburdened, lighter,
light-hearted, in America. In America, she was sure, she could be
free. And who am I to say her nay? She had this boy here, and he
grew up along the streets of this city, and he played in the muds and
watched the Indians on TV and he ate ice creams played Cowboys
& Indians, made Los Angeles into a place in his mind which was
his streets, his school, the girls he wanted to fuck, the girls he

wanted more than anything, and cars and things to put inside his house and more moneys; a good (paying) job; and he didn't see the river that once ran through the place (except the flood every five years on his street), and he didn't see the Gabrielino girls alongside the riverbanks, didn't know of Crespí or Mulholland, only the names of streets, the names of soda pop, pop stars, television Shows, songs on the radio (and his mother's reluctant cumbersome five, like enigmatic river stones).

Are you my grandmother? It would be a comfort and more than easy to see it so, say it so here and then make it into something: Mr Washington has monuments and mythic battles, may I not have my Marta girl and my nene in the same page and back again and again from their countries, their deaths, from the unwritten histories?

THE SCHOOLTEACHER died (your christ in the pit; hanged by the wrists) and as easily as the criminal, and even incriminates himself in the end; he lost his faiths; he pisses shits himself; bleeds like a hog; hates now those whom he vowed to teach (the Indians in the Highlands). And see how the soldiers laugh at his killing dying: see how they mock him feed him the salty pissed water the shitted biscuits; they break his knees like stones with stones; remove his fingers with blunt knives for luck-beads, the maggots in his wounds lift their heads to the chorus of his cries when they remove his penis with a red-hot coffee cutting implement.

And had he risen to heaven (but not the Heaven of the administration building) then a different world perhaps. Or the same world, the addled story. But who to rise him up, Marta? And who to relay each story with a proverbial yell? And who, finally, to put him into the icon's grave, engrave him onto the stone tympanum, over the mountains, to arrive, eventually, to Acul and your small blue and pink church; the cypress without nails then; a belfry for the innocent; a plaza without cobbled stone or graded asphalt. It is I, darling. Because the storyteller is the god. The storymakers the future masks of past civilizations: not what takes place, but what takes place in books; not to see, but to scribe—from the cradle to the grave; see how death hangs over my head? I have placed his hand in a book, I have shown you it, his arched scythe as it reaches toward my neck. I have killed you also, again and again. A repetition of returns, of the gods.

Imagine their joy when he rises! The ecstasy of eternal life has saved him, finally, from despair from his god's abandonment to the human to pain, to what suffers, a knife cut and the bone pushes out through flesh. The wide river'd sorrow that the human animal can make (so easily, dear Reader!) and the he suffers, O sorrow, for a lifetime and the children and his children also: have I not, also, had some of it (a paltry amount perhaps, but *some*) from my mother and her burdened phrases of that distant and dead town, Kharphert, and the Der Zor which holds the bones of some died people who could have been the great-grandmother or aunties or second second cousins; the Der Zor offers us bones like you offer me the tortilla from your hand, a cold and hot drink on hot and cold days.

PERHAPS you can never entirely hide the blood, Marta, or bind what cannot hold—it cannot be erased, the nation-state dream has its leaks and holes and interstitial lives, rivers: we are here, we have survived, and the half-Armenian boy, the Ixil girl, are blooded now, bolder now that we can know it, that I have known you: see my nene in the sunlight, her glorious brown hair; see my corpse and her yellow teeth—they have lost their hair and teeth in my dream and I awake and think that I can hear children in the back of the house: they are laughing; they are playing. O, to play! Glorious animals at play, wild and they show me their asses their sex their eyes are open, seeing, they say you are fat ugly I love you I am hungry: glorious unlying children, how happy I am inside their laughter as it moves around my body, inside organs, makes music and I think that I too ought to play, jump, find a girl for fun and love and *play*—they are not ashamed by their asses their tiny cocks and tits—they are open; free if and for as long as the adult allows it; move through the room like rockets, speed, and joy. I want a boy, Marta, a son in his glory—I could love him, I could cradle his form inside my arms, it's small and does not destroy sorrow or undo lonely forms, but joy, beauty, play, love and the possibility of a boy—and I'll take him out of this country to yours, eat tortilla beans grown by your brother's hands and eat a meal made by yours: we shall eat together, dine on the dirt floor of your rebuilt home— I'll bring some money to help build it, the American has his monies, only let me and my son come to you, arrive in Acul, I'll take him out of America and bring him into America so he can find a home, a place where the gods live inside trees and stones and mountains, so that his soul can alight on the tops of things and we'll share money and food, make history from the impossible notevents of History.

I'll sleep now I think. I am so tired, Marta, this book has tired me, pained me, the kidney again, pain as a talisman, and the essay, the black slants, always beyond the reach of my paltry talents. I sit in my chair now, and the sun is beginning its demise over the hills, the Washingtonias are tall and elegant as always, but less sunnily alert (permanently bent) and the old trees of Europe don't look so out of place alongside them. The air is browner today, Los Angeles has become more crowded as I write this to you for you, the freeways and roads filled with the metal beasts filled with one alone driver who makes his way and hers to work school shops meetings, not looking at the other drivers, not loving them or wanting their bodies' odors or what ails them or why it is that we have voluntarily put ourselves into the beasts for hours at a time to seek what does not arrive: freedom and love; why it is that we so easily give up the soul and the real for a half-lived life.

IT ISN'T COMPLICATED. It was simple. Do you love me anymore any longer? I asked of the divorcée when she was my wife. No, she said. I don't love you any longer, and perhaps, she continued, me sitting in the green armchair, I never did. We've no idea how to love any longer, I could have told her, could have said that fucking her was always an obligation and sometimes a pleasure but never the feeling of my soul rushing to the surface and out through my cock;

never was I god-like when we fucked. But a good husband, perhaps.
Paid bills. Worked. Smiled accordingly at all of our dinner parties
and the neighbors and colleagues ate foods at our house and we
talked of mortgages and retirement benefits and the economy and
the News and the price of petrol and which new (fastest) cars and
which new (better) television Shows, new films, new actresses, new
deals at the big and bigger stores, new things.

The divorcée lives in another city now. I can't remember the
smell of her cunt anymore, I hardly knew it then (the perfumes the
hairs removed douche and then I didn't want to suck her into my
mouth either). She has children, perhaps. She's not forgotten the
boy we might have had, the boy who died on the way to hospital
inside her flesh, the five month boy we didn't name but buried in
a plot of land.

She called me yesterday. She told me it rained in her city; that
it was colder and that if I wanted to I could return her calls.

This too could be a fiction: the wife the green armchair the
house on Hollyline Av—Reader, how will you decide? Who will
be allowed into the realm of your real? Will you allow some small
space for our Marta-girl? Any room for me, also? And the faceless
then cockless boy in the pit at the Polytechnic? The brother tied to
cypress? The Marta-girl in Chimaltenango, she is still there fucking for money. In the pit with the boy? She is sucking her torturer's
cock now.

Do I need to have a wife? Leave off the wife. Or the unlived
son? He too you may jettison from these pages your mind. Think
of the girl. Think of cypress, rain, clouds like girls, the cold land
and the walk from Acul to Nebaj. Give the Bone Boy some
American dollars to buy school books not bombs. See the children
that died before the age of five in the Highlands. Fight kidney dis-

ease. Eat good food. Buy. Eat. Fuck your wife as if she were a god, also. I don't need a wife a son or a house on Hollyline Av. I don't need to be in Los Angeles or driving along the streets of this city. There is no need for my parents or other family members. Just this I which writes speaks delineates the world here. See it see me, not as spectacle or Show, but as you yourself.

THEY COME in droves and I am killing them in droves, but they do not abate, Marta, I cannot stop them their thievery, their kidney works words, they live in my rooms, inside the television set, beneath my nail beds, and inside my mind they are stealing me. They are preening day and night and cleaning and flying inside my eyes and the noise does not abate, stops and starts, the cycle of diptera girls; forelegs aft, cleans and rubs; and if they would suck my cock or bring your cells up into me—vomit your flesh onto my skin?— then I could bear them, I could be happier; they could return a son to me, or your blackened toenails. But they don't; wont; cannot (I am no fool, not either here among these pages)—they cannot fly the distance, make the geographic leaps from Acul Nebaj down the Pan American Highway to the capital, or up across the jungles of the Petén, see the beautiful jungle monkeys, see how they throw rocks at your head on the steps of the ancient Mayan temples, and up northern borders and the Mixtec girls Nahua girls Tlaxcalan to- ward Tijuana and passing a check stand and hellos to the policemen, and cash their quetzales for pesos for dollars! and then continue along the 405 Freeway for three hours—there is a traffic jam—until they find me at home (east on Ventura Boulevard, turn right onto

Stansbury Street, a left turn then, and a right onto Hollyline Av, straight from your village which until 1983 had no roads or cars, only the ancient spoor across the mountains; the soft noises of hard feet); find me; fuck me with their bilious bodies and give me, finally, some of your sweet flesh and a bit, if I am lucky, of this soul for which we have no words in my modern language. What do you call it in yours?

(Is it the English words world, the language itself, which constrains me? How difficult it is to see in English; its rules, its History, blindnesses grammars on the man mind, the words now without gods, do not vibrate me home, the out of body, and how it itself limits this book, the book can only allude to what I once knew outside of my English inside of my body.)

THIS the sad truth of it, of us,—Marta. That the damned exiled races (now roam these Americas) care no more for the damned unexiled races of these Americas than Priam's dogs for their master's corpse. And for this I am sorry and bereaved even; for what is us, human I suppose, that does not make a man more likely or likely to love another and hated man if he—this man in the deserts of Mesopotamia in the mountains of Guatemala—has known pain and sorrow and the soldier's cut and fist upon his brow: compassion is not the child of suffering. And this gives me rare comfort in these Americas; yes: we survived, darling, like you and we made our way by boat and aeroplane and automobile to America New York City or the basin of Los Angeles, the angels for Christ's mother herself here by the river which we didn't know was a river, and

alone now, but fat, comfortable, sad, a half-Armenian boy who did
not know his grandmother's clan (the dead) and did not know you
either (the dead) and has longed for you here amidst the emigrant
plants and animals: the tall eucalyptus in his garden, the birds of
paradise in his garden, and the swift birds from Europe and Asia—
we all here and eating and sunning ourselves and walking, driving,
along the streets of this city without recourse (for the dead grandmothers and deader great-grandfathers) and eclipsed like the sun
from an old village which poor and distant was, nevertheless, ours
(like these new myths we've inherited here? of Providence Pilgrims
and to reason to purchase). I too lost my tongue on this uterine
journey: English is in my mouth and my mind is filled with it, like
absent vowels, and your tongue was cut out with a farmer's implement, and Spanish did not ever fill your cerebral mountains and distant plains and you are still poorer, your feet are dirty and your nails
blackened and you stink from afar and you have no table manners
and your fathers bow and kiss the foreigners' feet and ankles as
you, trudging up into the hills and looking seeking the day long for
some small kind of edible fruit or green plants because you are always hungry, you ate grass in the Mesopotamian desert stories of
summer 1915, will eat anything offered you, and still I never loved
you while the bombs rained down on your head from the Cessna
A37-B and the Army is saying there is no such thing as killing the
Ixil in the Highlands of Guatemala, or they are saying that it is the
guerrilla that is killing and killing and that they, innocent defend-
ers of the state, serve only the father- mother-lands while the young
boy lies prostrate on the floor of his home; and the Indians are
happy! Mr Ríos Montt says: See them happy! And you are crying
now perhaps, disgusted with the dead children in your arms, with
the bombed-off faces and feet and small child's hands, with that

kind of human meat that never, once it has made a picture in the human mind, recants;—with the boy from afar who, although he swore it, swore outrage against such killings and murders from his television set and from his living room and from his bed—did not come down into your village on a Thursday in April; did not find you on the road to the capital (or buy your open-legged invitations); did not descend into the pit of putrefied and petrified, the sad diptera children in the Polytechnic, in the capital of your country which has not been, since its inception in 1821, yours.

I have been lonely, yes, in this city and the distance of bones and old stories and the epic dogs upon the threshold . . . but I have not, consequently, been braver; a good American boy, yes, a buyer and eater and to fuck in the night with the lights taken down and a good American girl to love him, chide him his dirty underwear, washes his clothes and dishes and likes the rings he puts on her fingers, and the fat clothes they buy in shops and the Shows that they can watch and laugh over together in their new paradise (she doesn't know about the Mesopotamian desert in his mind or the bones that lie there, accusing, and the old smells of the old country; the stink of the food and of sorrow and shame and his mother's songs (and the one Armenian song he can't remember, not yet), a thick kind of sorrow for America, and hidden and his wife never saw it, his shame, he kept it buried deeply, like a stone in a concrete riverbed, beneath the concrete, mixed up there with some other boy's ancestors, the old Gabrielinos who once made villages alongside a river in Los Angeles before it was such a city, and before the air was browner and after his wife departed for another city inside America—he can hardly remember her now: what was my wife's name, Marta? And what is my name also?).

I AM SURE, Marta, that like you, I did not choose to be an American. And at night and I am lying in my bed, in the moments or seconds before sleep descends with its black and red curtain—such a despair overtakes me then, these perhaps the interstitial moments when I pen my unthought thoughts to you, when you come down to me from the invisible tangible world of the dead, and you speak to me, or I, almost dreaming, not fully unawake, discard the costumes and customs of my era, of my Americanness, and of my things, and I become you and we are not one, but I can see you in the basement of the Polytechnic, I hear your screams there, how they hanged you by your hands and then no hands with which to torture you more, the slashed breast, and your brother's face, the lost babes in the river, you as you run into the mountains with the neighbor child strapped to your back and another in your hand and the invisible boy in your belly, and seeking refuge on high—and then I am asleep. Then I dream of houses and boxes and running slowly, as if I am losing the ability to run. And I can no more take it in those moments, all of the living behind masks and the how-are-you's and the bosses' cocktail hours and the money I have made and the money I will make and suddenly, at night, on the threshold of sleep which is also the doorway to awakefullness, I can see: you, myself, the look of all of my American brethren, how sad they are, how lonely, their faces like porcelain tooth masks, creased with worry, fatigue, and with this tight fear that we all wear like scuttled dogs;—we are all of us dying; the fattest people to roam the earth with our chemical foods and improvements, and we are dying we are not living, we deny the soul the gaze, we don't love properly, because too afraid to love—what if we lose our things? our house? our car? our selves?—and so marriage is another mask and costume, and so friendship and love affairs, none of it real in my unreal Los Angeles city, how sad to call it by María's angels here, when the angels so determinedly denied, their heat has deserted us, their quick and sun—the gods almost gone now. In the stones? In the concrete river? Beneath the freeways and driveways?

And the dead

And the spirit in the rocks rivers and mountain

Walk with me down to the river. It is like a highway with its one-lane channel cuts through the San Fernando Valley; its two inches of water in the summer and a torrent after it rains. There are fences line the river. We are not allowed to touch the autochthonous waters; we don't drink them either—our water from the north and east. But O, we might take a small sip from the river in Acul, might wash our clothes along its banks, beat them with sticks on the rocks, and then afterwards walk the dirt path to the dirt house and drink some tea. No, not tea, some atol or thin coffee. And I will tell you about another city on a rise in a different plain, an ancient city where my grandmother once walked the dirt paths and played in the shadows of the seventeenth century maple tree, a girl who saw her town ruined and her father disappeared and her mother and sisters removed and then later denied (the Armenians elided from the History of Turkey): the Armenian girl who could never return and the Ixil girl who can return only at the threshold of dreams, she has died, in an American's mind, we the two of us now of America— born here and living here, and you have not died like the sun has not died and your dead in the ground and although mine scattered across the earth, perhaps I can lie in your XXMUJER grave awhile yet, feel comfort by trees and flowers and sunlight in America, get out of this city and reseek the old spoors, or if not, run down to death as if running into the concrete river and sit with you awhile yet in the sunlight, and drink your mother's milk when your children are born, and love you, love the smell of your legs, your cunt, your beautiful dark looks that see me and seeing me, destroy the old in-dividual American and love him unto death.

IT's WHAT we all know, as if knowing were sitting beneath the cy-press and at once the roots and at once the branches suspended in air speak like a tree: that these chemical feelings which fly around the air like birds or black flies, or suspended as if branches and brush my cheek mouth your skin, our sorrows, and betrayals the flow of loves of sex and disappointments and bald-faced lies to all of this—that we know more than reason, more than we say, can say: know to be: that I did not love my wife, married her, yes, fucked her, yes, and admired her form or respected her work-ways and weed-pulls in the garden and meals she made me, the house she kept for me, but it was not love, admiration, affection, simplicity and similarity of fears: yes: but no Love, not like you, Marta, and me in ether, across time and space, when you have come into me and I am you in the basement in the Polytechnic and at the sides of roads—sorrow, yes, to have felt it, seen their mauling hands and this pain, but life also: to have lived for a breath, inside of us, a freedom for the soul which I have not heeded, and scared, had scarcely known.

AND HAVE I, Marta, collected the corpses in reality? or have I simply sat in my green and sun-faded armchair thinking the smells while the black flies made their party in the hot afternoon sun? Have I loved you, really? Have I driven and then flown walked down our continent to find you, see you, on the road to your capital, the paths to Acul and Nebaj, up the dirt road to the Ixil Area? Have I seen your brother tied to the cypress, O saddest of trees in my mother's lexicon, and the machetes they cut him apart with, the boulders upon which the babes were torn open, the girls in the river, the old men in the six foot deep pit they are digging for their sons and nephews—Has this been fiction, or rather, has Reality created a plain like a jail to which the modern American boy has been banished, cannot see beyond the schooled ideas of it: of Washington the Washingtonias in the distance school-clocks and books about History and morality like a good compass to move the small christs by . . . For these fictions then, which have banished the real into the realm of the dead gods and now we, this boy, here in the dream-made world of America which is like a black road, it can be hot, there is speed, and I have orgasms inside the girls' cunts, but the bones have been shut-up shut-out and the dead will have their return willy-nilly, like a carnival in the moment just before I fall to sleep at night. And I must bear the Real as you bore your jailors, the young boys who killed you and for no ascertainable reasons— the communist scourge, subversives guerrilla and—cut up your face and breasts, removed your hands. I have tried to essay the real here, find it amidst the fiction, get out from under the Shows and the business meetings the shop clerk conversations and radio News television News newspapers, to see a girl on the path to Acul, the grandmother who died in a war, five sentences which have been his millstone, his invisible record, as if justice compelled him, truth were a sound the tympanum could suddenly detect outside of its moral mortal borders: we were killed like dogs, she whispered, and this she is you, Marta, and it is the Bone Boy's lament also: he too is haunted by the Armenians; and an Ixil girl made this boy real, I could turn the TV on off, and sit with you awhile longer in my house, this green and comfortable armchair, the black and blue flies buzz above us, land on my skin with your soul inside the sounds and bites.

You died, Marta, in these pages and in the Polytechnic, in the mountains, along the banks of the river in Acul, behind the administration building, on the Pan American Highway, and (you lived also and) I have died also toward the end of the book, when we will find my sad and bloated stinking corpse for the other corpse-collectors in America—the half-lived seeking the dead, reading the dead, trying to find the quick and soul and life again in the deadest places, in books.

And small hopes? The Ixil girls grind corn at four a.m.; the cocks crow the day long and the wild and domesticated dogs bark throughout the grey and black nights in Acul; the small girls tend sheep in the new cemetery and run, they are laughing, across the filled-to six foot deep fifteen foot long pit. The blue white and pink hydrangeas are beautiful in the cemetery and the mist sits on the surrounding mountains in the Valley of Acul like girls. There is beauty in the girls, in the mountains, in the men walking to the fields. There are Ixil men girls and boys and women in the houses; the chimney smoke is visible day and night; your sister, the one you carried on your back to Nebaj when you were girls, is grinding the corn with her young daughters; they have survived. And in my grandmother's village, I have seen a boy with my grandmother's eyes—he doesn't speak the autochthonous tongue (Turkish only), he doesn't know that the strange markings on the antique metal bowls in his home are from the time before (and a people before) and spell out a boy's name (in Armenian: Dickran), but he knows the light on the wheat fields in late August just as my grandmother once did, and just as the new girls know the grey mists of the valley in Acul, and the sounds from the dairy farm of bells tinkle, the zzac zzac of small birds. Good-bye to some things and girls (my grandmother, you) and hellos to others—the new Marta girls; listen in the trees to their stories sorrows and Achilles can rage while he mourns, and Priam's grief could be my own: the dead stories the old myths and an American boy in Los Angeles, an Ixil girl in the Highlands, running, living, loving each other here amidst the black and desiccate marks in eternal booktime.

IT IS NOT ONLY the gods in the world, Marta, it is the gods in me. They are in me and sit and rest awhile, like blue black flies, preen and howl and cry out for vengeance, in anger, love, a sexual starving, the passions, to hate my neighbor, to love the girl so many thousand miles from me, and love her more, hate her also: she smells, she is savage, she is natural and distant from me—all gods, these. The gods in trees, in the magnetic sequoia of my childhood mountain days, of the cypress in the plaza which was no more than a dirt patch, the rocks in the rivers, at the wash's end, in my liver sometimes, the kidneys, throat, chest and knees and groin: gods. And to deny them is to cancer it all up, sicken ourselves unto death or half-death: it cannot be erased or pushed out, away, to nothing— it is not possible. Because we also cannot stop breath, or if we do it kills us: we are dying, Marta, but will something new be born? Here is the question for the Americas: not damage and contamina- tion and tarmac and machines even, but a certain disintegration, a definite denial and lying, a repressed howl that will emerge out from the small cracks in things: this interstitial book itself: what will come from it? The Christians preach Apocalypse and Heaven for the righteous, faithful—but what of us? The riparian novels and boys and girls, the one seeking to uncontain the concrete river of Los Angeles, the other seeking the bones of her mother brother in its flow: it is a maze of possibilities, it is not clear down which road we may travel, only that this road is no tarmac road with its lying bouts of freedom, for the tarmac road can only take you down what is on the map already, it is not the free way, a man cannot choose his road but sits there inside the machine and metals plastics and rage fills his soul as it hits with the thousand thousand other ma- chines and sole passengers inside them on the tarmac freeways headed to a place which the road directs him to: not free to choose the road for his own soul, or free to say that he will take off his clothes and be an adam, or that he wont work anymore and wont buy things and he'll sell his houses things cars and televisions and he'll turn his gaze from the theatrical screens and look see what he can, into the eyes of girls, down their pupiled roads, into souls and beneath trees, feel the vibrations of the dirt of the leaves of the girls, of rain: feel it fully and without shame or remorse or humility: but happy to be as he is and to see, discard the tarmac roads and metallic masks and girls with layers of dung-heaped shame and bitter envy—it is good, he'll say, this me, it is me, and I am not you, Marta (you know this, I am sorry to have to say it for my own soul in these pages, but I am Whitman's American son, singing now, enraptured, *with the twirl of my tongue I encompass worlds and volumes of worlds*): and we are not one, but we are, darling, in touch, together, a soul at the edges of his self, adjacent passages and phrases juxtaposed—the massacre at your village and a massacre of his soul—we Americans here; black grey green—colors like electric stars, and you visited me and I let you sit awhile and speak to me, this American man in his green and modern upholstered chair, sat in front of the window and saw Hollyline Av, the neighbor's white house, the red rooftops and the white-barked birches, their branches like dresses; the evergreen cypress spoke also and I tried to learn, if not to learn, then to listen— and the half-alive man wanted to live, Marta, to become, to play and dance and fuck and labor: to be a man as is his right, either here in this city or there in your village—less alone in these pages, alive together and dead together for eternity, which could be as the gods, as Hektor and Achilles in the last days before their demise.

YOU WERE NEVER named in my News or newspapers, in History books, or political tracts or art Shows or postcards or Laws: so I named you here so that all may know you: Marta, girl with the black pupils, blackbrown hair in a plait, with her pain and her joy and her lovely strong muscle hands; the veins like a river in her hands; the feet small and black with this disease; the cunt black and red and beautiful, like a painting.

And later when there was an inquiry, after the wars ended and moved on to other places (back, I think, to my mother's old place) because the Cold War abated, and the Interests no longer interested and so the Army Generals agreed for a "peace treaty," which was something like a small theatrical piece for newspaper men and the políticos, and then there was an inquiry made by the Church, and they did ask the people in the villages and towns of your Highlands to tell them *what happened to you?* And they did, in the end, record what you knew for thirty-four years: that the Army went up into the mountains and slaughtered you like dogs, in Acul, in the Ixil Area, and in the basement of the capital. And afterwards, the bishop who commissioned the inquiry, Monseñor Gerardi, had his head broken apart by a concrete block (on the day after the publication of the findings)—a crime of passion, the authorities said— and who, finally, could disagree with them?

IT IS CERTAIN

that my mother's five sentences given me in Los Angeles, like a half-built house and then unbuilt by my own forgetting (of the dead in the distance as if walkers through the Der Zor) did not change me or make me a better man—a different man who could see your suffering on the evening News (you were not on it), a man who would make the trek down the Santa Monica Mountains toward the Pacific coast and passing San Diego and the border,

Tijuana, and farther—Hermosillo Escuinapa Oaxaca—until he arrives in Chiapas and you are closer now and he is making a joke of geography, a record here in the mind which is better than a fearful and desolate heart, he sees the temples of the ancient cities sees the modern capital, the Polytechnic built like a cartoon castle, then passes into the mountains, it is cold now, grey and greener in his mind, until he arrives at Nebaj (the corpses in the plaza have been removed), waves a hello to the guards inside the cathedral and keeps walking now, he will not drive any longer because there is no road yet, he becomes again a walker and removes his shoes walks over the mountain pass—metallic blue butterflies blue beetles and yellow moths—he sees the grazing cows at the peak of the mountain and then down the steep and rocky but not mudded path (it is not the rainy season today) to your village, the old one before it was burnt, before your brother was killed, mother and the others, and rebuilt into its Model form, and the cocks will not stop their continual language of the days and the dogs and crows have not eaten your brother's face and feet and you yourself have such beautiful hands and fingers to make food and grind corn.

It could be rage—it could be despair or the loneliness of these Christian things, which is like our modernity; or nostalgia which is this other disease: but none of it changes or changes makes a better man: the man whose grandmother died on the telephone; whose mother gave him reluctantly these allochthonous sentences like the father also reluctantly beat his face and hands; and perhaps he has been possessed by the phrases, by you and the corpses he has driven over the landscape of this city to essay connections where there are none, where there can only be (in books in poetry), as if the dead themselves were pounding inside his (foreign) English language and trying, terribly, to be removed or returned and risen. What would you say to me in your Ixil? Merely that I shut the doors now and my mother could whisper to her mother in Armenian like a chalice: Mother, why did you abandon me here? (and *me* in this city?) And perhaps even the others who remained behind: why did you abandon us here, also?

[

And let me tell you the story that my mother did not tell me in America

like a city of bones beneath the tarmac world beneath the phrases she gave me beneath American History and the History of your nation: that:

the Armenians are an ancient tribe

the sun

the mountain—Ararat—is the holy mountain (even still, see it rise high above the unreturnable nation, of Turkey)

that: Kharphert was built more than one thousand years ago by Armenian kings

that: the tribes lived on the land for one thousand years of history before that

that: in 1915 there were invisible edicts and

that: the Armenians were killed then (the men; her father), and taken at night and notreturned

and the rest removed (the women children and old men and boys: her mother and sisters and nieces nephews)—to the Der Zor Desert and starved and beaten and massacres and the babes pulled from their mothers' bellies like stones from a river that: this ancient tribe of men no longer resides in their place (Anatolia)

that: others remained there or taken there afterwards: Kurd and Turk

that: I didn't learn the story of my tribe: whom they love what they adore to which gods they prayed for whom the sacrifice is made: not the language or psalms or epic battles or midday customs, or marriage rites or rites of passage or rules of decorum or the knowledge that the guest is sacred: a messenger of the gods

that: I didn't learn you either: Ixil girl of Acul, Nebaj, the Polytechnic for the disappeared boys and girls, a long night of shame and red death and black earth, the earth made blacker during the thirty-four year moil; your hands; your sorrow

or of the Gabrielino girls and boys, Komiivet they called themselves in this place before it was this place; Yaanga they called it, and they lived alongside the old river for millennia

that: these books my books the notbooks of invisible tribes and invisible connections and invisible lovers, like invisible bone cities: you and me

and:

the myths of genocide, the girls of yesterday, the boy his sorrow.

]

AND YOU are not the sea, Marta, or a dog, and I no corpse-collector on the streets of this city; metaphors for men, to kill a girl in her mountain village on a Thursday in April 1982—and to make the clouds, which sit like girls today on the mountains: these all made or re-made in this book. Men make fictions, likenesses, comparisons of this to that in the circular ruins of emotional soul'd time, to know less, to kill, to resurrect and unthink what we know; for seeing better; for calling down the gods; for the vibrating words because we know that we are not dogs men (nor a sea for a General's offensive plans), nor civilized nor contained, but men, and to know what we have known but now will not (desire to) know: that men are ancient animals, part of the cosmos and its plans.

And I am the driver and you the girl prostrate in a cell of the Polytechnic, you die now, finally, and death is a relief release, you have longed to die for so long, the duration of this essay, to lie again in your mother's arms in the black fiery arms of the cosmos of Love and behind or alongside the News Shows, my drives your breaths

(Reader: you also breathe)

And then not breathing the heart stops now the brain quiets its electric nerve routes and the final bowel movement, your shit and piss pushed out involuntarily and you are off. At rest. The pages off also, at their fin, in this middle, muddle, breath   hhuh

And the cannibal of history of words of love and ideas and of an Ixil girl—I eat you and your brethren and all of my books—ingest it—eat shit like a black diptera girl eats it, corpses, all of the boys bullies books and my mother's phrases and her sorrow and the memories of my grandmother; love: to live, I did it (*I must live,* said the soul.)

IT IS because I was dying, Marta, and up until the moment of my demise writing I imagined death to be of no real existence; I feared death as I feared the ghosts of my childhood, the devils in the black paintings, in the cinema around the table as we played the séance games and lifted the lightest girl with our fingers and the Ouija board flew to the ground as an expression of the ghost's anger which we had inspired because of our inquiries; the ghouls of my daydreams were like the paper boats I drew on the lined school paper; colors;—as I feared the bullies on the playground in their yellow and orange parkas; the teacher's looks and what she never saw (the boys holding my head to the pavement, their blows); a row of uneven chairs, broken apart; unlined; my father's hands;—but not now, we are back in *now* and a now-knowing, as if this *to die* arrives like a motorcar and parks in front of my home, in a concrete driveway which, waiting, waits, material, like an engine runs, which are pistons? which is gasoline moves the pistons? (see how little I know), taken from my thinking imagining and put inside my kidney and has me by the flesh, and flesh dissolves and its pain is something to live inside like a glass house and I don't wish it—to be inside; blood sacrificed—and it has come to me and will not leave me, this dying kidney machine, which takes up residence in the flesh like a bird or spider, mechanical now, and makes a home here, and there is no undoing of its undoing me, the cells apace unmake my kidney first the right then the left and remake it into a city of lies, of deadly machinery, unmake pistons making a man know what he would not like to know—how what I wish cannot matter; the seeing of no use; I shall miss the days most of all; how America has been for naught, meaning less now while my kidneys make roads into the spine; and the suffering has been for naught, meaningless also: the girl who sat by the river in Los Angeles before it was Los Angeles and gave Mr Crespí an acorn from her hands and she smiled into the Spaniard's face like a good barbarian and you at the river washing the clothes and I cross the concrete sluice in my car and never knew it when it was dirted and tore through the houses of this city; made floods;—there is a river here?—for centuries until I am older and quieter now, demising as I am writing you in these sentence breaks.

And to imagine the days without a consciousness to imagine them? A man whose blood is tainted now—sick in his dorsal kidney like I am sick for you all of these years as a man; making you, unmaking you, loving you from the time I made boats on unlined and then lined school paper—ah, these lines lies like the easy sentences of TO DO, to make business, to marry a girl at twenty-six and make half of a boy at thirty; and the we traveled! and the we took a vacation on an island nation! and the people are like this: I hate them those, these people she is a dog we are like the dogs—I would like to suck her kneecaps for my breakfast . . . My living like a small dose of raw kidneyed meats. But this dying, the as it is, the unable to make the body stop its undoing of itself—a car is like a bird or a spider builds unbuilds makes a kidney from the red meats; a machinery of machines: to clean to drive to make a man think clearly, his hair grows nicely; he is not afraid—what could have been possible: the auto has unmade us, Marta? the ubiquitous motorcar which promised to us (by the company men) individual freedom! Sunday drives! O happy maidens in our arms and on our arms as we drive the roads of paradise; made us like stone corpses beneath the palm fronds which falling, slipping, do not disappear into the asphalted earth.

LET US SPEAK of your brother. Let us speak of your mother. This pains me and I am glad (happy!) for this pain, a sadness like a cancer: did it make me a sick man? a dying man? a man of disease and woe like a man who didn't love his living until he was seeing that he would not have eyes very soon and without to see and without to breathe and his blood uncleaned now and his hair falls into the garbage bins unwarranted and unkindly; black sheaves. And I will miss the days most of all; sunlight; not the despair of my bedroom at seven o'clock, that light which makes a man lonelier in his home (the television blares day and night in this city),—or: not the distance of flesh, the divides of ether, how culture shuts the girls' thighs like doors; not these doors; you from me; how we can act and what is sayable buyable, though all of these things have also killed our unknown souls. And the artifacts we could find together: baskets bowls painted tombstones the stela and stone grave markers in Anatolia in the jungles of the Petén, but never in Los Angeles? [the burial grounds kitchen-middens beneath your car-ways, drive ways?] For this, Marta, I have lived? Yet. Yet. Don't kill me; I would not like to demise for this

What is your name, Marta?

and: before   after   ?

Can I make You faster than I, which is no I, some other me, unmakes me? Are my cells mine then, like the dirt of my ancestors? of yours? of the girl holds the acorn for the Father and soldiers and surgeon making their way along the Alta California spoors? If they unmake me then I am unmaking myself, dying myself, and to do it I'll make you first—story you for a while because I don't wish it, to be narrated graphed striven, to live in this house on this green armchair (the television Shows; colors, black and whites; a three month old boy is sitting in the television and cries) and think that I wont live any longer which makes me want to kill all of the others, my dead mother, the divorcée in another city; and why has my kidney built its deadly juices like edifices inside this flesh? I want god now. No. I want life, its living. You before and after (and my half-boy back, as always, to live after me, recount, perhaps, my own unwitnessed demise in some other, ethereal, mind book).

I DREAMED of my grandmother's town, Marta. And I returned to it in this dream to find the old and diminutive woman come to me in the early morning and held a small boy's body in her arms, singing softly to him this song which although forgotten did not leave me, although the words themselves had evaporated for a time into the ether, like the lake in the Owens Valley. Such a dry bed of salts and soda now in the mind, and the grandmother in Kharphert sits in her ancestral home with her brothers and they are playing like thieves in the garden and the little blue-eyed sister has not been born yet and perhaps they are Armenian or the Ixil children—or none of these things because it is in the days before the nationalist wars, before the girl would see her mother and aunties walked out into the bright and desiccate yellow-gold plains (to Der Zor), survive, and make a girl in another place make a boy in America who dreams this dream of the old and sick grandmother sang to him who died from him (in another war, in the Lebanon) and who then came back to give him this essay these songs for the girl in the Cuchumatanes, for the black at the beginning of this book, the boy that boys tied to a Mercedes-Benz and took up into the mountains of the Lebanon, for the Komiivet at the river, the boy in the San Fernando Valley—each one has died, but her corpse his talisman and in this city he sought the dead so that he might live, and the dead came back to him out of pity or earnestness or simply because they had never left him, only they, like the other old ways, have not gone, but leave their traces, like petroglyphs and rock ruins of the old citadel in Kharphert City, of the temples in the Petén, and the red thick labia'd god in Los Angeles; and fragments of old books strewn onto his mind.

I dreamed that I had not died.

MARTA, I went home (in dreams, this book) and I am a complete stranger in the old paradise and the dogs do not know me, the girls will not speak my name, and I don't have the language for them, their smells have become a foreign thing their dance steps stumble in my feet across the landscape and how to say thank you and the rules and the place has not become a paradise, nor has it aged like a dark channel of the mind, but rather has its own is and more histories rush down there now and perhaps there is not a grandmother in Kharphert or her father (and how would I speak to them anyway?), we divided by land by language and time and wars, or understand his eyes speaking or her hands or the rules of decorum culture and love: I am in exile, yes, but it is alright, I think, to find comfort and joy at the Turkish wedding in my great-grandfather's village and dance the circle dance beneath the canopy of rain and wet and mudded and the boys and men are holding my arms and we are dancing and I am dancing with my enemies' grandsons and although I cannot remember the rhythms or music (and they don't remember or recognize the returned me), they do hold my arms graciously and kindly for the dance, and guide me up and back and feet crossing, carry me along as the guest, the foreigner arrived from another place, American now, with his girl in his mind and his mother's sentences for gifts to bring him back and take him to a wedding in old Turkey which could be Kharphert and the plains lighted up at dusk, the wheat and sweet manure and hanging figs pomegranates and waters running feeding the three hundred year old maple on the top of the rise and the white mulberry the hanging gourds and cucumbers and the souls of the living; the basking cows and long-eared donkey; the dogs and new cats; there are black flies throughout the days and the quiet earth and slow time: now I understand what it is that she longed for and her sadness to not see the afternoon light in summer and its gold-brown shadows on the fields and the boy brings the cows down and into the barns at the end of each day and this light makes the world its center and the gods donkey cows and the boy who brings them back: I am sorry you could not return, Nene, that I didn't know you better across the distances of America—have more than Mother's five phrases of you, and that I didn't care to know didn't know my soul paid in full for the not-knowing and know Marta now, behind the phrases of the Cold War, Guerrilla Warfare, Operation Ixil, and

Draining the Sea, and in this dream essay we can see it as it is and not what it could have been or should be and perhaps it's alright, perhaps the lake where they massacred your father, Nene, is now surrounded by houses and hotels and the children bathe in its water and we can have a meal alongside its banks (perhaps one day we shall dine along the river in Acul, Marta) and the meat and salads and hot fresh breads from the oven, this place, and fill our stomachs and drink the autochthonous waters and be happy for a moment in our dream, in our sad essay, and when the saz player pulls out his instrument and the duduk lifts our sorrow like swallows rising in flight, then we are dancing together, held, then we are home, then waking could be like dying and driving the streets of this city inside the maze like a man collecting corpses, a man seeking invisible roads, a man who is happy.

MARTA, I refused, finally, the mean separateness of things. Of every thing for this modern: the mind his laughs and loves machines, his grandmother in Turkey then Lebanon, and an Ixil girl in Acul then Guatemala City and how he feels thinks; the science of TO DO to love to make and build and progress like an animal and the animal knows everything as everything, not separate, not only in the mind, it passes through his heart and liver also (again): our record: we are Americans, he says, you and I, and here we are together, known together, and I opposed this separate reality reason the idea'd world the mechanical man unto the cosmic end . . . We are in a book together, and I loved this Marta girl, her hands and thighs; her sad look in the mountains in the Polytechnic on the road to the capital; not his idea'd girl, no writer's plastic muse, but a girl of flesh and mind and sinewed spirited vowels: breath as you breathe, dear Reader, and breathe up the girl, imagine her as she walks, she is wounded and she suffers, and he is lonely, in love, you can see them together, and don't they live then? Will they not survive two thousand seven hundred epic years?

O MONSTROUS unkind masks we formed in this city in the schools on the roads and in shops and restaurants and how to hate the fat girls and evil trespassers of the laws, put them on to live here, and to see is then masked because to see the dead is to remember that I am alive, Marta, for this I collected them up like marbles or plastic figurines and cars: *I wanted to live* but too afraid to do it, unable to do it in my America, and I sought you here because on the morn and the morn I became the good driver again at six o'clock in the morning, time of the clock, and I rise and eat and dress shower with perfumed "clean" soap and driving and it is Monday and work and then it is evening, I turn the television set on at dusk and off for sleeping, o hum of it, these Shows to keep up the façades, to keep out the dead, to shut-up my wife (who complaining bitterly, my soft cock, the shriveled soul, unmet needs) which remind us that we could be the living! (my wife divorced me but she hardly figures into these pages because these pages are the tiny interstitial soul pages—and she and I did not have our souls together bared like ancient stones in the dry heat of high summer landscapes, not ever, or only once a decade ago and for a (fucking) moment). But you crept in, Marta, interstitial archetypal girl: girl inside the maze, labyrinthal girl from my childhood, the grandmother's ghost inside you also, a mother's latenight whisper, each girl in each shop who unknowingly and for a second of eternity—such sad and self-loathing creatures—but they too can lift their animal eyes and the soul has seeped out, tiny escapes of the soul! and I see that she too must needs merge with this boy, if only to fuck him, fat ugly man! But so fast is the train of reason and well-trained Angeleno girls, and TO DO, and He is not Handsome, He is Fat Ugly Low-Born, and she is disgusted by me, my form, my unguarded deathly black desires: fuck me unto death—terrified of her desires, her terrifying shut-down of the soul—to merge, which for the half-deads is more painful than the death which awaits all of us. And without it we do not Live, of course, this why we are the half-deads in America and half alive and have then killed desecrated the ancient lands out of sheer progressive rage and an unending appetite for things, we are allowed things in my America, Marta, we need them, crave their thingéd solace like cocaine and porno tittied girls. And the girl across the mountains, over the borders, and into your country, you arrive in me at night, sad girl, frightened girl, handless and orphaned now, your brother on the cross of the plaza tree, your mother has died in the river, the father of his own bitter susto and rage (at what his own hands unmade: his son and nephews)—how to put all of us and all of this into this book? Slim, a man's essay into the girl and the boy across distance and rivers and a river which he didn't know because how can you see that which is no longer see-able? Yet I *know* that I have found you, as I must have known there was once a riparian dreamer near my home, and although I cannot or dare not do not tell another living person—who would believe it, so I write it,—and that you also have re-found me, albeit ruined now, but that is something, here we are together in the barest moments when you can break through the veil tarmac or I can let you back in through the smallest and high cracks of Reason, which is also the veil of the deadened living who refuse the dead their spirit, who take spirit from the rocks and rivers and the gods themselves denied, although not banishable, not entirely, for every road, even the terrible machined freeways and highways of this city, lead and have always led unto you, to spirit or love or what is, this immaterial thing which these things we make to cover up and fill up and in the world, our America, can never do it, only lie that it is not what it is, that we can be happy in the New Paradise of California's converted desert landscape, that the soul will be fed on sweets and TV more than spirit more than god more than the trees and a slow summer river.

WHY, darling, you may wonder, or simply in your rages and fierce quiet silent rages, demand that I honestly entail, describe and then say whence you come, this archetype in the mind, more, in the soul of the man, so that every woman he fucks is Marta, every girl whose cunt he has adored and sucked from and desired to enter more fully into the sublime, into her form: you there on the edges of all of the American girls, waiting, breath in the soul, as he puts his penis inside, ejaculates, breaks all of the rules of the possible, it is you he has sought found again and again. To undrain the sea for you? to undo time? unmake geography science and its reasonable lessons? Yes I will do it, for I have loved you thus: to destroy everything for you? or save the animal forms (otters trout and grizzly bear), the waters which once desiccated cannot be put back (the brown and

greys of the Dry Lake, the Sierra Nevada, and the White
Mountains like smaller girls in the same valley; the Cuchumatanes
distant in my mind and green). Was it, perhaps,—let me be an honest writer, we liars we writers, for form or fame or approvements
or an entertaining plotline! or girls we would like to fuck—that as
a boy you were the servant in our home and you had very few
words in our English, and in your language, which could have been
Ixil, you held a boy's hand at night in front of the television set and
I listened holding her hand to the News and Shows on the Spanish
channels and wanted so desperately to understand you, the language, your smells and differences, your differences unlike my
mother's—outside inside the American home, it was home: the
foods the body smells and limits, my mother, and then this girl who
cleaned the kitchen and floors and bathrooms and my bedroom: she
was in my mind before memory and during the beginnings of what
I remembered: the servant: what was her name? The small hands
and small feet and tortilla smell on her hands; not her look, which
I can't recall, just this one day she left us; one day she was five
months pregnant or my mother told me that her boy was in her
country—her country? was my home her bedroom not her country?—and that she missed him, and she returned to him. And this
boy's body who loved it and her in her room at night, sneaking into
her bed and placing my hands on her belly, longing for the cunt
which I didn't know yet, just to smell her form, just to touch her
pendulous breast and fat stomach thighs and black hair eyes—like
my mother, ah beauty of the smell of the real in this woman's form,
and so lonely afterwards in my America, Los Angeles, its northern
valley, without her, bleached out desires, like the hair of so many
girls here: denied the form her smells foods and distant forms of all
of my brethren who we all of us making distance lies and money

for our days of sunned hot afternoons on our walled-out properties, gated doors and pools and drives:—afraid isolates in this
America.

I took the buses across the streets of this city as a boy, before I
became the driver and collected the dead, and I was always searching for her after she left me in the city, she returned to a country
for which I had no name or maps, to her boy? wasn't I her boy any
longer? hadn't I tried to give it her: my own soul in each look I offered at breakfast, and plantains in butter, and black beans—and
didn't I try to learn all of the foreign languages things flora in the
house off of Mulholland Dr, the birches from England, the cypress
from Syria, the Washingtonias from Sonora, Mexico, and the girl
from Guatemala. I couldn't find her in Europe or either in this
America, these Los Angeles, just the half-dead girls, the pretty-
glossy ones on TV and in the shops, pretty unsexed and contained
girls with their covered up smells, hairs, souls and frightened and
cruel. And wasn't I always a failure, an ugly and lonely man, the
driver become a businessman, whose soul had seeped out from his
eyes and into his fingers, he turned dials on the radio and television
computer keyboard and he gave up on the project of love (bought
his girls on Hollywood Blvd and on the telephone when he wished
it and hiding it and lying of it) to find a wife, but every girl was still
her for the second which is eternity of fucking her, when even the
modern can be undone, the Angeleno boy himself, so stoic and stiff
in his postures and nice clean clothes of business fashion, his blue
and red neckties, he is the judge, hates the fat girls, the ugly girls,
the smelly stink of their armpits and cunt hairs which he tells them
to remove and cut off, and then inside of these girls, his wife also,
if on a bright and summer night in the Valley when there is this
quiet breeze and slivered moon and the trees have been planted and

the fescue grasses have grown high, hates them which is this hatred of his life, of what he has become, because even he can re-have (o timeless second) what has been his human right: to be out, in Love, across time and the boundaries of highways and roads and the clocks and machinery and even the sea: not paradise, darling, more than paradise or an oasis of high sloped and winded Washingtonias: but You and You and You: and we are undone and in union . . . I re-find the mythic girl of my childhood.

I AM DRIVING along the 405 Freeway; it is a Sunday afternoon and for today the traffic is not so terrible; the sky is blue and brown along its edges. I don't have any thoughts in my head except to arrive home and that my wife left me never loved me (not as I must needed to be loved), could not see the darkness in me, and I could not show it to her: didn't know it existed below the workdays and Shows and gatherings at restaurants with friends. I am driving quickly and Marta you have not existed for me, although I dreamed once of a girl whose brown and sad look looked at me from a yellow and white barred window on the Pan American Highway and I wanted to save her, didn't know the highway, your country, only that look from the metal trellis. But I have none of these thoughts now and I am moving faster and faster through the mountain pass and know that soon enough I will come to the top of the rise and then will see the San Fernando Valley down below (as you also come to the top of the rise from Nebaj to Acul, and see the beautiful green and quiet, the dairy farm in the distance, cow bells and cocks crowing and the dogs are barking, before and after massacre, this is the Valley of Acul). And something catches my eye—a dead animal on the side of the highway—it could be dog or coyote or large raccoon and before I can make any thoughts in my mind, I have pulled over to the side of the freeway and I have parked my car and I walk back the three yards to the carcass. And then I am crying, hysterical—uncontrollably—a man who never cries, he has been unable to cry since he was a boy, he is a man on the side of the freeway, howling for the dead mongrel bitch at the side of the road. She has the long pulled-out teats of a mother, sucked up and dried; her teeth push through the snout from the impact of the car, her organs spilling from her form—and I know that I have found her, that she was mine, and I lift the beast into my arms and walk her up to the place I have left my car; the cars rush by me on the road, the heavy bloody and stink of the bitch in my arms (the dipteras the beetles arrived already; maggots devour the flesh) and I can't stop any of it: what I am doing, the sobs which erupt out from some pit in the inside of the man, some desire to save to bury to call back the animal from her death: and I know that I can't do it, and that to try is a futile enterprise, but I do it all the same. And I am covered in dog blood and grime and the maggots fall from her entrails onto me. It would be strange and wrong even to say that I was happy to do it: find and then keep the corpse of the old mother—but I did it all the same, and kept her in my trunk until she became the bones and fur and the stink did not bother me, although yes it did cross the threshold of trunk to car cabin—but I didn't mind it, loved it for its reminder of my life, that I was alive and that there was *to feel* inside beneath these chest bones, my own feelings and not packaged boxed sugary wheated Shows; and, Marta, she led me directly unto you: made me the corpse-collector here in these pages: the Bone Boy came home also, and a grandmother lifted her maggoty head and the five forgotten phrases of my childhood also resurrected and put into relief and I was singing a song in Armenian that I did not know that I knew, and we all of us: you, my nene, your brothers and father and uncle and mother and my own unlived son: we had a time together here, returned to the real from the dream of America. To live, Marta. To feel. To love as we were made to do it: out and out and free.

HERE is the secret, a mystery, Reader: that I was once as you, read books and loved them, before Shows and drives, and snuck my consciousness up against the phrases and my soul alighted on the buoyant and downtrodden river, and myself against the selves in nottime, in books, and I was Achilles and then his slain foe and then Priam at the threshold of the soon-to-be destroyed city of Troy. The frightening joy and love and the grief, rage, and reign of our stories, our wide and riven histories, our gods—and to have essayed, Reader, the man! his sorrow his love for a girl in a distant place, his loneliness like an inheritance or thing he has purchased or not purchased and yet had purchase upon him; the girl herself in Acul, waited for him, beckoned him back, made him into her and she into him and then we all, less lonely, became the You for whom the book was made—the gods in us and the gods in the natural things and our godlikeness when we sit quiet and read this phrase end this book see death awaits us all upon the horizon.

Will you, dear Sirs Madams, take the phrases inside your crania and let them live awhile longer than Marta me, and you perchance a little less lonely today on your drives across the city?

Know that a boy once loved his distant girl, and that the real resides in books, where we can, finally, loafe and invite the soul.

We listen to our inmost selves—and do not know which sea we hear murmuring.

LIFE AS IT IS, Marta, our small and grand *to be*—and not life as the christ-makers would make it, the políticos and teachers and laws or moral tyrants or bosses for capital, or the killers either, your brother's on the road up into the Cuchumatanes; or the History books of nation-states and obscenity laws for girls; concrete rivers, roads and automobiles;—the white and tall granite mountains of the Sierra Nevada, the brown and greys of my Santa Monica, the green flush and low clouds like girls of your Cuchumatanes: is. A wild dog does not question his desires, his longings or paths or pissiness or fucking the bitch in his path; he shits when he feels it or licks his ass and balls and sticks it into the girls because it is good, because it is flow, because everything moves him to do it; perhaps the domesticate has been trained to shit in a pot, but is he then ashamed of his shit? or live inside a dog-made mask as if shitting never happened at all, falls into water, porcelain, silent and clean, like his ashamed and furtive sex? The rain is neither moral or immoral. The granite and maize and stones of the river—they don't feel sadness, sorrow, but *is* something—these pulls from the mountains as we ramble up the old spoors; the moon waxes wanes pulls on our pants and organs; gravitas; gravity,— graves; the gods in trees and rocks and rivers in me, and not in the machines, subdued in metals, subdued by the sheer functionality of machined things: the car drives, she cannot love me or sing inside my skin or caress the urges the to feel: drives: moves me around as if I were the mechanical beast now, capable of only one or two functions: to work, to eat, and then to fuck like a machine also, denied myself a man, an adam animal in his own garden with his gods in abundance, not abeyance, an abundance of desires, of flow, of energy light and electric being—and I too could call down the deus ex machina for a nice party to end our tirade and goat-skinned tragedy; we have worn the masks for your pleasure or for business and the requirements of capital and property, propriety and what the neighbors will say, all of our modern TO DO's.

But perhaps I'll lie here awhile yet with you in my unthingéd arms, I hold you and drink your sweat, you are sweating now, and soon we can make love again and then again, silly man, I know, to desire it so much, even now at the end of things, my life and this work, the man who collected corpses in these books, words and despicable failures for pages and phrases: ah, Marta—such loneliness to have been a half-dead man, a modern, whilst the sun pulled the shadows across the earth and sunlight on the mountains and the rain shadows too—how did I bear it so long? I could not do it one more day. What then? It was a comfort to me in this city, and a man made what he could and how he could do it: if I had been a carpenter it would have been a box for us; and a driver? the corpse-collector? his thing to you these books in his mind and the things he had not been able to think in so many years, he *knew* it as a boy;—"We must get back into relation, vivid and nourishing relation to the cosmos and the universe," a man said to me in a book; he is a corpse now also, and I collected his and other phrases here, and you chose me, dead girl, so that I might re-find the quick I knew as a boy, the togetherness in ourselves, and a little less lonely then, and I hoped, I swear it, that you also could be revived from your garden, from the river, the mountains and the basement in the Polytechnic: an eternal flame of a girl, an Ixil girl with beauty in the iris in the air, an archetype of love: the American half-Armenian boy and his Ixil girl—he half-dead and trying for life light before his own death alighted, and you? to live here for the breathy moments that I said you, and that someone, someone else in ether, reads your name. Dear Reader, please do it.

Taa.

COLLECTED PHRASES

The stories about the war in Guatemala in this book are grounded in historical fact. Between 1962 and 1996, a civil war raged in the small Central American republic—currently a population of 11.2 million, 50 to 60 percent of which is indigenous—making it the longest and bloodiest of Latin America's Cold War civil wars. In 1997, shortly after the signing of the peace accords, a UN-sponsored truth commission—the Commission for Historical Clarification (CEH)—was established to clarify human rights violations and acts of violence perpetrated during the war. Their final report, issued in 1999, *Guatemala: Memory of Silence*, concluded that more than 200,000 people had been killed or "disappeared," and more than one million displaced—state forces and related military groups were found responsible for 93 percent of these acts of violence. The report also confirmed that 83 percent of the victims of the conflict were indigenous Maya, largely from the rural peasantry; the report concluded by stating that the state committed acts of genocide against four Mayan groups during the counterinsurgency "scorched-earth" campaigns of 1981–1983, including the Ixil. As stipulated by the peace accords, the CEH was not allowed to name individuals responsible for human rights crimes in its report. This book is, in many ways, an interrogation into untold or denied histories—it is, however, a work of fiction.

PAGE x. *"Oh, take pity on me . . ."* Homer, *The Iliad*. Translated by Richmond Lattimore (Chicago: University of Chicago Press, 1951), pp. 436–437.

PAGE xi. *"In the sound of these foxes . . ."* James Agee, *Let Us Now Praise Famous Men* (Boston: Houghton Mifflin, 1941), pp. 469–470.

PAGE 11. *"Where would you like to go . . . to Heaven or to Hell?"* "He was pointing to the people . . . the guilty one, let's say, for being a guerrilla fighter, they sent him to hell and the other to heaven, in other words two things were named, nothing else. One, 'This one to heaven,' he said, and another man who was pulled out, 'Ah, this one goes to hell.' And that's how the people learned [where they were to go], one by one." *Guatemala: Memoria del Silencio,* Anexo 1: Volumen 2, Caso Ilustrativo 107. Trans. author. http://shr.aaas.org/guatemala/ceh/mds/spanish/anexo1/vol2/no107.html.

PAGE 14. *"Roots which hold one teaspoonful of water . . ."* "Civilians in the mountains suffered extreme hardship with no shelter, no clothing, no medicines, and no stable food or water sources. People survived by eating roots and weeds. Families dedicated most of their time to the search for edible plants. Much anxiety was focused on thirst and the desperate search for and digging up of small roots that contained approximately one teaspoon of water per root. In the case of Acul, survivor testimony indicates that one-third of massacre survivors died in the mountains from hunger and diseases associated with exposure to the elements and starvation." Victoria Sanford, *Buried Secrets: Truth and Human Rights in Guatemala* (New York: Palgrave Macmillan, 2003), p. 131.

PAGE 16: *"They made the Ixil prisoners, branded them and took them slaves."* + *"The impact of the conquest must have been disastrous for the Ixil."* + *"As a reward to Spanish settlers, the land and its Indian inhabitants were parceled out in large groupings called* encomiendas, *under a system already applied in Spain to 'reconquered' Moorish territories."* "Indians were placed under the tutelage of an encomendero, who was to protect them, direct their work, Christianize them, and collect tribute. These Indians were held by the encomendero and passed on to his heirs. . . . Gibson characterizes the first encomienda generation in the New World as 'one of generalized abuse and particular atrocities' . . . Indians were used in all forms of labor, were overworked and overtaxed." + *"The encomenderos . . . jailed them, killed them, beat them and set dogs on them. They seized their goods, destroyed their agriculture, and took their women. They used them as beasts of burden. They took tribute from them and sold it back under compulsion at exorbitant profits. Coercion and ill-treatment were the daily practices of their overseers."* + *"Such a drastic change must have had a profound effect on the Ixil population, and must have added a great burden to the logistics of corn growing, harvesting, and transporting. (On the other hand, logistical problems may have been alleviated with the drop in population caused by concentrating the people and making them more vulnerable to the devastating epidemics of the period. A reduced population would not have so far to go in the surrounding countryside to till their fields.)"* Benjamin N. Colby and Pierre L. van den Berghe, *Ixil Country: A Plural Society in Highland Guatemala* (Berkeley: University of California Press, 1969), pp. 42, 44–46.

PAGE 18. *"Bo pointn to his niga."* (Written on the bottom of a photograph of the lynching of Thomas Shipp and Abram Smith, framed photograph also includes victim's hair). James Allen et al., *Without Sanctuary: Lynching Photography in America* (Santa Fe, NM: Twin Palms), plate 32.

PAGE 22. *"The Army never arrived on 22 April."* "On the 22nd of April, 1982, around six in the morning, approximately seventy Army regulars arrived to Acul from the military attachment in Nebaj." *Guatemala: Memoria del Silencio.* Anexo 1: Volumen 2, Caso Ilustrativo 107. Trans. author. http://shr.aaas.org/guatemala/ceh/mds/spanish/anexo1/vol2/no107/html.

PAGE 22. *"Not a brother or crucified . . ."* Based in part on the execution of eighteen-year-old Domingo Cedillo López, who "they tied to the cypress that today still stands in front of the church. In front of a great number of villagers, Domingo was tied to the tree by his hands and feet and accused of belonging to the guerrilla." Ibid. http://shr.aaas.org/guatemala/ceh/ mds/spanish/anexo1/vol2/no107.html.

PAGE 27. *"The man of action . . ."* "I repeat, and repeat emphatically: all spontaneous people, men of action, are active *because* they are stupid and limited." Fyodor Dostoyevsky, *Notes From Underground*, trans. Jessie Coulson (New York: Penguin, 1972), p. 26.

PAGE 27. *"We are not dogs."* Interview with Acul massacre survivor Doña Elena; in Sanford, p. 103.

PAGE 42. *"His mother discards him at six . . ."* This section is loosely based on a survivor interview with an ex-Kaibil (Kaibiles are the special operations force of the Guatemalan army; their motto is: "If I advance, follow me. If I stop, urge me on. If I retreat, kill me") who spoke of how his mother "gave me to a finca owner when I was six," and how "many times you joined the army for a pair of shoes." He also described training to become a Kaibil: "They took us to the mountains. Each of us had to carry a live dog that was tied up and over our shoulders. I was thirsty. There was no water. . . . When we were ordered to pick up stray dogs on the street, I thought we were going to learn how to train them. . . . But when we arrived to the camp, we were ordered to kill them with our bare hands. . . . We were ordered to put their meat and blood in a big bowl. Then we had to eat and drink this dog . . . that was in a bath of blood. Whoever vomited had to vomit into the shared bowl and get back in line to eat and drink more. We had to eat it all, including the vomit, until no one vomited." In Sanford, pp. 182–184.

PAGE 47. *"He said that the devils lived . . ."* "We found a great number of books in these letters, and since they contained nothing but superstitions and falsehoods of the devil we burned them all, which they [the Maya] took most grievously, and which gave them great pain." Friar Diego de Landa, *Yucatan Before and After the Conquest*, trans. William Gates (New York: Dover, 1978), quoted from the back cover.

PAGE 50. *"Dear Sir: You are a man . . ."* President Reagan described Ríos Montt as a "man of great personal integrity and commitment" who "is totally dedicated to democracy . . . And frankly, I'm inclined to believe they've been getting a bum rap." Weekly Compilation of Presidential Statements, December 13, 1982.

PAGE 55. *"Why are you all so sad? You shouldn't be sad. It is not just here that there are problems. There are dead everywhere. There are dead in Cotzal and Chajul. So, you have to have a little, too. Why are you so sad? It has to be this way."* Interview with Acul massacre survivor Don Sebastián; in Sanford, p. 93.

PAGE 71. *"The Indians educated . . ."* "Señorita, imagine the Indians with education, with arms, with money! If they are learning to better themselves it is a great danger, you see, to the whites. The Indians educated, armed, could take the country away from us!" Erna Fergusson, *Guatemala* (New York: Knopf, 1946), p. 290.

PAGE 79. *"The palm at the end of the mind."* From "Of Mere Being" by Wallace Stevens, in *The Palm at the End of the Mind: Selected Poems and a Play,* ed. Holly Stevens (New York: Vintage Books, 1972), p. 398.

PAGE 79. *"Why is it* (that you can . . ." "What is it about foreigners that they can only comprehend us by how close we come to fitting some European precedent? Why are we, as just ourselves, so invisible?" Jennifer Harbury, *Bridge of Courage* (Monroe, ME: Common Courage, 1994), pp. 79–80.

PAGE 82. *"The soldiers piss and shit upon your heads . . ."* After the description of torture by an ex-"confidant" for the Army: "They put them in a pit filled with water. . . . There one had to urinate and defecate into the pit." In *Guatemala: Memoria del Silencio,* Anexo 1, Volumen 2, Caso Ilustrativo 17. Trans author. http://shr.aaas.org/guatemala/ceh/mds/spanish/anexo1/vol 2/no17.html.

PAGE 83. *"American Empire for Liberty."* Daniel J. Boorstin, Brooks Mather Kelley, and Ruth Frankel Boorstin, *A History of the United States* (Needham, MA: Prentice Hall, 2005), p. 159.

PAGE 87. *"Man is born . . ."* "Death and birth are solitary experiences. We are born alone and we die alone." Octavio Paz, *The Labyrinth of Solitude: Life and Thought in Mexico* (New York: Grove, 1961), p. 196.

PAGE 89. *"Where will we leave . . ."* "Without the trees, where will we leave our sorrow?" Author interview with ex–guerrilla fighter, Ixil Area, July 2004.

PAGE 91. *"Food is a weapon in a world at war."* Sanford, p. 37.

PAGE 91. *"We are always . . ."* " 'We are always afraid' and 'the fear never leaves' were among the most common statements survivors of La Violencia shared in testimonies." Ibid., p. 144.

PAGE 94. *"These things in . . ."* "These things in my head I give to you. These things I unload before it is impossible." Micheline Aharonian Marcom, *Three Apples Fell From Heaven* (New York: Riverhead Books, 2001), p. 211.

PAGE 105. *"Others form man . . ."* Michel de Montaigne, *The Complete Works,* trans. Donald M. Frame (New York: Everyman's Library, 2003), p. 740.

PAGE 105. *"The settlement of new countries . . ."* Robert F. Heizer and Alan J. Almquist, *The Other Californians* (Berkeley: University of California Press, 1971), p. 26.

PAGE 105. *"When the Indians had died . . ."* William McCawley, *The First Angelinos: The Gabrielino Indians of Los Angeles* (Banning, CA: Malki Museum Press, 1996), p. 198.

PAGE 109. *"What have you observed here . . ."* "Don Sebastián remembers, 'Then, they asked us, 'What have you observed here? What is it that you have seen?' We did not answer them because we knew that they had killed our sons. We just didn't respond. The soldiers did. They said, 'You don't answer us because you don't take good care of your sons. These sons of yours are involved with the guerrilla. That's why you don't answer us. Now you've seen the dead. You have to return to your homes. You must go tranquil. Go home and eat, relax, and sleep. Don't do anything. You have done good work here. Go home. Go home tranquil.' " Interview with Acul massacre survivor Don Sebastián; in Sanford, p. 93.

PAGE 116. *"A christ, his face removed . . ."* "They took me to another door and in this door there were some boards in the ceiling. Have you seen the crucifixion? Well here there was almost a Jesus Christ, there was a man, he was half a man—the most horrible thing I have ever seen in my life—, a totally disfigured man, a man who already had worms, he had no teeth, he didn't have hair, his face was disfigured, hanging, in other words, hanged by his hands. A man from the Judicial arrived and he had a small scythe, a small one like for cutting coffee, red hot, and he grabbed the man's penis and he cut it off, and the man gave a scream which I have never forgotten, he screamed in such agony that for many years I remembered it." Archbishop of Guatemala, Office of Human Rights, *Nunca Más: Los Mecanismos del Horror* (Guatemala City: ODHAG, 1998), pp. 62–63. Trans. author.

PAGE 131. *"200 Reported Killed . . ."* Excerpted from the article "200 Reported Killed in Guatemalan Villages," *Los Angeles Times*, March 12, 1981.

PAGE 144. *"How long have you . . ."* All the "questions posed" taken from *Guatemala: Memoria del Silencio*, Anexo 1: Volumen 2, Caso Ilustrativo 17. Trans. author. http://shr.aaas.org/guatemala/ceh/mds/spanish/anexo1/vol2/no17.html.

PAGE 151. *"Lord, if thou hadst . . ."* John 11:21. Holy Bible, King James Version (New York: New American Library, 1974).

PAGE 151. *"He has excited domestic . . ." Declaration of Independence* (New York: Dover, 2000), p. 8.

PAGE 157. *"I loafe and invite my soul, I lean and loafe at my ease."* Walt Whitman, "Song of Myself," in *The New Oxford Book of American Verse* (New York: Oxford University Press, 1976), p. 207.

PAGE 167. *"One of the fundamental . . ."* "One of the fundamental aspects of the new government philosophy is respect for human rights. Incorrect information published abroad, and which the Guatemalan government lacks the funds to refute effectively, has led to a wide-spread belief among foreigners that it is carrying out massacres of the Indian farmers. But the government of President Ríos Montt has ample evidence disproving these charges and which it is happy to share with foreign journalists visiting Guatemala." Message to the international press in Tegucigalpa, Honduras, by President Efraín Ríos Montt, December 1982.

PAGE 201. *"The guerrilla is the fish . . ."* General Ríos Montt, as quoted by Bob Harris in "Guatemala: Bill Clinton's Latest Damn-Near Apology," *Mother Jones,* March 16, 1999.

PAGE 201. *"We should wish to know . . ."* Mircea Eliade, *The Myth of the Eternal Return, or Cosmos and History* (Princeton, NJ: Princeton University Press, Bollingen Series XLVI, 1971), p. 151.

PAGE 220. *"The soldiers bashed the children's heads . . . cut them into pieces"* "What do they do to the children? They cut them into pieces. I mean, they cut them up with machetes; they cut them into pieces." Case 2052, Chamá, Cobán, Alta Verapaz, *Guatemala Never Again! Recovery of Historical Memory Project* (Guatemala City: The Official Report of the Human

Rights Office, Archdiocese of Guatemala, Abridged English Translation, 1999), p. 32.

PAGE 225. "*Նորից գարուն եկավ, գարուն աննրման.*" Armenian song, trans. author: "New spring arrives, beautiful spring." As found in Marcom, *Three Apples Fell from Heaven* (dedication page) and *The Daydreaming Boy* (New York: Riverhead Books, 2004), p. 97.

PAGE 236. "*Urge and urge and urges denied.*" "Urge and urge and urge / Always the procreant urge of the world." Whitman, p. 208.

PAGE 243. "*He cuts her belly open . . .*" "A man with long eyelashes and a dimpled chin who slices my belly open wide, like a mouth." Marcom, *Three Apples Fell from Heaven,* p. 229.

PAGE 261. "*One must realize . . .*" Carey McWilliams, *California: The Great Exception* (Berkeley: University of California Press, 1999; originally pub. 1949), p. 51.

PAGE 261. "*To yield entirely . . .*" D. H. Lawrence, *Apocalypse* (New York: Viking, 1932), p. 196.

PAGE 267. "*Virtually every village . . .*" "In 1986, municipal authorities in each of the three main towns of the Ixil Triangle—in which the military indiscriminately burned and attacked virtually every rural Indian settlement in the area—estimated that approximately one-third of their rural population had been killed." Jennifer Schirmer, *The Guatemalan Military Project: A Violence Called Democracy* (Philadelphia: University of Pennsylvania Press, 1998), p. 56.

PAGE 269. "*The total past felt nothing when destroyed.*" Stevens, "Esthétique du Mal," p. 252.

PAGE 292. *"With the twirl of my tongue I encompass worlds and volumes of worlds."* Whitman, p. 227.

PAGE 296. *"Komiivet . . ."* "The Gabrielino of the Los Angeles area called themselves *Komiivet,* from the word *Komii,* meaning *east."* McCawley, p. 10.

PAGE 296. *"Yaanga . . ."* "The Gabrielino community of Yaanga . . . is largely regarded as the Indian precursor of modern Los Angeles." Ibid., p. 57.

PAGE 312. *"Out and out . . ."* "Know this: I loved you in my mind and in my internal organs fleshy place I gave it all to you and I could have saved all of us—the three of us uncaged, unhanded, out and out and free." Marcom, *The Daydreaming Boy,* p. 157.

PAGE 313. *"We listen to our inmost selves—and do not know which sea we hear murmuring."* Martin Buber, *Ecstatic Confessions* (San Francisco: Harper & Row, 1985) p. 11.

PAGE 314. *"We must get back into relation, vivid and nourishing relation to the cosmos and the universe."* D. H. Lawrence, *Sex, Literature and Censorship* (New York: Viking, 1959), p. 106.

PAGE 315. *"Taa."* The name "Marta" in Ixil.

LIST OF PHOTOGRAPHS

PAGE 2. 405 Freeway, Santa Monica Pass, Los Angeles, United States.

PAGE 2. House, Acul, Guatemala.

PAGE 104. The Bone Boy, Der Zor Desert, Syria.

PAGE 104. The Polytechnic School, Guatemala City, Guatemala.

PAGE 150. *Washingtonia robusta*, Los Angeles, United States.

PAGE 150. The Pan American Highway, Chimaltenango, Guatemala.

PAGE 200. The Los Angeles River, Los Angeles, United States.

PAGE 200. The Los Angeles River, Los Angeles, United States.

PAGE 260. Cemetery in Acul, Guatemala. Site where the victims of the massacre were killed and dumped into a mass grave. (The site was later exhumed, and the victims reinterred.)

PAGE 260. Entrance to Kharphert (Harput), Turkey.

VICTIMS OF THE ACUL MASSACRE

EXECUTION

  Andrés Brito

  Andrés Brito

  Andrés Brito de León

  Antonio Brito

  Antonio Cobo Cobo

  Antonio Santiago Cobo

  Diego Cobo Avilés

  Diego Hernández Baca

  Diego Raymundo

  Diego Raymundo de León

  Diego Sánchez Raymundo

  Diego de León Marcos

  Francisco de Paz Raymundo

  Gaspar Raymundo

  Jacinto Brito Brito

  José Raymundo

  Mateo Maton Raymundo

  Miguel Meléndez

  Nicolás Ceto Cobo

  Nicolás Gusaro

  Pedro Cedillo Cedillo

  Pedro Marcos Bernal

  Pedro Solís de León

  Miguel Raymundo

TORTURE, EXECUTION

  Domingo Cedillo López

TIMELINE

ca. 10,000 B.C.	Seafaring culture in modern-day southern California.
ca. 9,000 B.C.	Settlement in the Cuchumatán Mountains of Guatemala.
ca. A.D. 1–500	Arrival of Gabrielinos in the Los Angeles Basin.
Before A.D. 200	Evidence of Ixil-Maya population in the Ixil Area.
600 to 1200	Nebaj settlement in full flower.
1492	Christopher Columbus encounters the Arawak in the Bahamas.
1523	The conquistador Pedro de Alvarado enters the territory of Guatemala.
1530	The Spanish defeat the Ixil at Nebaj.
1542	The Cabrillo Expedition becomes the first European group of record to observe the Gabrielinos.
1562	Diego de Landa destroys at least 5,000 "idols" and twenty-seven hieroglyphic rolls in an auto-de-fé in the Yucatán.
1769	August 2. Fray Juan Crespí of the Portolá Expedition makes a close observation of the Gabrielinos at the village of Yangna.
1771	Establishment of Misión San Gabriel Arcángel.
1781	Establishment of El Pueblo de Nuestra Señora la Reina de los Angeles del Río de Porciúncula.
1821	Guatemala wins independence from Spain.
1847	At the battle of Río San Gabriel, the Americans defeat the Mexicans and take control of Los Angeles.
1848	Treaty of Guadalupe Hidalgo cedes the whole of California, Nevada, and Utah plus parts of Colorado,

New Mexico, Arizona, and Wyoming to the
United States.

1850   Los Angeles incorporates.

1870s   Dictator Justo Rufino Barrios passes debt-peonage
statutes and abolishes hundreds of Mayan land titles in
order to create an army of seasonal laborers for the huge
coffee plantations along Guatemala's Pacific piedmont.
Hundreds of thousands of indigenous farmers conscripted to work in the coastal *fincas* as coffee pickers.

1907   Voters approve bond to build the Los Angeles
Aqueduct from the Owens Valley.

1913   Completion of the Los Angeles Aqueduct.

1915–1917   Massacre and "deportations" of Armenians in the
Ottoman Empire. Hundreds of thousands of
Armenians marched to the Der Zor Desert. Between 1
and 1.5 million Armenians perish.

1936   Dictator Jorge Ubico replaces debt-peonage statutes
with vagrancy laws in Guatemala, obligating all peasants owning less than two hectares of land to do manual labor for a minimum of one hundred days a year.
Two hundred Nebaj residents march to the courthouse
in opposition to the vagrancy law. Seven men are exe-
cuted the next day by firing squad.

1939   Construction begins on the Water Improvement
Project for the Los Angeles River, to make a fifty-one-
mile concrete "river freeway."

1944   The dictator General Jorge Ubico is forced from power
in Guatemala, and general elections are held for the
first time. Juan José Arévalo is elected president, initi-
ates many reforms, including a minimum wage, the
legalization of unions, laws to protect workers,
elimination of vagrancy laws, and national health care.
Guatemala's "Ten Years of Spring" commences.

1950 Another reformer, Jacobo Arbenz, wins the presidential election. Institutes an agrarian reform law requiring very large estates not under cultivation to be distributed to people needing land. Large landowners, including the United Fruit Company, feel threatened. United Fruit Company uses its close ties with the U.S. government to promote an overthrow of the Arbenz administration.

This decade marks the only time in Guatemalan history when leaders committed to improving living conditions and human rights hold office and implement major social reforms.

1954 At height of the Cold War, the United States accuses the Arbenz government of being communist. The CIA organizes a coup against Arbenz, Operation PBSuccess, replacing him with Colonel Carlos Castillo Armas. Some 9,000 people—mostly peasant and labor leaders—are arrested during and after the coup and many are tortured. The 1954 coup paves the way for the long line of military dictators who will rule Guatemala—except for a brief period in the 1960s— for the next thirty-two years.

1962 The Internal Armed Conflict begins in Guatemala.

1974 The Civil War begins in Lebanon.

1980 The Guatemalan army doubles in size from 20,000 to 40,0000 to make it the largest standing army in Central America.

1981 Scorched-earth campaign begins under dictator General Romeo Lucas García.

1982 March 23. Coup d'état of Efraín Ríos Montt. Scorched-earth campaign intensifies under his Plan Victoria 82 campaign.

1982 April 22. Massacre at Acul. (Some sources say the massacre at Acul occurred in 1981. For the purposes of the narrative in this book, I have used the 1982 date.)

1982   December 5. General Ríos Montt and Ronald Reagan meet at a press conference in Tegucigalpa, Honduras.

1989   October 22. Taif Accords signed, Lebanese Civil War ends.

1996   December 29. Peace Accord signed between Guatemalan army and guerrilla factions.

1996   Two thousand troops come down out of the mountains.

1997   Exhumation of mass grave in Acul.

1998   April 24. The Archbishop of Guatemala, Monseñor Gerardi, presents the findings of a yearlong study into his country's violence—*The Recuperation of Historical Memory Project*, or REHMI. Two days later, he is found dead outside of his parish home, bludgeoned to death with a concrete block.

I never felt sadder in my life. LA is the loneliest and most brutal of American cities.

—Jack Kerouac, *On the Road*

ACKNOWLEDGMENTS

I would like to thank the brilliant, generous people who make up the Lannan Foundation. In so many ways—books, travels, a computer, time, belief—you made this book possible.

In Guatemala, Silvia Donoso López, old and dear friend, allowed me to stay with her on many occasions and also accompanied me to the Ixil Area up the long steep drive on the dirt road to Nebaj. Victoria Sanford, eminent anthropologist and fierce *luchadora*, took a risk and took an unknown American to the Ixil Area for the first time and introduced me to her friends and showed me a beautiful grace and an immense generosity, the likes of which I have rarely encountered. Thanks to Doña María and Don Jacinto for inviting me into their home; and to Señoras Ana and Magdalena also, for their hospitality and welcome. I am grateful to the folks at CIRMA, Center for Regional Investigations of Mesoamerica, in Antigua, Guatemala, including Tani Adams and Ingrid Molina, who assisted me with my research about Guatemala and the Internal Armed Conflict.

I would like to thank Sona Tatoyan and the Knadjian family in Aleppo, Syria, for their hospitality and the amazing trip to the Der Zor Desert, where we saw the bones. I am also indebted to Sona and her husband, José Rivera, for including me on their honeymoon to Turkey and our journey together to the old towns of Kharphert and Mezre in Anatolia, now known as Harput and Elazig. Thanks also to Paxton Winters, for driving us across eastern Anatolia, for interpreting, for inviting us into his circle, and for making me laugh when the sadness would descend. And to Sila and Aylin of Istanbul, for their company and friendship and conversations.

Hrag Varjabedian came from Armenia to accompany us on our trip to Der Zor and to offer, as always, his unflagging kindness and calm.

In Los Angeles, Cristina Garcia offered me her home on many occasions for quiet and a place to stay and work, and a view of the sea.

I would like to thank David Parsons for his constant support of this book during the many years, and travels, that it took to complete.

Marc Anthony Richardson did a fine job with the two maps. Pascal Huwart was very helpful with all of the Ixil words.

Sandy Dijkstra, as always, championed this book. And many thanks to Sean McDonald, for his diligence and care during the months leading to publication.

I am grateful to my father, who gave me a love of books and mountains. And to my mother, as always, who taught me that one must continually fight for what is just.